THE LAST GUARDIAN

A beautiful woman with flame-red hair approached Shannow.

'I will help you,' she said . . . but in her hand was a knife. Shannow backed away.

'Leave me alone,' he told her. But she advanced and the knife came up to sink in his chest. Darkness engulfed him. Then there was the noise of great roaring and he awoke.

He was sitting in a small seat, surrounded by crystal set in steel. Upon his head was a tight-fitting helmet of leather. Voices whispered in his ear.

'Calling Tower. This is an emergency. We seem to be off course. We cannot see land . . . Repeat . . . We cannot see land.'

Shannow leaned over and looked through the crystal window. Far below he could see the ocean. He glanced back. He was sitting in a metal cross, suspended in the air below the clouds which flashed by above him with dizzying speed.

'What is your position, Flight Leader?' came a second voice.

'We are not sure of our position, Tower. We cannot be sure just where we are . . . We seem to be lost . . .'

'Assume bearing due west.'

'We don't know which way is west. Everything is wrong . . . strange . . .'

The cross began to tremble violently and Shannow scrabbled at the window. Ahead, the heavens and the sea appeared to merge. All around the window the sky disappeared, and blackness swamped the cross. Shannow screamed . . .

Also in Legend by David Gemmell

The Siptrassi Tales
WOLF IN SHADOW
GHOST KING
LAST SWORD OF POWER

The Drenai Saga
LEGEND
KING BEYOND THE GATE
WAYLANDER

KNIGHTS OF DARK RENOWN

THE LAST GUARDIAN

David A. Gemmell

First published in 1989 by Legend Books,
Century Hutchinson Ltd

7 9 10 8 6

This Legend edition 1990

Random House UK Ltd, 20 Vauxhall Bridge Road, London SW1V 2SA

Random House Australia (Pty) Limited
20 Alfred Street, Milsons Point, Sydney,
New South Wales 2061, Australia

Random House New Zealand Limited
18 Poland Road, Glenfield
Auckland 10, New Zealand

Random House South Africa (Pty) Limited
PO Box 337, Bergvlei, South Africa

Random House UK Limited Reg. No. 954009

A CIP catalogue record for this book
is available from the British Library

ISBN 0 09 964330 8

Printed and bound in Great Britain by
Cox & Wyman Ltd, Reading, Berkshire

This novel is
dedicated with
love to my children
Kathryn and Luke who,
thankfully, are still
too young to know
what fine people
they are.

1

SOUTH OF THE PLAGUE LANDS – 2341 AD

But he did not die. The flesh around the bullet wound over his hip froze as the temperature dropped to thirty below zero, and the distant spires of Jerusalem blurred and changed, becoming snow-shrouded pine. Ice had formed on his beard and his heavy black, double-shouldered topcoat glistened white in the moonlight. Shannow swayed in the saddle, trying to focus on the city he had sought for so long. But it was gone. As his horse stumbled, Shannow's right hand gripped the saddle pommel and the wound in his side flared with fresh pain.

He turned the black stallion's head, steering the beast downhill towards the valley.

Images rushed through his mind: Karitas, Ruth, Donna; the hazardous journey across the Plague Lands and the battles with the Hellborn, the monstrous ghost ship wrecked on a mountain. Guns and gunfire, war and death.

The blizzard found new life and the wind whipped freezing snow into Shannow's face. He could not see where he was heading, and his mind wandered. He knew that life was ebbing from his body with each passing second, but he had neither the strength nor the will to fight on.

He remembered the farm and his first sight of Donna, standing in the doorway with an ancient crossbow in her hands. She had mistaken Shannow for a brigand, and feared for her life and that of her son, Eric. Shannow had never blamed her for that mistake. He knew what people saw when the Jerusalem Man came riding – a tall, gaunt figure in a flat-crowned leather hat, a man with cold, cold eyes that had seen too much of death and despair. Always it was the same. People would stand and stare, first at his expressionless face and then their eyes would be drawn down to his guns, the terrible weapons of the Thunder Maker.

Yet Donna Taybard had been different. She had taken Shannow to her hearth and her home and, for the first time in two weary decades, the Jerusalem Man had known happiness.

But then had come the brigands and the war-makers and finally the Hellborn. Shannow had gone against them all for the woman he loved, only to see her wed another.

Now he was alone again, dying on a frozen mountain in an uncharted wilderness. And, strangely, he did not care. The wind howled about horse and man and Shannow fell forward across the stallion's neck, lost in the siren song of the blizzard. The horse was mountain bred; he did not like the howling wind, nor the biting snow. Now he angled his way through the trees into the lee of a rock-face and followed a deer trail down to the mouth of a high lava tunnel that stretched through the ancient volcanic range. It was warmer here and the stallion plodded on, aware of the dead weight across his back. This disturbed him, for his rider was always in balance and could signal his commands with the slightest pressure or flick of the reins.

The stallion's wide nostrils flared as the smell of smoke came to him. He halted and backed up, his iron hooves clattering on the rocky floor. A dark shadow moved in front of him . . . in panic he reared and Shannow tumbled from the saddle. A huge taloned hand caught the reins and the smell of lion filled the tunnel. The stallion tried to rear again, to lash out with iron-shod hooves, but he was held tight and a soft, deep voice whispered to him, a gentle hand stroking his neck. Calmed by the voice, he allowed himself to be led into a deep cave, where a camp-fire had been set within a circle of round flat stones. He waited calmly as he was tethered to a jutting stone at the far wall; then the figure was gone.

Outside the cave Shannow groaned and tried to roll to his belly, but he was stricken by pain and deep cold. He opened his eyes to see a hideous face looming over him. Dark hair framed the head and face and a pair of tawny eyes gazed down at him; the nose was wide and flat, the mouth a deep slash, rimmed with sharp fangs. Shannow, unable to move, could only glare at the creature.

Taloned hands moved under his body, lifting him easily, and he was carried like a child into a cave and laid gently by a fire. The creature fumbled at the ties on Shannow's coat, but the thick paw-like hands could not cope with the frozen knots. Talons hissed out to sever the leather thongs and Shannow felt his coat eased from him. Slowly, but with great care, the creature removed his frozen clothing and covered him with a warm blanket. The Jerusalem Man faded into sleep – and his dreams were pain-filled.

Once more he fought the Guardian Lord, Sarento, while the *Titanic* sailed on a ghostly sea and the Devil walked in Babylon. But this time Shannow could not win, and he struggled to survive as the sea poured into the stricken ship, engulfing him. He could hear the cries of drowning men, women and children, but he could not save them. He awoke sweating and tried to sit. Pain ripped at his wounded side and he groaned and sank back into his fever dreams.

*

He was riding towards the mountains when he heard a shot; he rode to the crest of a hill and gazed down on a farmyard where three men were dragging two women from their home. Drawing a pistol, Shannow kicked his stallion into a run and thundered towards the scene. When the men saw him they flung the women aside and two of them drew flintlocks from their belts; the third ran at him with a knife. He dragged on the reins and the stallion reared. Shannow timed his first shot well and a brigand was punched from his feet. The knife-man leapt, but Shannow swung in the saddle and fired point-blank, the bullet entering the man's forehead and exiting from the neck in a bloody spray. The third man loosed a shot that ricocheted from the pommel of Shannow's saddle to tear into his hip. Ignoring the sudden pain, the Jerusa-

lem Man fired twice. The first shell took the brigand high in the shoulder, spinning him; the second hammered into his skull.

In the sudden silence, Shannow sat his stallion gazing at the women. The elder of the two approached him and he could see the fear in her eyes. Blood was seeping from his wound and dripping to the saddle, but he sat upright as she neared.

'What do you want of us?' she asked.

'Nothing, Lady, save to help you.'

'Well,' she said, her eyes hard, 'you have done that, and we thank you.' She backed away, still staring at him. He knew she could see the blood, but he could not – would not – beg for aid.

'Good day to you,' he said, swinging the stallion and heading away.

The younger girl ran after him; blonde and pretty, her face was leathered by the sunlight and the hardship of wilderness farming. She gazed up at him with large blue eyes.

'I am sorry,' she told him. 'My mother distrusts all men. I am so sorry.'

'Get away from him, girl!' shouted the older woman, and she fell back.

Shannow nodded. 'She probably has good reason,' he said. 'I am sorry I cannot stay and help you bury these vermin.'

'You are wounded. Let me help you.'

'No. There is a city near here, I am sure. It has white spires and gates of burnished gold. There they will tend me.'

'There are no cities,' she said.

'I will find it.' He touched his heels to the stallion's flanks and rode from the farmyard.

*

A hand touched him and he awoke. The bestial face was leaning over him.

'How are you feeling?' The voice was deep and slow and slurred, and the question had to be repeated twice before Shannow could understand it.

'I am alive – thanks to you. Who are you?'

The creature's great head tilted. 'Good. Usually the question is *what* are you. My name is Shir-ran. You are a strong man to live so long with such a wound.'

'The ball passed through me,' said Shannow. 'Can you help me to sit?'

'No. Lie there. I have stitched the wounds, front and back, but my fingers are not what they were. Lie still and rest tonight. We will talk in the morning.'

'My horse?'

'Safe. He was a little frightened of me, but we understand each other now. I fed him the grain you carried in your saddlebags. Sleep, Man.'

Shannow relaxed and moved his hand under the blankets to rest on the wound over his right hip. He could feel the tightness of the stitches and the clumsy knots. There was no bleeding, but he was worried about the fibres from his coat which had been driven into his flesh. It was these that killed more often than ball or shell, aiding gangrene and poisoning the blood.

'It is a good wound,' said Shir-ran softly, as if reading his mind. 'The issue of blood cleansed it, I think. But here in the mountains wounds heal well. The air is clean. Bacteria find it hard to survive at thirty below.'

'Bacteria?' whispered Shannow, his eyes closing.

'Germs . . . the filth that causes wounds to fester.'

'I see. Thank you, Shir-ran.'

And Shannow slept without dreams.

*

Shannow awoke hungry and eased himself to a sitting position. The fire was burning brightly and he could see a large store of wood stacked against the far wall. Gazing around the cave, he saw it was some fifty feet across at the widest point and the high domed ceiling was pitted with fissures, through which the smoke from the fire drifted lazily. Beside Shannow's blankets were his water canteen, his leather-bound Bible and his guns, still sheathed in their oiled leather scabbards. Taking the canteen, he pulled clear the brass-topped cork and drank deeply. Then in the bright firelight he examined the bullet wound in his hip; the flesh around it was angry, bruised and inflamed, but it looked clean and there was no bleeding. Slowly and carefully he stood, scanning the cave for his clothes. They were dry and casually folded atop a boulder on the other side of the fire. Dried blood still caked the white woollen shirt, but he slipped it on and climbed into his black woollen trousers. He could not buckle his belt on the usual notch, for the leather bit into his wound, bringing a grunt of pain. Still, he felt more human now he was clothed. He pulled on socks and high riding boots and walked to where his stallion was tethered at the far wall. Shannow stroked his neck and the horse dropped his head and nuzzled him in the chest. 'Careful, boy, I'm still tender.' He half-filled the feed-bag with grain and settled it over the stallion's head. Of Shirran there was no sign.

Near the wood-store was a bank of rough-hewn shelves. Some carried books, others small sacks of salt, sugar, dried fruit and meat. Shannow ate some of the fruit and returned to the fire. The cave was warm and he lay back in his blankets and took up his guns, cleaning them with care. Both were Hellborn pistols, single or double action, side-feed weapons. He opened his saddlebag and checked his shells. He still had forty-seven, but when these were gone the beautifully balanced pistols would be useless. Delving deep into the saddlebag he found his own guns, cap and ball percussion pistols that had served him well for twenty years. For these he could make his own powder and mould ammunition. Having cleaned them, he wrapped them in oilskin and returned them to the depths of the saddlebag. Only then did he take up his Bible.

It was a well-thumbed book, the pages thin and gold edged, the leather cover as supple as silk. He banked up the fire and opened the pages at The Book of Habakkuk. He read the section aloud, his voice deep and resonant.

'How long, O Lord, must I call for help, but you do not listen? Or cry out to you, "Violence," but you do not save? Why do you make me look at injustice? Why do you tolerate wrong? Destruc-

tion and violence are before me, there is strife, and conflict abounds. Therefore the law is paralysed and justice never prevails. The wicked hem in the righteous so that justice is perverted.'

'And how does your God answer, Jon Shannow?' asked Shir-ran.

'In his own way,' Shannow answered. 'How is it you know my name?'

The huge creature ambled forward, his great shoulders bowed under the weight of the enormous head. He sank to the floor by the fire and Shannow noticed that his breathing was ragged. A thin trickle of blood could be seen coming from his right ear, matting the dark hair of his mane. 'Are you hurt?' asked Shannow.

'No. It is the Change, that is all. You found food?'

'Yes. Some dried fruit in crystallised honey. It was good.'

'Take it all. I can no longer stomach it. How is your wound?'

'Healing well – as you promised. You seem in pain, Shir-ran. Is there anything I can do?'

'Nothing, Shannow. Save, perhaps, to offer me a little company?'

'That will be a pleasure. It is too long since I sat by a fire, secure and at peace. Tell me how you know me?'

'Of you, Shannow. The Dark Lady speaks of you – and your deeds against the Hellborn. You are a strong man. A brave friend, I think.'

'Who is this Dark Lady?' countered Shannow, uncomfortable with the compliments.

'She is who she is, dark and beautiful. She labours among the Dianae – my people – and the Wolvers. The Bears will not receive her, for their humanity is all gone. They are beasts – now and for ever. I am tired, Shannow. I will rest . . . sleep.' He settled down on his belly, taloned hands supporting his head. His tawny eyes closed – then opened. 'If . . . when . . . you can no longer understand me, then saddle your stallion and ride on. You understand?'

'No,' replied Shannow.

'You will,' said Shir-ran.

Shannow ate some more fruit and returned to his Bible; Habakkuk had long been a favourite. Short and bitter-sweet were his words, but they echoed the doubts and the fears in Shannow's heart and, reflecting them, calmed them.

For three days Shannow sat with Shir-ran, but although they talked often the Jerusalem Man learned little of the Dianae. What meagre information the creature did impart told Shannow of a land where men were slowly changing into beasts. There were the People of the Lion, the Wolf and the Bear. The Bears were finished, their culture gone. The Wolvers were dying out. Only the Lion people remained. Shir-ran spoke of the beauty of life, of its pains and its glories, and Shannow began to realise that the great creature was dying. They did not speak of it, but day by day Shir-ran's body changed, swelling, twisting, until he could not stand upright. Blood flowed from both ears now and his speech was ever more slurred. At night in his sleep he would growl.

On the fourth morning Shannow awoke to hear his stallion whinnying in terror. He rolled from his bed, his hand sweeping out and gathering a pistol. Shir-ran was crouched before the horse, his head swaying.

'What is wrong?' called Shannow. Shir-ran swung – and Shannow found himself staring into the tawny eyes of a huge lion. It advanced on him in a rush and leapt, but Shannow hurled himself to his right, hitting the ground hard. Pain lanced his side, but he swivelled as the lion surged at him, its roaring filling the cave.

'Shir-ran!' bellowed Shannow. The lion twisted its head and for a moment Shannow saw the light of understanding in its eyes . . . then it was gone. Again the beast leapt. A pistol shot thundered in the cave.

The creature that had been Shir-ran sank to the floor and rolled to its side, eyes locked to Shannow's own. The Jerusalem Man moved forward and knelt by the body, laying his hand upon the black mane.

'I am sorry,' he said. The eyes closed and all breathing ceased.

Shannow laid aside his pistol and took up his Bible. 'You saved my life, Shir-ran, and I took yours. That is not just, yet I had no choice. I do not know how to pray for you, for I do not know if you were man or beast. But you were kind to me, and for that I commend your soul to the All-High.' He opened his Bible.

Laying his left hand on Shir-ran's body, he read, '*The Earth is the Lord's, and everything in it, the world, all who live in it, for he founded it upon the seas and established it upon the waters. Who may ascend the Hill of the Lord? Who may stand in his Holy place? He who has clean hands and a pure heart, who does not lift up his soul to an idol, or swear by what is false.*'

He walked to the trembling stallion and saddled him. Then he gathered what remained of the food, stepped into the saddle and rode from the cave.

Behind him the fire flickered . . . and died.

2

THE CITY OF AD – 9364 BC

The Temple was a place of great beauty still, with its white spires and golden domes, but the once tranquil courtyards were now thronged with people baying for the blood sacrifice. The white tent at the entrance to the Holy Circle had been removed and in its place stood a marble statue of the King, regal and mighty, arms outstretched.

Nu-Khasisatra stood in the crowd, his limbs trembling. Three times had the vision come to him and three times had he pushed it aside.

'I cannot do this, Lord,' he whispered. 'I do not have the strength.'

He turned away from the spectacle as the victim was brought out, and eased his way through the crowds. He heard the new High Priest chant the opening lines of the ritual, but he did not look back. Tears stung his eyes as he stumbled along the corridors of white marble, emerging at last at the Pool of Silence. He sat at the Pool's edge; the roar of the crowd was muted here, yet still he heard the savage joy which heralded the death of another innocent.

'Forgive me,' he said. Gazing down into the Pool, he looked at the fish swimming there and above them his own reflection. The face was strong and square, the eyes deep-set, the beard full. He had never considered it the face of a weak man. His hand snaked out, disturbing the water. The sleek silver and black fish scattered, carrying his reflection with them.

'What can one man do, Lord? You can see them. The King has brought them wealth, and peace; prosperity and long life. They would tear me to pieces.' A sense of defeat settled upon him. In the past three months he had organised secret meetings, preaching against the excesses of the King. He had helped the outlawed Priests of Chronos to escape the Daggers, smuggling them from the city. But now he shrank from the last commitment; he was ashamed that love of life was stronger than love of God.

His vision swam, the sky darkened and Nu-Khasisatra felt himself torn from his body. He soared into the sky and hovered over the gleaming city below. In the distance a deeper darkness gathered, then a bright light shone beyond the darkness. A great wind blew and Nu trembled as the sea roared up to meet the sky. The mighty city was like a toy now as the ocean thundered across the land. Huge trees disappeared under the waves, like grass beneath a river flood. Mountains were swallowed whole. The stars flew across the sky and the sun rose majestically in the West.

Looking down upon the city of his birth, Nu-Khasisatra saw only the deep blue-grey of an angry sea. His spirit sank below the waves, deeper and deeper into the darkness. The Pool of Silence was truly silent now, and the black fish were gone. Bodies floated by him . . . men, women, tiny babes. Unencumbered by the water, Nu walked back to the central square. The statue of the King still stood with arms outstretched, but a huge black shark brushed against it. Slowly, the statue toppled striking a pillar. The head sheared off and the body bounced against the mosaic tiles.

'No!' screamed Nu. 'No!'

His body jerked, and once more he was sitting by the Pool. Bright sunlight streamed above the temple and doves circled the wooden parapets of the Wailing Tower. He stood, swept his sky-blue cloak over his shoulder and marched back to the Courtyard of the Holy Circle. The crowd was milling now and the priests were lifting the victim's body from the flat grey sacrifice stone. Blood stained the surface, and had run down the carved channels to disappear through the golden vents.

Nu-Khasisatra strode to the steps and walked slowly towards the sacrifice stone. At first no one made a move to stop him, but as he drew nearer to the stone a red-robed priest intercepted him. 'You cannot approach the Holy Place,' said the priest.

'What holy place?' countered Nu. 'You have corrupted it.' He thrust the man aside and walked to the stone. Some people in the crowd had watched the altercation, and now began to whisper.

'What is he doing?'

'Did you see him strike the priest?'

'Is he a madman?'

All eyes turned to the broad-shouldered man at the stone as he removed his blue cloak; beneath it he wore the white robes of a Priest of Chronos. Temple guards gathered at the foot of the steps, but it was forbidden to carry a weapon to the Holy Place and they stood their ground, uncertain.

Three priests approached the man at the sacrifice stone.

'What madness is this?' asked one. 'Why do you desecrate this Temple?'

'How dare you speak of desecration?' countered Nu-Khasisatra. 'This Temple was dedicated to Chronos, Lord of Light, Lord of Life. No blood sacrifice was ever made here.'

'The King is the living image of Chronos,' the priest argued. 'The conqueror of worlds, the Lord of Heaven. All who deny this are traitors and heretics.'

'Then count me among them!' roared Nu and his huge hands took hold of the sacrifice stone and wrenched it clear of its supports. Forcing his fingers under the stone, he lifted it high above his head and hurled it out over the steps, where it shattered. An angry roar rose from the crowd.

Nu-Khasisatra leapt to stand upon the altar base. 'Faithless people!' he shouted. 'The end of all days is upon you. You have mocked the Lord of Creation, and your doom will be terrible. The seas will rise against you and not one stone will be left upon another. Your bodies will be dashed to the deep and your dreams will be forgotten, even as you are forgotten. You have heard that the King is the living god. Blasphemy! Who brought the Rolynd Stones from the vault of Heaven? Who led the chosen people to this bountiful land? Who dashed the hopes of the wicked in the Year of Dragons? It was Chronos, through his prophets. And where was the King? Unborn and unmade. He is a man, and his evil is colossal. He will destroy the world. You have wives and sons; you have loved ones. All will die. Not one of you listening to these words will be alive at year's end.'

'Drag him down!' shouted someone in the crowd.

'Kill him!' yelled another, and the cry was taken up by the mob.

The Temple guards drew their swords and ran up the steps. Lightning seared amongst them, leaping from sword to sword, and the guards, their flesh blackened, toppled to the stone. A great silence settled on the crowd.

Smoke drifted up from the bodies of the guards as Nu-Khasisatra raised his hands to the heavens.

'There is no turning back now,' he said. 'All will be as I have told it. The sun will rise in the West, and the oceans will thunder across the land. You will see the Sword of God in the heavens – and despair!'

He stepped down from the altar and walked slowly past the dead guards. The crowd parted before him as he marched from the Temple.

'I recognise him,' said a man, as he passed by. 'That was Nu-Khasisatra, the shipbuilder. He lives in the south quarter.'

The name was whispered amongst the mob and carried from the Temple, coming at last to the woman Sharazad.

And the hunt began.

3

For three days Shannow travelled south, the trails winding ever down into a long valley of half-frozen streams and tall stands of pine, wide meadows and rolling hills. He saw little game, but came across tracks of deer and elk. Each day, around mid-morning he would halt in a spot shielded from the wind and clear the snow from the grass, allowing the stallion to eat, while Shannow himself sat by a small fire reading his Bible or thinking about the journey ahead.

His wounds were healing fast; Shir-ran had done a fine job on them. He thought of the strange Man-beast often, and came to the conclusion that Shir-ran had wanted his company for just the purpose it had served. The Man-beast had stitched his wounds, then left his guns by his side. Yet within the sanctuary of the cave he had no need of weapons. The doomed creature had spoken of the Change and it had been awesome to witness – the move from humanity to bestiality. What could cause such a transformation Shannow had no idea, but in the strange world after Armageddon there were many mysteries.

Two years before, in a bid to rescue Samuel Archer and the reformed Hellborn, Batik, Shannow had seen at first hand a new race of people called Wolvers, part man and part animal. Archer himself had spoken of other such creatures, though Shannow had yet to see them.

It was warmer here in the valley and as he moved further south the snow thinned, great patches of verdant grass shimmering on the hillsides. Every day Shannow scanned the skies, looking for the signs of wonder. But ever the heavens remained blue and clear.

On the fourth day, as dusk gathered, Shannow guided the stallion into a wood, seeking a camp-site. Ahead, through the tall trees, he glimpsed a glittering fire.

'Hello, the camp!' he yelled. At first there was no answer, then a gruff voice called out, beckoning him in. Shannow waited for a moment and then delved into his pack, bringing out the short-nosed percussion pistol and tucking it into his belt just inside the flap of his long coat. Then he rode forward.

There were four men sitting around the fire and five horses tethered to a picket line. Shannow stepped from the saddle and tied his stallion's reins to a jutting root. On the fire a large black pot was hanging from a tripod, and within it Shannow could smell a simmering broth. Casually he moved to the fire and squatted down, his eyes sweeping the group. They were hard men, for the most part lean and wolf-like; Shannow had known men like these all his life. His gaze halted on a burly, round-shouldered man with a short-cropped salt-and-pepper beard and eyes that were merely slits under heavy lids.

There was a tension in the air, but it did not affect the Jerusalem Man though he acknowledged it. His eyes locked to the burly man and he waited.

'Eat,' said the man at last, his voice low.

'After you,' said Shannow. 'I would not wish to be impolite.'

The man smiled, showing stained teeth. 'The wilderness is no place for manners.' He reached out and ladled some broth into a metal dish and the others followed suit. As the tension grew, Shannow took a dish with his left hand and placed it before the fire. Then, still with his left hand, he lifted the ladle and filled the bowl, drawing it to him. Slowly he finished the meal and pushed the plate from him.

'Thank you,' he said into the silence. 'It was most welcome.'

'Help yourself to more,' offered the leader.

'No, thank you. There will not be enough left for your scout.'

The leader swung round. 'Come in, Zak, supper's waitin'!' he called. Across from the fire a young man rose from the bushes, a long rifle in his hands. He walked slowly to the fire, avoiding Shannow's gaze, and sat beside the leader with the rifle by his side.

Shannow rose and moved to his stallion, untying his blanket roll and spreading his bed beside the horse. Loosening the cinch, he lifted the saddle and dropped it to the ground; then, taking a brush from his saddlebag, he ducked under the stallion's neck and, with smooth even strokes, groomed the horse. He did not look at the men around the fire, but the silence grew. The Jerusalem Man had been tempted to finish his meal and ride on, to be clear of the immediate danger – but such a move would be foolishness, he knew. These men were brigands and killers and to ride on would display weakness like the scent of blood to a wolf-pack. He patted the stallion's neck and returned to his bed. Without a word to the men he removed his hat and lay down, pulling a blanket over him and closing his eyes.

At the fire the young man reached for his rifle, but the leader gripped his arm and shook his head.

The youth pulled his arm clear. 'What the Devil's wrong with you?' he whispered. 'Let's take him now. That there is one Hell of a horse, and his guns . . . you see them guns?'

'I saw,' answered the leader, 'and I saw the man who wears 'em. You see how he rode in? Careful. He spotted you rightaways, and hunkered down where you couldn't get no shot. And all through the meal he only used his left hand. And where was his right? I'll tell you where. It was inside that long coat, and it weren't scratching his belly. Now you leave it be, boy. I'll think on it.'

Towards midnight, with all the men asleep in their blankets, the youth rose silently, a double-edged knife in one hand. He crept forward towards where Shannow slept. A dark figure loomed behind him and a pistol clubbed across the youth's neck; he fell without a sound. The leader holstered his pistol and dragged the boy back to his blankets.

Twenty feet away Shannow smiled and returned his own gun to its scabbard.

The leader walked across to him. 'I know you ain't asleep,' he said. 'Who the Hell are you?'

Shannow sat up. 'That boy will have a sore head. I hope he has sense enough to thank you for it.'

'The name's Lee Patterson,' the man answered, thrusting out his right hand. Shannow smiled at him, but ignored the offer.

'Jon Shannow.'

'Jesus God Almighty! You hunting us?'

'No. I'm riding south.'

Lee grinned. 'You wanna see them statues in the sky, eh? The Sword of God, Shannow?'

'You have seen them?'

'Not me, man. They call that the Wild Lands. There's no settlements there, no way for a man to make a living. But I seen a man once who swore he'd stood under 'em; he said it gave him religion. Me, I don't need no religion. You sure you're not huntin' us?'

'You have my word. Why did you save the boy?'

'A man don't have too many sons, Shannow. I had three. One got killed when I lost my farm. Another was shot down after we . . . took to the road. He was hit in the leg; it went bad and I had to cut it from him. Can you image that, Shannow, cutting the leg from your son? And he died anyway, 'cause I left it too long. It's a hard life, and no mistake.'

'What happened to your wife?'

'She died. This is no land for women, it burns them out. You got a woman, Shannow?'

'No. I have no one.'

'I guess that's what makes you dangerous.'

'I guess it does,' Shannow agreed.

Lee stood and stretched. He looked down. 'You ever find Jerusalem, Shannow?'

'Not yet.'

'When you do, ask *Him* a question, will you? Ask Him what the Hell is the point of it all.'

*

4

Nu-Khasisatra ran from the Temple, out on to the broad steps and down into the teeming multitudes who thronged the city thoroughfares. His courage was exhausted and reaction had set in; his limbs were trembling as he pushed his way through the crowds, trying to lose himself among the thousands who packed the market streets.

'Are you a priest?' a man asked him, clutching his sleeve.

'No,' snapped Nu. 'Leave me alone!'

'But you wear the robes,' the man persisted.

'Leave me!' roared Nu, wrenching the man's hand from him. Once more swallowed by the throng, he cut left into an alleyway and walked swiftly through to the Street of Merchants. Here he bought a heavy cloak; it had a deep hood, which he pulled over his dark hair.

He stopped at an eating house on the Crossroads corner, taking a table by the east window where he sat staring out on to the street, overwhelmed by the enormity of his deed. He was a traitor and a heretic. There was nowhere in the Empire to hide from the wrath of the King. Even now the Daggers would be hunting him.

'Why you?' Pashad had demanded the previous night. 'Why can your God not use someone else? Why must you throw away your life?'

'I do not know, Pashad. What can I say?'

'You can give up this foolishness. We will move to Balacris – put this nonsense behind us.'

'It is not nonsense. Without God I am nothing. And the King's evil must be opposed.'

'If your Lord Chronos is so powerful, why does he not strike the King dead with a thunderbolt? Why does he need a shipbuilder?'

Nu shrugged. 'It is not for me to question Him. All I

have is His. All the world is His. I have been a Temple student all my life – never good enough to be a priest. And I have broken many of His laws. But I cannot refuse when He calls upon me. What kind of a man would I be? Answer me that?'

'You would be a live man,' she said.

'Away from God there is no life.' He saw the defeat in her dark eyes, saw it born in the bright tears that welled and fell to her cheeks.

'What of me and the children? A traitor's wife suffers his fate – have you thought of that? Do you wish to see your own children burning in the fires?'

'No!' The word was torn from him in a cry of anguish.

'You must get away from here, beloved. You must! I spoke to Bali this afternoon and he says you can go to him tomorrow night; he has something for you.'

They had talked for more than two hours, making plans, then Nu had gone to his tiny prayer room where he knelt until the dawn. He begged his God to release him, but as the dawn streaked the sky he knew what he must do . . .

Go to the Temple and speak against the King.

Now he had – and death awaited him.

'Are you eating or drinking, Highness?' asked the House-keeper.

'What? Oh. Wine. The best you have.'

'Indeed, Highness.' The man bowed and moved away. Nu did not notice his return, nor the jug and goblet he placed upon the table. The House-keeper cleared his throat and Nu jerked, then delved into his purse and dropped a large silver coin into the man's hand. The House-keeper counted out Nu's change and placed it on the table. Nu ignored the money and absently poured the wine; it was from the south-west, rich and heady. He drained the goblet and refilled it.

Two Daggers moved into sight beyond the window and the crowd parted for them, people jostling and pushing to avoid contact with the reptiles.

Nu averted his eyes and drank more of the wine.

A figure moved into the seat opposite. 'To know the future is to be assured of fortune,' he said, as he spread out a series of stones on the table.

'I do not need my future read,' replied Nu. But the seer swept up two small silver pieces from the change on the table. Then he scattered the stones.

'Pick three,' he said.

Nu was about to order the man away when the two Daggers entered the room. He swallowed hard. 'What did you say?' he asked, turning to face the newcomer. 'Pick three stones,' the seer repeated and Nu did so, leaning forward so that his hood fell further over his face. 'Now give me your hand,' ordered the seer.

The man's fingers were long and slender, cold as knife-blades as he studied Nu's palm for several seconds.

'You are a strong man, but then I need no special skill to see that,' he said, grinning. He was young, hawk-faced, with deep-set brown eyes. 'And you are worried.'

'Not at all,' whispered Nu.

'Curious,' said the man suddenly. 'I see a journey, but not over water, nor yet over land. I see a man with lightning in his hands and death in his dark fingers. I see water . . . rising . . .'

Nu wrenched his hand away. 'Keep the money,' he hissed. He looked into the seer's eyes and saw the fear there. 'How does a man travel, and yet not move over land or water?' he asked, forcing a smile. 'What kind of seer are you?'

'A good one,' said the man softly. 'And you can relax, for they have gone.'

'Who?' Nu asked, not daring to look up.

'The reptiles. You are in great danger, my friend. Death stalks you.'

'Death stalks us all,' Nu replied. 'No man avoids him for ever.'

'There is truth in that. I do not know where you are going – nor do I want to know. But I see a strange land and a grey rider. His hands hold great power. He is the man of thunder. He is the doom of worlds. I do not know if he is a friend or an enemy, but you are linked to him. Walk warily.'

'Too late for that,' said Nu. 'Will you join me in a drink?'

'Your company is – I think – too perilous for me. Go with God.'

5

Beth McAdam climbed down from the wagon, gave the broken wheel a hard kick and cursed long and fluently. Her two children sat in amused silence on the tailboard. 'Wouldn't you just know it?' said Beth. The wooden rim had split and torn free the metal edge; she kicked it again. Samuel tried to stifle the giggle with his fist, but it exploded from him in a high peal. Beth stormed round to the rear of the wagon, but the boy squirmed up over the piled furniture where she could not reach him.

'You little snapper-gut!' she yelled. Then Mary began to laugh and Beth swung on her.

'You think it's funny to be trapped out here with the wolves . . . and the enormous lions?'

Mary's face fell and Beth was instantly contrite. 'I'm sorry, honey. There ain't no lions. I was only joking.'

'You promise?' said Mary, gazing out over the plain.

'I do. And even if there was, he'd know better than to come anywhere near your Ma when she's angry. And you come down from there, Samuel, or I'll rip out your arms and feed 'em to the wolves.'

His blond head peeped over the chest of drawers. 'You ain't gonna whack me, Ma?'

'I ain't gonna whack you, snapper-gut. Help Mary get the pots unloaded. We're going to have to camp here and figure a way to mend the wagon.'

While the children busied themselves preparing a campfire, Beth sat on a boulder and stared hard at the wheel. They would need to unload everything, then try to lever up the empty wagon while she manhandled the spare wheel into place. She was sure she could do it, but could the children handle the lever? Samuel was big for a seven-year-old, but he lacked the concentration necessary for such a task, and Mary, at eight, was wand-thin and would never muster the power needed. But there had to be a way . . . there always was.

Ten years ago, when her mother was beaten to death by a drunken father, the twelve-year-old Beth Newson had taken a carving-knife and cut his throat in his sleep. Then, with seven silver Barta coin, she had walked seventy miles to Seeka Settlement and spun a terrible tale of brigands and killers raiding the farm. For three years the Committee made her live with Seth Reid and his wife, and she was treated like a slave. At fifteen she had set her cap at the powerful logger, Sean McAdam. The poor man had no chance against her wide blue eyes, long blonde hair and hip-swinging walk. Beth Newson was no beauty, with her heavy brows and large nose, but by Heaven she knew what to do with what God had given her. Sean McAdam fell like a poleaxed bull and they were wed three months later. Seven months after that Mary had been born, and a year later Samuel. Last Fall, Sean had decided to move his family south and they had purchased a wagon from Meneer Grimm and set off with high hopes. But the first town they reached had been hit by the Red Death. They had left swiftly, but within days Sean's huge body had been covered with red weeping sores; the glands under his arms swelled and all movement brought pain. They had camped in a high meadow and Beth tended him day and night, but despite his awesome strength Sean McAdam lost the fight for life, and Beth buried him on the hillside. Before they could move on, Samuel was struck down by the illness. Exhausted, Beth continued to nurse the boy, going without sleep and sitting by his bedside dabbing at the sores with a damp cloth. The child had pulled through, and within two weeks the sores had vanished.

Without the strength of Sean McAdam the family had pushed on, through snow and ice, through spring floods, and once across a narrow cliff trail under threat of avalanche. Beth had twice driven wolves from the six oxen, shooting one great beast dead with a single shot from Sean's double-barrelled flintlock. Samuel's pride in his mother's achievement was colossal.

Five days ago he found another source for pride when two brigands had accosted them on the road – sour-looking men, bearded and eagle-eyed. Beth laid down the reins and took up the flintlock pistol.

'Now, you scum-tars don't look too bright to me, so I'll speak slow. Give me the road or, by God, I'll send your pitiful souls straight to Hell!'

And they had. One even swept his hat from his head in an elaborate bow as she passed.

Beth smiled at the memory now, then returned her gaze to the wheel. Two problems faced her: one, finding a length of wood to use as a lever; and two, figuring out how to do both jobs – levering and fitting the wheel – herself.

Mary brought her some soup; it was thin but nourishing. Samuel made her a cup of herb tea; there was too much sugar in it, but she thanked him with a bright smile and ruffled his hair. 'You're a pair of good kids,' she said. 'For a pair of snapper-guts, that is!'

'Ma! Riders comin'!' cried Mary and Beth stood and drew the flintlock from her wide belt. She eared back the hammers and hid the weapon in the fold of her long woollen skirt. Her blue eyes narrowed as she took in the six men and she swallowed hard, determined to show no fear.

'Wait in the wagon,' she told the children. 'Do it now!' They scrambled up the tailboard and hid behind the chest.

Beth walked forward, her eyes moving from man to man, seeking the leader. He rode at the centre of the group, a tall, thin-faced rider with short-cropped grey hair and a red scar running from brow to chin. Beth smiled up at him. 'Will you not step down, sir?' she asked. The men chuckled but she ignored them, keeping her eyes fixed to Scar-face.

'Oh, we'll step down right enough,' he said. 'I'd step down into Hell for a woman with a body like yours.' Lifting his leg over the saddle pommel, he slid to the ground and advanced on her. Taking a swift step forward, she curled her left arm up over his shoulder, drawing him down to a passionate kiss. At the same time her right hand slid up between them and the cold barrels of the flintlock pressed into his groin. Beth moved her head so that her mouth was close to his ear.

'What you are feeling, pig-breath, is a gun,' she whispered. 'Now tell your men to change the wheel on the wagon. And touch nothing in it.'

'Ain't ya gonna share her, Harry?' called one rider.

For a moment Scar-face toyed with the idea of making a grab for the pistol, but he glanced down into Beth's steely blue eyes and changed his mind.

'We'll talk about it later, Quint,' he said. 'First, you boys change that wheel.'

'Change . . . we didn't ride in here to change no damned wheel!' roared Quint.

'Do it!' hissed Scar-face. 'Or I'll rip your guts out.'

The men swung down from their mounts and set to work – four of them taking the weight of the wagon and the fifth, Quint, hammering loose the wheel-pin and manhandling the broken wheel free. Beth walked Scar-face to the edge of the camp, where she ordered him to sit on a round boulder. She sat to the right of him, leaving his body between her and the working men; out of sight, the flintlock remained pressed now to his ribs.

'You're a smart bitch,' said Scar-face, 'and – except for that big nose – a pretty one. Would you really shoot me?'

'Sooner than spit,' she assured him. 'Now, when those men have finished their chore you'll send them back to wherever your camp is. Am I making myself clear, dung-brain?'

'It's done, Harry. Now do we get down to it?' called Quint.

'Ride back to camp. I'll see you there in a couple of hours.'

'Now wait a goddamned minute! You ain't keepin' the whore to yourself. No ways!' Quint turned to look to the others for support, but the men shifted nervously. Then two of them mounted their horses and the others followed.

'Dammit, Harry. It ain't fair!' protested Quint, but he backed to his mount and stepped into the saddle nevertheless.

As they rode from the camp, Beth lifted the heavy pistol from the scabbard at Scar-face's hip. Then she stood and moved away from him. The children climbed out of the wagon.

'What you going to do now, Ma?' asked Samuel. 'You gonna kill him?'

Beth passed the brigand's gun to Mary; it was a cap and ball percussion revolver. 'Get the pliers and pull off the brass caps, girl,' she said. Mary carried the gun to the wagon and opened the tool box; one by one she stripped the caps from the weapon, then returned it to her mother. Beth threw it to Scar-face and he caught it deftly and slid it home in its scabbard.

'Now what?' he asked.

'Now we wait for a while, and then you go back to your men.'

'You think I won't come back?'

'You'll think about it,' she admitted. 'Then you'll realise just how they'll laugh when you tell them I held a gun to your instrument and forced you to mend my wagon. No, you'll tell them I was one Hell of a lay and you let me ride on.'

'They'll be fightin' mad,' he said. Then he grinned. 'Sweet Jesus, but you're a woman worth fightin' over! Where you headed?'

'Pilgrim's Valley,' she told him. There was no point in lying; the wagon tracks would be easy to follow.

'See those peaks yonder? Cut to the right of them. There's a trail there – it's high and narrow, but it will save you four days. You can't miss it. A long time ago someone placed out a stone arrow, and cut signs into the trees. Follow it through and you'll find Pilgrim's Valley is around two days beyond.'

'I may just take your advice, Harry,' she said. 'Mary,

prepare some herb tea for our guest. But don't get too close to him; I'd like a clear shot if necessary.'

Mary stoked up the fire and boiled a kettle of water. She asked Harry if he took sugar, added three measures and then carried a steaming mug to within six feet of him. 'Put it on the ground,' ordered Beth. Mary did so and Harry moved to it cautiously.

He sipped the tea slowly. 'If I'm ever in Pilgrim's Valley, would you object if I called on you?' Harry asked.

'Ask me when you see me in Pilgrim's Valley,' she told him.

'Who would I ask for?'

'Beth McAdam.'

'Greatly pleased to meet you, ma'am. Harry Cooper is my name. Late of Allion and points north.'

He went to his horse and mounted. Beth watched as he rode east, then uncocked the flintlock.

Harry rode the four miles to the camp, his mind aflame with thoughts of the spirited woman. He saw the camp-fire and cantered in, ready with his tale of satisfied lust. Tying his horse to the picket line, he walked to the fire . . .

Something struck him in the back and he heard the thunder of a shot. He swung, dragging his pistol clear and cocking it. Quint rose from behind a bush and shot him a second time in the chest. Harry levelled his own gun, but the hammer clicked down on the empty nipple. Two more shots punched him from his feet and he fell back into the fire which blazed around his hair.

'Now,' said Quint. '*Now* we all share.'

6

Nu-Khasisatra eased his huge frame into the shadows of a doorway, pulling his dark cloak over his head and holding his breath. His fear rose, and he could feel his heart beating in his chest. A cloud obscured the moon and the burly shipbuilder welcomed the darkness. The Daggers were patrolling the streets and if he was caught he would be dragged to the prison buildings at the centre of the city and tortured. He would be dead by the dawn, his head impaled on a spike above the gates. Nu shivered. The sound of distant thunder rumbled above the City of Ad, and a jagged spear of lightning threw momentary shadows across the cobbled street.

Nu waited for several seconds, calming himself. His faith had carried him this far, but his courage was near exhausted.

'Be with me, Lord Chronos,' he prayed. 'Strengthen my failing limbs.'

He stepped out on to the street, ears straining for any sound that might warn him of the approach of the Daggers. He swallowed hard; the night was silent, the curfew complete. He moved on as silently as he could until he reached Bali's high-towered home. The gate was locked and he waited in the shadows, watching the moon rise. At the prearranged hour he heard the bolt slide open. Stepping into the courtyard beyond, he sank to a seat as his friend shut the gate, locking it tight.

Bali touched a finger to his lips and led the dark-cloaked Nu into the house. The shutters were closed and curtains had been hung over the windows. Bali lit a lantern and placed it on an oval table.

'Peace be upon this house,' said Nu. The smaller Bali nodded his bald head and smiled.

'And the Lord bless my guest and friend,' he answered.

The two men sat at the table and drank a little wine; then Bali leaned back and gazed at his friend of twenty years. Nu-Khasisatra had not changed in that time. His beard was still rich and black, his eyes bright blue and ageless beneath thick jutting brows. Both men had managed to purchase Sipstrassi fragments at least twice to restore youth and health. But Bali had fallen on hard times, his wealth disappearing with the loss in storms at sea of three of his prize ships, and now he was beginning to show the signs of age. He appeared to be in his sixties, though he was in fact eighty years older than Nu, who was one hundred and ten. Nu had tried to acquire more Sipstrassi, but the King had gathered almost all the Stones to himself and even a fragment would now cost all of Nu's wealth.

'You must leave the city,' Bali said, breaking the silence. 'The King has signed a warrant for your immediate arrest.'

'I know. I was foolish to speak against him in the temple, but I have prayed hard and I know the Great One was speaking through me.'

'The Law of One is no more, my friend. The Sons of Belial have the ears of the King. How is Pashad?'

'I ordered her to denounce me this morning, and seek the severing of the Knot. She at least will be safe, as will my sons.'

'No one is safe, Nu. No one. The King is insane, the slaughter has begun . . . even as you prophesied it. There is madness in the streets – and these Daggers fill me with terror.'

'There is worse to come,' Nu told him sadly. 'In my prayer dreams I have seen terrible sights: three suns in the sky at one time, the heavens tearing, and the seas rising to swamp the clouds. I know it is close, Bali, and I am powerless to prevent it.'

'Many men have dreams that do not presage evil days,' said Bali.

Nu shook his head. 'I know this. But my dreams have all come true so far. The Lord of All Things is sending these visions. I know he has ordered me to warn the people, and

I know also that they will ignore me. But it is not for me to question His purpose.'

Bali poured another goblet of wine and said nothing. Nu-Khasisatra had always been a man of iron principles and faith, devout and honest. Bali liked and respected him. He did not share his principles, but he had come to know his God – and for that gift alone, he would give his life for the shipbuilder.

Opening a hidden drawer below the table, he removed a small purse of embroidered deerskin. For a moment he held it, reluctant to part with it, then he smiled and pushed it across the table.

'For you, my friend,' he said. Nu picked it up and felt the warmth emanating from within the purse. Then he opened it with trembling fingers and tipped out the Stone within. It was not a fragment but a whole Stone, round as if polished, golden with thin black veins. He closed his hand around it, feeling the power surging in him. Gently he placed it on the table top and gazed at the bald, elderly man before him.

'With this you could be young again, Bali. You could live for a thousand years. Why? Why would you give it to me?'

'Because you need it, Nu. And because I never had a friend before.'

'But it is worth perhaps ten times as much money as is contained in the entire city. I could not possibly accept it.'

'You must. It is life. The Daggers are seeking you and you know what that means. Torture and death. They have closed the city and you cannot escape, save by the Journey. There is a gateway within the stone circle the princes used to use, to the north of the seventh square. You know it? By the crystal lake? Good. Go there. Use these words and hold the Stone high.' He passed Nu a small square of parchment.

'The Enchantment will take you to Balacris. From there you will be on your own.'

'I have funds in Balacris,' said Nu, 'but the Lord wants me to stay and continue to warn the people.'

'You gave me the secret of the Great One,' Bali told him,

'and I accept His will overrides any wishes of our own. But similarly you have done as He commanded. You gave your warnings, but their ears were closed to you. Added to this, Nu my friend, I prayed for a way in which I might help you, and now this Stone has come into my possession. And yes, I wanted to keep it, but the Great One touched me and let me know it was for you.'

'How did you come by it?'

'An Achean trader brought it to my shop. He thought it was a gold nugget and wished to sell it to me in return for the money to buy a new sail.'

'A sail? With this you could buy a thousand sails, perhaps more.'

'I told him it was worth half the price of a sail, and he sold it to me for sixty pieces of silver.' Bali shrugged. 'It was with such dealings that I first became rich. You must go now. The Daggers surely know we are friends.'

'Come with me, Bali,' Nu urged. 'With this Stone we could reach my new ship. We could sail far from the reach of the King and his Daggers.'

'No. My place is here. My life is here. My death will be here.' Bali rose and led the way to the gate. 'One thing more,' he told his friend as they stood in the moonlight. 'Last night, as I held the Stone I had a strange dream. I saw a man in golden armour. He came to me and sat beside me. He gave me a message for you; he said you must seek the Sword of God. Does it mean anything to you?'

'Nothing. Did you recognise him?'

'No. His face shone like the sun, and I could not look at him.'

'The Great One will make it plain to me,' said Nu as he reached out to embrace the smaller man. 'May He watch over you, Bali.'

'And you, my friend.'

Bali silently opened the gate and peered out into the shadows. 'It is clear,' he whispered. 'Go quickly.'

Nu embraced him once more, then stepped into the shadows and was gone. Bali re-bolted the gate and returned to his room, where he sank into his chair and tried to repress his regrets. With the Stone he could have rebuilt his empire and enjoyed eternal youth. Without it? Penury and death.

He moved back into the main house, stepping over the body of the Achean sailor who had brought him the Stone. Bali had not even possessed the sixty silver pieces the man had requested, but he still owned a knife with a sharp blade.

The sound of crashing timber caused him to spin and run back towards the garden. He arrived to see the gate on its hinges and three dark-armoured Daggers moving towards him, their reptilian eyes gleaming in the moonlight, their scaled skin glistening.

'What . . . what do you want?' asked Bali, trembling.

'Where iss hee?'

'Who?'

Two of the Daggers moved around the garden, sucking the air through their slitted nostrils.

'He wass here,' hissed one of them and Bali backed away. One of the Daggers lifted a strangely shaped club from a scabbard at his side, pointing it at the little trader.

'Lasst chance. Where iss he?'

'Where you will never find him,' said Bali, and drawing his knife he leapt at the Dagger. A sound like thunder came from the small club in the reptile's hand, and a hammer smote Bali in the chest. The little man was hurled on his back to the path where he lay sprawled, staring sightlessly up at the stars.

A second shot sounded and the Dagger pitched to the ground, a black hole in his wedge-shaped head. The other creatures spun to see the golden-haired woman, Sharazad. 'I wanted Bali alive,' she said softly. 'And my orders will be obeyed.'

Behind her a dozen more Daggers crowded into the garden.

'Search the house,' she ordered. 'Rip it apart. If Nu-Khasisatra escapes, I will see you all flayed alive.'

7

Of all the seasons God had granted it was the Spring that Shannow loved above others, with its heady music of life and growth, its chorus of bird-song and richly coloured flowers pushing back the snow. The air too was clean and a man could drink it in like wine, filling his lungs with the essence of life itself.

Shannow dismounted before the crest of a hill and walked to the summit, gazing out over the rippling grass of the plain. Then he squatted on the ground and scanned the rolling lands before him. In the far distance he could see a wandering herd of cattle, and to the west several mountain sheep grazing on a hillside. He moved back from the skyline and studied the back-trail through the mountain valley, memorising the jagged peaks and the narrow ways he had passed. He did not expect to return this way, but if he did he needed to be sure of his bearings. He unbuckled the thick belt which carried his gun scabbards and removed his heavy topcoat, then swung the guns around his hips once more and buckled the belt in place before rolling his coat and tying it behind his saddle. The stallion was contentedly cropping grass and Shannow loosened the saddle cinch.

Taking his Bible he sat with his back to a boulder, slowly reading the story of King Saul. He always found it hard to avoid sympathising with the first King of Israel. The man had fought hard and well to make the nation strong, only to have a usurper preparing to steal his crown. Even at the end, when God deserted him, Saul still fought gallantly against the enemy and died alongside his sons in a great battle.

Shannow closed the book and took a long cool drink from his canteen. His wounds were almost healed now, and last night he had cut the stitches with the blade of his hunting-knife. Although he could not yet move his right arm with customary speed, his strength was returning.

He tightened the saddle and rode out on to the plain. Here and there were the tracks of horses, cattle and deer. He rode warily, watching the horizon, constantly hitching himself in the saddle to study the trail behind.

The plain stretched on endlessly and the far blue mountains to the south seemed small and insubstantial. A bird suddenly flew up to Shannow's left. His eyes fastened to it and he realised that he was following its flight with the barrel of his pistol; the weapon was cocked and ready. He eased the hammer back into place and sheathed the gun.

A long time ago he would have been delighted with the speed at which he reacted to possible danger, but bitter experience had long since corroded his pride. He had been attacked outside Allion by several men and had killed them all; then a sound from behind had caused him to swivel and fire . . . and he had killed a child who happened to be in the wrong place at the wrong time.

That child would have been a grown man by now, with children of his own. A farmer, a builder, a preacher? No one would ever know. Shannow tried to push the memory from his mind, but it clung to him with talons of fire.

Who would want to be you, Shannow? he asked himself. *Who would want to be the Jerusalem Man*?

The children of Allion had followed him during his nightly tours, copying the smooth straight-backed walk. They carried wooden guns thrust in their belts and they worshipped him; they thought it wonderful to be so respected and feared, to have a name that travelled the land ahead of you.

Is it wonderful, Shannow?

The people of Allion had been grateful when Jon Shannow put the brigands to flight – or buried them. But when the town was clean they had paid him and asked him to move on. And the brigands returned, as they always did. And perhaps the children followed *them* around, copying their walks and fighting pretend battles with their wooden guns.

How far to Jerusalem, Shannow?

'Over the next mountain,' he answered aloud. The stallion's ears pricked up and he snorted. Shannow chuckled as he patted the beast's neck and urged him into a run over the level ground. It was not a sensible move, he knew; a rabbit-hole or a loose rock could cause the horse to stumble and break a leg, or throw a shoe. But the wind in his face felt good and life was never without perils.

He let the horse have his head for about a half mile, then drew back on the reins as he saw wagon tracks. They were fresh, maybe two days old; Shannow dismounted and examined them. The wheels had bit deep into the dry earth – a family moving south with all their possessions. Silently he wished them good fortune and remounted.

By mid-afternoon he came upon the broken wheel. By now he knew a little of the family: there were two children and a woman. The children had gathered sticks and dried cattle droppings for fuel, probably depositing them in a net slung under the tailboard. The woman had walked beside the lead oxen; her feet were small, but her stride long. There was no sign of a man but then, thought Shannow, perhaps he is lazy and rides in the wagon. The broken wheel, though, was a mystery.

Shannow studied the tracks of the horsemen. They had ridden to the camp and changed the wheel, then returned the way they had come. The woman had stood close to one of the riders, and they had walked together to a boulder. By the wagon tracks Shannow found six brass caps, still with their fulminates intact. At some time during the encounter someone had unloaded a pistol. Why?

He built a fire on the ashes of the old one and sat pondering the problem. Perhaps the caps were old and the woman – for he knew now there was no man with them – had doubted their effectiveness. But if the caps were old, then so would be the wads and charges and these had not been stripped clear. He read the track signs once more, but could make no more of them – save that one of the horsemen had ridden to the right of the main group, or had left at a different time. Shannow walked out along the trail and a hundred paces from the camp he saw a hoofprint from the lone horse which had overstamped a previous print. So then, the lone rider had left *after* the main group. He had obviously sat talking with the woman. Why did they not all stay?

He prepared himself some tea, and ate the last of the fruit from Shir-ran's store. As he delved at the bottom of the sack his fingers touched something cold and metallic and he drew it out. It was like a coin, but made of gold, and upon the surface was a raised motif that Shannow could not make out in the gathering dusk. He tucked the coin into his pocket and settled down beside the fire. But the tracks had disturbed him and sleep would not come; the moon was bright and he rose, saddled the stallion and rode off after the horsemen.

When he came to their camp-site they were gone, but a man lay with his head in the ashes of a dead fire, his face burned. He had been shot several times and his boots and gun were missing, though the belt and scabbard remained. Shannow was about to return to his horse when he heard a groan. He could hardly believe life still survived in that ruined body. Unhooking his canteen from the saddle, he knelt by the man, lifting the burnt head.

The man's eyes opened. 'They gone after the woman,' he whispered. Shannow held the canteen to his lips, but he choked and could not swallow. He said no more and Shannow waited for the inevitable. The man died within minutes.

Something glinted to Shannow's right. Under a bush, where it must have fallen, lay the man's gun. Shannow retrieved it. The caps had been removed; he had no chance to defend himself against the attack. Shannow pondered the evidence. The men were obviously brigands who had shot down one of their own. Why? Over the woman? But they had all been at the camp. Why leave?

A group of men had come across a woman and two

children by a wagon with a broken wheel. They had mended the wheel and left – save one, who followed after. His pistol had been tampered with. But then surely he would have known that? When he arrived his . . . friends? . . . had shot him. Then they had headed back to the woman. There was no sense in it . . . unless he had stopped them from taking the woman in the first place. But then, why would he unload his gun before returning?

There was only one way to find out.

Shannow stepped into the saddle and searched for the tracks.

*

'Why did God kill my Dad?' asked Samuel, as he dipped his flat baked bread in the last of his broth. Beth put aside her own plate and looked across the camp-fire at the boy, his face white in the moonlight, his blond hair shining like silver threads.

'God didn't kill him, Sam. The Red Fever done that.'

'But the Preacher used to say that nobody died unless God wanted them to. Then they went to Heaven or Hell.'

'That's what the Preacher believes,' she said slowly, 'but it don't necessarily mean it's true. The Preacher used to say that Holy Jesus died less than four hundred years ago, and then the world toppled. But your Dad didn't believe that, did he? He said there were thousands of years between then and now. You remember?'

'Maybe that's why God killed him,' said Samuel, ''cos he didn't believe the Preacher.'

'Ain't nothin' in life that easy,' Beth told him. 'There's wicked men that God don't kill, and there's good men – like your Pa – who die out of their time. That's just life, Samuel; it don't come with no promises.'

Mary, who had said nothing throughout, cleared away the dishes, carrying them beyond the camp-site and scrubbing them with grass. Beth stood and stretched her back. 'You've a lot still to learn, Samuel,' she said. 'You want something, then you have to fight for it. You don't give ground, and you don't whinge and whine. You take your knocks and you get on with living. Now help your sister clear up, and put that fire out.'

'But it's cold, Ma,' Samuel protested. 'Couldn't we just sleep out here with the fire?'

'The fire can be seen for miles. You want them raiders coming back?'

'But they helped us with the wheel?'

'Put out the fire, snapper-gut!' she stormed and the boy leapt to his feet and began to kick earth over the blaze. Beth walked away to the wagon and stood staring out over the plain. She didn't know if there was a God, and she didn't care. God had not helped her mother against the brutality of the man she married – and, sure as sin, God had never helped her. Such a shame, she thought. It would have been nice to feel her children were safe under the security of a benign deity, with the faith that all their troubles could be safely left to a supreme being.

She remembered the terrible beating her mother had suffered the day she died; could still hear the awful sounds of fists on flesh. She had watched as he dragged her body out to the waste ground behind the house, and listened as the spade bit into the earth for an unmarked grave. He had staggered back into the house and stared at her, his hands filthy and his eyes red-streaked. Then he had drunk himself into a stupor and fallen asleep in the heavy chair. 'Jus' you an' me now,' he mumbled. The carving-knife had slid across his throat and he had died without waking.

Beth shook her head and stared up at the stars, her eyes misting with unaccustomed tears. She glanced back at the children, as they spread their blankets on the warm ground beside the dead fire. Sean McAdam had not been a bad man, but she did not miss him as they did. He had learned early on that his wife did not love him, but he had doted on his children, played with them, taught them, helped them. So devoted had he been that he had not noticed his wife's affection growing, not until close to the end when he had lain, almost paralysed, in the wagon.

'Sorry, Beth,' he whispered.

'Nothin' to be sorry for. Rest and get well.'

For an hour or more he had slept, then his eyes opened and his hand trembled and lifted from the blanket. She took hold of it, squeezing it firmly. 'I love you,' he said. 'God's truth.'

She stared at him hard. 'I know. Sleep. Go to sleep.'

'I . . . didn't do too bad . . . by you and the kids, did I?'

'Stop talkin' like that,' she ordered. 'You'll feel better in the morning.'

He shook his head. 'It's over, Beth. I'm hanging by a thread. Tell me? Please?'

'Tell you what?'

'Just tell me . . .' His eyes closed and his breathing became shallow.

She held his hand to her breast and leaned in close. 'I love you, Sean. I do. God knows I do. Now please get well.'

He had slipped away in the night while the children were sleeping. Beth sat with him for some time, but then considered the effect on the children of seeing their father's corpse. So she had dragged the body from the wagon and dug a grave on the hillside while they slept.

Lost in her memories now she did not hear Mary approach. The child laid her hand on her mother's shoulder and Beth turned and instinctively took her in her arms.

'Don't fret, Mary love. Nothing's going to happen.'

'I miss my Pa. I wish we were still back home.'

'I know,' said Beth, stroking the child's long auburn hair. 'But if wishes were horses then beggars would ride. We just got to move on.' She pushed the girl from her. 'Now, it's important you remember what I showed you today, and do it. There's no tellin' how many bad men there are 'twixt here and Pilgrim's Valley. And I need you, Mary. Can I trust you?'

'Sure you can, Ma.'

'Good girl. Now get to bed.'

Beth stayed awake for several hours, listening to the wind over the grass of the plain, watching the stars gliding by.

Two hours before dawn she woke Mary. 'Don't fall asleep, girl. You watch for any riders and wake me if you see them.'

Then she lay down and fell into a dreamless sleep. It seemed to last for only a few moments before Mary was shaking her, but the sun was clearing the eastern horizon as Beth blinked and pushed one hand through her blonde hair.

'Riders, Ma. I think it's the same men.'

'Get in the wagon. And remember what I told you.'

Beth lifted the flintlock pistol and cocked both barrels; then she hid the gun once more in the folds of her skirt and scanned the group for sign of Harry. He wasn't with them. She took a deep breath and steadied herself as the horsemen thundered into the camp and the man she remembered as Quint leapt from the saddle.

'Now, Missy,' he said. 'We'll have a little of what old Harry enjoyed.'

Beth raised the flintlock. Quint stopped in his tracks. She loosed the first barrel and the ball took Quint just above his nose, ploughing through his skull. He fell back into the dust with blood pumping from a fatal wound in his head as Beth stepped forward.

The sudden explosion had alarmed the horses and the four remaining riders fought to settle them as Quint's mount galloped out over the plain. In the silence that followed, the men glanced at one another. Beth's voice cut into them.

'You whoresons have two choices: ride, or die. And make the choice fast. I start shooting when I stop speaking.' The gun rose and pointed at the nearest man.

'Whoa there, lady!' the rider shouted. 'I'm leaving.'

'You can't take all of us, bitch!' shouted another, spurring his horse. But a tremendous explosion came from the wagon and the brigand was whipped from the saddle, half his head blown away.

'Any other doubters?' asked Beth. 'Move!'

The three survivors dragged on the reins and galloped away. Beth ran to the wagon, took her powder horn and reloaded the flintlock. Mary climbed down from the tail-board with the shortened rifle in her arms.

'You did well, Mary,' said Beth, ramming home the wad over the ball and charge. 'I'm proud of you.'

She took the rifle and leaned it against the wagon, then cradled the trembling child in her arms. 'There, there. It's all right. Go and sit at the front; don't look at them.' Beth guided Mary to the driving platform and helped her up, then walked back to the bodies. Unbuckling Quint's pistol belt, she strapped it to her own waist and then searched the body for powder and ammunition. She found a small hide sack of caps and transferred them to the wagon, then took a second pistol from the other body and hid it behind the driver's seat. Sean McAdam had never been able to afford a revolving pistol; now they had two. Beth gathered the oxen, hitched them to the wagon and then walked to the brigand's horse, a bay mare, and pulled herself into the saddle. Awkwardly she rode alongside where Mary sat.

'Take up the reins, child. And let's move.'

Samuel clambered up beside Mary and grinned at his mother. 'You look just like a brigand, Ma.'

Beth smiled back at him, then transferred her gaze to Mary who was sitting white-faced, staring ahead.

'Take the reins, Mary, goddammit!' The girl flinched and unhooked them from the brake. 'Now let's go!' Mary flicked the reins and Beth rode up alongside the lead ox and whacked her palm across its rump.

High above, the carrion birds had begun to circle.

8

Nu-Khasisatra reached the old stone circle an hour before dawn. He waited, hidden in the trees, searching for any guards who might be patrolling here, but there were none that he could see. Under the bright moonlight he studied the words on the parchment, memorising them. Then, Stone in hand, he ran from the trees on to the open ground before the circle.

At once there was a thin, piercing whistle. Shadows darted for him and a woman's voice cried out: 'Alive! Take him alive!'

Nu sprinted for the stone circle, its tall grey slabs promising sanctuary. A reptilean figure in black armour ran into his path but Nu swung his huge fist into the creature's face, dashing him to the grass. Hurdling the falling body, he made it to the shadows of the stones. Once there, he swung to see more Daggers closing on him.

He lifted his hand. '*Barak naizi tor lemmes!*' he shouted. Lightning flashed across his eyes, blinding him, and his mind was filled with whirling colours. All sense of weight and strength left him, and he tumbled like a wind-blown feather into a storm. With a sickening lurch he felt the ground under his feet, stumbled and fell. His eyes opened, but at first he could see nothing save flickering lights. Then his vision cleared and he found himself in a small clearing. Close by was a dead man, his face hideously burnt. Nu got to his feet and moved to the body. The man was wearing strange apparel and he studied it; the clothing was unlike anything he had encountered. He walked out of the clearing and stared at the surrounding landscape. There was no city of Balacris, no view of a distant ocean. Grasslands drifted to a blurred horizon where jagged mountains soared to meet the sky.

Returning to the clearing, Nu sat and examined his Stone. The black veins in the gold had swelled. He had no way of knowing how much power the journey had sucked from the Sipstrassi.

Moving to his knees, Nu-Khasisatra began to pray. For some time he gave thanks for his deliverance from the hands of Sharazad and her Daggers; then he asked for his family to be protected. Finally he sought the silence in which the voice of God could be heard.

The wind whispered about him, but he heard no words within it. Sunlight bathed his face, but no visions came. At last he stood. It would be safer, he knew, if his clothing matched that of the people of this land. The Stone glowed warm in his hand, and his robes and cloak shimmered and changed. Now he was wearing trousers and boots, shirt and long jacket identical to those of the dead man.

'Be careful, Nu,' he warned himself. 'Do not waste the power.'

He recalled the words of Bali: 'Seek the Sword of God.' He had no idea in which direction to travel, but looking down at the ground he saw the tracks of a horse, heading towards the mountains. With no other omen to guide him, Nu-Khasisatra followed them.

*

Sharazad sat at an ornate table, her ice-blue eyes locked to the face of Pashad, wife of the traitor Nu-Khasisatra.

'You denounced your husband yesterday. Why?'

'I discovered he was plotting against the King,' she answered, averting her eyes and gazing at the surface of the desk on which lay a curious white-handled ornament of silver.

'With whom was he plotting?'

'The merchant, Bali, Highness. He was the only one I knew.'

'You know that the family of a traitor shares his sentence?' whispered the golden-haired inquisitor and Pashad nodded.

'Yet he had not been declared a traitor when I denounced

him, Highness. Also, I am no longer of his family, for after denouncing him I divorced him.'

'So you did. Where is he hiding?'

'I do not know, Highness. The list of our property was taken this morning. There are only five houses, and three store buildings by the dock. Other than that, I cannot help you.'

Sharazad smiled. Then reaching into the pocket of her pearl-embroidered tunic, she drew out a red-gold stone and placed it upon the desk. Three words of power she uttered. 'Place your hand over the stone,' she told the slim, dark-haired girl before her. Pashad did so.

'Now I will ask you some more questions, but I want you to be aware that if you lie the stone will kill you instantly. Do you understand this?'

Pashad nodded, but her eyes showed her fear.

'Do you know the whereabouts of the man, Nu-Khasisatra?'

'I do not.'

'Do you know the names of any of his friends who may have been involved in the plot?'

'That is difficult to answer,' said Pashad, sweat glistening on her brow. 'I know some of his . . . friends, but I would have no way of knowing whether they shared his treason.'

'Do you share his treason?'

'No. I do not understand any of it. How can I tell if the King is a god? My life has been spent in making my husband happy and raising his children. What should it matter to us whether the King is a god or not?'

'If you did know the whereabouts of the man, Nu-Khasisatra, would you tell me?'

'Yes,' answered Pashad. 'Instantly.'

Sharazad's surprise was genuine. Lifting Pashad's hand, she took the stone and replaced it in her pocket.

'You are free to go,' she said. 'If you hear any news of the traitor, then make sure I know of it.'

'I will, Highness.'

Sharazad watched the woman leave and then leaned back

in her chair. A curtain by the left wall parted and a young man stepped through – tall and wide-shouldered, yet slim of hip. He grinned and sat down in a nearby chair, lifting his booted foot to rest on the table.

'You owe me,' he said. 'I told you she would know nothing.'

'Always so smug, Rhodaeul?' she snapped. 'But I am somewhat taken aback. From all I have heard of this ship-builder, he adored his wife. I would have expected him to have taken her into his confidence.'

'He's a careful man. Have you any idea where he has gone?'

'Yes,' she said, smiling, 'as a matter of fact, I have. You see, the Circle has been linked to the world we discovered two months ago. Nu-Khasisatra thought he was escaping, but instead he has travelled to our latest field of conquest. It is the land that has brought us these strange weapons.' She lifted the pistol from the desk-top and tossed it to Rhodaeul; it was silver-plated, with grips of carved white bone. 'The King wishes you to become proficient with these . . . these guns.'

'Will he equip the army with them?'

'No. The King believes them to be vulgar. But my Daggers will prove their potency in war.'

Rhodaeul nodded. 'And Nu-Khasisatra?'

'He is stranded in that strange land. He does not speak the language, nor does he know a way back. I will find him.'

'So sure of yourself, Sharazad? Beware!'

'Do not mock me, Rhodaeul. If I am arrogant, it is with good cause. The King knows my talents.'

'We all know your talents, dear Sharazad. Some of us have even enjoyed them. But the King is right. These weapons are vulgar beyond description; there is no honour in despatching an enemy with such a monstrosity.'

'You fool! You think there is more honour in an arrow, or a lance? They are merely weapons of death.'

'A clever man can dodge an arrow, Sharazad, or sidestep a lance. But with these, death strikes a man unawares. And their mastery takes no skill.' He walked to the window and stepped out into the courtyard beyond. Two prisoners were tied to stakes; wood had been piled around their feet and legs.

'Where is the skill?' asked Rhodaeul, cocking the pistol smoothly. Two shots rang out and the victims at the stakes sagged against their ropes. 'All a man needs is a good eye and a swift hand. But with the sword, there are over forty different variations on the classic block and riposte, sixty if you count the sabre. But – if it is the King's wish – I will learn how to handle the thing.'

'It is the King's wish, Rhodaeul. Perhaps you will be able to polish your skills in my new world. There are men there who are legends because of their skill with such weapons. I will hunt them down for you, and have them brought back for your . . . education.'

'How sweet of you, Sharazad. I will look forward to it. Can you give me a name to disturb my dreams?'

'There are several. Johnson is one, Crowe another. Then there is Daniel Cade. But above them all, there is a man called Jon Shannow. They say he seeks a mythical city and they call him the Jerusalem Man.'

'Bring them all, Sharazad. Since our conquests in the north, we have been sadly lacking in good sport.'

9

Shannow knew from the moment he set off in pursuit that he would be too late to help the woman and her family, and anger burned in him. Even so he rode with care, for in the light of the moon he could not clearly see the ground ahead. It was dawn before he came upon the bodies; they had been disturbed by carrion-eaters, the faces and hands stripped of flesh. Shannow sat his horse and stared down at them.

His respect for the unknown woman soared. Dismounting he examined the ground, finding the spot from which Beth McAdam had fired. Judging by the angle at which the other corpse lay, the second shot must have come from the wagon. Shannow remounted and headed towards the mountains.

The land rose sharply, becoming thickly wooded with towering pine. The stallion was tired and stumbled twice; Shannow stepped down and led the horse up and into the trees. They came to a crest on the mountainside and Shannow gazed down on a sprawling camp with six fires and a dozen tents. Men were working under torchlight in an immense pit from which jutted a towering structure of metal, almost triangular but with one side slightly curved. There was a wide stream to the south of the camp and, beside it, a wagon. The Jerusalem Man led his mount down into the camp-site, tethering him at a picket line and removing the saddle. A man approached him.

'You got word from Scayse?' the man asked, and Shannow turned.

'No. I've just come in from the north.' The man swore and walked away.

Shannow made his way to the largest tent and stepped into the lantern-lit interior. There were a dozen or so men inside, eating and drinking, while a large-boned, well-fleshed woman in a leather apron was ladling food into round wooden bowls. He joined the queue and took a bowl of thick broth and a chunk of black bread, carrying it to a bench table near the tent opening. Two men made room for him and he ate in silence.

'Looking for work?' asked a man across the table and Shannow looked up. The speaker was around thirty years of age, slender and fair-haired.

'No . . . thank you. I am heading south,' Shannow replied. 'Can I purchase supplies here?'

'You could see Deiker, he may have some spare. He's on site at the moment; he should be in any time now.'

'What are you working on?'

'It's an old metal building from before the Fall. We've found some interesting artefacts. Nothing of great value yet, but we're hopeful. It has given us a great insight into the Dark Times; they must have been living in fear to build such a great iron fortress here.'

'Why in fear?' Shannow asked.

'Oh, you can only see a section of the building from here. It goes on and on. There are no windows or doors for over a hundred feet from the foundation base, and then when you do find them they are too small to allow anyone to climb through. They must have had terrible wars in those days. By the way, my name is Klaus Monet.' The young man thrust out his hand and Shannow accepted the grip.

'Jon Shannow,' he said, watching for any response. There was none.

'And another thing,' Monet went on. 'It is all built of iron, and yet there are no significant iron ore deposits in these mountains, nor trace of any mines – save the silver mines at Pilgrim's Valley. So, the inhabitants must have carted ore right across the Big Wide. Incredible, isn't it?'

'Incredible,' agreed Shannow, finishing his meal and rising.

Outside the tent he walked to the edge of the pit and watched the men below; they were finishing their work and packing their tools away. He waited until they reached the upper level.

'Meneer Deiker!' Shannow called.

'Who wants him?' asked a thickset man with a black and silver beard.

'I do. I am looking to buy some supplies – grain, dried fruit and meat. And some oats if you have them.'

'For how many?'

'Just myself.'

The man nodded. 'I think I can accommodate you, but Pilgrim's Valley is only two days away. You'd get better prices there.'

'Always take food where you can find it,' Shannow said.

'There's wisdom in that,' Deiker agreed. He led Shannow to the store tents and filled several small sacks. 'You want sugar and salt?'

'If you can spare it. How long have you been working on this site?'

'About a month; it's one of the best. There will be a lot of answers here, mark my words.'

'And you think it is a building?'

'What else can it be?' asked Deiker, with a broad grin.

'It is a ship,' Shannow told him.

'I like a man with a sense of humour, Meneer. I estimate that it is over three hundred feet long – most of it still buried. And it is made of iron. Did you ever see anyone float a piece of iron?'

'No, but I have seen an iron ship before – and considerably bigger than this one.'

Deiker shook his head. 'I am an Arcanist, Meneer. I know my business. I also know you do not get ships at the centre of a land mass. That will be three full Silvers.'

Shannow said no more but paid for the food with Barta coin and carried it back to his saddle, stowing it in his cavernous bags. Then he walked back through the camp towards the wagon by the stream. He saw a woman sitting by a blazing fire with her two children asleep in blankets by her feet.

She looked up as he approached and he watched her hand slide towards the pistol scabbard on her belt.

*

Beth McAdam looked long at the tall newcomer. His hair was shoulder-length and dark, with silver streaks at the temples, and a white fork at the chin showed in the close-trimmed beard he wore. His face was angular and strong, his blue eyes cold. By his side were two pistols in oiled leather scabbards.

He sat down opposite her. 'You coped well with a perilous journey. I congratulate you. Very few people would have dared to cross the Big Wide without the protection of a wagon convoy.'

'You get straight to it, don't you?' she said.

'I do not understand you?'

'Well, I do not need a guide, or a helper, or a man around me. Thank you for your offer. And good night.'

'Have I offended you?' Shannow asked softly, his blue eyes locked to her own.

'I don't offend easily. Neither do you, it seems.'

He scratched at his beard and smiled; in that moment his face lost some of its harshness. 'No, I do not. If you would prefer me to leave, I will do so.'

'Help yourself to some tea,' she said. 'After that, I would like some privacy.'

'That is kind of you.' As he leaned forward to lift the kettle he froze, then stood, turning to face the darkness. Two men walked into the firelight; Beth eased her hand around the butt of her pistol.

'Meneer Shannow, do you have a moment?' asked Klaus Monet. 'There is someone I would like you to meet.' He gestured to his companion, a small, balding figure with a sparse white beard. 'This is Boris Haimut; he is a leading Arcanist.' The man dropped his head in a short bow and offered his hand. Shannow took it.

'Meneer Deiker told me of your conversation,' said Haimut. 'I was fascinated. I have thought for some time that we were studying a vessel of some kind, but it seemed so improbable. We have only excavated some one-fifth of the . . . the ship. Do you have an explanation as to how it got here?'

'Yes,' replied Shannow. 'But I fear we are intruding on the lady's privacy.'

'But of course,' agreed Haimut. 'My apologies, Frey . . .'

'McAdam. And Meneer Shannow is correct; I do not wish the sleep of my children disturbed.'

The three men bowed and silently left the camp-site. Beth watched them vanish into the shadows and then reappear on the torch-lit slopes of the site.

She poured herself some tea and sipped it, Shannow's face hovering in her mind. Was he brigand or Landsman? She shook her thoughts clear of him. What difference did it make? She would not see him again. Throwing the remains of her tea to the ground, she settled down under her blankets.

But sleep did not come easily.

*

'You have to understand, Meneer Shannow,' said Boris Haimut with an apologetic smile, 'that Meneer Deiker is Oldview. He is a Biblical man and believes the world is currently enduring the Last Days. To him Armageddon was a reality that began – to the best of our knowledge – three hundred and seventeen years ago. For myself, I am a Longview scholar. It is my belief that we have seen at least a thousand years of civilisation following the death of the man, Jesus; that civilisation knew wonders that are now lost to us. This find has already cast great doubts on the Oldview. If it is a ship . . . the doubts could become certainties.'

Shannow sat silently, uncomfortable within the small tent and acutely aware that the bright lantern was casting shadows on the canvas. He knew he should be in little danger here, but years of being both hunter and hunted left him uneasy when sitting in exposed places.

'I can tell you little, Meneer,' he said. 'More than a

thousand miles from here is a tall mountain. High on a ledge there is a rotting vessel of iron, around a thousand feet long. It was a ship – I learned this from people who lived close by it and knew its history. It seems this land mass was once at the bottom of an ocean, and many ships sank during storms.'

'But the ancient cities we have found?' questioned Haimut. 'There are even ruins less than two miles from here. How is it they were built at the bottom of an ocean?'

'I too wondered this. Then I met a man named Samuel Archer – a scholar like yourself. He proved to me that the world had toppled not once, but twice. The cities themselves are indeed ancient – from an empire called Atlantis that sank below the oceans before the time of Christ.'

'Revolutionary words, Meneer. In some areas you could be stoned to death for saying them.'

'I am aware of that,' said Shannow. 'However, when you excavate more of the ship you will find the great engines that powered it, and a wheelhouse from where it was steered. Now, if you will excuse me, I need to rest.'

'A moment, sir,' put in Klaus Monet, who had been sitting in silence as the two older men spoke. 'Would you stay with us – become part of the team?'

'I do not think so,' answered Shannow, rising.

'It is just that . . .' Monet looked to the elderly Haimut for support, but the scholar shook his head and Monet lapsed into embarrassed silence.

Shannow stepped from the tent and made his way to his horse. He fed the beast some grain, then spread his blankets on the ground beside it. He could have told them more: the glowing lights that burned without flame, the navigational devices – all the knowledge he had gained from the Guardians during the Hellborn War. But what would it serve? Shannow was caught in the no-man's land of the Arcane debate.

Instinctively he longed for the Oldview to be correct, but events had forced a different understanding on him. The old world was gone. Shannow had no wish to see it rise from the ashes.

Just as he was drifting to sleep, he heard a gentle footfall on the earth. He drew a pistol and waited.

The slender figure of Klaus Monet crouched beside him. 'I am sorry to intrude on you, Meneer Shannow. But . . . you seem a man of action, sir. And we sorely need someone like you.'

Shannow sat up. 'Explain yourself.'

Monet leaned in close. 'This expedition was led by Boris; we won the finance from a group of Longviewers in the east. But since we have been here, a man named Scayse has become involved in the project. He has put his own men – led by Deiker – in charge, and now some of the finds are being sent to him in Pilgrim's Valley.'

'What kind of finds?'

'Gold bars, gems from steel boxes in one of the deep rooms. It is theft, Meneer Shannow.'

'Then put a stop to it,' Shannow advised.

'I am a scholar, sir.'

'Then study – and do not interfere with matters beyond your strength.'

'You would condone such thievery?'

Shannow chuckled. 'Thievery? Who owns this ship? No one. Therefore there is no theft. Two groups of men desire what is here. The strongest will take what he wills. That is the way of life, Meneer Monet; strength always decides.'

'But with you, we would be stronger.'

'Perhaps . . . but you will never know. I leave in the morning.'

'Are you afraid, Meneer Shannow, or do you just desire more coin? We can pay.'

'You could not afford me, sir. Now leave me to sleep.'

The morning sky was grey and rain on his face woke Shannow soon after dawn. He rose from his blankets and rolled them into a tight bundle, tying them with strips of oiled hide. Then he put on his heavy, double-shouldered topcoat and saddled the stallion. Two men came walking towards him through the misty rain and Shannow turned and waited.

'Looks like you beat us to it,' said the first, a broad-shouldered man with a gaping gap where his front teeth should have been. His comrade was shorter and more lean; both were wearing pistols. 'Well, don't let us stop you,' continued the big man. 'Be on your way.'

Shannow remained silent.

'Are you deficient in the hearing?' the second man asked. 'You are not wanted here.'

A small crowd had gathered in the background and Shannow caught sight of Haimut and Klaus Monet. Of Deiker there was no sign.

'That's it, let's help him on his way,' said the big man, stepping in; but Shannow's hand shot up with fingers extended, and hammered into his throat. He fell back choking, then sank to his knees. Shannow's eyes fixed on the second man.

'Be so kind as to tie my blanket roll to my saddle,' he said softly.

The man swallowed hard and licked his lips, his hand hovering over the pistol butt.

'Today,' stated Shannow, 'is not a good day to die. A man should at least see the sun in the heavens.'

For several seconds the man stood tense; then he cast a nervous glance at his comrade who was kneeling and holding his throat, his breathing hoarse and ragged. He knew he should grab for his pistol, but could not make his hand obey him. His eyes flicked up to meet Shannow's.

'Damn you!' he whispered. His hand fell away from the gun and he moved to the blanket roll, swinging it over the back of the saddle and tying it into place.

'Thank you,' said Shannow. 'And now see to your friend.' He stepped into the saddle and swung the stallion towards the north. The crowd parted and he resisted the urge to glance back. Now was the moment of greatest danger. But there was no shot. He angled the stallion down to where Frey McAdam's wagon had been camped; it was gone.

Shannow was angry with himself. There was no need to have shamed the men Deiker had obviously sent to see him on his way. He should have mounted and left as they had asked him. Only pride had prevented him from doing just that, and pride was a sin in the eyes of the Almighty.

That is why you cannot find Jerusalem, Shannow, he told himself. Your sins burden you down.

There is no Jerusalem!

The thought leapt unbidden to his mind and he shivered. He had seen so much in these last few years and his doubts were many. But what choice do I have, he wondered. If there is no Jerusalem, then all is in vain. And so the search must go on. *For what purpose?* For me! For as long as I search, then Jerusalem exists – if only in my mind. And that is enough. I need no more. *You lie, Shannow!* Yes, yes, I lie. But what does that prove? I must search. I must know. *Where next will you search?* Beyond the Great Wall. *And if not there?* To the ends of the earth and the borders of Hell!

Coming to the top of the rise, he turned west seeking the pass through the mountains. He rode the deer trails for more than two hours before joining the main track, which was scarred by the rims of wagon wheels and the hooves of many horses. The rain had ceased and the sun broke clear of the clouds. He rode more warily now, halting often and studying his surroundings. With the sun at its height he stopped and rested in the shadow of a looming natural pillar of stone. It was cool here and he read his Bible for an hour, enjoying the Song of Solomon. By mid-afternoon the Jerusalem Man had passed the mountains and was following a narrow track down into the valley beyond.

To the west he could see the McAdam wagon, following the wider trail which led into the town. To the north, beyond the buildings, the valley stretched for miles, ending in a huge wall that vanished into the distance. Shannow drew a long glass from his bags and through it he scanned the Wall. It was massive and even at this distance he could make out the flowers and lichens sprouting between its great blocks. He transferred his gaze to the sky, seeking the wonders beyond the Wall, but only huge white clouds could be seen gently rolling across the vault of Heaven. Hitching himself round in the saddle, he focused on the McAdam wagon. The woman was at the reins; he could see her honey-blonde hair and the flesh of her right leg as it rested against the brake. The children were walking behind, leading the horse. They would be in the town long before Shannow. He studied the buildings below. Most were wood structures – some timber, some log – but there were stone dwellings of several storeys, mostly at the eastern end. There appeared to be one main thoroughfare stretching for around four hundred paces and then, in the shape of a 'T', buildings branched north and south of it. It was a thriving community and many more dwellings were in the process of completion. Beyond the town was a meadow packed with tents, large and small, and Shannow could see more than a dozen cook-fires. Families were moving in to settle the land and soon Pilgrim's Valley would house a city.

Shannow considered avoiding the town and riding on to the Wall, and beyond. But the stallion needed rest and grain feeding and the Jerusalem Man had not slept in a bed in what seemed an age. He rubbed at his chin and imagined a long, hot bath and the feel of a razor on his face. His clothes too were way overdue for a cleaning, and his boots were leaf-thin. Flicking a glance at the wagon, he could no longer see the driver nor the flesh of her leg at the brake.

10

Oshere eased his swollen, misshapen frame into the room and tried to sit down in a wide chair. The discomfort was supreme; the muscles of his back no longer stretched as they should. He rose and squatted on his haunches, watching the Dark Lady as she sat, statue still, at the huge desk. Her eyes were closed, her spirit absent from her body. Oshere knew where she flew. She was deep down inside the drying smear of his blood that stained the crystal on her desk. Oshere sat silently until Chreena stretched her back and opened her eyes. She cursed softly.

'You must not be impatient,' said Oshere.

The black woman turned and smiled. 'Time races away from me,' she replied. 'How are you feeling?'

'Not good, Chreena. Now I know how Shir-ran felt . . . and why he left. Perhaps I should go too.'

'No! I will not hear such talk. I am close, Oshere; I know I am. All I need to find out is *why* the daughter molecules depart from the norm. They should not; it is against nature.'

Oshere chuckled. 'Are we not against nature, my dear? Did God ever intend a lion to walk like a man?'

'I am not worthy to discuss God's aims, Oshere. But your genetic structure was altered hundreds of years ago and now it is reverting. There must be a way to halt it.'

'But that is what I am saying, Chreena. Perhaps God wants us back the way he created us.'

'I should never have told you the truth,' Chreena whispered.

His tawny eyes locked on her dark face. 'We have left the others in the joy of their myths, but it is better for me to know the truth. Dear Lord, Chreena, I am a lion. I should be padding the forests and the mountains. And I will be.'

'You were born as a human,' she told him, 'and you grew into a man. A fine man, Oshere. You were not intended to prowl the wilds – I know it.'

'And Shir-ran was? No, Chreena. You are a fine scientist, and you have cared for the People of the Dianae. But I think your emotions are ruling your intellect. We always thought that we were the Chosen People. We saw the statues in the cities and believed that Man was once subservient to us. The truth may not be as palatable, but I can live with it. It will not change the Law of the One that Oshere becomes a lion.'

'Nor if he does not,' said Chreena. 'Someone, a long time ago, began an experiment on chromosome engineering. The reasons I can only guess at. But the chain of life was altered in several species and this was successful – until now. What could be done then, can be done now. And I will find a way to reverse the process.'

'The Bears have all reverted,' he pointed out. 'The Wolvers are dying. And did you not make the same promise to Shir-ran?'

'Yes, damn you, I did. And I'll say it to the next unfortunate. I'll keep saying it until I make it true.'

Oshere looked away. 'Forgive me, Chreena. Do not be angry.'

'Dear God, I'm not angry with you, my dear. It is me. I have the Books inside my head, and the knowledge. But the answer eludes me.'

'Take your mind from it for a while. Walk with me.'

'I can't. I have no time.'

Oshere pushed himself painfully to his feet, his great head lolling to one side. 'We both know that a tired mind will find no answers. Come. Walk with me on the hillside.'

He put out his hand, sheathing the talons that leapt unbidden from the new sockets at the ends of his swollen fingers. She put her fingers into the black mane on his cheek and kissed him gently. 'Just for a little while, then.'

Together they walked along the statue-lined hall and out into the bright sunlight blazing down on the terraced gardens. He stopped at a long marble bench and stretched himself along it. She sat beside him with his head resting on her lap.

'Tell me again of the Fall,' he said.

'Which one?'

'The disaster that destroyed Atlantis – the one with the Ark.'

'Which Ark?' she asked him. 'During the Between Times there were more than five hundred legends involving Great Floods. The Hopi indians, the Arabs, the Assyrians, the Turks, the Norse, the Irish – all had their own racial memories of the day the world toppled. And each had their Ark. For some it was gopherwood, for others reeds. Some were giant vessels, others huge rafts.'

'But the Between Times people did not believe the legends, did they?'

'No,' she admitted. 'It was part arrogance. They knew the earth had changed, that the axis was no longer what it was, but they believed it was a gradual happening. However, the evidence was there. High water marks on the sides of mountains, seashells found in deserts; huge bone graveyards of animals found in mountain caves, where they must have gathered to escape the floods.'

'And why did the earth topple, Chreena, that first time?'

She smiled down at him. 'Your desire for knowledge is insatiable. And you know I will not tell you the secrets of the Second Fall. You are too guileless to attempt cunning, Oshere.'

'Tell of the First Fall. Tell me.'

'I do not have all the answers. There was tremendous seismic activity. Tidal waves rolled across the lands – thousands of feet of rushing water. There are indications in legends I have read of the sun and the moon reversing their motions, the sun rising in the West. That phenomenon could only have been caused by the earth suddenly rolling. One of my teachers believed it was the result of a meteor striking the earth; another claimed it was the increasing weight of ice at the poles. Perhaps it was both. Many legends talk of the Atlanteans finding a source of great power and disturbing the balance of the world. They did indeed find such a power source. Who knows the truth? Whatever the answer, the roaring seas destroyed much of the world. And most of the continent that had been Atlantis sank beneath the new oceans.'

'Did no Atlanteans escape?'

'Some who lived in the far north survived. Another group lived on a large island which had once been a mountain range; it used to be called the Canaries. They lived there undisturbed until the middle 1300s AD; then they were discovered by a seafaring nation called the Spanish. The Spanish butchered them all, and the language and the culture were destroyed for all time.'

'The Between Times people were unusually harsh,' said Oshere. 'Most of your stories concerning them deal with death and destruction.'

'They were harsher than you could possibly imagine,' Chreena responded.

'And the Second Fall was worse than the first?'

'A thousand times worse. By then the world's population had multiplied many times, and almost eighty per cent of them lived in lands that were at best no more than 100 feet above sea level. Some were below it, and relied on sea walls or dykes. When the earth toppled, they were destroyed utterly.'

'And yet Man survived, as did the People of the Dianae.'

'We are tough, Oshere – and incredibly resourceful. And God did not want us all to die.'

'But is Human Man still evil and harsh? Does he still slaughter his fellows Beyond the Wall?'

'He does. But not all men are evil. There are still those who resist the Spell of the Land.'

'When they breach the Wall, will they come peacefully?'

'I don't know, Oshere. Now I must return to my work.'

*

Oshere watched the woman walk to her laboratory. Her

skin was ebony dark and glistened as if oiled, and the undulating sway of her hips was a joy to behold. He realised he was now appreciating her beauty on a more aesthetic plane – yet another sign of the impending change. He raised himself from the bench and ambled down the terraces until he came to the main street. Everywhere there were people moving about their business. They saw him and bowed low – as befitted a man soon to be a god. A god?

The humour of it touched him fleetingly. Soon his mind would lose its intelligence, his voice would become a roar and he would spend the rest of his days driven not by a lust for knowledge, but by the desire to fill a swaying belly.

He remembered the first day when the woman known as Chreena had arrived at the city. Crowds had gathered to gaze on the blackness of her skin. Priests had bowed down before her and Oshere's older brother, the Prince Shir-ran, had been smitten by her unearthly beauty. She had a child with her then, a sickly boy with wide sorrowful eyes, but he had died within the first two months of her stay. The physicians had been powerless; his blood, they said, was weak and diseased. Chreena had mourned him for a long time. Shir-ran, tall and handsome, and the finest athlete among the Dianae, had spent his days walking with her, telling her of the legends of the Dianae; showing her statues and holy buildings. At last – when they had become lovers – he had taken her on the long walk to the mountains of the Sword. She had returned dazed from the experience.

Then the Change had begun in Shir-ran. The priests gave thanks and blessed him, and a great celebration was ordered for the dwellers of the city. But Oshere had noticed that Chreena did not join in the festivities.

One night he found her in the ancient medi-chamber of the palace, poring over Scrolls of the Lost Ones. And he remembered her words:

'Damn you, you bastards! Was there no end to your arrogance?'

Oshere had walked forward. In those days he too had been tall and well formed, his eyes wide-set and tawny, his hair dark and gleaming, held in place by a band of gold. 'What troubles you, Chreena?'

'Your whole stupid civilisation!' she stormed. 'You know, once upon a time a people called the Incas believed that they could make people gods by cutting out their hearts.'

'Stupidity,' Oshere agreed.

'You are no different. Shir-ran is being mutated into some kind of beast and you all drink to it. I have never mocked your legends, nor sought to fill you with the arcane knowledge I possess. But this?'

'What are you saying, Chreena?'

'How can I explain this to you? You have seen that dust and water combine to make clay. Yes? Well, all living organisms are the same. We are all a combination of parts.'

'I know all this, Chreena. Heart, lungs, liver. Every child knows it.'

'Wait,' she commanded. 'I don't mean just the organs, or the bones or the blood. Oh, this is impossible . . .'

Oshere sat down facing her desk. 'I am not slow-witted. Explain it to me.'

Slowly she began to talk of the genetic material that was vital to all living organisms. She did not use its Between Times name – *deoxyribonucleic acid* – nor the initials by which it became better known. But she did try to explain its importance in terms of controlling hereditary characteristics. For an hour she spoke, accompanying her words with sketches.

'So,' said Oshere at last, 'you are saying that these magic chains divide themselves into exact replicas? For what purpose?'

With extraordinary patience Chreena moved on to talk of genes and chromosomes. At last the light of understanding dawned in Oshere.

'I begin to see. How fascinating! But how does this make us stupid? Until we are told – or discover – new knowledge, we cannot be accused of foolishness. Can we?'

'I guess not,' said Chreena, 'but that is not what I meant. What I am saying is that Shir-ran's genetic structure is changing, mutating. The daughter chains are no longer identical to the parent – and now I know why.'

'Tell me.'

'Because you are not people. You are . . .' she stopped suddenly and looked away and Oshere's tawny eyes narrowed.

'Finish what you were saying.'

'Someone – some group – in the Between Times inserted a different gene into your ancestors – into your basic genetic code, if you like. Now – once in maybe five generations – the structure breaks down and reverts. Shir-ran is not becoming a god – he's becoming what his ancestor was. A lion.'

Oshere rose. 'There are statues in the old cities which show lion-headed gods. They were worshipped. I have been educated to believe in the religion of my ancestors and I will not throw it aside. But I will speak to you again; I will learn which is correct.'

Chreena rose and took his arm. 'I'm sorry, Oshere. I should never have told you. You must not mention it to anyone else – especially Shir-ran.'

'It is rather too late for that,' said Shir-ran as he ambled into the room, his huge leonine head tilted. 'I am sorry, Chreena. It was rude to listen, but I could not help myself. I don't know about you, Oshere, but I do know I never felt less like a god.'

Oshere had seen tears in the great tawny eyes and had backed away from the former lovers.

Shir-ran had fled the city three months later, passing from the land without comment. Oshere had spent the time since then with Chreena, learning in secret all the dark lore of the Between Times – save how it fell. Then – a month ago – Oshere himself had woken in the dawn to find his muscles racked with pain and his face strangely distended.

Chreena had worked ceaselessly to help him. But to no avail.

Now all he wanted was to learn as much as he could

about the land, the stars and the Lord of All Things. And he had one dream he held in his heart like a jewel.

He wanted to see the Ocean. Just once.

*

Her dreams were troubled. She was sitting at a feast, the only woman present. Around her the men were handsome and tall, their smiles easy, full of warmth and friendliness. She reached out to touch her companion and her hand rested on his arm, felt the fur. Then she recoiled and looked up into tawny eyes that chilled her, saw the long fangs that could rend her flesh. She sat frozen as, one by one, the men became lions, their eyes no longer friendly.

She awoke in a cold sweat and swung her long legs from the bed. The night was cool and the breeze from the balcony window caressed her naked body as she walked to the balcony and gazed over the moonlit city.

The People of the Dianae slept now in blissful ignorance of the real doom that awaited them. She shivered and returned to the bedroom. Sleep would not come again, but she was too tired to work. Wrapping herself in a warm woollen blanket, she pulled a chair to the balcony and sat beneath the stars.

'I miss you, Samuel,' she said, picturing the kindly face of the husband she had lost, the father of the son she had lost. 'If all men had been like you, the world would have remained Eden.'

But all men were not as Samuel Archer had been. They were driven by greed, or lust, hate or fear. She shook her head. The People of the Dianae had never known war. They were gentle and conciliatory, kind and understanding. Now, like a perverse cosmic jest, they were beginning a reversion to savagery.

The Bear-people had long since lost their humanity. Chreena had journeyed with Shir-ran to one of their settlements close to the Pool of the Sword and what she had seen there was terrifying. Only one human was left among them, and he had begun to revert.

'Go away from us,' he had said. 'We are cursed.'

Now their settlement was deserted, the tribe moving to the high timberlands away from prying eyes; far from pity or loathing.

A hunting roar sounded in the distance from the pride that roamed the plain before the city and Chreena shivered. Some thirty lions were living there, preying upon the deer and antelope. Yet once they had been men and women who talked and laughed, and sang.

Her eyes scanned the ancient buildings. Just four hundred of the Dianae remained – not enough to survive and grow.

'Why do you see the lions as gods?' Chreena had asked the old Priest, Men-chor. 'They lose the power of speech and become mindless.'

'The tale of Elder days,' he replied, smiling as he closed his eyes and began to recite the opening of the Book. 'First there was the goddess Marik-sen, who walked under the sun and knew no words, nor ancient stories, nor even the name of her father, nor even that her father had a name. The Law of the One touched her and her name was born. And she knew. Yet in knowing she also realised that she had lost a great gift – something wonderful – and it grieved her. Her son was born, but was no god. He was a man. He spoke like a man, and walked like a man. He knew his name and the name of his mother, and many more names. But he too sensed a loss: an empty place in the depths of his soul. And he was the father of the Dianae, and the people grew. And they lived in the Great Garden, with the walls of crystal. But one day the Law of the One was assailed by many enemies. The land was in turmoil, the walls split asunder and great waters destroyed the garden. The Dianae themselves were almost destroyed. Then the waters subsided and the people gazed upon a different world. The Law of the One visited his presence upon Pen-ran, and he became the Prophet. He told us what was lost and what was gained. We had lost the Road to Heaven, we had gained the Path to Knowing. He was the first to lead us here, and the first to leave the Path and find the Road.'

The old man opened his eyes. 'There is far more, Chreena, but only the Dianae could understand.'

'You believe that knowledge prevents you from seeing Heaven?'

'It is the great barrier. The soul can exist only in purity. Knowledge corrupts, it fills us with dreams and desires. Such ambition keeps our eyes from the Law of the One.'

'Yet a savage lion knows only hunger and lust.'

'Perhaps. But he does not slay wantonly, and if his belly is full a young antelope can walk to a pool beside him and drink in safety.'

'You will forgive me for not sharing your . . . faith?'

'Even as you have forgiven me for not sharing yours. Perhaps we are both correct,' said Men-chor. 'For do we not have similar origins? Did you not also originate in a Garden, and were you not also cast from it? And did you not also, with the sin of Adam and the crime of Cain, lose the Road to Heaven?'

Chreena had laughed then, and politely conceded the argument. She liked the old man. But she had one last question.

'What happens when, like the Bears, all the Dianae are lions?'

'We will all be close to God,' he told her simply.

'But there will be no more songs.'

'Who knows what songs are heard in the heart of a lion? But can they be more discordant than the songs of death we hear from Beyond the Wall?'

11

Shannow left the stallion at the stock paddocks, paid the hostler to grain-feed and groom the beast, then hitched his saddlebags over his left shoulder and made his way to the Traveller's Rest, a three-storey building to the west of the town. They had one room vacant but the owner – a thin, sallow-faced individual called Mason – asked Shannow if he could wait for an hour while they 'cleaned it up'.

Shannow agreed and paid for a three-day stay. He left his saddlebags behind the counter and walked into the next room where a long bar stretched some fifty feet. The barman smiled as he entered.

'Name it, son,' he said.

'Beer,' ordered Shannow. He paid for the drink and took the brimming jug to a corner table where he sat with his back to the wall. He was tired and curiously on edge; his thoughts kept drifting to the woman with the wagon. Slowly the bar began to fill with working men – some straight from the mine, their clothes black, their faces streaked with grime and sweat. Shannow cast his eyes swiftly over each newcomer. Few wore pistols, but many carried knives or hatchets. He was ready to move to his room when a young man entered. He was wearing a white cotton shirt, dark trousers and a fitted jacket of tanned leather; and he wore a pistol with a smooth white grip. Watching him move, Shannow felt his anger rise. He pulled his eyes from the newcomer and finished his beer. They always looked the same, bright-eyed and smooth as cats: the mark of the hunter, the killer, the warrior.

Shannow left the bar, collected his belongings and climbed the two flights to his room. It was larger than he had expected, with a brass-fitted double bed, two easy chairs and a table on which sat an oil light. He dumped his bags behind the door and checked the window. Below it was a drop of around forty feet. Stripping off his clothes, he lay back on the bed and slept for twelve hours. He awoke ravenous, dressed swiftly, strapped on his guns and returned to the ground floor. The owner, Mason, nodded to him as Shannow approached.

'I could do with a hot bath,' he said.

'Outside and turn to your left. About thirty paces. You can't miss it.'

The bath-house was a dingy shed in which five metal tubs were separated by curtains hung on brass rings. Shannow moved to the end and waited while two men filled the bath with steaming water, then he stripped and climbed in. There was a bar of used soap and a hard brush. He lathered himself clean and stepped from the tub; the towel was coarse and gritty, but it served its purpose. He dressed, paid the attendants and wandered across the main street, following the aroma of frying bacon.

The eating house was situated in a long cabin under the sign of The Jolly Pilgrim. Shannow entered and found a table against the wall, where he sat facing the door.

'What will you have?' asked Beth McAdam.

Shannow glanced up and reddened. Then he stood and swept his hat from his head. 'Good morning, Frey McAdam.'

'The name's Beth. And I asked what you wanted?'

'Eggs, bacon . . . whatever there is.'

'They've got a hot drink here made from nuts and tree bark; it's good with sugar.'

'Fine. I'll try some. It did not take you long to find work.'

'Needs must,' she said and walked away. Shannow's hunger had evaporated, but he waited for his meal and forced his way through it. The drink was bitter, even with the sugar, and black as the pit, but the after-taste was good. He paid from his dwindling store of Barta coins and walked out into the sunshine. A crowd had gathered, and he saw the young man from the night before standing in the centre of the street.

'Hell man, it's easy,' he said. 'You just stand there and drop the jug any time you're ready.'

'I don't want to do this, Clem,' said the man he was addressing, a portly miner. 'You might kill me, goddammit!'

'Never killed no one yet with this trick,' said the pistoleer. 'Still, there's always a first time.' The crowd hooted with laughter. Shannow stood against the wall of the eating house and watched the crowd melt away before the two men, forming a line on either side of them. The fat miner was standing some ten feet from the pistoleer, holding a clay jug out from his body at arm's length.

'Come on, Gary. Drop it!' someone shouted.

The miner did so as Shannow's eyes flicked to the pistoleer. His hand swept down and up and the crack of the shot echoed in the street. The jug exploded into shards and the crowd cheered wildly. Shannow eased himself from the wall and walked around them towards the hotel.

'You don't seem too impressed,' said the young man, as Shannow passed.

'Oh, I was impressed,' Shannow assured him, walking on, but the man caught up with him.

'The name's Clem Steiner,' he said, falling into step.

'That was exceptionally skilful,' commented Shannow. 'You have fast hands and a good eye.'

'Could you have done it?'

'Never in a million years,' Shannow replied, mounting the steps to the hotel. Returning to his room, he took the Bible from his saddlebag and flicked through the pages until he came to the words that echoed in his heart.

'And he carried me away in the spirit to a mountain great and high and showed me the Holy City, Jerusalem, coming down out of Heaven from God. It shone with the glory of God, and its brilliance was like that of a very precious jewel, like a jasper, clear as crystal. It had a great high wall with twelve gates and with twelve angels at the gates . . . The city does not need the sun or the moon to shine on it for the glory of God gives it light, and the Lamb is its lamp . . . Nothing impure will ever enter it, nor will anyone who does what is shameful or deceitful . . . '

Shannow closed the book. *A great high wall.* Just like the one at the end of the valley.

He hoped so. By God, he hoped so . . .

*

Awoken by the sound of gunshots, Shannow rolled from the bed and moved to the side of the window, glancing down into the moonlit street below. Two men lay sprawled in the dust; still standing was Clem Steiner, a pistol in his hand. Men were running from the drinking houses and the sidewalks. Shannow shook his head and returned to his bed.

In the morning he took his breakfast in the Long Bar, a simple bowl of hot oats and a large jug of the black drink, called Baker's after the man who had introduced it to the area some eight years before.

Boris Haimut approached his table. 'Do you mind if I join you, sir?' he asked diffidently. Shannow shrugged and the small, balding Arcanist pulled up a chair and sat. The barman brought him a Baker's and Haimut sat in silence for a while sipping it.

'An interesting mixture, Meneer Shannow. Do you know it also cures headaches and rheumatic pain? It is also mildly addictive.' Shannow put down his jug. 'No, no,' said Haimut, smiling. 'I mean that one acquires a taste for it. There are no harmful effects. Are you staying long in Pilgrim's Valley?'

'Two more days. Maybe three.'

'It could be a beautiful place, but I fear they will have more trouble here.'

'You have finished work on the ship?' Shannow asked.

'We . . . Klaus and I . . . were ordered to leave the site. Meneer Scayse has taken over.'

'I am sorry.'

Haimut spread his hands. 'There was not much more to see. We dug further and found the ship was only a piece – it must have broken up as it sank. But any theory of it being a building was destroyed.'

'What will you do now?'

'I will wait here for a wagon convoy and then journey back to the east. There is always an expedition to somewhere. It is my life. Did you hear the shootings last night?'

'Yes,' said Shannow.

'Fourteen people have died violently here in the last month. It is worse than the Big Wide.'

'There is wealth here,' said Shannow. 'It draws men of violence, weak men, evil men. I have seen it in other areas. Once the wealth is gone, the boil bursts.'

'But there are some men, Meneer Shannow, who have a talent for lancing such boils, are there not?'

Shannow looked into the man's pale blue eyes. 'Indeed there are, Meneer Haimut. But it seems there are none such in Pilgrim's Valley.'

'Oh, I think there is one, sir. But he is disinterested. Do you still seek Jerusalem, Jon Shannow?'

'I do. And I no longer lance boils.'

Haimut looked away – and changed the subject. 'I met a travelling man two years ago who said he had been south of the Great Wall. He talked of astonishing wonders in the sky – a great sword that hung below the clouds, a crown of crosses above its silver hilt. Less than a hundred miles from it there was a ruined city of incredible size. I would sell my soul to see such a city.'

Shannow's eyes narrowed. 'Do not say that – even lightly. You might be taken up on it.'

Haimut smiled. 'My apologies, sir. I forgot – momentarily – that you are a man of religion. Do you intend to venture past the Wall?'

'I do.'

'It is a land of strange beasts and great danger.'

'There is danger everywhere, Meneer. Two men died on the street last night. There is no safe place in all the world.'

'That is increasingly true. Since the last full moon there have been – in Pilgrim's Valley alone – six rapes, eight murders, six fatal shootings and innumerable injuries from knife fights and other brawls.'

'Why do you retain such figures?' asked Shannow, finishing his Baker's.

'Habit, sir.' He produced a wad of paper and a pencil from the bulging pocket of his coat. 'Would you do me the kindness, sir, of telling me the whereabouts of the giant ship you saw in your travels?'

For almost half an hour Haimut questioned the Jerusalem Man about the ghost ship and the ruined cities of Atlantis. Finally Shannow rose, paid for his breakfast and strolled on to the street. For most of the morning he toured the town. It was quiet at the western end, where most of the houses betrayed the wealth of the inhabitants, but towards the east where the buildings were more mediocre and flimsy he saw several scuffles outside taverns and drinking-houses. At the end of the town was a vast meadow, filled by tents of various sizes. Even here there were drinking areas, and he saw drunkards sitting or lying on the grass in various stages of stupor.

The town had sprung up around a silver mine and this had attracted vagrants like ants to a picnic. And with the vagrants came the brigands and the thieves, the dice rollers and the Carnat players. He left the Tent Town and moved back along the main thoroughfare. The sound of children singing came from a long, timber-built hall. He stopped for a while and listened to the tune, trying to place it. It was a pleasant sound, full of youth and hope and innocent joy; at first it lifted him, but this was followed by a sense of melancholy and loss and he walked on.

Outside the Traveller's Rest a large crowd had gathered and a man's voice could be heard, deep and stirring. Shannow joined the crowd and looked up at the speaker who was standing on a barrel. The man was tall and broad-shouldered, with thick red hair tightly curled. He wore a black robe belted at the waist with grey rope, and a wooden cross hung from a cord around his neck.

'And I say to you, brothers, that the Lord is waiting for you. All he wants is a sign from you. To see your eyes lifted from the mud at your feet, lifted towards the glories of

Heaven. To hear your voices say, "Lord, I believe." And then, my friends, the joys of the Spirit will flow in your souls.'

A man stepped forward. 'And then he'll make us wear pretty black dresses like that one? Tell me, Parson, do you have to squat to piss?'

'Such is the voice of ignorance, my brothers,' began the Parson, but the man shouted him down.

'Ignorance? You puking son of a bitch! You can take your puking Jesus and tell him go . . .'

The Parson's booted foot flashed out, catching the man under the chin and catapulting him from his feet. 'As I was saying, dear friends,' he continued, 'the Lord waits with love in His heart for any sinner who repents. But those who persist in evil ways will fall to the Sword of God, to burn in lakes of Hellfire. Put aside evil and lust and greed. Love your neighbour as yourself. Only then will the Lord smile on you and yours and your rewards will be all the greater.'

'Do you love *him*, Parson?' shouted another man in the crowd, pointing down at the unconscious heckler.

'Like my own son,' replied the Parson, grinning. 'But children must first learn discipline. I will stand bad language, for that is the way of sinful man. But I will not stand for blasphemy, or any insult to the Lord. Faced with such, I will smite the offender hip and thigh as Samson among the Philistines.'

'How do you feel about drinking, Parson?' called a man at the back.

'Nice of you to ask, my son. I'll have a strong beer.' As the laughter began, the Parson raised his arms for silence.

'Tomorrow is the Sabbath, and I will be holding a service beyond the Town of Tents. There will be singing and praise, followed by food and drink. Come with your wives, your sweethearts and your children. We'll make a day of it in the meadow. Now where's that beer I was promised?' He stepped down from the barrel and moved to the fallen man. Hoisting him to his feet, the Parson lifted the man to his shoulder and marched up the steps into the Traveller's Rest.

Shannow remained in the sunlight.

'Impressive, is he not?' asked Clem Steiner. When Shannow turned, the young man's eyes were bright and challenging.

'Yes,' Shannow agreed.

'I hope the little fracas didn't trouble you in the night?'

'No, it did not. Excuse me,' replied Shannow, moving away.

Steiner's voice floated after him. 'You bother me, friend. I hope we will not fall out.'

Shannow ignored him. He returned to his room and checked his remaining Barta coin, finding he had seven full silvers, three halves and five quarters. He searched his pockets and came up with the gold coin he had found in Shir-ran's food store. It was just over an inch in diameter and upon the surface was stamped the image of a sword surrounded by stars; the reverse of the coin was blank. Shannow took it to the window to examine it more closely. The sword was of an unusual design, long and tapering, and the stars were more like crosses in the sky.

The thunder of hooves sounded from the street and a large group of riders came hurtling into sight. Shannow opened the window to see the body of a beast being dragged in the dust behind two of the riders, and a large crowd gathering. The horsemen pulled up their mounts and Shannow was amazed to see the bloodied beast rise up on all fours, and then lurch to its hind legs.

It ran – but a rope pulled it up. Two shots exploded and gaping wounds appeared on the creature's back. Several more of the onlookers produced guns and the beast was smashed from its feet. Shannow left his room and moved swiftly down the stairs. On the street beside the Traveller's Rest was a store, outside which stood several barrels and a stack of long wooden axe- or pick-handles. Lifting one of them, Shannow walked down into the milling group of riders and stopped before a bearded man on a black horse.

The pick-handle slashed through the air to hammer into the man's face; his body flew back over the saddle and hit the ground, raising a cloud of dust. Shannow dropped the club on the rider's body and, taking hold of the pommel of the saddle, vaulted to the stallion's back.

There was silence now as Shannow eased the horse past the stunned riders. He tugged on the reins, turning the stallion to face the group.

'When he awakes, point out to him the perils of stealing a man's horse,' Shannow told them. 'Make it clear to him. I will leave his saddle with the hostler.'

'He'll kill you for this, friend,' said a young man close to him.

'I am no friend of yours, child. Nor ever will be.'

Shannow rode on, pausing only to glance down at the dead beast. It looked almost exactly as Shir-ran had in those last days – the spreading lion's mane, the hideously muscled shoulders. Shannow touched his heels to the stallion's flanks and cantered down to the stables, where the hostler came out to meet him.

'I'm sorry, Meneer, but I couldn't stop them. There were eight . . . ten of them. They took three other horses that weren't theirs.'

'Who were they? The thieves?'

'They ride for Scayse,' replied the man, as if that answered everything.

Shannow dismounted and led the stallion into the stable. He stripped the saddle from him and flung it in a corner; then he groomed the horse, rubbing the lather from him and brushing the gleaming back.

'It's a fine horse,' said the hostler, limping forward. 'Must be seventeen hands. I'll bet he runs like the wind.'

'He does. What happened to your leg?'

'Timber cracked in the mine, years ago. Busted my knee. Still, it's a damn sight better living above ground than below. Not so much coin, but I breathe a lot easier. What was all the shooting?'

'They killed the lion they captured,' Shannow told him.

'Hell, I'd like to have seen that. Was it one of them Man-demons?'

'I do not know. It ran on its hind legs.'

'Lord, what a thing to miss! There ain't so many as there was, you know. Not since the gates vanished on the Wall. We used to see them often in the Spring. They killed a family near Silver Stream. Ate them all, would you believe it? Was it male or female?'

'Male,' said Shannow.

'Yep. Never seen no females. Must be Beyond the Wall, I reckon.'

'Does anyone ever go there?'

'Beyond the Wall?' queried the hostler. 'No way. Not ever. Believe me, there's beings there to frizzle a man's soul.'

'If no one goes there – how can you know?'

The hostler grinned. 'No one goes there *now*. But five years ago there was an expedition. Only one man – of forty-two who started out – got back alive. It was him that told about the sword in the sky. And he only lived a month, what with the wounds and the gashes in his body. Then, two years ago, the gateways vanished. There were three of them, twenty feet high and as broad. Then one morning they were gone.'

'Filled in, you mean?'

'I mean *gone*! Not a trace of them. And no mark of any breaks in the Wall. Lichens and plants growing over old stones, like there never was no gates at all.'

*

She knew the problem and could see the results. Yet she was powerless to change the process . . . just as she had been powerless to save her son. The woman known as Chreena prowled the medi-chamber, her dark eyes angry, her fists clenched.

One small Sipstrassi Stone could change everything; one fragment with its gold veins intact could save Oshere and others like him. Little Luke would have been alive, and

Shir-ran would still have been standing beside her, tall and proud.

She had searched the mountains and the valleys, had questioned the Dianae. But no one had ever seen such a Stone, black as coal and yet streaked with gold, warm to the touch and soothing to the soul.

She blamed herself, for she had carried her own Stone to this distant land and had used it to seal the Wall – one great surge of Sipstrassi power to wipe out the gates which would have allowed Man to corrupt the lands of the Dianae. And then she had made the great discovery – Man had already corrupted them . . . back before the Second Fall.

The People of the Dianae. The People of the DNA. The Cat-people. There had been mutants and freaks in the world for hundreds of years. Chreena had been educated to believe they were the result of the poisons and toxic wastes which littered the land, but now she was beginning to see the true wickedness that was the legacy of Between. Genetic engineering gone rogue in a hostile environment. New races birthed; others, like the Dianae, slowly dying.

The priests here believed that the Changes were gifts from Heaven. But they were happening more frequently, whole families showing signs of reversion.

Chreena's anger rose. She had seen the books and the records back at Home Base. Many diseases of the Between Times had been treated by producing bacterial DNA and using it in commercial production. Insulin for diabetics was one such. Food production had been boosted by inserting genes for growth into pigs and cattle – promoter genes, these had been called. But the Betweeners had gone much further.

May you rot in Hell! she thought. Suddenly she smiled. Because, of course they *were* rotting in Hell. Their disgusting world had been swept away by the power of nature, like blood washing the pus from a boil.

And yet it had not affected the core of the infection – Man himself: the ultimate carnivore, the complete killer.

Even now they warred amongst themselves, butchering and plundering.

The Spell of the Land was at work. Colossal radiation levels, toxic wastes in the air they breathed – all coming together to create abnormally high levels of aggression and violence.

The circle of history spun on. Already Man had rediscovered guns and had risen to the level the world had known in the middle 1800s. It would not be long before they took to the skies, before nations were formed and wars spread.

Slowly she climbed the stairs to the observatory platform. From here she could see the streets of the city and watch the people moving about their business. Further out she could see the farmlands, and the herds of cattle. And away into the distance, like a shimmering thread, the Wall between Worlds. She could almost hear Man beating upon it, venting his rage upon the ancient stones.

Chreena transferred her gaze to the south, where heavy clouds drifted over the new mountains and the Sword of God was hidden. She shivered.

A sudden storm broke in the east and she swung to watch the lightning fork up from the ground, the dark thunder-clouds swirling furiously. A cold wind screamed across the plain and she shivered again and stepped inside.

The city would withstand the storm, as it had withstood the First Fall and the terrible fury of the risen ocean.

As she turned away, she failed to see a glimmer of blue within the storm, as if a curtain had flickered in the wind, showing clear skies amid the lowering black clouds. At the centre of the blue shone the golden disc of a second sun so that, for no more than a heartbeat, two shadows were cast on the streets of the city.

12

The riders dismounted and gathered around the fallen man. His nose was crushed and both eyes were swelling fast; his upper lip was split and bleeding profusely. Two men lifted him, carrying him from the street to the sidewalk outside the Jolly Pilgrim.

The owner, Josiah Broome, took a bowl of fresh water and a towel and moved to join them, kneeling beside the injured man. He immersed the towel in the cool water and then folded it, placing it gently over the man's blackened eyes.

'It was a disgrace,' he said. 'I saw it. Unwarranted violence. Despicable!'

'Damn right about that,' someone agreed.

'People like him will ruin this valley, even before we get a chance to build something lasting here,' said Broome.

'He stole a horse, goddammit!' exclaimed Beth McAdam, before she could stop the words. Broome looked up.

'These men were hunting a beast that could have devoured your children and they took the first mounts they could find. All he had to do was to ask the man for his horse. But no. Men like him are always the same. Violence. Death. Destruction. It follows them like a plague.'

Beth held her tongue and walked back into the eating-house. She needed this job to swell the funds she had hidden in her wagon, and to pay for the children to remain at the Cabin School. But men like Broome annoyed her. Sanctimonious and blinkered, they saw only what they wished to see. Beth had been in Pilgrim's Valley for only two days, but already she knew the political structure of the settlement. These riders worked for Edric Scayse, and he was one of the three most powerful men in Pilgrim's Valley. He owned the largest mine, two of the stores and, with the man Mason, the Traveller's Rest and several of the gambling-houses on the east quarter. His men patrolled the Tent City, extorting payment for their vigilance. Any who did not pay could guarantee to see their wagons or their belongings lost through theft or fire. In the main, Scayse's men were bullies or former brigands.

Beth had watched the beast dragged in and shot down, and had seen Shannow recover his horse. The man who stole it was bruised but alive. Shannow could have asked for its return, but Beth knew the chances were the man would have refused and almost certainly that would have led to a gun battle. Broome was a dung-brain of the first order. But he was also her boss and, in his own way, a nice man. He believed in the nobility of Man, that all disputes could be settled by reason and debate. She stood in the doorway and watched him tend the injured victim. Broome was tall and thin, with long, straight, sandy hair and a slender face dominated by large protruding blue eyes. He was not an unhandsome man, and his manner towards her had been courteous. He was a widower with no children, and as such Beth had scrutinised him carefully; she knew it would be wise to find a good man with a solid base so that she could ensure security for her children. But Broome could never fill her requirements.

The injured man regained consciousness and was helped to a table. Beth brought him a cup of Baker's and he sipped it.

'I'll kill the whoreson,' he mumbled. 'So help me God, I'll kill him!'

'Don't even think like that, Meneer Thomas,' Broome urged. 'What he did was appalling, but further violence will not eradicate it.'

The man pushed himself to his feet. 'Who's with me?' he asked. Two men joined him, but the others hung back. Thomas pulled his pistol from his belt and checked the loads. 'Where'd he go?'

'He took the stallion back to the stable,' said a short lean man.

'Thanks, Jack. Well, let's find him.'

'Please, Meneer . . .' began Broome, but Thomas pushed him aside. Beth eased her way back through the kitchen and out into the yard, then she hitched up her long skirt and ran behind the buildings, cutting through an alleyway and on to the main street ahead of the three men. At the end of the street she saw Shannow talking to the hostler in the doorway of the stable. Quickly she crossed to him.

'They are coming for you, Shannow,' she said. 'Three of them.'

He turned to her and smiled softly. 'It was kind of you to think of me.'

'Never mind kindness. Saddle up and move.'

'My belongings are still in my room. I would suggest that you wait here.'

'I said, there are three of them.'

'Is the man I struck among them?'

'Yes,' she told him. Shannow nodded, removed his coat and laid it across the stall beam. Then he moved out into the sunlight. Beth crossed to the doorway and watched him make his way to the centre of the street. There he stood and waited with arms hanging by his sides. The sun was high now, shining in the faces of the three pistoleers. They came closer, the two on the outside angling themselves away from Thomas in the centre. Beth felt the tension rise.

'Now how do you feel, you whoreson?' shouted Thomas. Shannow said nothing. 'Cat got your tongue?' Closer now they came until only about ten paces separated them. Then Shannow's voice sounded, low and clear.

'Have you come here to die?' he asked. Beth saw the man on the right rub sweat from his face and glance at his friend. Thomas grabbed for his pistol, but a single shot punched him from his feet. His legs twitched in the dust, and a slow stain spread on the front of his trousers.

The other two men stood statue-still. 'I would suggest,' said Shannow quietly, 'that you carry him off the street.' They hurried to obey as he walked back to Beth and the hostler.

'I thank you again, Frey McAdam. I am sorry that you needed to witness such an act.'

'I've seen dead men before, Meneer Shannow. But he has a lot of friends and I don't think it will be safe for you here. Tell me, how did you know those others would not fight?'

'I did not,' he told her. 'But he was the man carrying the anger. Will you be going to the Parson's gathering tomorrow?'

'Might be.'

'I would be privileged if you and your children would accompany me.'

'I am sorry, Meneer,' said Beth. 'I think you are now in some peril, and I will not allow my children to be in your dangerous company.'

'I understand. You are correct, of course.'

'Were I without children . . . the answer might have been different.'

He bowed and walked out into the sunshine.

'Damn, but he's cool,' said the hostler. 'Well, Thomas ain't gonna be missed, not by a long shot.'

Beth did not reply.

*

The Jerusalem Man paused on the street where only a dark patch of blood showed where a life had been taken. He felt no regret. The dead man had made his own decision and Shannow recalled the words of Solomon: *Such is the end of all who go after ill-gotten gain; it takes away the lives of those who get it.*

It was a long walk back to his rooms and Shannow could feel the eyes of many upon him as he strode along the dusty street. The former riders were now grouped around the eating-house, but they did not speak as he passed. Clem Steiner was waiting inside the Traveller's Rest; the young man rose as he entered.

'I knew,' he said. 'Something told me you were a fighter

when I first seen you sitting in the Long Bar. What is your name, friend?'

'Shannow.'

'I should have guessed it: the Jerusalem Man. You're a long way from home, Shannow. Who sent for you? Brisley? Fenner?'

'No one sent for me, Steiner. I ride where I please.'

'You realise we may have to go up against one another?'

Shannow stared at the young man for several seconds. 'That would not be advisable,' he said softly.

'Damn right there. You'd better remember that. Meneer Scayse would like a few words with you, Shannow. He's in the Long Bar.'

Shannow turned away and made for the stairs.

'You hear what I said?' Steiner called, but Shannow ignored him and climbed to his room. He poured himself a cup of water from a stone jug and sat down to wait in a chair by the window.

*

Edric Scayse stepped from the Long Bar. 'He's gone, Mr Scayse,' said Steiner. 'Want me to fetch him back?'

'No. Wait here for me.'

He was a tall man, broad-shouldered, his raven-black hair cut short and swept back over his head without a parting. Clean-shaven, his face was strong and angular, the dark eyes deep-set, and he moved with smooth assurance. Reaching the door of Shannow's room he knocked once.

'Come in. It is open,' came a voice from within.

Scayse stepped inside. His eyes fastened on the man sitting in the chair by the window, and he re-evaluated his plan. He had intended to offer Shannow employment, but this was now an option that would serve only to make the man before him more of an enemy.

'May I sit, Mr Shannow?'

'I thought the term was Meneer in this part of the country.'

'I am not from this part of the country.' He walked to

the chair opposite the Jerusalem Man and lowered himself into it.

'What is it that you want, Mr Scayse?'

'Merely to apologise, sir. The man who stole your horse worked for me. He was a hot-headed youngster. I wished to assure you that there will be no revenge attacks – I have made that clear to all my riders.'

Shannow shrugged, but his expression did not change. 'And?'

Scayse felt a flicker of anger but suppressed it, forcing a smile instead. 'There is no "and". It is merely a call of courtesy, sir. Do you intend staying long in Pilgrim's Valley?'

'No. It is my intention to ride further south.'

'To seek the wonders in the sky, no doubt. I envy you that. It will be at least three months before I have assembled a force to cross the Wall.'

'A force? For what purpose?' asked Shannow.

'*Out of his mouth comes a sharp sword with which to strike down the nations*,' quoted Scayse. '*He will rule them with an iron sceptre*.'

He watched Shannow's expression change from open hostility to wariness.

'So you read your Scripture, sir. But what does it mean to you?'

Scayse leaned forward, pressing home his advantage. 'I have gathered information about the land Beyond the Wall, and the wonders there. There are great signs in the sky. Of this there is no doubt. There is a shining sword, surrounded by stars and crosses, and upon the sword is a name that no one can read. Exactly as the Scripture says. What is more, the land is peopled by beasts who walk like men and worship a dark goddess – a witch who performs obscene rites among them. Or as the Scripture has it, Mr Shannow: "*There I saw a woman sitting on a scarlet beast that was covered with blasphemous names*." Or there again: "*The Beast I saw resembled a leopard, but had feet like those of a bear and a mouth like that of a lion*." All these things are Beyond the Wall,

Mr Shannow. I intend to go there and find the Sword of God.'

'And for this you gather brigands and pistoleers?'

'You would have me take farmers and teachers?'

Shannow stood and moved to the window. 'I am no debater, sir. Nor am I a judge.' Behind him Scayse masked a smile of triumph and remained silent. Shannow turned, his pale eyes fixing on Scayse. 'But neither am I a fool, Mr Scayse. You are a man who seeks power – domination over your fellows. You are not a seeker after truth. Down there your men are feared. But that is no business of mine.'

'You are correct, Mr Shannow, when you talk of the pursuit of power. But that is not an evil thing in itself, surely? Was not David the son of a farmer, and did he not rise to be King over Israel? Was not Moses the child of a slave? God gives a man talents and therefore it is right that he should use them. I am no wilful murderer, nor brigand. My men may be . . . boisterous and rough, but they pay for their wares and treat the folk of this community with respect. Not one of them has been found guilty of murder or rape, and those who have been caught stealing have been dealt with by me. There will always be rulers, Mr Shannow. It is not a sin to become one.'

Shannow returned to his chair and poured a mug of water which he offered to Scayse, who refused it with a smile. 'As I said, I am no judge. I will not be in this community for long. But I have seen other such communities. The violence will grow, and there will be many more deaths unless order is established. Why is it, sir, that with your quest for power you have not established such order?'

'Because I am not a tyrant, Mr Shannow. The gambling places in the eastern sector are not under my jurisdiction. I have a large farm and several herds of dairy and beef cattle – and I own the largest silver mine. My lands are patrolled by my men, but the town itself – though I have interests here – is not my concern.'

Shannow nodded. 'Did you find anything of interest in the wreck of the ship?'

Scayse chuckled. 'I heard about your . . . altercation. Yes, I did, Mr Shannow. There were some gold bars and several interesting pieces of silver plate. But nothing as grand as you saw on the *Titanic*.'

Shannow betrayed no surprise, he merely nodded and Scayse went on: 'Yes, I have seen the *Titanic*. I know of the Sipstrassi Demon Stone that resurrected it, and of your battle with Sarento. I also am no fool, sir. I know that the world of the past contained wonders beyond our imaginings, and that they are lost to us, perhaps for ever. But this new world has power also. And I will find it Beyond the Wall.'

'The Demon Stone was destroyed,' said Shannow. 'If you know of Sarento, you know of his evil and of the Hellborn War he caused. Such power is not suited to men.'

Scayse rose. 'I have been honest with you, Mr Shannow, because I respect you. I do not seek a confrontation with you. Do not misunderstand me; I do not speak from fear. But I want no unnecessary enemies. Sipstrassi is merely a power source, not unlike the guns you wear. In evil hands, it will create evil. But I am not an evil man. Good day to you.'

Scayse moved back into the hallway and continued down the stairs to where Steiner waited.

'You want me to take him out, Mr Scayse?'

'Stay away from him, Clem. That man would kill you.'

'Is that a joke, Mr Scayse? There's no one could take me with a pistol.'

'I didn't say he could beat you, Clem. I said he would kill you.'

13

For two long, hot days Nu-Khasisatra walked across the Great Wide. The mountains seemed no closer, but his strength was ebbing. As a shipbuilder and a craftsman, he had long been proud of the enormous strength he could bring to bear, lifting great weights of wood or stone. But this seemingly endless walk called not for strength but for stamina, and on this count Nu realised he was lacking. He sat down in the shade of a shallow gully and took the Sipstrassi Stone from the deep pocket of his coat. He was loath to use its power, not knowing how much was left, nor how much was needed to allow him to return home to Pashad and his children. Unlike many from the City of Ad, Nu had taken only one wife, the daughter of Axin the sailmaker. He had loved her from the first moment their hands had touched, and he loved her still. There was little strength in Pashad, fragile as a spring flower, but there was a well of giving in her without which Nu felt lost.

The last time Nu had been in possession of Sipstrassi it had been a fragment, a sliver no bigger than a torn finger-nail. Its power had been used up in a day – fuelling his strength; forcing back the awesome power of time, turning his greying hair black and filling his muscles with the strength of youth. But what he held now was twenty times larger, the gold veins thick and pulsing with power.

Nu had escaped the Daggers, but he had not journeyed to Balacris. He had come to some foreign land far across the sea, where men wore strange raiment. *Use your mind, you fool!* he told himself. *How can you return home unless you first know from where you are starting?* According to legend, the Elder Priests had used Sipstrassi to free their spirits to fly the universe. If they could do it, so could Nu-Khasisatra. He moved to his knees and prayed to the Great One, using ten of the thousand names known to Man, then he gripped the stone tightly and pictured himself rising through the gathering clouds above. His mind swam and he felt suddenly free, like a ship whose anchor falls away. Opening his eyes, he found himself staring down at a white wilderness of mountains and valleys with not a trace of life. Above him the sky was blue and clear, but the landscape below was ghostly and silent. Fear swept through him. Where had he flown? He dropped towards the snow-covered world . . . and passed into the clouds.

For a time he was blind, then he broke through the grey-white mist and saw the land far below, green and lush, sectioned by snow-topped mountains and ribbon rivers, great valleys and dales, forests and plains. He scanned the horizon for signs of life, for cities or towns, but there was nothing save the vastness of nature. Nu's spirit swooped closer to the plain. Now he could see his own tiny figure in the gully below and, some miles to the west, a camp of wagons with white canvas covers and oxen feeding on the hillside.

He ventured further, over the mountains, and saw an ugly township with squat wooden buildings and a large gathering of people in a meadow. Passing over them, he continued south. A great wall, similar in structure to the sea wall at Ad, met his eyes and he dropped towards it. The stones were hewn in the same way, but they were far older than Pendarric's Wall. He moved on, wondering how a nation which could erect such a wall could have regressed to creating such hideous buildings as he had seen in the small town. Then he saw the city – and his heart sank.

There was the domed palace, the marble terraces, the long statue-lined Road of Kings – and to the south the curving line of the dock. But beyond it there was no glittering ocean, only fields and meadows. Nu hovered, scanning the people strolling the streets. Everything was as he remembered, yet nothing was the same. He sped to the temple and halted by the statue of Derarch the Prophet.

The prophet's face was worn away, the holy scrolls in his hands reduced to no more than white sticks.

Shaken beyond endurance, Nu fled back to the sky.

What he had seen was like a vision from the Fires of Belial.

And he knew the truth. This was not some strange, distant land; this was home, this was the City of Ad. He recalled his vision of the sea roaring up, and the three suns in the sky. This was the world of the future.

He returned to his body and wept for all that had been lost: for Pashad and his sons, for Bali and his friends, and for all the people of a world soon to die . . . of a world that had already died.

Nu-Khasisatra wept for Atlantis.

*

At last his tears dried and he lay back against a rock, his body aching, his heart heavy. What point was there in his warnings to the people? Why had the Lord Chronos used him, if there was no hope?

No hope? You of all men should know the folly of that thought.

His first ship had been caught in a terrible storm. All his money had been tied into the venture, and more. He had borrowed heavily, pushing himself and his family into awesome debt. As the voyage was nearing completion with the cargo secure in the hold and his fortune assured, the winds had turned foul, the sea had roared; great waves pummelled the vessel, hurling it towards the black cliffs poised like a hammer above them.

Most of his crew had panicked, flinging themselves over the side and risking almost certain death in the raging sea. Not so Nu-Khasisatra. Holding to the tiller, straining with all the power in his formidable frame, he locked his gaze to the black monstrosity looming over him. At first there had been no response, but then the sleek craft began to turn. Nu's muscles had been stretched to tearing point, but his ship missed the cliff and raced on towards the peril of a hidden reef.

Only three out of thirty crew members remained with him, and these clung to the timbers, unable to aid their master for fear of being washed overboard.

'The anchor!' yelled Nu into the teeth of the storm. Salt spray lashed his face, hurling the words back at him. Lifting one arm from the tiller, he pointed at the rope brake by the iron anchor and one of his crewmen began to haul himself back to the stern. A huge wave hit him and he lost hold; his body slid down the deck. Nu released the tiller and dived for the man, catching his tunic just as he was about to topple over the side. Clamping his right hand to a stay, Nu hauled the seaman to safety. The ship sped towards the reefs, hidden like the fangs of a monster below the foaming waves. Nu staggered upright and forced a path to the tiller. The seaman struggled with the anchor brake . . . suddenly it gave and the iron weight hissed over the side.

The ship shuddered and Nu let out a cry of despair, for he believed they had struck the reef. But it was only the anchor biting hard into the coral below them. The ship bobbed and the cliff which had been such a threat now became a shelter from the ferocity of the storm.

The wind died down in the bay. 'We're still shipping water,' shouted the crewman Nu had rescued.

'Start the pump, and see where the problem lies,' Nu ordered, and the man raced below. The two other crewmen followed him and Nu sank to the wet deck. The moon broke clear of the storm clouds as he glanced to port. Rows of jagged rocks, black and gleaming, could be seen above the swell. Had the ship struck any of them, it would have been ripped open from prow to stern. Nu hauled himself upright and moved to the starboard side. Here too the reef could be seen. Somehow – by some miracle – he had steered the vessel through a narrow channel between the reefs.

The crewman returned. 'The level is dropping. The ship is sound, master.'

'You have earned a good bonus, Acrylla. I'll see you get it.'

The man grinned, showing broken front teeth. 'I thought we were finished. It looked so hopeless.'

Nu-Khasisatra's fortune had been built on that first adventure, and his reply to Acrylla was now carved on the tiller of each of his ships:

'*Nothing is ever hopeless – as long as courage endures.*'

The memory of that night came flooding back to him and he pushed himself to his feet. Despair, he realised, was as great an enemy as Sharazad or the King's Daggers. His world was doomed, but that did not mean Pashad must die. He had a Sipstrassi Stone and he was alive.

'I will come for you, my love,' he said. 'Through the vaults of time or the Valleys of the Damned.' He glanced up at the sky. 'Thank you for reminding me, Lord.'

*

Beth sat on the hillside under a spreading pine and watched the children playing on the makeshift swing-boards and see-saw planks down by the stream. The high meadow was seething with townspeople, farmers and miners, enjoying the bright sunshine and the food at the stalls. Elsewhere there were games of strength or skill, knife and hatchet hurling, rifle shooting, wrestling and boxing. The miners held a jousting tourney, where one man sat upon the shoulders of another gripping a mock lance with a wooden ball at either end. A similar team would rush at them, and there was much shouting of encouragement as the riders proceeded to hammer their opponents to the ground. The barbecue fires were lit and the smell of roasting beef – compliments of Edric Scayse – filled the air. Beth leaned her back to the tree and relaxed for the first time in days. Her small hoard of coin was swelling, and soon she would move the family out to the rich southland north of the Wall, and there build a farm of her own on land leased from Scayse. It would be a hard life, but she would make it work.

A shadow fell across her and she looked up to see Jon Shannow standing hat in hand.

'Good morning . . . Beth. Your children are far from us, and in little danger. May I join you?'

'Please do,' she said and he swung round and sat with his back to the tree. She moved out to sit in front of him. 'I know who you are,' she told him. 'The whole town knows.'

'Yes,' he said wearily. 'I expect they do. It is a fine gathering and people are enjoying themselves. That is good to see.'

'Why did you come here?' she pressed.

'It is only a stopping place, Beth. I shall not be staying. I was not summoned here; I have not come to deal death to all and sundry.'

'I did not think for one moment that you had. Is it true that you seek Jerusalem?'

'Not, perhaps, with the same fervour as once I had. But, yes, I seek the Holy City.'

'Why?'

'Why not? There are worse ways for a man to live. When I was a child I lived with my parents and my brother. Raiders came and slaughtered my family. My brother and I escaped and were taken in by another family, but the raiders hit them too. I was older then and I killed them. For a long time I was angry, filled with hate for all brigands. Then I found my God and I wanted to see Him, to ask Him many things. I am a direct man. So, I look for Him. Does that answer your question?'

'It would have, were you younger. How old are you? Forty? Fifty?'

'I am forty-four years old, and, yes, I have been searching since before you were born. Does that make a difference?'

'Of course it does,' she told him. 'Young men – like Clem Steiner – see themselves as adventurers. But surely with maturity a man would come to see that such a life is wasted?'

'Wasted? Yes, I suppose it has been. I have no wife, no children, no home. But for all people, Beth McAdam, life is like a river. One man steps into it and finds it is cool and sweet and gentle. Another enters and finds it shallow and cold and unwelcoming. Still another finds it a rushing torrent that bears him on to many perils; this last man cannot easily change his course.'

'Just words, Mr Shannow – and well you know it. A strong man can do anything he pleases, live any life he chooses.'

'Then perhaps I am not strong,' he conceded. 'I had a wife once. I put aside my dreams of the Holy City and I rode with her seeking a new life. She had a son, Eric, a shy boy who was frightened of me. And we rode, unknowingly, into the heart of the Hellborn War . . . and I lost her.'

'Did you look for her? Or did she die?' Beth asked.

'She was taken by the Hellborn. I fought to save her. And – with the help of a fine friend – I did. She married another man – a good man. I am what I am, Beth. I cannot change. The world we live in will not allow me to change.'

'You could marry. Start a farm. Raise children.'

'And how long before someone recognises me? How long before the brigands gather? How long before an old enemy hunts me or my children? How long? No, I will find Jerusalem.'

'I think you are a sad man, Jon Shannow.' She opened the basket by her side and produced two apples, offering one to the Jerusalem Man. He took it and smiled.

'Less sad in your company, Lady. For which I thank you.'

Angry words instantly gathered in her mind, but she saw the expression on his face and swallowed them back. This was no clumsy attempt to bed her, nor the opening shots in a campaign to woo her. It was merely a moment of genuine honesty from a lonely fellow traveller.

'Why me?' she whispered. 'I sense you do not allow yourself many friends?'

He shrugged. 'I came to know you when I rode in your tracks. You are strong and caring; you do not panic. In some ways we are very alike. When I found the dying brigand, I knew I would be too late to help you. I expected to find you and your children murdered and my joy was great when I found your courage had saved you.'

'They murdered Harry,' she said. 'That is a shame. He asked if he could call on me in Pilgrim's Valley.' Beth lay down, resting on her elbow, and told Shannow the story of the brigands. He listened in silence until she had finished.

'Some women have that effect on a man,' he said. 'Harry respected your courage, and hung on to life long enough to send me to help you. For that I think the Almighty will look kindly on him.'

'You and I have different thoughts on that subject.' She looked down the hill and saw Samuel and Mary making their way up towards them. 'My children are returning,' she said softly.

'And I will leave you,' he replied.

'Will you take part in the pistol contest?' she asked. 'It is being held after the Parson gives his sermon. There is a prize of 100 Bartas.'

He shrugged. 'I do not think so.' He bowed and she watched him walk away.

'Damn you, Beth,' she whispered. 'Don't let him get to you.'

*

The Parson knelt deep in prayer on the hillside as the crowd gathered. He opened his eyes and looked out over the throng, and a deep warmth flowed within him. He had walked for two months to reach Pilgrim's Valley, crossing desert and plain, mountain and valley. He had preached at farms and settlements, performed marriages, christenings and funerals at isolated homes. He had prayed for the sick, and been welcomed wherever he walked. Once he had delivered a sermon at a brigand camp, and they had fed him and given him supplies of food and water to enable him to continue his journey. Now he was here, looking out over two thousand eager faces. He ran his hand through his thick red hair and stood.

He was home.

Lifting his borrowed pistols, he cocked them and fired two shots in the air. Into the silence that followed, his voice rang out.

'Brothers and sisters, welcome to God's Holy Day! Look at the sun shining in the clear blue heavens. Feel the warmth on your faces. That is but a poor reflection of the Love of God, when it flows into your hearts and your minds.

'We spend our days, brethren, grubbing in the dirt for wealth. Yet true wealth is here. Right here! I want each one of you to turn to the person beside you and take their hand in friendship. Do it now! Touch. Feel. Welcome. For the person beside you is your brother today, or your sister. Or your son. Or your daughter. Do it now! Do it now in love.'

A ripple ran through the crowd as people turned, mostly in embarrassment, to grasp and swiftly release the hands of the strangers beside them.

'Not good enough, brethren,' shouted the Parson. 'Is this how you would greet a long-lost brother or sister? I will show you.' He strode down amongst them and took an elderly woman in a deep hug, kissing both her cheeks. 'God's love upon you, mother,' he said. He seized a man's arm and swung him to face a young woman. 'Embrace her,' he ordered. 'And say the words with meaning. With belief. With love.'

Slowly he moved through the crowd, forcing people together. Some of the miners began to follow him, taking women in their arms and kissing them soundly on the cheeks. 'That is it, brethren!' shouted the Parson. 'Today is God's Day. Today is love!' He moved back to the hillside.

'Not that much love!' he shouted at a miner who had lifted a struggling woman from her feet. The crowd bellowed with laughter, and the tension eased.

'Look at us, Lord!' The Parson raised his arms and his face to the heavens. 'Look down on your people. Today there is no killing. No violence. No greed. Today we are a family in your sight.'

Then he launched into a powerful sermon about the sins of the many and the joys of the few. He had them then, as his powerful voice rolled over them. He talked of greed and of cruelty, the mindless pursuit of wealth and the loss of joy it created.

'For what does it profit a man if he gain the world, and yet lose his soul? What is wealth without love? Three hundred years ago the Lord brought Armageddon to the world of sin, toppling the earth, destroying Babylon the Great. For in those days evil had spread across the earth like a deadly plague, and the Lord washed away their sins even as Isaiah had prophesied. The sun rose in the West, the seas tipped from their bowls and not one stone was left upon another. But what did we learn, brethren? Did we come to love one another? Did we turn to the Almighty? No. We threw our noses into the mud and we scrabbled for gold and silver. We lusted and we fought, we hated and we slew.

'And why? Why?' he roared. 'Because we are men. Sinful, lustful men. But not today, brethren. We stand here in God's sunshine, and we know peace. We know love. And tomorrow I will build me a church on this meadow, where the love and peace of today will be sanctified; where it will be planted like a seed. And those of you who wish to see God's love remain in this community will come to me here, bringing wood and hammers and nails and saws, and we will build a church of love. And now, let us pray.'

The crowd knelt and he blessed them. He allowed the silence to grow for more than a minute, then, 'Up, my brethren. The fatted calf is waiting, the fun and the joy are here for all. Up and be happy. Up and laugh!'

People surged away to the tents and stalls, the children racing down the hill to the swing-boards and the mud around the stream. The Parson walked down into the throng, accepting a jug of water from a woman selling cakes. He drank deeply.

'That was well spoken,' said a voice and the Parson turned to see a tall man with silver-streaked shoulder-length hair and a greying beard. The man was wearing a flat-brimmed hat and a black coat and two pistols hung from scabbards at his hips.

'Thank you, brother. Did you feel moved to repent?'

'You made me think deeply. That, I hope, is a beginning.'

'Indeed it is. Do you have a farm here?'

'No, I am a travelling man. Good luck with your church.' He moved away into the crowd.

'That was the Jerusalem Man,' said the woman selling cakes. 'He killed a man yesterday. They say he's come to destroy the wicked.'

'Vengeance is mine, says the Lord. But let us not talk of violence and death, sister. Cut me a slice of your cake.'

14

Shannow watched the pistol-shooting contest with interest. The competitors, twenty-two of them, lined up facing open ground and loosed shots at targets thirty paces away. Gradually the field was whittled down to three men, one of them Clem Steiner. Each was obliged to fire at plates which were hurled in the air by children standing to the right of the range. Steiner won the competition and collected his prize of 100 Bartas from Edric Scayse. As the crowd was beginning to disperse, Scayse's voice rang out.

'We have with us today a legendary figure, possibly one of the greatest pistol shots on the continent. Ladies and gentlemen – Jon Shannow, the Jerusalem Man!' A ripple of applause ran through the spectators and Shannow stood silently, crushing the anger welling up in him. 'Come forward Meneer Shannow,' called Scayse and Shannow stepped up to the line. 'The winner of our competition, Clement Steiner, feels that his prize cannot be truly won unless he defeats the finest competitors. Therefore he has returned his prize until he has matched skills with the Jerusalem Man.'

The crowd roared approval. 'Do you accept the challenge, Jon Shannow?'

Shannow nodded and removed his coat and hat, laying them on the wooden rail that bordered the range. He drew his guns and checked his loads. Steiner stepped alongside him.

'Now they'll see some real shooting,' said the young man, grinning. He drew his pistol. 'Would you like to go first?' he asked. Shannow shook his head. 'Okay. Throw, boy!' called Steiner and a large clay plate sailed into the air. The crack of the pistol shot was followed by the shattering of the plate at the apex of its flight. Shannow then cocked his pistol and nodded to the boy. Another plate flew up and disintegrated as Shannow fired. Plate after plate was blown to pieces until finally the Jerusalem Man called a halt.

'This could go on all day, boy,' he said. 'Try two.' Steiner's eyes narrowed.

Another boy was sent to join the first and two plates were hurled high. Steiner hit the first but the second fell to the ground, shattering on impact.

Shannow took his place and both plates were exploded. 'Four!' he called, and the crowd stood stock-still as two more boys joined the throwers. Shannow cocked both pistols and took a deep breath. Then he nodded to the boys and as the plates soared into the air his guns swept up. The shots rolled out like thunder, smashing three of the spinning plates before they had reached the top of their flight. The fourth was falling like a stone when the bullet smashed through it. The applause was thunderous as Shannow bowed to the crowd, reloaded his pistols and sheathed them. He put on his coat and hat and collected the prize from Scayse.

The man smiled. 'You did not enjoy that, Mr Shannow. I am sorry. But the people will not forget it.'

'The coin will come in useful,' said Shannow. He turned to Steiner. 'I think it would be right for us to share this prize,' he suggested. 'For you had to work much harder for it.'

'Keep it!' snapped Steiner. 'You won it. But it doesn't make you a better man. We've still to decide that.'

'There is nothing to decide, Meneer Steiner. I can hit more plates, but you can draw and shoot accurately with far greater speed.'

'You know what I mean, Shannow. I'm talking about man to man.'

'Do not even think about it,' advised the Jerusalem Man.

*

It was almost midnight before Broome allowed Beth to leave the Jolly Pilgrim. The morning's entertainment had spilled over into the evening and Broome wanted to stay open to cater for the late-night revellers. Beth was not concerned about the children for Mary would have taken Samuel back to the wagon and prepared him some supper, but she was sorry to have missed an evening with them. They were growing so fast. She moved along the darkened sidewalk and down the three short steps to the street. A man stepped out in front of her from the shadows at the side of the building; two others joined him.

'Well, well,' he said, his face shadowed from the moonlight by the brim of his hat. 'If it ain't the whore who killed poor Thomas.'

'His stupidity killed him,' she said.

'Yeah? But you warned the Jerusalem Man, didn't you? You went running to him. Are you his whore, bitch?'

Beth's fist cracked against his chin and he staggered; she followed in crashing a second blow with her left that spun him from his feet. As he tried to rise she lashed out with her foot, catching him under the chin. 'Any other questions?' she asked. She walked on but a man leapt at her, grabbing her arms; she struggled to turn and kick out, but another man grabbed her legs and she was hoisted from her feet.

They carried her towards the alley. 'We'll see what makes you so special,' grunted one of her attackers.

'I don't think so,' said a man's voice and the attackers dropped Beth to the ground. She scrambled to her feet and looked up to see the Parson was standing in the street.

'You keep your puking nose out of this,' said one of the men, while the other drew a pistol.

'I do not like to see any among the brethren behaving in such a manner towards a lady,' said the Parson. 'And I do not like guns pointed at me. It is not polite. Go on about your business.'

'You think I won't kill you?' the gunman asked. 'Just because you wear a black dress and spout on about God? You're nothing, man. Nothing!'

'What I am is a man. And men do not behave as you do.

Only the basest animals act in such a manner. You are filth! Vermin! You do not belong in the company of civilised people.'

'That's it!' shouted the man, his pistol coming up and his thumb on the hammer. The Parson's hand swept out from behind his cassock and his gun roared. The man was hurled backwards by the force of the shell as it hit his chest, then a second bullet smashed through his skull.

'Jesus Christ!' whispered the survivor.

'A little late for prayers,' the Parson told him. 'Step forward and let me see your face.' The man stumbled towards him and the Parson lifted his hand and removed the man's hat, allowing the moonlight to illuminate his features.

'Tomorrow morning you will report to the meadow where you will help me build my church. Is that not so, brother?' The gun pushed up under the man's chin.

'Whatever you say, Parson.'

'Good. Now see to the body. It is not fitting that it should lie there to be seen by children in the morning.'

The Parson moved to Beth. 'How are you feeling, sister?'

'I've had better days,' Beth told him.

'I shall walk you to your home.'

'That will not be necessary.'

'Indeed no. But it will be a pleasure.' He took her arm and they walked off in the direction of Tent Town.

'I thought your God looked unkindly on killing,' said Beth.

'Indeed he does, sister. But the distinction he makes concerns murder. The Bible is full of killing and slaughter, and the Lord understands that among sinful men there will always be violence. There is an apt section in Ecclesiastes: *There is a time for everything, and a season for every activity. A time to be born, and a time to die, a time to plant and a time to uproot, a time to kill, and a time to heal* . . . There is more, and it is very beautiful.'

'You speak well, Parson. But I'm glad you also shoot well.'

'I've had a lot of practice, sister.'

'Call me Beth. I never had no brothers. Do you have a name?'

'Parson is fine. And I like the sound of Beth; it is a good name. Are you married?'

'I was. Sean died on the journey. But my children are with me. I expect they're sleeping now – or they damn well better be.'

They made their way through the tents and wagons until they reached the McAdam camp-site. The fire was low and the children asleep in their blankets beside the wheels. The oxen had been led to a second meadow where they grazed with other cattle. Beth stoked up the fire.

'Will you join me for tea, Parson? I always drink a cup before sleeping.'

'Thank you,' he answered, sitting cross-legged by the fire. She boiled some water, added herbs and sugar and poured the mixture into two pottery mugs.

'You come far?' she asked, as they drank.

'Very far. I heard God calling me, and I answered. But what of you? Where are you bound?'

'I'll be staying in the valley. I am going to lease some land from Meneer Scayse – start a farm. I have some seed corn and other such.'

'Hard work for a woman alone.'

'I won't be alone long, Parson. It's not my way.'

'No, I can see that,' he answered without embarrassment. 'By the way, where did such a charming young mother learn the rudiments of the left hook? It was a splendid blow with all your weight behind it.'

'My husband Sean was a fist-fighter. He taught me that – and much more.'

'He was a lucky man, Beth.'

'He's dead, Parson.'

'Many men live a long lifetime and never meet a woman like you. They, I think, are the unlucky ones. And now I must bid you good night.' He rose and bowed.

'You come again, Parson. You're always welcome.'

'That is nice to know. I hope we will see you in our new church.'

'Only if you have songs. I like to sing.'

'We will have songs just for you,' he told her, and walked away into the shadows.

For a while Beth sat quietly by the dying fire. The Parson was a strong man, and extraordinarily handsome with that fine red hair and easy smile. But there was something about him that disturbed her and she thought about it, trying to pin down her unease. Physically she found him attractive, but there was about him a tightness, a tension that left her wary. Her thoughts strayed to Jon Shannow. Similar men, and yet not so. Like thunder and lightning. Both were companion to inner storms. But Shannow was aware of his own dark side. She was not sure about the Parson.

Beth stripped off her long woollen skirt and her white blouse and washed in cold water. Then she slipped into a full-length bed-gown and settled down into her blankets. Her hand moved under the pillow, curling round the walnut butt of her pistol.

And she slept.

*

During the night there were two killings and a woman was raped behind a gambling-house in the east section. Shannow sat silently in the corner of the Long Bar drinking a Baker's and listening to the tales. It seemed the Parson had killed one man who was attacking a woman but the other shooting was a mystery, save for the fact that the dead man had won a large amount of coin playing Carnat at a gambling house run by a man named Webber.

Shannow had seen it all before: crooked gamblers, thieves and robbers congregating in a community that had no law. When would the upright citizens ever learn, he wondered? There were around two thousand people in Pilgrim's Valley, and no more than a hundred villains. Yet the brigands swaggered around the town and the good people stepped aside for them. He stared sourly into the dark depths of the drink before him, and knew that he was tempted to cut away the disease afflicting the community; to storm the bastions of the Ungodly and root out the evil. Yet he would not.

I no longer lance boils – that's what he had told Boris Haimut. And it was true. A man could take only so much of rejection and the contempt of his fellows. It always began with fine words and promises. 'Help us, Mr Shannow.' 'We need you, Mr Shannow.' 'Good work, Mr Shannow.' 'That will show them, sir.' And then . . . 'But do you have to be so violent, Mr Shannow?' 'Is the bloodshed necessary?' 'When will you be moving on?'

But no more. If the town was diseased it was a problem for those who lived here, who wanted to work here, raise children in the valley. It was for them now to put their house in order.

He had said as much to the merchants Brisley and Fenner who had waited for him that morning. Brisley, fat and gregarious, had extolled the virtues of the community, blaming its ills on men like Scayse and Webber.

'No better than brigands, sir, I assure you. Scayse's men are arrogant and ill-mannered. And as for Webber, the man is a thief and a killer. Four times in the last month, men who have won large amounts of money have been slain close to his establishment. And he killed two others in gun battles over alleged cheating. It is insufferable, sir.'

'Then do something about it,' advised Shannow.

'That's what we are doing,' put in Fenner, a dark-eyed young man of slender build. 'We have come to you.'

'You do not need me. Get together twenty men. Go to Webber. Close him down. Order him from the community.'

'His men are thugs and villains,' said Brisley, wiping the sweat from his face. 'They thrive on violence. We are merchants.'

'You have guns,' said Shannow simply. 'Even a merchant can pull a trigger.'

'With respect, sir,' Fenner interposed, 'it takes a certain kind of man to be able to kill a human being in cold blood.

Now I don't know if killing will be necessary. I hope not. But surely a man with your reputation would find it more easy to stamp his authority on the villains?'

'In cold blood, Meneer?' responded Shannow. 'I do not consider it in those terms. I am not a wanton slayer, nor am I a kind of respectable brigand. Mostly the men I have killed have died in the act of trying to kill me. The rest have been in the process of wilfully attacking others. However, such points are meaningless in the current circumstances. I have no wish to give birth again to seven devils.'

'You have me at a loss, sir,' said Fenner.

'Read your Bible, Meneer. Now leave me in peace.'

Shannow finished his drink and returned to his room. For a while he sat thinking about the problems posed by the Wall, but Beth McAdam's face kept appearing before his mind's eye.

'You are a fool, Shannow,' he told himself. Loving Donna Taybard had been a mistake, and one he had come to regret. But it was folly of the worst kind to allow another woman to enter his heart.

He forced her from his mind and took up his Bible, leafing through to the Gospel of Matthew.

'*When an evil spirit goes out of a man, it goes through arid places seeking rest and does not find it. Then it says, "I will return to the house I left." When it arrives it finds the house unoccupied, swept clean and put in order. Then it goes and takes with it seven other spirits more wicked than itself and they go in and live there. And the final condition of that man is worse than the first.*'

How often had the Jerusalem Man seen the truth of that? In Allion, Cantastay, Berkalin, and a score of other settlements. The brigands had fled before him – or been buried because of him. Then he had ridden on and the evil had returned. Daniel Cade had visited Allion two weeks after Shannow left, and the town had been ruined by his attack.

It would not happen here, he decided.

In Pilgrim's Valley the Jerusalem Man was merely an observer.

15

The pistol competition had left Shannow short of shells for his Hellborn pistols. There were twenty-three left, including the ten in the cylinders of his guns. Pilgrim's Valley boasted one gunsmith and Shannow made his way to the man's small shop in the eastern section. It was a narrow building, lit by lanterns, the wall behind the service area filled with weapons of every kind from flintlock pistols to percussion rifles, flared-barrelled blunderbusses alongside sleek gravity-fed weapons with walnut stocks. But there were no pistols like Shannow's.

The shop-owner was a short, bald elderly man who identified himself as Groves. Shannow drew one of his guns and laid it on the double plank unit that served as a long table between the gunsmith and his customers. Groves sniffed and lifted the weapon, flicking open the gate and ejecting a shell. 'Hellborn,' he said. 'There are a lot of these in the north now. We're hoping to get some – but they're mighty expensive.'

'I need bullets for it,' said Shannow. 'Can you make them?'

'I'd have no trouble with the moulds, or the fulminates. But these brass cases? It will not be easy, Mr Shannow. Nor cheap.'

'But you can do it?'

'Leave me five shells with which to experiment. I will do what I can. When are you leaving?'

'I was due to ride on today.'

Groves chuckled. 'I need at least a week, sir. How many do you require?'

'One hundred would suffice.'

'That will cost fifty Bartas. I would appreciate half now.'

'Your price is very high.'

'So is the level of my craftsmanship.'

Shannow paid the man and returned to the hotel where he found Mason sitting in a comfort chair by an open window, dozing in the sun.

'I need the room for another week,' he said.

Mason blinked and stood. 'I thought you were moving on, Meneer Shannow.'

'I am, sir, but not for a week.'

'I see. Very well. A week, then.'

Shannow walked to the stable and saddled the stallion. The hostler grinned at him as he rode out and Shannow waved as he steered the horse to the south, heading for the Wall. He rode for two hours, crossing rich grassland and cutting high into the timberline of the hills. He saw cattle grazing, and a herd of antelope moving along the line of a stream. The Wall grew ever nearer. From the high ground where he rode, Shannow could see over the colossal structure and the rolling hills beyond it. There was no sign of life; no cattle, sheep, goats or deer. Yet the land looked rich and verdant. Angling the stallion downwards, he halted on the hillside, drawing his long glass from the saddlebag. He followed the line of the Wall first to the east where it disappeared in the blue haze of the mountains; then he swung the glass west. As far as he could see the Wall went on for miles, unbroken and unbreachable; he focused the glass on a section of it some half a mile away, and saw a group of men camped nearby. Then he continued his descent and rode on. The Wall now reared above him and he estimated its height at more than sixty feet. It was constructed of giant rectangular blocks each approximately ten feet wide and more than six feet high.

Shannow dismounted and approached the edifice. He drew his hunting-knife and tried to push the blade between two stones, but the fit was too tight and there was no sign of mortar. From the hill above he had judged the Wall to be at least ten feet thick. He sheathed his knife and ran his fingers over the blocks, seeking handholds that might permit him to climb. But apart from lichens and curious shells imbedded in the surface, there was no purchase.

He stepped into the saddle and followed the line of the Wall west until he reached the camp-site where Boris Haimut was chipping away at one of the blocks with a hammer and chisel. The scholar put down his tools and waved.

'Fascinating, is it not?' said Haimut, grinning cheerfully. Shannow dismounted, his eyes scanning the small group of men who continued with their work. To the far right he could see the two men who had tried to force him to leave the site of the shipwreck; they avoided his gaze, and continued to chip away at the blocks.

Shannow followed Haimut to the camp-site where a large pot of Baker's was brewing. Haimut wrapped a cloth around the handle and lifted the pot, filling two mugs. He passed one to Shannow.

'Have you ever seen anything like it?' asked Haimut and Shannow shook his head. 'Neither have I. There are no windows, no towers and no gates. It could not have been built for defence; any invading army would simply throw grappling lines over the top and climb it. There are no parapets. Nothing. Just a colossal Wall. Take a look at this.' He fished in his pocket and produced a shining shell, slightly larger than a Barta coin. Shannow took it, turning it over and holding it to the light. There were many colours glistening within the grooves – purple, yellow, blue and white.

'It is very pretty,' Shannow said.

'Indeed it is. But it is also from the sea, Mr Shannow. This towering structure was once below the ocean.'

'This whole land was once under water,' Shannow told him. 'There was a civilisation here – a great civilisation. But the seas rose up and devoured them.'

'So then, you are saying this is an Oldworld site?'

'No. The Oldworld sites are now mostly beneath the seas. I learned several years ago that the earth had toppled not once, but twice. The people who lived beyond this Wall were destroyed thousands of years ago. I have no way of knowing, but I would guess it happened about the time of the Flood described in the Book.'

'How do you know all this?' asked Haimut.

Shannow considered telling him the whole truth, but dismissed the thought. What credibility he had would disappear if he explained how the long-dead King of Atlantis had come to his rescue in the battle against the Guardians during the Hellborn War.

'Two years ago, with a friend, I rode into the ruins of a great city. There were statues everywhere. Beautifully carved. While there, I met a scholar named Samuel Archer. He was a fine man: strong, yet gentle. He had studied the ruins and others like them for many years and had even managed to decipher the language of the ancients. The city was called Balacris, the land was known as Atlantis. I learned much from him before he died.'

'I'm sorry that he is dead. I would like to have met him,' said Haimut. 'I too have seen the inscriptions on gold foil. But to meet a man who could read them . . . How did he die?'

'He was beaten to death because he would not work as a slave in a silver mine.'

Haimut looked away and sipped his Baker's. 'This is not a contented world, Meneer Shannow. We live in strange circumstances, fighting over scraps of knowledge. Everywhere there are isolated communities, and no central focus. In the wildlands the brigands rule, and in settled communities there are wars with rivals. There is no peace. It is most galling. Far to the east there is a land where women are not allowed to show their faces in public and men who deny the Book are burned alive. To the north there are communities where child sacrifice has become the norm. Last year I visited an area where women are not allowed to marry; they are owned by the men and used as breed cows for the community. But wherever you go there is violence and death, and the rule of the powerful. Have you been to Rivervale?'

'I have,' replied Shannow. 'I lived there once.'

'Now that is an oasis. It is ruled by a man named Daniel Cade. They have laws there, good laws; and families can raise their children in peace and prosperity. If only we could all find such a way. You say you lived there? Do you know Daniel Cade?'

'I know him,' said Shannow. 'He is my brother.'

'Good Lord! I never knew that. I have heard of you, of course. But no one ever spoke of a brother.'

'We were parted as children. Tell me, what do you hope to achieve here?'

'Meneer Scayse is looking for a way to breach the Wall. He has asked me to examine it. And I need the coin, in order to be able to return home.'

'I thought you disapproved of him?'

'I do. He is – like all men who seek power – eminently selfish. But I cannot afford too many scruples. And I harm no one by examining this edifice.'

Shannow finished his drink and rose.

'Will you stay the night, Meneer?' Haimut asked. 'It would be good to have some intelligent conversation.'

'Thank you, no. Another time perhaps. Tell me, what do you know of Scayse?'

Haimut shrugged. 'Very little. He came here a year ago with a great deal of coin and a large herd of cattle. He is said to be from the far north. He is a clever man.'

'I don't doubt that,' said Shannow.

*

Shannow returned to the settlement just before dusk. He left the stallion at the stable, paid the hostler to groom and feed him and then walked to the Jolly Pilgrim. Beth McAdam smiled as he entered and moved across to greet him.

'Haven't seen much of you, Shannow,' she said. 'Food not good enough?'

'The food is fine. How are you faring?'

'Can't complain. You?'

'Well enough,' Shannow replied, aware of a rising tension. 'Would you bring me some food? Anything hot that you have.'

'Sure,' she told him. He sat quietly facing the door and glanced around the room. There were eight other diners – they studiously avoided looking at him. Beth brought him a bowl of thick broth and some dark bread and cheese. He ate it slowly and considered ordering a Baker's, but then he remembered Haimut's warning about the drink being habit-forming and decided against. Instead he asked for a glass of water.

'Are you all right, Shannow?' asked Beth, as she brought it to his table. 'You seem a little . . . preoccupied.'

'I have been studying the Wall,' he told her, 'looking for a way through. It looks as if I will have to climb it and proceed on foot. I do not like travelling that way.'

'Then ride around it. It cannot stretch across the world, for goodness' sake.'

'That could take weeks.'

'And you, of course, are a man with no time on his hands.'

He grinned at her. 'Will you join me?'

'I can't; I'm working. But tomorrow morning I get a free hour at noon. You could come then.'

'Perhaps I will,' he said.

'Maybe, if you do, you should consider getting that coat brushed and cleaning your other clothes. You smell of dust and horses. And that silver-forked beard makes you look like Methuselah.'

Shannow scratched his chin and smiled. 'We will see.' Just then Alain Fenner entered. He spotted Shannow and approached.

'May I sit down, Meneer?' he asked.

'I thought we had concluded our conversation,' said Shannow, annoyed that the interruption caused Beth to leave.

'It is only advice I am seeking.'

Shannow gestured to the chair opposite. 'How can I help you?'

Fenner leaned forward, lowering his voice. 'We are going to close down Webber tonight. As you suggested there will be a group of us – Brisley, Broome and a few others. But we are none of us men used to sudden violence. I would appreciate your thoughts.'

Shannow looked into the man's open, honest face and realised that he liked him. Fenner had courage, and he cared. 'Who will be your spokesman?' he asked.

'I will.'

'Then it is you the ungodly will look to for action. Do not allow Webber or anyone else to take the lead. Do not enter into any discussion. Say what you want and make it happen. Do you understand me?'

'I think so.'

'Keep all talk to a minimum. Move in, get Webber out and close the place. If there is the least suggestion of opposition, shoot someone. Keep the mob off balance. But it is Webber you must control. He is the head of the snake – cut him off and the others will stand and wonder what to do and while they are wondering, you will have won. Can you trust the men with you?'

'Trust them? What do you mean?'

'Are they close-mouthed? Will Webber know of your plan before you arrive?'

'I do not think so.'

'I hope you are right. Your life depends on it. Are you married?'

'I have a wife and four sons.'

'Think of them, Fenner, when you walk in. If you make a mistake, it is they who will pay for it.'

'Can it be done without shooting anyone?'

'Perhaps. I did not say you should walk in with guns blazing. I am trying to tell you how to stay alive. If Webber starts to talk and you respond his men will begin to gather themselves – and your men will start to waver. Be strong, be swift and be direct. No shades of grey, Meneer Fenner. Black and white. Win or lose. Live or die.'

Fenner took a deep breath. 'I will try to follow your advice. Thank you for your time.'

'It cost me nothing. If trouble starts – or even looks like starting – kill Webber.' But Shannow knew he would not, for even as he said it the young man's eyes wavered from his direct gaze. 'Do your best, Meneer.'

When the young man had left, Beth returned to the table. 'He's a good man,' she said.

'He may not live very long,' Shannow told her.

*

There were eight armed men in the group that entered Webber's gambling-house. It was crowded with more than twenty tables and a long bar packed with customers. Webber himself sat at a Carnat table to the rear and Fenner led the group through to him.

'You will come with us, Meneer Webber,' he said, drawing his pistol and pointing it at the gambler. As the revellers realised what was happening a silence fell on the room. Webber stood and folded his arms. He was a tall man, running to fat but powerfully built; his eyes were black and deep-set and he smiled at Fenner. Gleaming gold flashed in his grin and Fenner saw that the teeth on either side of his incisors were moulded from precious metal.

'Why in the Devil's name should I?' Webber asked.

Fenner cocked the pistol. 'Because you'll be dead if you don't,' he told him.

'Is this fair?' Webber thundered. 'What have I done? I run a gambling-house. I have killed no one – save in fair battle.'

'You are a thief and a scoundrel,' said Josiah Broome, pushing forward, 'and we are closing you down.'

'Who says I am a thief? Let him stand forward,' Webber shouted.

Fenner waved Broome back, but the man pushed on.

'People who win from you are killed. Do you deny any responsibility?'

'Why is that my fault, Meneer? A man who wins a great deal of coin is seen by many other – unluckier – gamblers.'

Fenner glanced around. The crowd had fallen back now and Webber's men ringed the group. Brisley was sweating heavily and two of the others were shifting uneasily. Fenner's pistol levelled at Webber's chest.

'You will move now, Meneer. Or suffer the consequences.'

'You would shoot me down? Murder me, Meneer? What sort of law is this you are proposing?'

'He . . . he's right, Alain,' whispered Broome. 'We didn't come here to kill anyone. But let this be a lesson to you, Webber! We'll not stand for any more violence.'

'I stand and quake in my shoes, Meneer Bacon-server. Now all of you put down your weapons, or my men will blow you into tiny pieces.' Brisley's gun clattered to the floor and the others followed . . . all save Alain Fenner. His eyes locked to Webber's and understanding flowed between them.

But Fenner was no killer. He uncocked the pistol and thrust it deep into the scabbard at his hip, but as he did so Webber drew his own pistol and shot Fenner twice in the chest. The young man scrabbled for his gun and fell to his knees, but a third shot struck his breastbone and spun him back to the floor.

'Emily . . .' he whispered. Blood bubbled from his lips and his body twitched.

'Get the fool out of here,' ordered Webber. 'There's a game in progress.'

Brisley and the others hauled Fenner out into the street and back past the Traveller's Rest. Shannow was sitting on the porch; a great sadness weighed down on him as he stood and walked to the group.

'He just shot him down,' said Broome. 'Alain was putting away his gun, and Webber just shot him down.'

Shannow leaned over and touched his hand to Fenner's neck. 'He's dead. Put him down.'
'Not in the street,' Broome protested.
'Put him down!' stormed Shannow. 'And wait here.' He took off his coat and left it by the body, then walked swiftly to Webber's establishment. He entered and stalked across the room where the gambler was drinking and joking with his men. Then he drew his pistol, cocked it and slid it against Webber's lips.
'Open your mouth!' said Shannow. Webber blinked twice and saw the light of fury in Shannow's eyes. He opened his mouth and the barrel slid between his teeth. 'Now stand!' Webber eased himself to his feet. Shannow walked him slowly back through the throng and out of the door into the street. He did not need to look back to know that everyone in the gambling-house had followed. Word spread to other establishments and the crowd grew. Webber backed away, the gun almost making him choke. His own pistol was still in its holster, but he kept his hands well away from it. Shannow halted by the body of Alain Fenner, and turned slightly to look at the crowd.
'This young man risked his life for many of you. And now he lies dead, and his wife is a widow, and his sons have been robbed of a father. And why? Because you have no courage. Because you allow the vermin to walk among you. This man died as a result of sin.' His eyes swept the crowd. 'And as the Book says, "The Wages of Sin is death"!'
Shannow pulled the trigger. Webber's brains mushroomed from his skull and the body fell back to the earth with dark powder-smoke streaming from the blackened mouth.
'Now you listen to me!' Shannow roared into the stunned silence that followed. 'I know many of you brigands. If you are in Pilgrim's Valley come morning, I will hunt you down and kill you on sight. You may be sitting breaking your fast, or sleeping snug in a warm bed, or quietly playing Carnat with friends. But I will fall upon you with the wrath of God.

Those with ears to hear, let them understand. Tomorrow you die.'

A stocky man stepped from the crowd, wearing two guns thrust into his belt. 'You think you can tackle all of us?' he challenged.

Shannow's pistol boomed and the man flew from his feet, his skull smashed.

'There will be no questions,' declared the Jerusalem Man. 'Tomorrow I will hunt you down.'

16

The long night had begun. Shannow sat in his room with his Hellborn pistols on the table beside him, his trusted cap and ball weapons in the scabbards at his side. He had cleaned the old guns and reloaded them; he had only sixteen shells for the Hellborn revolvers, and if the night turned sour he would need more than that. He had moved his chair away from the window and now sat in the darkness of his room. The pillows of his bed had been rolled tight and placed under the blankets to imitate a sleeping form, and now the Jerusalem Man had nothing to do but wait for the inevitable.

As the first hour crept by he heard the sound of horsemen leaving the town. He did not look from the window to check the numbers. At least two-thirds of the brigands would be leaving before dawn, but it was not the runners who worried Shannow.

He sat in the darkness, his fury gone, blaming himself for Fenner's death; he had known deep in his soul that the young man could not survive, and yet he had let him walk into the Valley of the Shadow.

Am I my brother's keeper? The answer should have been yes. He recalled the shocked looks on the faces of the mob as he had blown Webber to Hell, and he knew what they had seen: the crazed fanatic the world knew as the Jerusalem Man taking one more helpless victim. They would forget that Webber had mercilessly murdered poor Alain Fenner, but they would remember the tormented Webber, standing in the moonlight with a pistol barrel in his mouth.

And so would Shannow. It was not a good deed. He could convince himself of its necessity, but not of its virtue. There was a time when Jon Shannow would have fought Webber man to man, upright and fearless. But not now.

His powers and his speed were waning. He had seen that well enough when he watched Clem Steiner shoot the jug. Once, maybe, the Jerusalem Man could have duplicated such a feat. Not any more. Not even close.

A floorboard creaked in the corridor outside. Shannow hefted a pistol, then heard a door open and close and the sound of a man sitting down on a mattress. He relaxed, but left the pistol cocked.

Rivervale. That was where his life had changed. He had ridden through the wild lands and found himself in a predominantly peaceful community. There he had met Donna Taybard. Her husband, Tomas the carpenter, had been murdered, and she herself was under threat. Shannow had helped her and had grown to love her. Together they had journeyed with Con Griffin to a hoped-for new life in a world without brigands and killers. Griffin had called it Avalon.

Yet what had they found? Shannow had been wounded by the Carns, a strange race of cannibals, and rescued by the saintly Karitas, a survivor of the Fall of the world. Donna had believed Shannow dead and had married Griffin.

And something in Jon Shannow had given up the ghost and died. He remembered his father once saying: 'Better to have loved and lost than never to have loved at all.' But it was not true.

He had been more content before he met Donna. Perhaps not happy, but he knew who he was and what he was . . .

The soft scuff of a boot sounded on the roof above his head.

Come then, my would-be killers. I am here. I am waiting. He heard the stretching groan of a rope and saw a booted foot in a loop easing down outside the window.

Lower and lower it came until a man's body appeared. He was holding the rope with his left hand while in his right was a long-barrelled pistol. As his torso came level with the window he sighted on the bed and fired twice. At the same time, the door to Shannow's room was smashed open and two men rushed in.

The Jerusalem Man shot them both with his left-hand pistol, then twisted his right and fired point-blank into the belly of the man on the rope, who screamed and pitched back out of sight. Shannow lifted his pistols high and blasted three shots through the ceiling. He heard a man yell; the rope sailed past the window and he heard the thumping crash of the body splitting the planks of the sidewalk.

Silence fell. The room stank of gunfire and a fine mist of powder and cordite hung in the air.

Outside in the corridor Shannow could hear whispered commands, but there was no movement.

Swiftly he reloaded his pistols with the last of his shells.

Two shots came from the corridor. A man screamed and a body thudded against the wooden landing.

'Hey, Shannow,' called Steiner. 'It's clear out here. Can I come in?'

'Your hands better be empty,' Shannow replied.

Steiner stepped across the bodies and entered the room. 'There were only two of them,' he said, smiling. 'Damn, but you do make life interesting. You know, at least thirty men have already left the settlement. What I wouldn't give for a reputation like yours!'

'Why did you help me?'

'Hell, Shannow, I couldn't take the risk of someone else killing you. Where in the world would I find an opponent like you?'

Steiner eased his way to the side of the window and pulled the thick curtain across it, then he struck a match and lit the lantern on the table. 'Mind if I move these bodies into the hall – they're starting to stink up the place?' Without waiting for a response he moved over to the corpses. 'Both shot through the head. Pretty good. Pretty damn good!' He grabbed the collar of the first man and dragged him out into the hall. Shannow sat and watched as he pulled the second corpse after it. 'Hey, Mason!' Steiner shouted. 'Can you get some men up here to move this dead meat?'

Stepping back inside, he wedged the broken door shut and returned to his seat. 'Well, Shannow, you going to thank me, or what?'

'Why should I thank you?'

'For taking out the two on the stairs. What would you have done without me? They had you trapped in here like snared game.'

'Thank you,' said Shannow. 'And now you should leave. I'm going to get some sleep.'

'You want me to walk with you tomorrow, when the hunting starts?'

'That will not be necessary.'

'Man, you are crazy. There're still twenty, maybe thirty men who won't be run out. You can't take them all.'

'Good night, Meneer Steiner.'

*

The following morning, after three hours' sleep, Jon Shannow made his way down to the lobby and called Mason to him. 'Send someone out to find me six children who can read. Have them brought here.'

Then the Jerusalem Man sat down at a table with six large sheets of paper and a charcoal stub. Slowly and carefully he spelled out a simple message on each sheet.

Shannow made the children read aloud the message and then sent them to the gambling and drinking houses in the east section with instructions to hand a notice to each of the owners, or barmen. The message was simple:

WARNING

ANYONE CARRYING A GUN WITHIN THE TOWNSHIP OF PILGRIM'S VALLEY WILL BE CONSIDERED A BRIGAND AND A WARMAKER AND WILL BE DEALT WITH AS SUCH.

SHANNOW

When the children had left, Shannow sat back and waited patiently, emptying his mind of fear and tension. Mason brought him a cup of Baker's and sat down opposite.

'For what it's worth, Shannow, the room is free – and any food or drink you consume.'

'That is kind of you, Meneer.'

Mason shrugged. 'You are a good man. This will make you no friends, however.'

'I am aware of that.' He looked into the man's cadaverous face. 'I do not think you were always a room-keeper?'

Mason gave a thin smile. 'You chased me out of Allion – put a bullet in my shoulder. When it rains, it hurts like the Devil.'

Shannow nodded. 'I remember you; you rode with Cade. I am glad you found something more productive.'

'A man gets older,' said Mason. 'Most of us took to the road because we were forced from our farms, either by raiders, or drought, or men with more power. But it's no life. Here I have a wife, two daughters and a roof over my head. My meals are regular, and in the winter I have a large log fire to keep out the cold. What more can a man rightly ask for?'

'Amen to that,' Shannow agreed.

'What will you do now?'

'I'll wait until noon and then root out whoever is left.'

'This isn't Allion, Shannow. There you had townspeople who backed you. There was a Committee, I recall – all good with rifles – and they protected your back. Here it is suicidal. They will wait for you in alleys, or shoot you as you appear on the street.'

'I have spoken the words, Meneer, and they are iron.'

'I guess so,' agreed Mason, rising. 'God's luck be with you.'

'It generally is,' said the Jerusalem Man.

From where he sat, he could see the sun slowly ascending the heavens. It looked to be a beautiful day; a man could not choose a more beautiful day to die. One by one the children returned and Shannow gave them each a coin, asked them where they had taken the notices and what had been the response. In most cases the recipients had read them aloud to the gathering, but in one instance a man had read out the notice and then torn it to pieces. The crowd had laughed, the boy told Shannow.

'Describe the place.' The boy did so. 'And did you see men with guns there?'

'Yes. One was sitting by a window with a long rifle aimed at the street. There were two others on a balcony above and to the right of the door. And I think there was another man hidden by some barrels at the far wall by the bar.'

'You are an observant boy. What is your name?'

'Matthew Fenner, sir.' Shannow looked into the boy's dark eyes and wondered why he had not seen the resemblance to the martyred farmer.

'How is your mother?'

'She's been crying a lot.'

Shannow opened the hide pouch in which he kept his coin and counted out twenty pieces. 'Give these to your mother. Tell her I am sorry.'

'We are not poor, sir. But thank you for the thought,' said Matthew. The boy turned and walked from the room.

It was almost noon. Shannow returned the coin to his pouch and stood.

He left the Traveller's Rest by the back door and stepped swiftly into the alley, moving to his right with gun poised. The alley was deserted. He walked along behind the buildings until he came to the side of the gambling-house the boy had described. It was run by a man named Zeb Maddox and Mason had told him Maddox was a fast man with a pistol: 'Damn near as sudden as Steiner. Don't give him no second chances, Shannow.'

The Jerusalem Man paused outside a tiny service door to the rear, took a deep breath and then eased open the latch. Stepping inside, he saw the back of a man who was kneeling behind some barrels. Beyond him everyone's eyes were on the front door. Shannow moved forward and cracked his pistol against the back of the kneeling man's neck. As he grunted and slid sideways, Shannow caught him by the collar and eased him to the floor.

Just then someone shouted, 'There's a crowd gathering, Zeb.'

Shannow watched as a tall, thin man in a black shirt and leather trousers emerged from behind the bar and moved to the door. He was wearing a pistol scabbard of polished leather which housed a short-barrelled gun with a bone handle.

From outside came a voice.

'You men inside, listen to me; this is the Parson speaking. We know you are armed, and we are ready to give battle to you. But think on this: There are forty men out here, and when we rush the place the carnage will be terrible. Those we do not kill will be taken to a place of execution and hanged by the neck until dead. I suggest you put down your weapons and walk – in peace – to your horses. We will wait for a few minutes, but if we are forced to storm in you all will die.'

'We got to get out of here, Zeb,' shouted a man Shannow could not see.

'I'll not run from a pack of Townies,' hissed Zeb Maddox.

'Then run from me,' said Shannow, moving forward with pistol raised.

Maddox turned slowly. 'You going to try to put that pistol in my mouth, Shannow, or will you be a man and face me?'

'Oh, I'll face you,' said Shannow as he strode forward and pushed his pistol into Maddox's belly. 'Draw your gun and cock it.'

'What the Hell is this?'

'Do it. Now put it against my stomach.' Maddox did so. 'Fine. There's your chance. I'll count to three and we'll both pull the triggers,' whispered Shannow coldly.

'You're crazy. We'll both die, for sure.'

'One,' said Shannow.

'This is mad, Shannow!' Maddox's eyes were wide with terror.

'Two!'

'No!' screamed Maddox, hurling away his pistol and throwing himself backwards, his hands over his face.

The Jerusalem Man looked around at the waiting gunmen. 'Live or die,' he told them. 'Choose now.'

Guns clattered to the floor. Shannow walked to the doorway and nodded to the Parson and the men gathered with him. Broome was there. And Brisley . . . and Mason . . . and Steiner. Beth McAdam was standing beside them, her pistol in her hand.

'I killed no one,' said Shannow. 'They are ready to go. Let them ride.' He walked away, his gun hanging at his side.

'Shannow!' screamed Beth and the Jerusalem Man spun as Zeb Maddox fired from the doorway. The shell punched Shannow from his feet; his vision misting, he returned the fire. Maddox doubled over, then staggered upright, but a volley of shots from the crowd lifted him and hurled him back through the doorway.

Shannow struggled to his feet and staggered. Blood was dripping to his cheek. He bent to retrieve his hat . . .

And darkness swallowed him.

*

Bright colours were everywhere, hurting his eyes. And blood flowed upon his face. Flames flickered at the edge of his vision and he saw a terrible beast stalking towards him, holding a rope with which to throttle him. His pistol blazed and the creature staggered, but came on, blood pouring from its wound. He fired again. And again. Still the beast advanced until finally it slumped to its knees before him, its taloned claws opening.

'Why?' the beast whispered.

Shannow looked down and saw that the creature was carrying not a rope but a bandage. 'Why did you kill me, when I was trying to help you?'

'I'm sorry,' whispered Shannow. The beast vanished and he rose and walked to the cave-mouth. Hanging in the sky, awesome in its scale, was the Sword of God, with around it crosses of many colours – green and white and blue. Below it was a city, teeming with life: a huge, circular city, ringed with walls of white

stone and a massive moat which boasted a harbour where wooden ships with banks of oars were anchored.

A beautiful woman with flame-red hair approached Shannow. 'I will help you,' she said . . . but in her hand was a knife. Shannow backed away.

'Leave me alone,' he told her. But she advanced and the knife came up to sink in his chest. Darkness engulfed him. Then there was the noise of a great roaring and he awoke.

He was sitting in a small seat, surrounded by crystal set in steel. Upon his head was a tight-fitting helmet of leather. Voices whispered in his ear.

'Calling Tower. This is an emergency. We seem to be off course. We cannot see land . . . Repeat . . . We cannot see land.'

Shannow leaned over and looked through the crystal window. Far below he could see the ocean. He glanced back. He was sitting in a metal cross, suspended in the air below the clouds which flashed by above him with dizzying speed.

'What is your position, Flight Leader?' came a second voice.

'We are not sure of our position, Tower. We cannot be sure just where we are . . . We seem to be lost . . .'

'Assume bearing due west.'

'We don't know which way is west. Everything is wrong . . . strange . . . we can't be sure of any direction – even the ocean doesn't look as it should . . .'

The cross began to tremble violently and Shannow scrabbled at the window. Ahead, the heavens and the sea appeared to merge. All around the window the sky disappeared, and blackness swamped the cross. Shannow screamed . . .

'It's all right, Shannow. Calm. Stay calm.'

His eyes opened to see Beth McAdam leaning over him. He tried to move his head, but sickening pain thundered in his temple and he groaned.

Beth laid a cool towel on his brow. 'You're all right, Shannow. You were turning as the bullet struck you. It did not pierce the skull, but it gave you a powerful blow. Rest now.'

'Maddox?' he whispered.

'Dead. We shot him down; the others we hanged. There

is a Committee now, patrolling the town. The brigands have gone.'

'They will return,' he said. 'They always return.'

'Sufficient unto the day is the evil thereof,' came another voice.

'That you, Parson?'

'Yes,' answered the man, leaning over him. 'Take it easy, Shannow. All is peaceful.'

Shannow slept without dreams.

17

'I see you have two Bibles,' said the Parson, sitting by Shannow's bedside and holding the leather-covered books. 'Surely one is enough?'

Shannow, his head bandaged, his left eye swollen and blue, reached out and took the first. 'I carried this with me for many years. But last year a woman gave me the second; the language is more simple. It lacks the majesty, but it makes many passages easier to understand.'

'I have no trouble in understanding it,' said the Parson. 'Throughout it makes one point – God's law is absolute. Live by it and you prosper, both here and in the Afterlife. Defy it and you die.'

Shannow eased himself back into the pillows. He was always wary of men who claimed to understand the Almighty, yet the Parson was good company, by turns witty and philosophical; he had an active mind and was strong on debate.

His presence made Shannow's enforced rest less galling.

'How goes the church building?' Shannow asked.

'My son,' said the Parson, grinning, 'it is no less than a miracle. Every day scores of the brethren hurl themselves into work with gusto. You have never seen such spirit.'

'Could it have anything to do with the Committee, Parson? Beth tells me that miscreants are now sentenced to work on the church or hang.'

The Parson chuckled. 'Faith without works is dead. These lucky . . . miscreants . . . are finding God through their labours. And only three were offered the ultimate choice. One proved to be a fine carpenter and the others are developing like skills, but most of the workers are townspeople. When you are well enough you must come along and hear one of my sermons. Though I say it myself, the Spirit moves me powerfully at such times.'

Shannow smiled. 'Humility, Parson?'

'I am exceptionally proud of my humility, Shannow,' the Parson replied.

Shannow chuckled. 'I do not know what to make of you, but I am glad of your company.'

'I do not understand your confusion,' said the Parson seriously. 'I am as you see me, a servant of the Almighty. I wish to see His plan fulfilled.'

'His plan? Which one?'

'The new Jerusalem, Shannow, coming down from Heaven in glory. And the secret is here, in the southlands. Look at the world we see. It is still beautiful, but there is no cohesion. We search for God in a hundred different ways in a thousand different places. We must gather together, work together, build together. We must have laws that hold like iron from ocean to ocean. But first we must see Revelation fulfilled.'

Shannow's unease grew. 'I thought it had been. Does it not speak of terrible catastrophes, cataclysms that will destroy most of Mankind?'

'I am talking of the Sword of God, Shannow. The Lord sent it to scythe the land like a sickle – yet it has not. And why? Because it is over an unholy place, peopled by the beasts of Satan and the Whore of Babylon.'

'I think I am ahead of you, Parson,' said Shannow wearily. 'You seek to destroy the beasts, bring down the Whore? Yes?'

'What else should a God-fearing man do, Shannow? Do you not wish to see the work of the Lord fulfilled?'

'I do not believe it to be fulfilled by slaughter.'

The Parson shook his head, eyes wide with disbelief. 'How can you, of all men, say that? Your guns are legendary, and corpses mark the road of your life. I thought you were well read, Shannow. Recall you not the Cities of Ai, and the curse of God upon the heathen? Not one man or woman or child was to be left alive among the worshippers of Molech.'

'I have heard this argument before,' said Shannow, 'from a Hellborn king who worshipped Satan. Where is the talk of love, Parson?'

'Love is for those of the Chosen People, created in the image of Almighty God. He made Men and he made the beasts of the earth. Only Lucifer would have the brazen gall to mould beasts into men.'

'You are swift to judge. Perhaps you are swift to misjudge.'

The Parson rose. 'You may be right, for I appear to have misjudged you. I thought you a warrior for God – but there is a weakness in you, Shannow, a doubt.'

The door opened and Beth entered, carrying a tray on which was some sliced dark bread and cheese and a jug of water. The Parson eased his way past her with a friendly smile, but left without farewells. Beth set the tray down and sat at the bedside.

'Do I sense angry words?' she asked.

Shannow shrugged. 'He is a man touched by a dream I do not share.' He reached out and took her hand. 'You have been kind to me, Beth McAdam, and I am grateful. I understand it was you who went to the Parson and got him to form the Committee which came to my aid.'

'It was nothing, Shannow. The town needed cleaning, and men like Broome would have spent a year debating the ethics of direct action.'

'Yet he was there, I recall.'

'The man doesn't lack courage – just common sense. How's your head?'

'Better. There is little pain. Would you do something for me? Would you fetch me razor and soap?'

'I'll do better than that, Jerusalem Man. I'll shave you myself. I'm longing to see what kind of a face you have hidden under that beard.'

She returned with a stiff badger-fur brush and a razor, borrowed from Mason, plus a cake of soap and a bowl of hot water. Shannow lay back with his eyes closed as she softened his beard with lather. The razor was cool on his cheek as she expertly scraped away the bristle and hair. At last she wiped his face clean of soap and handed him a towel. He smiled at her.

'What do you see?'

'You are not unhandsome, Shannow, but you'll win no prizes. Now eat your lunch. I'll see you this evening.'

'Don't go, Beth. Not just yet.' His hand reached up and took her arm.

'I have to work, Shannow.'

'Yes. Yes, of course. Forgive me.'

She stood and backed away, forced a smile and left. Outside in the corridor she stopped and pictured again the look in his eyes as he asked her to stay.

'Don't be a fool, Beth,' she told herself.

Why not? There's an hour before you are expected back. Swinging on her heel, she opened the door once more and stepped inside. Her hand moved to the buttons of her blouse.

'Don't you read too much into this, Shannow,' she whispered as she dropped her skirt to the floor and slid into bed beside him.

*

For Beth McAdam it was a revelation. Afterwards she lay beside the sleeping Shannow, her body warm and wonderfully relaxed. Yet the surprise of his love-making had been in the inexperience he showed; in the passive, grateful manner in which he had received her. Beth was no stranger to the ways of men and she had enjoyed lovers long before she met and seduced Sean McAdam. She had learned that there was a great similarity about the actions of the aroused male. He fumbled, he groped, and then he drove himself into a rhythmic frenzy. Not so with Shannow . . .

He had opened his arms to her and stroked her shoulders and back. It was she who had made all the moves. For all his awesome powers in dealing with situations of peril, the

Jerusalem Man was untutored and surprisingly gentle in the arms of a woman.

Beth slid from the bed and Shannow awoke instantly.

'You are going?' he asked.

'Yes. Did you sleep well?'

'Wonderfully. Will you come back this evening?'

'No,' she said firmly. 'I must see to my children.'

'Thank you, Beth.'

'Don't thank me,' she snapped. She dressed swiftly and pushed her fingers through her blonde hair, roughly combing it. At the door she paused. 'How many women have you slept with, Shannow?'

'Two,' he answered, without trace of embarrassment.

She walked across the street to the Jolly Pilgrim where Broome was waiting, his face red with anger.

'You said an hour, Frey McAdam, and it has been two. I have lost customers – and you will lose coin.'

'Whatever you decide, Meneer,' she said, moving past him to where the dishes waited for cleaning. There were only two customers and both were finishing their meals. Beth carried the plates to the rear of the eating-house and scrubbed them clean with water from the deep well. When she returned the Pilgrim was empty.

Broome approached her. 'I am sorry for losing my temper,' he said. 'I know he is wounded and needs attention. You will keep the coin. I was wondering . . . if you would join me at my house this evening?'

'For what purpose, Meneer?'

'To talk . . . have a little meal . . . get to know one another. It is important for people who work together to understand each other.'

She looked into his thin face and saw arousal in his eyes. 'I am afraid not, Meneer. I am seeing Meneer Scayse this evening to discuss a business matter.'

'A lease of land, I know,' he said and her eyes darkened. 'Do not misunderstand, Frey McAdam. Meneer Scayse spoke to me because I know you. He wishes to be sure of your . . . integrity. I told him I felt you were honest and hard-working. But do you really want the lonely life of a farm widow?'

'I want a home, Meneer.'

'Yes, yes.' She could see him building towards a proposal and headed him off. 'I must get on with my work,' she told him, easing past him to the rear of the building.

That evening she was welcomed to Scayse's permanent rooms at the Traveller's Rest by a servant, who led her through to a long room where a log fire blazed in a wide hearth. Scayse rose from a deep, comfortable chair and took her hand, lifting it to his lips.

'Welcome, madam. Might I offer you some wine?'

A handsome man, he was even more striking in the light from the fire – his swept-back hair gleaming, his sharp powerful features almost savage. 'No, thank you,' she said. He led her to a chair, waited as she sat and then returned to his own.

'The land you wish to lease is of little use to me. But tell me, Frey McAdam, why you approached me? You will know that no one has title to land. A man takes what he can hold. You could merely have driven your wagon to a spot of your choosing and built a home.'

'Were I rich, Meneer, with fifty riders, I would have done just that. But I am not. It remains your land – and if I am troubled I will come to you for assistance. You have men riding the high pastures, and it is known that brigands rarely trouble you. I hope the same will be true of me.'

'You have learned a great deal in your short time here. You are obviously a woman of great intelligence. I find it rare that a woman should combine beauty with wit.'

'How curious, I find exactly the same thing with men.'

He chuckled. 'Will you dine with me?'

'I don't think so. Is the price agreed?'

'I will waive the price – in return for dinner.'

'Let us be clear, sir. This is a business arrangement.' She opened the small bag she carried and counted out thirty silver coins. 'That is for the first year. And now I must be leaving.'

'I am disappointed,' he said, rising with her. 'I had great hopes.'

'Hold on to them, Meneer. They are all any of us have.'

*

After Beth had gone, Shannow sat up. He could still smell the perfume of her body on the sheets, and feel the after-warmth of her presence. Never before had he experienced a phenomenon like her. Donna Taybard had been soft, gentle and passive, deeply loving and wonderfully comforting. But Beth . . . there had been with her a power, an almost primordial hunger that had both drained him physically and elevated him emotionally.

He eased himself from the bed and stood. For a moment he swayed, and the room spun; but he held on, breathing deeply until it passed. He had wanted to dress and walk out into the air, but he knew he was too weak. A child with a short stick could lay him low in this condition. Reluctantly he returned to his bed. The bread and cheese were still on the tray nearby and he ate them, discovering to his surprise that he was ravenous. He slept for several hours and awoke refreshed.

A light knock came at the door. He hoped it was Beth. 'Come in!' he called.

Clem Steiner stepped into view.

'Now there's a sight,' said Steiner, grinning. 'The Jerusalem Man laid up and shaved. You don't look half as formidable without that silver-forked beard, Shannow.' The young man reversed a chair and sat facing the Jerusalem Man. Shannow looked into the other's eyes.

'What is it you want, Steiner?'

'I want something you can't give me. It's something I shall have to take from you – and that's a shame, because I like you, Shannow.'

'You make more noise than a pig with wind. And you are too damned young to understand it. What I have – whatever it is – is beyond you, boy. It always will be. You only get it when you don't want it. Never when you do.'

'Easy for you to say, Shannow. Look at you, the most famous man I've ever seen. And who's heard of me?'

'You want to see the price of fame, Steiner? Look in my saddlebags. Two worn-out shirts, two Bibles and four pistols. You see a wife anywhere, Steiner? A family? A home? Fame? I wasn't looking for fame. And I wouldn't care a jot if it all left me – and it will, Steiner. Because I'll keep travelling, and I'll find a place where they've never heard of the Jerusalem Man.'

'You could have been rich,' said Steiner. 'You could have been like some king of olden times. But you threw it away, Shannow. On you fame has been wasted. But I know what to do with it.'

'You know nothing, boy.'

'I haven't been called "boy" in a long time. And I don't like it.'

'I don't like the rain, boy, but there's not much I can do about it.'

Steiner pushed himself to his feet. 'You really know how to push a man, don't you, Shannow? You really know how to goad?'

'Hungry to kill me, Steiner? Your fame would be sky-high. Meet the man who shot Shannow in his bed.'

Steiner relaxed and returned to his seat. 'I'm learning. I won't shoot you down in the dark, Shannow, or in the back. I'll give it to you straight. Out on the street.'

'Where everyone can see?'

'Exactly.'

'And then what will you do?'

'I'll see you get a great funeral, with tall black horses and a fine stone to mark your grave. Then I'll travel, and maybe I'll become a king. Tell me, why did you pull that stunt with Maddox? You could have blown each other apart.'

'But we didn't, did we?'

'No. He almost killed you. Bad misjudgement, Shannow. It's not like what I've heard of you. Has the speed gone? Are you getting old?'

'Yes to both questions,' answered Shannow. Easing himself up on the pillow he turned his gaze to the window, ignoring the young man. But Steiner chuckled and reached out to pat Shannow's arm.

'Time to retire, Shannow – if only they'd let you.'

'The thought has occurred to me.'

'But not for long, I'll bet. What would you do? Grub around on the land, waiting for someone who recognises you? Waiting for the bullet, or the knife? Always staring at the distant hills, wondering if Jerusalem was just beyond the horizon? No. You'll go out with guns blazing on some street, or plain, or valley.'

'Like they all do?' put in Shannow softly.

'Like we all do,' Steiner agreed. 'But the names live on. History remembers.'

'Sometimes. You ever hear of Pendarric?'

'No. Was he a shootist?'

'He was one of the greatest kings who ever lived. He changed the world, Steiner; he conquered it, and he destroyed it. He brought about the First Fall.'

'What of it?'

'You'd never heard of him. That's how well history remembers. Tell me a name you do remember.'

'Cory Tyler.'

'The brigand who built himself a small empire in the north – shot through the head by a woman he'd spurned. Describe him, Steiner. Tell what he dreamed of. Tell me where he came from.'

'I never saw him.'

'Then what difference does his name make? It is just a sound, whispered into the air. In years to come, some other foolish boy may wish to be like Clement Steiner. He will not know either whether you were tall or short, fat or thin, young or old, but he will chant the name like a talisman.'

Steiner smiled and rose. 'Maybe so. But I will kill you, Shannow. I'll make my own tracks.'

18

Nu-Khasisatra could see something was seriously wrong with the wagon convoy long before he reached it. The sun was up and yet there was little movement from amongst the twenty-six wagons. A dead body lay close to the convoy, and Nu could see other corpses laid side by side some thirty paces away.

He stopped and decided to pass them by, but a voice called out to him from the long grass beside the track and Nu turned to see a young woman lying in a gulley; she was cradling a babe in her arms. Her words were unintelligible, the language coarse and unknown to Nu. Her face was pinched and drawn, and red, open sores scarred her cheeks and throat. For a moment Nu drew back in horror, then he looked into her eyes and saw the fear and the pain. He took his Stone and moved to her side. She was terribly thin and as Nu laid his hand on her shoulder he could feel the sharpness of her bones beneath the grey woollen dress she wore. As he touched her, the whispered words she spoke became instantly clear to him. 'Help me. For the sake of God, help me!' He touched the Stone to her brow and the sores vanished instantly, as did the hollow dark rings below her large blue eyes. 'My babe,' she said, lifting the tiny bundle towards Nu.

'I can do nothing,' he told her sadly, staring at the corpse. A terrible moaning cry came from the woman and she hugged the child to her. Nu stood and helped her to her feet, leading her back to the wagons. Some twenty paces ahead on the road a man was lying on his back, dead eyes staring up at the sky. They passed him by. As they entered the camp, an elderly woman with iron-grey hair ran towards him. 'Get back!' she shouted. 'There is plague here.'

'I know,' he told her. 'I . . . I am a healer.'

'There's nothing more to be done,' said the woman. Then she noticed the girl. 'Ella? Dear God, Ella. You are well?'

'He couldn't save my baby,' whispered Ella. 'He was too late for my little Mary.'

'What is your name, friend?' asked the woman, taking his arm.

'Nu-Khasisatra.'

'Well, Meneer New, there are more than seventy people bad sick here, and only four of us that are holding the plague at bay. I pray to God you *are* a healer.'

Nu looked around him. Death was everywhere. Some bodies lay uncovered, flies settling on the still weeping sores, while others had blankets casually tossed over them. Several paces to his right he saw a child's arm protruding from a large section of sackcloth. Moans and cries came from the wagons and here and there helpers – themselves stricken – staggered from victim to victim, giving aid where they could, helping the sick to drink a little water. Nu swallowed hard as the elderly woman touched his arm. 'Come,' she said. He looked down at her hand and saw the ugly red blotches that stained her lower arm. Taking his Stone, he reached out and stroked her hair. 'God's Love,' he told her. The sores disappeared.

She stared down at her arms, feeling the rush of strength as if she had just awoken from a deep refreshing sleep. 'Thank you,' she whispered. 'God's blessing on you. But come quickly, for there are others in sore need.'

She led him to a wagon where a woman and four children lay under sweat-soaked blankets. Nu laid the Stone on each of them, and the fever passed. From wagon to wagon he moved, healing the sick and watching as the black veins in the Stone swelled. As dusk came, he had healed more than thirty of the company. The elderly woman, whose name was Martha, busied herself preparing food for the survivors and Nu was left to himself. Under the moonlight he studied the Stone. There was more black than gold now and, under cover of darkness, he slipped away into the night.

He had no choice, he told himself. If ever he was to see Pashad and the children again, he had to leave some power in the Stone. But with each step he took, his heart became heavier.

At last he sat down under the bright moonlight and prayed. 'What would you have me do?' he asked. 'What are these people to me? You are the giver of life, the bringer of death. It was you who brought this plague to them. Why can you not take it away?' There was no answer, but he recalled his boyhood days in the temple under the great teacher Rizzhak.

He could see the old man's hooded eyes and his hawk nose, the white straggly beard. And he remembered the story Rizzhak had told of Heaven and Hell:

'I prayed to the Lord of All Things to let me see both Paradise and the Torment of Belial. And in my vision I saw a door. I opened it and there, in a great room, was a sumptuous feast placed on a great table. But all the guests were wailing, for the spoons in their hands had long, long handles and, though they could reach the food the spoons were too long for them to place it in their mouths. And they were cursing God and starving. I closed the door and asked to see Paradise. Yet it was the same door that stayed before me. I opened it and inside was an identical feast, and all the guests had the same long-handled spoons. But they were feeding each other and praising God in the thousand names known only to the angels.'

Nu stared up at the moon and thought of Pashad. He sighed and stood.

Back at the wagons he moved amongst the sick, healing them all. He laboured long into the night, and at the dawn he stared down at the Stone in his hand. It was black now, with not a trace of gold.

Martha came and sat beside him, giving him a cup in which was a dark, bitter drink.

'I've heard of them,' she said, 'but I never saw one before. It was a Daniel Stone. Is it used up?'

'Yes,' said Nu, dropping it to the ground in front of the fire.

'It saved many lives, Meneer New. And I thank you for it.'

Nu said nothing.

He was thinking of Pashad . . .

*

Beth McAdam was thoughtful and silent as she steered the wagon south over the rolling grasslands towards the Wall. The children were sitting on the tailboard squabbling, but the noise passed her by. Shannow was making good progress, but still confined to his room at the Traveller's Rest, and the Parson had been a frequent caller at their campsite in Tent Town. Now there was Edric Scayse, tall and confident, courteous and gallant. He had taken her to dinner twice, and amused her with stories of his upbringing in the far north.

'They have cities there now, and elected leaders,' he had told her. 'Some of the areas have formed treaties with neighbouring groups and there was talk last year of a Confederation.'

'They won't get together,' said Beth. 'People don't. They'll row over everything and fight over nothing.'

'Don't be too sure, Beth. Mankind cannot grow without organisation. Take the Barta coin – that's universally accepted now, no matter which community you enter. Old Jacob Barta, who first stamped the coins, had a dream of one nation. Now it looks as if it has a chance. Just imagine what it would be like if laws were as readily accepted as Barta coin?'

'Wars will just get bigger,' she said with certainty. 'It's the way of things.'

'We need leaders, Beth – strong men to draw us all together. There's so much we don't know about the past, that could help us with the future . . . so much.'

The lead oxen stumbled, jerking Beth back to the present and she hauled on the reins, giving the beast time to recover its footing. She was attracted to Scayse, drawn by his strength, but there was something about him that left her with a vague sense of unease. Like the Parson, he had a dangerous, uncertain quality. With Shannow, the danger was all on the surface – what you saw was what you got. How much easier life would have been had she found Josiah Broome attractive. But the man was such a blinkered fool.

'I dread to think of people who look up to men like Jon Shannow,' he had told her one morning, as they waited for the first customers of the day. 'Loathsome man! A killer and a war-maker of the worst kind. People like him wreck communities, destroy any sense of civilised behaviour. He is a cancer in our midst and should be ordered to leave.'

'When has he stolen anything?' she countered, holding the anger from her voice. 'When has he been disrespectful? When? When has he killed a man without first being threatened with death himself?'

'How can you ask such a thing? Did you not see on the night poor Fenner died? When he stood before the crowd, and that man asked him if he thought he could take on all of them? Shannow shot him down without warning; the man did not even have a gun in his hand.'

'You'll never understand, Meneer Broome. I am surprised you have lived this long. If Shannow had let the moment pass, they would all have turned on him and he would have been shot to pieces. As it was, he held them, he took the initiative . . . unlike poor Fenner. I spoke to Shannow about him. Did you know Fenner went to Shannow for advice? The Jerusalem Man told him to give Webber an order and not engage in any conversation; he said that as soon as Webber is allowed to debate you will lose the moment. Fenner understood this, Meneer Broome. But he was betrayed, by you and all those with you. Now he is dead.'

'How dare you accuse me of betrayal? I went there with Fenner; I did my part.'

'Your part?' she hissed. 'You got him killed and crawled away like a gutless snake.'

'There was nothing we could do. Nothing anyone could do.'

'Shannow did it. Alone. So don't criticise him to my face. The man's worth ten of you.'

'Get out! You don't work here any more. Out, I say!'

With her job lost, Beth saw Scayse who agreed to let her move on to the land immediately. He even offered men to help her with building her home, but she refused him.

Now she was almost there. The oxen were tired as they laboured up the last rise before the land she had leased, and she was ready to allow them a breather at the top of the hill. But when they reached it, Beth looked down into the vale and saw five men shaping felled trees into logs. Close by was a roped-off area which had been stamped out to form the dirt floor of a cabin. Beth's fury rose and she drew her pistol and stepped down from the wagon, walking back to where her horse was tethered at the rear. Telling the children to stay where they were, she rode down where the men were working. As she approached, one of them put down his hatchet and strolled across to her, doffing his leather hat and grinning.

'Mornin', Frey. Nice day for it, what with the sun and the breeze.'

The pistol came up and the man's smile vanished. 'What the Hell are you doing on my land?' she asked him, cocking the pistol.

'Hold up, lady,' he said, lifting his hands. 'Meneer Scayse asked us to give you a hand with the footings – felling the trees and suchlike. We've also taken water bearings to see how the land lies.'

'I asked for no help,' she told him, the pistol steady in her hands.

'I don't know nothin' about that. We ride for Meneer Scayse. He says jump, we don't say why – we just jump.'

Beth uncocked the pistol and returned it to her scabbard. 'Why did you choose this spot for the cabin?'

'Well,' he said, the smile returning, 'it's got a good range of open ground to front and rear, there's water close by and the front windows will catch the evening sun.'

'You chose well. What is your name?'

'They call me Bull, though my name is rightly Ishmael Kovac.'

'Bull it is,' she told him. 'You carry on. I'll fetch the wagon.'

19

The first tremor hit the city just after dawn. It was no more than an insistent vibration that rattled plates upon shelves and many slept through it; others awakened and rose, rubbing sleep from their eyes and wondering if a storm was due. The second tremor came at noon and Chreena was working in the laboratory when it struck. The vibration was stronger now. Books fell from shelves and she ran to the balcony to see people milling in the streets. A twelve-foot statue toppled near the main square, but no one was hurt. The tremor passed.

Oshere limped in to the laboratory. 'A little excitement,' he said, his words more slurred than usual.

'Yes,' said Chreena. 'Have there been quakes before?'

'Once, twelve years ago,' he told her. 'It was not serious, though some farmers lost cattle and there were many still-born calves. How is your work progressing?'

'I'll get there,' she replied, looking away.

He squatted on the mosaic floor and looked up at her. 'I wonder if we are tackling the problem in the right way,' he said.

'What other way is there? If I can find out what causes the genetic structure to regress, I might be able to stop it.'

'That's what I mean, Chreena. You are staring into the heart of the problem and you cannot see the whole. I have been looking at the records of the others who have gone through the Change before me. All were male, and all under twenty-five years of age.'

'I know that. It is not a great help,' she snapped.

'Bear with me. Almost all the Changelings were about to be married. You did not know that, did you?'

'No,' she admitted. 'But how is that important?'

He smiled, but she did not recognise the expression in

his swollen, leonine face. 'Our custom is for the groom to take his lady to the southern mountains, there to pledge his love beneath the Sword of the One. Everyone does it.'

'But the women go too, and they are not affected.'

'Yes,' he said. 'I have given great thought to this. I do not understand your science, Chreena, but I understand how to solve a problem. First look for the deviation and then ask – not where is the problem, but where is *not* the problem. If all the Changelings journey to the Sword, but the women are unaffected, then what do the men do that is different? What did Shir-ran do while you were there?'

'Nothing that I did not,' she replied. 'We ate, we drank, we slept, we made love. We came home.'

'Did he not climb to the Chaos Peak and dive to the waters two hundred feet below?'

'Yes. The custom, as I understand it, is for the men to purify themselves in the water of the Golden Pool before they pledge themselves. But all men do this – and not all are affected.'

'This is true,' he agreed, 'but some men merely bathe in an easily accessible part of the Pool. Others dive from low rocks. But only the most foolhardy climb to the Chaos Peak and dive.'

'I still do not understand what you are trying to say.'

'Five of the last six changelings climbed that Peak. Eleven others who were unaffected only bathed in the Pool. That is the deviation: the greatest percentage of Changelings come from those who climb the Peak.'

'But what of you? You are not in love. You took no one to the Sword.'

'No, Chreena. I went alone. I climbed the Peak, and I dived. Oshere flew and pledged himself.'

'To what?'

'To love. I was going to ask . . . a woman to accompany me, but I did not know if I would have the courage to dive. So I went alone. Two weeks later, the Change began.'

Chreena sat down and stared at the Man-beast. 'I have

been a fool,' she whispered. 'Can you come with me, back to the Sword?'

'I may not survive the journey as a man,' he said. 'Do you still have the Thunder-maker you brought with you?'

'Yes,' she answered, opening the drawer of her desk and removing the Hellborn pistol.

'Best to bring it with you, Chreena.'

'I could never kill you, Oshere. *Never.*'

'And I believe I could never harm you. But neither of us knows, do we?'

*

Shannow pulled on his boots and settled his gun scabbards in place at his hips. He was still weaker than he liked, but his strength had almost returned. Beth McAdam had filled his thoughts ever since the afternoon when she had shared his bed; she had not returned to him since then. Shannow sat by the window and recalled the joy of the day. He did not blame her for avoiding him. What did he have to offer? How many women would want to be tied to a man of his reputation? The days of his convalescence had given him a great deal of time for thought. Had his life been a waste? What had he done that would live after him? Yes, he had killed evil men, and it could be argued that in so doing he had saved other innocent lives. Yet he had no sons or daughters to continue his line, and nowhere in this untamed world was he welcome for long.

The Jerusalem Man. The Killer. The Destroyer.

'Where is love, Shannow?' he asked himself.

He wandered down the stairs, acknowledged Mason's wave and stepped out into the daylight. The sun was shining in a clear sky and the breeze was lifting dust from the dried mud of the roadway.

Shannow crossed the street and made his way to the gunsmith's shop. Groves was not behind his counter and he walked through the shop and found the man crouching over a work bench.

Groves looked up and smiled. 'You set me a fair task, Meneer Jerusalem Man. These aren't rim-fire cartridges.'

'No. Centre-fire.'

'They have heavy loads. A man needs to shoot straight with such ammunition. A stray bullet would pass through a house wall and kill an occupant sitting quietly in his chair.'

'I tend to shoot straight,' said Shannow. 'Have you completed my order?'

'Is the sky blue? Of course I have. I also made some five hundred shells for Meneer Scayse to the same requirements. It seems his Hellborn pistols arrived – without ammunition.'

Shannow paid the man and left his store. A sharp pebble under his foot made him remember how thin were his boots. The town store was across the street and he bought a new pair of soft leather boots, two white woollen shirts and a quantity of black powder.

As the man was preparing his order, an earth tremor struck the town and from outside came the sound of screaming. Shannow gripped the counter to stop from falling, while all around him the store's wares – pots, pans, knives, sacks of flour – began to tumble from the shelves.

As quickly as it had come the tremor passed. Shannow moved back into the bright sunlight.

'Will you look at that!' yelled a man, pointing to the sky. The sun was directly overhead, but way to the south a second sun shone brightly for several seconds before suddenly disappearing.

'You ever seen the like, Shannow?' asked Clem Steiner, approaching him.

'Never.'

'What does it mean, do you think?'

Shannow shrugged. 'Maybe it was a mirage. I've heard of such things.'

'It fair makes your skin crawl. I never heard of a mirage that could cast a shadow.'

The storekeeper came out carrying Shannow's order.

The Jerusalem Man thanked him and tucked it under his arm, along with the package he had taken from Groves.

'Fixing to leave us?' Steiner asked.

'Yes. Tomorrow.'

'Then maybe we should complete our business,' said the young pistoleer.

'Steiner, you are a foolish boy. And yet I like you – I have no wish to bury you. You understand what I am saying? Stay clear of me, boy. Build your reputation another way.'

Before the young man could answer Shannow had walked away, climbing the steps of the Traveller's Rest. A young woman stood in the doorway with her eyes fixed on something across the street. Easing past her, Shannow glanced back to see that she was staring at a black-bearded man sitting on the sidewalk outside the Jolly Pilgrim. He looked up and saw her; his face lost all colour and he stood and ran back towards Tent Town. Puzzled, Shannow studied the woman. She was tall, and beautifully dressed in a shimmering skirt of golden yellow. A green shirt was loosely tucked into a wide leather belt and she wore riding boots of the softest doeskin. Her hair was blonde, streaked with gold, and her eyes sea green.

She turned and saw him looking at her and for a moment he felt like recoiling under the icy glare she gave him. Instead he smiled and bowed. Ignoring him, she swept past and approached Mason.

'Is Scayse here?' she asked, her voice low, almost husky.

Mason cleared his throat. 'Not yet, Frey Sharazad. Would you like to wait in his rooms?'

'No. Tell him we will meet in the usual place. Tonight.' She swung on her heel and stalked from the building.

'A beautiful woman,' Shannow commented.

'She makes my hair stand on end,' said Mason, grinning. 'Beats me where she comes from. She rode in yesterday on a stallion that must have been all of eighteen hands. And those clothes . . . that skirt is a wonder. How do they make it shine so?'

'Beats me,' said Shannow. 'I'll be leaving tomorrow. What do I owe you?'

'I told you once, Shannow, there's no charge. And it'll be that way if ever you return.'

'I doubt I'll come back – but thanks for the offer.'

'You hear about the Healer? Came in with the wagons this afternoon?'

'No.'

'Seems like the Red Plague hit the convoy and this man walked out of the wilderness with a Daniel Stone. He healed everybody. I'd like to have seen that. I've heard of Daniels before, but I never touched one. You?'

'I've seen them,' said Shannow. 'What did he look like, this Healer?'

'Big man with the blackest beard you ever saw. Big hands too. Like a fighter.'

Shannow returned to his room and sat once more at the chair by the window. The golden-haired woman had been staring with naked hatred at just such a man. He shook his head.

Nothing to do with you, Shannow.

Tomorrow you put Pilgrim's Valley far behind you.

20

Sharazad sat, seemingly alone, on a flat rock under the moonlight. The day had brought an unexpected pleasure: Nu-Khasisatra was here in this cursed land of barbarians. It had been a source of constant fury that he had escaped from Ad, and the King had been most displeased. Seven of her Daggers had been flayed and impaled, and she herself had lost ground in the King's affections. But now – Great be the Glory of Belial – the shipbuilder was within her reach once more. Her mind wandered back to the man she had seen staring at her in the hovel that passed for a resting place. Something about him disturbed her. He was not handsome, nor yet ugly, but his eyes were striking. A long time ago she had enjoyed a lover with just such eyes. The man had been a gladiator, a superb killer of men. Was that it? Was the barbarian a danger?

She heard the rumble of the wagon coming through the trees and wandered to the crest of the hill, gazing down at the two men who drove it. One was young and handsome, the other older and balding. She waited until they came closer, then stepped out on to the path.

The older man heaved on the reins and applied the clumsy brake. 'Good evening, Frey,' he said climbing down and stretching his back. 'You sure you want to unload here?'

'Yes,' she said. 'Just here. Where is Scayse?'

'He couldn't come,' said the younger man. 'I represent him. The name's Steiner.'

What do I care what your name is, thought Sharazad. 'Unload the wagon and open the first box,' she said aloud. Steiner loosened the reins of a saddled horse that was tied to the rear of the wagon and led the beast back a few paces. Then both men struggled with the heavy boxes, manhandling them to the ground. The older man drew a hunting-knife and prised open a lid. Sharazad stepped closer and leaned forward, pulling back the greased paper and lifting a short-barrelled rifle clear of the box.

'Show me how it works,' she ordered.

The older man opened a packet of shells and slid two into the side gate. 'They slide in here – up to ten shells; there's a spring keeps the pressure on. You take hold here,' he said, gripping a moulded section under the barrel, 'and pump once. Now there's a shell in the breech and the rifle is cocked. Pull the trigger and pump the action, and the spent shell is ejected and a fresh one slides home.'

'Ingenious,' admitted Sharazad. 'But, sadly, after this load we will need no more. We will make our own.'

'Ain't sad to me,' said the man. 'Don't make no difference to me.'

'Ah, but it does,' she said, smiling and she raised her hand. From the bushes all around them rose a score of Daggers, pistols in their hands.

'Sweet Jesus, what the Hell are they?' whispered the man, as the reptiles moved forward. At the back of the wagon Clem stood horror-struck as the demonic creatures appeared, then backed away towards his horse.

'Kill them,' ordered Sharazad. Clem dived for the ground, rolled and came up firing. Two of the reptiles were hurled from their feet. More gunfire shattered the night, spurts of dust spitting up around Clem's prone body. His horse panicked and ran but Clem dived for the saddle, grabbing the pommel as it passed. He was half-carried, half-dragged into the trees, shells whistling about him.

'Find him,' ordered Sharazad and six of the reptiles loped away into the darkness. She turned on the older man, who had stood stock-still throughout the battle. Her hand dipped into the pocket of her golden skirt and she lifted out a small stone, dark red and veined with black.

'Do you know what this is?' she asked. He shook his head. 'This is a Bloodstone. It can do amazing things, but it needs to be fed. Will you feed my Bloodstone?'

'Oh, my God,' he whispered, backing away as Sharazad drew a silver pistol and stared down at it.

'I am surprised that the greatest minds of Atlantis never discovered such a sweet toy. It is so clean, so lethal, so final.'

'Please, Frey. I have a wife . . . children. I never harmed you.'

'You offend me, barbarian, merely by being.' The pistol came up and the shell hammered through his heart; he fell to his knees, then toppled to his face. She turned him over with the toe of her boot and laid the Bloodstone on his chest. The black veins dwindled to nothing.

She sat by the corpse and closed her eyes, concentrating on her victory. An image formed in her mind and she saw Nu-Khasisatra waiting unarmed and ready to be taken. But a dark shadow stood between her and the revenge she desired. The face was blurred, but she focused her concentration and the shadow became recognisable. It was the man from the Traveller's Rest – only now his eyes were flames and in his hands were serpents, sharp-fanged and deadly. Holding the image, she called out to her mentor and his face appeared in her mind.

'What troubles you, Sharazad?'

'Look, Lord, at the image. What does it mean?'

'The eyes of fire mean he is an implacable enemy, the serpents show that in his hands he has power. Is that the renegade prophet behind him?'

'Yes, Lord. He is here, in this strange world.'

'Take him. I want him here before me. You understand, Sharazad?'

'I do, Lord. But tell me, why are we no longer dealing with Scayse? I thought their guns would be of more use.'

'I have opened other gates to worlds with infinitely more power. Your barbaric kingdom offers little. You may take ten companies of Daggers if you wish, and blood them on the barbarians. Yes, do it, Sharazad, if it would bring you pleasure.'

His face disappeared. Ten companies of Daggers! Never

had she commanded so many. And, yes, it would be good to plan a battle; to hear the thunder of gunfire, the screams of the dying. Perhaps if she did well she would be given a command of humans and not these disgusting, scaled creatures from beyond the gates. Lost in her dreams, she ignored the sounds of distant gunfire.

*

Clem Steiner had been hit twice. Blood seeped from the wound in his chest, and his left leg burned as sweat mixed with the blood at the outer edges of the jagged wound. His horse had been shot from under him, but he had managed to hit at least one of the creatures giving pursuit.

What in the Devil's name were they?

Clem hauled himself behind a rock and scrabbled further up the wooded hillside. At first he had thought them men wearing masks, but now he was not so sure. And they were so fast . . . they moved across his line of vision with a speed no human could match. Licking his lips, he held his breath, listening hard. He could hear the wind sighing in the leaves above him, and the rushing of a mountain stream to his left. A dark shadow moved to his right and he rolled and fired. The bullet took the reptile under the chin, exiting from the top of its skull, and it fell alongside Clem, its legs twitching. He stared, horror-struck, at the grey, scaled skin and the black leather body armour. The creature's hand had a treble-jointed thumb and three thick fingers.

Jesus God, they're demons! he thought. *I am being hunted by demons!*

He fought for calm and reloaded his pistol with the last of his shells. Then he gathered up the reptile's weapon and sank back against the rock. The wound in his chest was high and he hoped it had missed his lung. *Of course it has, you fool! You're not coughing blood, are you?*

But he felt so weak. His eyes closed but he jerked himself awake. *Got to move! Get safe!* He started to crawl, but loss of blood had weakened him terribly and he made only a few yards before his strength was spent. A rustling movement came from behind him and he tried to roll, but a booted foot lashed into his side. His gun came up, but was kicked from his hand. Then he felt himself being dragged from the hillside, but all pain passed and he slid into unconsciousness.

The pain awoke him and he found he had been stripped naked and tied to a tree. Four of the reptiles were sitting together in a close circle around the body of the creature he had killed on the hillside. As he watched, one of the others took a serrated knife and cut into the chest of the corpse, ripping open the dead flesh and pulling clear the heart. Clem felt nausea overwhelming him, but he could not tear his eyes from the scene. The reptiles began to chant, their sibilant hissing echoing in the trees; then the first cut the heart into four pieces, and the others all accepted a portion which they ate.

Then they knelt around the corpse and each touched his forehead to the body. Finally they rose and turned to face the bound man. Clem looked into their golden, slitted eyes, then down at the serrated knives they all held.

No glittering reputation for Clem Steiner, no admiring glances. No treasure would be his, no adoring women. Anger flooded him and he struggled at the ropes that bit into his flesh as the reptiles advanced.

'Behold,' said a voice and Clem glanced to his right to see Jon Shannow standing with the sun behind him, his face in silhouette. The voice was low and compelling, and the reptiles stood and stared at the newcomer. *'Behold, the whirlwind of the Lord goeth forth in fury, a continuing whirlwind: it shall fall with pain upon the heads of the wicked.'*

Then there was silence as Shannow stood calmly, the morning breeze flapping at his long coat.

One of the reptiles lowered his knife. He stepped forward, his voice a sibilant hiss.

'You sspirit or man?'

Shannow said nothing and the reptiles gathered together, whispering. Then the leader moved away from them, approaching the Jerusalem Man.

'I can ssmell your blood,' hissed the Dagger. 'You are Man.'

'I am death,' Shannow replied.

'You are a Truthsspeaker,' said the reptile at last. 'We have no fear, but we undersstand much that men do not. You are what you ssay you are, and your power iss felt by uss. Thiss day is yourss. But other dayss will dawn. Walk warily, Man of Death.'

The leader gestured to the other Daggers, then turned on his heel and loped away.

Time stood still for Clem and it seemed that Shannow had become a statue. 'Help me,' called the wounded man and the Jerusalem Man walked slowly to the tree and squatted down. Clem looked into his eyes. 'I owe you my life,' he said.

'You owe me nothing,' said Shannow. He cut Clem's bonds and plugged the wounds in his chest and leg; then he helped him dress and led him to the black stallion.

'There're more of them, Shannow. I don't know where they are.'

'Sufficient unto the day is the evil thereof,' said the Jerusalem Man, lifting Steiner into the saddle. He mounted behind him and rode from the hills.

*

Sharazad watched as Szshark and his three companions loped into the clearing. She lifted a hand and waved the tall reptile to her; he approached and gave a short bow.

'You found the man?'

'Yess.'

'And killed him?'

'No. Another claimed him.'

Sharazad swallowed her anger. Szshark was the leader of these creatures, had been the first of the reptiles to pledge allegiance to the King. 'Explain yourself,' she said.

'We took him – alive, as you ssaid. Then sshadow came. Tall warrior. Ssun at his back. He sspoke power wordss.'

'But he was human, yes?'

'U-man, yess,' Szshark agreed. 'I go now?'

'Did he fight? What? What happened?'

'No fight. He wass Death, Goldenhair. He wass power. We felt it.'

'So you just left him? That is cowardice, Szshark!'

His wedge-shaped head tilted, and his huge golden eyes bored into her own. 'That word for U-manss. We have no fearss, Goldenhair. But it would be wrong to die for nothing.'

'How could you know you would die? You did not try to fight him. You have guns, do you not?'

'Gunss!' spat Szshark. 'Loud noisses. Kill very far. No honour! We are Daggerss. Thiss man. Thiss power. He carry gunss. But not hold them. You ssee?'

'I see everything. Gather twenty warriors and hunt him down. I want him. Take him. Do you understand that?'

Szshark nodded and moved away from her. She did not understand, she would never understand. The Death man could have opened fire on them at any time, but instead he spoke words of power. He gave them a choice: life or death. As starkly simple as that. What creature of intelligence would have chosen anything but life? Szshark gazed around at the camp-site. His warriors were waiting for his word.

He chose twenty and watched them run from the camp.

Sharazad summoned him again.

'Why are you not with them?' she asked.

'I gave him thiss day,' he said, and walked away. He could feel her anger washing over him, sense her longing to put a bullet in his back. He walked to the stream and squatted down, dipping his head under the surface and revelling in the cool quiet of Below.

When the King of Atlantis led his legions into the jungles, the *Ruazsh* had fought them to a standstill. But Szshark had seen the inevitable outcome. The *Ruazsh* were too few to withstand the might of Atlantis. He had journeyed alone to seek out the King.

'Why have you come?' the King asked him, sitting before his battle tent.

'Kill you or sserve you,' Szshark answered.

'How will you determine which course of action?' the King enquired.

'Iss already done.'

The King nodded, his face stretching, baring his teeth. 'Then show me,' he said.

Szshark knelt and offered the King his curved dagger. The monarch took it and held the point to Szshark's throat.

'Now it seems I have two choices.'

'No,' said Szshark, 'only one.'

The King's mouth opened and a series of barking sounds disturbed the reptile. In the months that followed he would learn that this sound was laughter, and that it denoted good humour among humans. He rarely heard that sound now from Sharazad – unless something had died.

Now as he lifted his head from the water, a rippling of faint music echoed inside his mind. He answered the Calling.

'Speak, my brother, my son,' his mind answered.

A Dagger moved from the bushes and crouched low to the ground, his eyes averted from Szshark's face.

The music in Szshark's mind hardened and the language of the *Ruazsh* flowed in the corridors of his mind. 'Goldenhair wishes to attack the homes of the land humans. Her mind is easy to read. But there are few warriors there, Szshark. Why are we here? Have we offended the King?'

'The King is a Great Power, my son. But his people fear us. We are now . . . merely playthings for his bed-mate. She longs for blood. But we are pledged to the King and we must obey. The land humans are to die.'

'It is not good, Szshark.' The music changed again. 'Why did the Truthspeaker not kill us? Were we beneath his talents?'

'You read his thoughts. He did not need to kill us.'

'I do not like this world, Szshark. I wish we could go home.'

'We will never go home, my son. But the King has

promised never to re-open the gate. The Seed is safe, but we are the hostages to that promise.'

'Goldenhair hates us. She will see us all dead. There will be no one to eat our hearts and give us life. And I can no longer feel the souls of my brothers beyond the gates.'

'Nor I. But they are there, and they carry our souls. We cannot die.'

'Goldenhair comes!' The reptile climbed to his feet and vanished into the undergrowth.

Szshark stood, observing the woman. Her ugliness was nauseating, but he closed his mind to it, concentrating instead on the grossness of the language of Man.

'What you wissh?' he asked.

'There is a community close by. I wish to see it destroyed.'

'As you command,' he replied.

21

Shannow rode with care, holding the wounded man in place but stopping often to study his back-trail. There was no sign of pursuit as yet and the Jerusalem Man headed higher into the hills, riding across rocky scree that would leave little evidence of his passing. Steiner's chest wound had ceased to bleed, but his trouser-leg was drenched with blood and he had fallen into a feverish sleep, his head on Shannow's shoulder.

'Didn't mean it, Pa,' he whispered. 'Didn't mean to do it! Don't hit me, Pa!' Steiner began to weep – low moans, rhythmic and intense.

Shannow halted the stallion in a rough circle of boulders high on the hillside overlooking the great Wall. Holding on to Steiner, he dismounted, then lowered the unconscious man to the ground. The stallion moved off a few paces and began cropping grass as Shannow made up a bed and covered Steiner's upper body with a blanket. Taking needle and thread, he sewed the wounds in the pistoleer's leg. The gaping hole at the rear of the thigh caused him concern, for the shell had obviously ricocheted from the bone and broken up, causing a large exit wound. Shannow sealed this as best he could, then left Steiner to rest. He walked to the ridge and stared down over the countryside. Far in the distance he could see dark shadows moving, seeking a trail. He knew he and Steiner had a three-hour start, but loaded down with a wounded man that would mean nothing.

He considered riding back to Pilgrim's Valley, but dismissed the idea. It would mean setting a course that would take him across the line of the reptiles, and he didn't feel he could be as lucky a second time.

Shannow had left the settlement at dawn, but had been drawn to the east by the sound of gunshots. He had seen the black-clad reptiles dragging Steiner to the tree and stripping his clothes, and he had watched them eat the heart of their dead comrade. He had never seen the like of them, nor heard of any such creatures. It seemed strange that they should appear in Pilgrim's Valley unheralded.

According to local legend, there were beasts Beyond the Wall that walked like men, but never had he heard them described as scaled. Nor had he heard of any Man-beasts who sported weapons – especially the remarkable Hellborn pieces.

He put the problem from his mind. It did not matter where they came from – they were here now, and had to be faced.

Steiner began to weep again in his sleep and Shannow moved across to him, taking his hand. 'It's all right, boy. You're safe. Sleep easy.' But the words did not penetrate and the weeping continued.

'Oh please, Pa. Please? I'm begging you!' Sweat coursed on Steiner's face and his colour was not good. Shannow added a second blanket and felt the man's pulse; it was erratic and weak.

'You've two chances, boy,' said Shannow. 'Live or die. It's up to you.'

He eased back up to the ridge, careful not to skyline himself. To the east the dark shadows were closer now and Shannow counted more than twenty figures moving slowly across the landscape. Far to the west he could see a thin spiral of smoke that could be coming from a camp-fire.

Steiner was in no shape to ride, and Shannow did not have the firepower to stop twenty enemies. He scratched at the stubble on his cheek and tried to think the problem through. Steiner's mumbling had faded away and he went to him. The man was sleeping now, his pulse a little stronger. Shannow returned to the ridge and waited.

How many times had he waited thus, he wondered, while enemies crept upon him? Brigands, war-makers, hunters, Hellborn Zealots – all had sought to kill the Jerusalem Man.

He recalled the Zealots, frenzied killers whose Bloodstones had given them bizarre powers, enabling their spirits to soar and take over the bodies of animals and direct them to their purpose. Once Shannow had been attacked by a lion possessed by a Zealot; he had fallen from a high cliff and almost drowned in a torrent.

Then there were the Guardians, with their terrible weapons recreated from the Between Days, guns that fired hundreds of times per minute, screaming shells that could rip a man to pieces.

But none had mastered the Jerusalem Man.

Pendarric, the ghost King of Atlantis, had told Shannow he was Rolynd, a special kind of warrior with a God-given sixth sense that warned him of danger. But even with Pendarric's aid, Shannow had almost died fighting the Guardian leader, Sarento.

How much longer could his luck hold?

Luck, Shannow? He glanced at the sky in mute apology. A long time ago, when he was a child, a holy man had told him a story. It was about a man who came to the end of his days and, looking back, he saw his footprints in the sands of his life. And beside them was a second set, which he knew to be God's. But when the man looked closely he saw that in the times of his greatest trouble there was only a single set. The man looked at God and asked, 'Why is it that you left me when my need was greatest?' And God replied, 'I never left you, my son.' And when the man asked, 'Why then was there only one set of footprints?' God smiled and replied, 'Because those were the times when I carried you.'

Shannow grinned, recalling the days in the old schoolhouse with his brother Daniel. Many were the stories told by Mr Hillel, and always they were uplifting.

The figures out on the plain were closer now. Shannow could make out the black armour on their chests, and the grey scaled skin of their wedge-shaped faces. He eased himself back from the ridge and tethered the stallion to a rock, then took his spare pistols from the saddlebag and thrust them into his belt. Returning to the ridge he studied the slope before him, estimating distances between cover and choosing the best fields of fire.

He wished Batik was here. The giant Hellborn was a warrior born, fearless and deadly. Together they had fought their way through a vast stone fortress to free a friend. Batik had journeyed into the city of New Babylon to rescue Donna Taybard, and fought the Devil himself. Shannow needed him now.

The leading Dagger had found the scent and was waving the others forward. They gathered in a tight bunch some two hundred yards away, then loped towards the ridge. Shannow drew his Hellborn pistols and cocked them.

Just then a group of four horsemen appeared, coming from the west. They saw the reptiles and reined in, more curious than afraid. One of the reptiles fired and a man lurched in the saddle. As the other three returned the fire, Shannow took the opportunity to roll over the ridge and run to a large boulder half-way down the slope. The shooting continued for several seconds and he saw a horse go down, the rider lying flat, shielded by the body; the man had a rifle and was coolly sending shot after shot into the reptiles. Five of them were down and the rest began to run for cover. Shannow stepped out into their path with his pistols blazing – two were swept from their feet, a third fell clutching his throat. The shock of his sudden attack was too much for them and the survivors turned and ran back over the plain, their speed incredible. Shannow waited for several seconds, watching the bodies. One of the downed reptiles suddenly rolled, bringing up a pistol . . . Shannow shot him in the head. Then he walked out to the riders. Two men were dead, a third wounded; the fourth man stood cradling his rifle in his arms. He was sandy-haired, with a wide friendly face and narrow eyes. Shannow recognised him as one of the riders who had been present when he repossessed his horse.

'Very grateful for your assistance, Shannow,' said the man, holding out his hand. 'My friends call me Bull.'

'Glad to meet you, Bull,' said Shannow, ignoring the hand. 'You arrived at the right time.'

'That's a matter of opinion,' the rider answered, looking down at his dead comrades. The wounded man was sitting up, clutching his shoulder and cursing.

'There's another wounded man up on the ridge,' said Shannow. 'I suggest you ride into Pilgrim's Valley and have a wagon sent.'

'I'll do that. But looks like there's a storm brewing. I should get him to Frey McAdam's cabin – we finished it yesterday and at least he'll be under cover and in a bed.'

Bull gave Shannow directions, then he and the wounded man rode off towards the north. Shannow stripped the guns and ammunition from the dead men and walked back to the bodies of the reptiles, crouching to examine them. The eyes were large and protruding, golden in colour, the pupils long and oval like those of cats. Their faces were elongated, the mouths lipless and rimmed with pointed teeth. But what made Shannow most uneasy was that they all wore identical body armour, and that reminded him of the Hellborn. These creatures were not individual killers, they were part of an army . . . and that did not bode well. He gathered their guns and hid them behind a rock. Then returning to the ridge, he dragged the unconscious Steiner upright and pushed him across the saddle of the stallion. Gathering his blankets, he mounted behind Steiner and rode for Beth McAdam's cabin.

*

When Samuel McAdam walked from the new cabin and saw the man sitting on the ground in the shade of the building, his fear rose and he stepped back a pace, staring at the newcomer. The man was very large, with the blackest beard Samuel had ever seen; he was gazing intently at the distant wall.

'It is a hot day,' the man observed, without turning round.

Samuel said nothing.

'I am not a man to fear, child. I carry no weapon and I

am merely sitting here, enjoying the breeze before moving on.' The voice was low, deep and reassuring, but Beth McAdam's son had been warned many times about trusting strangers.

'Some,' Beth had told him, 'look fair, but feel foul. Others look foul and are foul. Treat them all the same. Keep away from them.' But this was difficult, for the man was sitting virtually in the doorway of their house. He had not come in, though, thought Samuel, which at least showed he had good manners. Beth was in the meadow with Mary, the oxen hitched to the plough, the long, arduous work of preparing the soil under way. Samuel wondered if he should just run back through the house and fetch his mother.

'I would appreciate a drink of water,' said the man, pointing to the well dug out by Bull and the others. 'Would it be permissible?'

'Sure,' Samuel replied, happy to be able to grant a favour to an adult, and enjoying the unaccustomed power that came with bestowing a gift. The man stood and walked over to the well and Samuel saw that his hands were huge and his arms long. He had a swaying walk, like a man unused to solid ground who feared it might pitch beneath him. He dropped the bucket into the well and hauled it up with ease, dipping the long-handled ladle into it and drinking deeply. Then he walked back slowly and sat watching Samuel.

'I have a son of your age,' he said. 'His name is Japheth. He has golden hair, and he too is forbidden to talk with strangers. Is your father home?'

'He died and went to Heaven,' Samuel told him. 'God wanted him.'

'Then he must be happy. My name is Nu. Is your mother here?'

'She's working and she won't want to be disturbed, especially not by no man. She can get awful angry, Meneer Nu.'

'I understand that. In my short time here I have discovered this to be a violent world. It is pleasant, however, to meet so many people who know of God and his works.'

'Are you a preacher?' asked Samuel, squatting down with his back to the wall.

'I am – after a fashion. I am a shipbuilder, but I am also an Elder of the Law of One and I preach in the Temple. Or rather I did.'

'Do you know about Heaven?' Samuel asked, his blue eyes wide.

'I know a little. Though, thankfully, I have not yet been called there.'

'How do you know my Dad is happy? Maybe he doesn't like it there. Maybe he misses us?'

'He can see you,' said Nu. 'And he knows the Great One . . . God . . . is looking after you.'

'He always wanted a fine house,' said the boy. 'Do they have fine houses there?'

Nu settled back and did not notice the blonde woman who moved slowly through the house with a large pistol in her hand. She halted in the shadow of the doorway listening. 'When I was a child I wondered that and I went to the Temple Teacher. He told me that the houses of Heaven are very special. He said there was a rich woman once who had been very devout, but not very loving to her neighbours; she prayed a lot, but never thought of being kind to others. She died and went to Paradise; when she arrived there she was met by an angel who said he would take her to her new home. They walked near great palaces of marble and gold. "Will I live here?" she asked. "No," the angel replied. They went further to a street of fine houses of stone and cedarwood. But they passed these by too. At last they came to a street of small houses. "Will I live here?" she asked. "No," replied the angel. They walked on until they came to an ugly piece of ground by a river. Here there were several rotting planks loosely nailed to form two walls and a roof, and a moth-eaten blanket for a bed. "Here is your home," said the angel. "But this is terrible," the rich woman said. "I cannot live here." The angel smiled and said, "I am sorry. It was all we were able to build with the materials you sent up." ' Nu grinned at the perplexed boy. 'If your father was a kind man, then he has a wonderful house,' he said.

Samuel smiled. 'He was kind. He really was.'

'Now you should tell your mother I am here,' said Nu, 'lest she be frightened when she sees me.'

'She's seen you,' said Beth McAdam. 'And the man ain't been born who could frighten me. What's your business here?'

Nu rose and bowed. 'I am seeking a way through the Wall, and I paused here to drink of your water. I will not stay.'

'Where's your gun?'

'I do not carry weapons.'

'That's a little foolish,' said Beth, 'but it's up to you. You're welcome to stay for a meal. I liked the story about Heaven; it may be nonsense, but I liked the sound of it.'

An earth tremor rippled across the valley and Beth pitched sideways into the door-frame, dropping her pistol. Samuel screamed and Nu staggered. Then it passed. He bent and picked up the pistol and Beth's eyes hardened, but he merely handed it to her.

'Look at that, Ma!' Samuel shouted.

Two suns were blazing in the sky, and twin shadows forked from the trees around the cabin. For several seconds the brightness remained, then the second sun faded and was gone.

'Wasn't that wonderful?' said Samuel. 'It was so hot, and so bright.'

'It wasn't wonderful,' said Nu softly. 'Not wonderful at all.'

Mary came running round the cabin. 'Did you see it?' she yelled, then pulled to a halt as she saw the stranger.

'We saw it,' replied Beth. 'You and Samuel go into the house and prepare the meal. One extra portion for our guest.'

'His name's Meneer Nu,' said Samuel, disappearing into the house. Beth gestured to Nu and the two of them walked out into the sunshine.

'What is happening?' she asked. 'I sense you know more about the weird signs than I do.'

'There are things that should not be,' he told her. 'There are powers Man should never use. Gateways that should not be opened. These are times of great danger, and greater folly.'

'You're the man with the Daniel Stone, aren't you? The one who cured the plague?'

'Yes.'

'They say the Stone was all used up.'

'It was. But it served a fine purpose – God's purpose.'

'I heard talk of them, but I never believed it. How can a Stone do magic?'

'I do not know. The Sipstrassi was a gift from Heaven; it fell from the sky hundreds of years ago. I spoke to a scholar once who said that the Stone was merely an enhancer, that through it the dreams of men could be made real. He claimed that all men have a power of magic, but it is submerged deep in our minds. The Sipstrassi releases that power. I have no idea if that is true, but I know the magic is real. We just saw it in the sky.'

'That is strong magic,' said Beth, 'if it can make another sun.'

'It is not another sun,' Nu told her, 'and that is why it is dangerous.'

22

'Your weapons are terrible indeed,' said Nu, as he looked down at the wound in Clem Steiner's chest. 'Swords can kill, but at least a man must needs face his enemy at close range, risking his own life. But these thunder-makers are barbaric.'

'We are a barbaric people,' answered Shannow, laying his hand on Steiner's brow. The man was sleeping now, his pulse still weak.

'You said something about reptiles, Shannow,' remarked Beth as the three of them walked back into the large living room. 'What did you mean?'

'I've not seen anything like them. They wear dark armour and carry Hellborn pistols. From what Steiner says, they are led by a woman.' He glanced at Nu. 'I think you know of her, Healer.'

'I am no healer. I had . . . magic. But it is gone. And, yes, I know of her. She is Sharazad; she was one of the King's concubines. But she has a lust for blood and he fulfils her desires. The reptiles are known as Daggers. They first came to the realm four years ago, from beyond a gateway to a world of steaming jungles. They are swift and deadly and the King has used them in several wars. With sword and knife they are without equal. But these weapons of yours . . .'

'What is all this about kings?' snapped Beth. 'There are no kings here that I have heard of. You mean Beyond the Wall?'

Nu shook his head, then he smiled. 'In a way, yes. But also, no. There is a city Beyond the Wall. I grew to manhood there, yet it is not my city. It is hard for me to explain, dear Lady, since I do not understand it all myself. The city is called . . . was called . . . Ad. It is one of the seven great cities of Atlantis. I was being hunted by the Daggers and I used my . . . Daniel Stone? . . . to escape. It was supposed to bring me to Balacris, another city by the coast. Instead it brought me here, into the future.'

'What do you mean, the future?' Beth asked. 'You are making no sense.'

'I am aware of that,' said Nu. 'But when I left Ad, the city was bordered by the sea and great triremes sailed on the bays. Yet here the city is landlocked, the statues worn away.'

'That happened,' Shannow told him softly, 'when the seas swallowed Atlantis twelve thousand years ago.'

Nu nodded. 'I guessed that. The Lord has granted me a vision of just such an upheaval. I am glad, however, that some understanding of our world survived. How did you hear of it?'

'I have seen Balacris,' said Shannow. 'It is a ruined shell, but the buildings survived. And once I met a man called Samuel Archer who told me of the first Fall of the World. But tell me, how many of the Daggers are there?'

'I do not know exactly, but there are several legions. Perhaps five thousand, perhaps less.'

Shannow wandered to a window, looking out over the night. 'I don't know how many are here,' he said, 'but I have a bad feeling. I shall stay outside and keep watch. I am sorry to bring trouble to your home, Beth, but I think you will be safer with me here.'

'You are welcome here . . . Jon. You do what you have to do and I'll see to Steiner. If he lasts the night, he has a chance.'

Shannow took some dried meat and fruit and walked out on to the hillside beyond the cabin, where he sat beneath a spreading pine and scanned the dark horizon. Somewhere out there the demons were gathering, and a golden-haired woman was dreaming of blood. He shivered and pulled his coat tight around him.

Nu joined him at midnight and the two men sat in comfortable silence beneath the stars.

'Why were they hunting you?' asked Shannow at last.

'I preached against the King. I warned the people . . . or I tried to . . . that a great doom was about to befall. They did not listen. The King's conquests have led to a great swelling of the treasuries. People are richer now than ever before.'

'So they wanted to kill you? That's always the way with prophets, my friend. Tell me about your god.'

'Not my god, Shannow. Just God. The Lord Chronos, creator of Heaven and Earth. One God. And you, what do you believe?'

For an hour or more the two men discussed their faiths, and were delighted to find great similarities between the two religions. Shannow liked the big shipbuilder and listened as he talked of his family, his gentle wife Pashad, and his sons; of the ships he had built and the voyages he had sailed. But when Nu asked about Shannow and his life the Jerusalem Man merely smiled, and returned to questions about Atlantis and the distant past.

'I would like to read your Bible,' said Nu. 'Would that be permissible?'

'Of course. I am surprised that the ancients of Atlantis speak our language.'

'I'm not sure that we do, Shannow. When first I came here, I could not understand a word of it. But when I touched the Stone to the brow of a woman in need of healing all the words became clear inside my head.' He chuckled. 'Perhaps when I return I will not be able to speak the language of my fathers.'

'Return? You say your world is about to fall. Why would you go back?'

'Pashad is there. I cannot leave her.'

'But you might go back merely to die with her.'

'What would you do, Shannow?'

'I would go back,' he replied without hesitation. 'But then I have always been considered less than sane.'

Nu clapped his hand on Shannow's shoulder. 'Not

insanity, Shannow. Love – the greatest gift God can bestow. Where will you go from here?'

'South, across the Wall. There are signs there in the sky. I'd like to see them.'

'What sort of signs?'

'The Sword of God is there, floating in the clouds. Perhaps Jerusalem is close by.'

Nu fell silent for a while. Then: 'I will travel with you. I too must see these signs.'

'It is said to be a land of great peril. How will it help you to return home?'

'I have no idea, my friend. But the Lord has commanded me to find the Sword and I do not question His will.'

'I can lend you a gun or two.'

'I do not need one. If the Lord has me marked for death, I will die. Your thunder-makers will not alter the situation.'

'That is too fatalistic for me, Nu,' Shannow told him. 'Trust in God, but keep your pistols cocked. I have found He likes a man who stays ready.'

'Does He talk to you, Shannow? Do you hear His voice?'

'No, but I see Him in the prairies and on the mountains. I feel His presence in the night breezes. I see His glory in the dawn.'

'We are lucky men, you and I. I spent fifty years learning the thousand names of God known to Man, and another thirty absorbing the nine hundred and ninety-nine names known to the Prophets. One day I will know the thousand that are sung only by angels. But all this knowledge is as nothing compared with the sense of knowing you describe. Few men experience it; I pity those who do not.'

A shadow flickered out in the valley and Shannow held up his hand for silence. He watched for several minutes, but saw nothing further.

'I think you should go inside, Nu. I need to be alone.'

'Have I offended you?'

'Not at all. But I need to concentrate – to feel the presence of my enemies. I need all my strength, Nu. And that only happens when I am alone. If you cannot sleep, take one of my Bibles from the saddlebag by the door. I will see you come the dawn.'

When the man had gone Shannow stood and moved silently into the trees. The shadow could have been a wolf or a dog, a fox or a badger.

But equally it could be a Dagger . . .

Shannow loosened the guns in their scabbards and waited.

*

Shannow remained alert until an hour before sunrise. Then his feeling of unease drifted away, his muscles relaxing; he put his back to a broad pine and slept.

Beth McAdam walked out into the early morning light and gazed at the sky. Dawn was always special to her – those few precious minutes when the sky was blue and yet the stars still shone. She glanced up to the wooded hillside and walked towards where Shannow slept. He did not hear her approach and for some minutes she sat down beside him, staring intently at his weatherbeaten face. His beard was growing again, silver at the chin, yet his features seemed strangely youthful in sleep.

After a while, he awoke and saw her. He did not jump or start, he merely smiled lazily.

'They were out there,' he said, 'but they passed us by.'

She nodded. 'You look rested. How long did you sleep?'

He glanced at the sky. 'Less than an hour. I do not need much. I have been having curious dreams. I see myself trapped within a crystal dome in a huge cross that hangs in the sky; I am wearing a leather helmet and there is a voice in my ear; it is someone called Tower giving me directions. But I cannot escape or move.' He took a deep breath and stretched. 'Are the children still asleep?'

'Yes. In each other's arms.'

'And Steiner?'

'His pulse is stronger, but he is not yet awake. Do you believe Nu? That he came from the past?'

'I believe him, Beth. The Daniel Stones are incredibly

powerful. I once stood on the wreck of a ship beached on a mountain, but by the power of a great Stone it sailed again. They can give a man immortality, cure any disease. Once I ate a honeycake that had been a rock; a Daniel Stone reshaped it. I think there is nothing such power cannot achieve.'

'Tell me about it.'

Shannow told her about the Hellborn and their crazed leader, Abaddon; then about the Guardians of the Past and the rebirth of the *Titanic*. And finally he spoke of the Motherstone, the colossal Sipstrassi meteorite that had been corrupted by blood and sacrifice.

'So there are two kinds of Stones?' she said.

'No, just one. Sipstrassi is the pure power; but the more it is used, the sooner it fades. If fed with blood, it swells again, but it can no longer heal or make food. Also it affects the mind of the user, bringing with it a lust for pain and violence. The Hellborn all had Bloodstones, but their power was drained during the War.'

'How did you survive, Jon Shannow, against such odds?'

He smiled and pointed to the sky. 'Who knows? I ask myself that question often – not just about the Hellborn Zealots, but about all the perils I have faced. Much is timing, more is luck or the will of God. But I have seen strong men cut down by enemies, or disease, or accident. When I was young I had another name; I was Jon Cade. I met a town tamer called Varey Shannow, who taught me about people and the ways of evil men. He could stand alone against a mob and they would turn away from his eyes. But one day a young man – no more than a boy – walked up to him as he was having breakfast. "Pleased to meet you," he said, holding out his hand. Varey took it. At the same time the boy produced a pistol in his left hand and shot Varey through the head. When they asked him later why he had done it, he said he wanted to be remembered. Varey was a man to walk the mountains with; he helped people to settle this wild land of ours. The boy? Well, he was remembered. They hanged him and put a marker on his grave that said, "Here lies the killer of Varey Shannow".'

'So you took his name? Why?'

Shannow shrugged. 'I didn't want to see it die. And also my brother, Daniel, had become a brigand and a killer. I was ashamed.'

'But did not Daniel become a prophet? Did he not fight the Hellborn?'

'Yes. That pleased me.'

'So a man can change, Jon Shannow? He can make a new life for himself?'

'I guess that he can – if he has the strength. But I do not.'

Beth sat silently for a moment, then she reached out and touched his arm. He did not pull away. 'You know why I never came back to you?'

'I think so.'

'But if you made the decision to change your life, my hearth *would* be open to you.'

He looked away at the far Wall and the lands rolling out beyond it. 'I know,' he said sadly. 'I have always been lonely, Beth. There is an emptiness in my life which has been there ever since my parents were murdered. But look at Steiner. Until yesterday the boy wanted nothing more than to kill me – to be the man who beat Jon Shannow. How long before some boy comes to me at breakfast and says, "Pleased to meet you"? How long? And could I sit at night at your table, wondering if your children will intercept a bullet meant for me? I do not have that kind of strength, Beth.'

'Change your name,' she said. 'Shave your head. Whatever it takes. I'd travel with you and we could build a home somewhere where no one has ever heard of you.' He said nothing, but she looked into his eyes and saw the answer. 'I'm sorry for you, Shannow,' she whispered. 'You don't know what you're missing. But I hope you are not fooling yourself. I hope you are not in love with what you are: the Jerusalem Man, proud and alone, bane of the wicked. Is there something to that? Do you fear putting aside your reputation and your name? Do you fear anonymity?'

'You are a very astute woman, Beth McAdam. Yes, I fear it.'

'Then you are a weaker man than you know,' she said. 'Most men fear dying. You just fear living.' She rose and walked back to the cabin.

23

Josiah Broome closed the front door of his small house and wandered along the street towards the Jolly Pilgrim. The sun was shining brightly, but Broome did not notice it. For days now he had been seething over the departure of Beth McAdam, and the hurtful untrue words she had hurled at him like knives.

How could she not see? Men like Jon Shannow were no help to civilisation. Violence and despair followed him, giving birth to yet more of the same. Only men of reason could change the world. But how the words stung! She had called him a fool and a coward; she had blamed him for Fenner's death.

Could you blame a man for a summer storm, or a winter flood? It was so unfair. Yes, Fenner would still be alive if they had walked into Webber's establishment and shot him down. But what would that have achieved? What would it have taught the youngsters of this community? That in certain situations murder was acceptable?

He remembered Shannow shooting down the man in the street, just after he had executed Webber. The man's name had been Lomax. He was a tough, arrogant man, but he had helped the Parson build his church and he had worked hard for Meneer Scayse to support a wife and two children. Those children were now orphans who would grow up knowing their father had been gunned down in the street to make a point. Who would blame them if they turned bad? But Beth McAdam did not see that.

Broome crossed the street and heard the sounds of gunfire coming from the west. More trouble-makers he thought, swinging to see the cause of the disturbance. His jaw dropped open to see hundreds of black-armoured warriors advancing with their guns blazing. Men and women were running and screaming. A shell whistled past Broome and he ducked instinctively and ran to an alley between two buildings. A man sprinted past . . . his chest exploded and he fell face forward in the dirt.

Broome turned and cut down the alley, arms pumping. He scaled a fence and ran out over the fields towards the newly-built church in the meadow.

At the Traveller's Rest Mason glanced out of his window to see the reptiles advancing down the main street killing all in their sights. He swore and took down his Hellborn rifle from its rack on the wall. Swiftly he fed shells into the side gate, then pumped one into the breech. He heard sounds of booted feet on the stairs and as the door exploded inwards he swivelled and fired. One reptile hurtled back into the hallway, but several more ran in. Mason's gun jumped in his hands as he pumped shell after shell into them, then a bullet took him high in the chest, spinning him against the window. Two more shells ripped into his belly and he plunged out of the window, toppling to the street below.

At the gunsmith's shop Groves grabbed two pistols, but he was shot to death before he could loose a single round.

Hundreds of reptiles surged through the town. Here and there men returned their fire, but the attack was so sudden there was no organised defence.

At the church the Parson had been delivering an impassioned sermon about the Whore of Babylon and the beasts Beyond the Wall. When the sounds of the battle reached them, men and women had streamed from the building. The Parson pushed his way through them and stared in horror at the flames beginning to spring from the town buildings. Josiah Broome staggered towards the milling crowd.

'Beasts from Hell!' he shouted. 'There are thousands of them!'

Men began to run but the Parson's voice stopped them cold. 'Brethren! To run is to die.' He looked around at the gathering. More than two hundred people were present, two-thirds of them women and children. The men had left their guns in the front porch. 'Gather your weapons,' he ordered. 'Broome, you and Hendricks lead the women and children to the south. There are woods there. Find hiding places and we will join you later. Go now!' He swung to the men who had gathered rifles and pistols. 'Follow me,' he said, striding off towards the town. For a moment they hesitated, then one by one they joined him. He stopped at the edge of the meadow where a shallow ditch had been built for drainage. 'Line up here,' he said, 'and do not open fire until I give the word.'

The fifty-six men who had joined him settled down in the dirt, their weapons held before them. The Parson stood, listening to the screams from the town; he would like to have charged in, bringing the vengeance of God on the killers, but he fought down the impulse and waited.

A large group of Daggers came into sight. Seeing the Parson they lifted their rifles, but just before they fired he jumped down into the ditch and the shots whistled harmlessly overhead. Twenty of the reptiles ran across the open ground.

'Now!' yelled the Parson. A ragged volley swept through them and only one was left standing; the Parson took up a pistol and shot the creature in the head. Scores more of the reptiles came surging through the alleyways. Glancing back, the Parson could see Broome and Hendricks leading the women and children to safety, but they were not sufficiently clear to allow the defenders to withdraw. The reptiles charged. There were no screams from them, no terrible battle cries; they ran forward with incredible speed, firing as they came. Three volleys smashed into their ranks and the charge broke.

'I'm out of ammunition,' shouted one of the men in the ditch. Someone else passed him a handful of shells. The Parson glanced to his right and saw more than a hundred reptiles running to outflank them.

Just then Edric Scayse and thirty riders came thundering from the east. The reptiles opened fire and horses and men fell. Scayse, two pistols in his hand, galloped in amongst the enemy, firing coolly. The surviving riders followed. The carnage was awful, but Scayse and seventeen men made it through to leap from their horses and clamber into the ditch.

'You're a welcome sight, man,' said the Parson, thumping Scayse's shoulder.

'Where the Hell are they from?' shouted Scayse.

'Beyond the Wall . . . sent by the Great Whore,' the Parson replied.

'I think we'd best get out of here,' Scayse urged.

'No, we must protect the women and children. I have sent more than a hundred of them to the south. We must hold these beasts for a while.'

'We can't do it here, Parson; it's too easy for them to go round us. I suggest we back off to the church and hold them there.'

The reptiles charged again. Bullets shredded their ranks, but four got through to leap in among the defenders. Scayse hammered his pistol into a grey scaled head, then fired at point-blank range into the beast's body. The others were despatched with knives, but not before they had killed three of the defenders.

'Fall back in two lines,' shouted the Parson. 'Every second man get back thirty paces, then cover the second group.'

The ground began to tremble violently. Men were pitched from their feet as a great, jagged crack opened in the meadow, snaking across the front of the ditch like the jaws of a giant beast. In the town buildings buckled and a second quake scored the earth. The Daggers fled towards open ground, the battle forgotten.

'Now's the time, Parson,' said Scayse and the defenders rose and sprinted back across the meadow. Clouds of dust obscured their passing, but the earth opened and two men fell into the depths of a vast pit. The rest managed to reach the church, which was sagging in the centre. The Parson stood and watched as the building slowly tore itself apart.

'Back to the woods,' he said. 'The Wrath of God is upon us.'

*

Josiah Broome sat and watched as the Parson organised the digging of a trench across the north side of the woods. Earth was being thrown up to form a rampart, the labour carried out in grim silence. Without tools the workers dug into the soft clay with their bare hands, casting nervous eyes to the north for the expected attack. Broome was in a state of shock; he sat grey-faced as people bustled around him.

It was all gone. The town was ruined, the community decimated, the survivors trapped in the woods with no food, no shelter and precious little ammunition for the few guns they carried. All that remained was to wait for death at the hands of the beasts. Broome blinked back tears.

Edric Scayse had rounded up three horses and had ridden to his own lands, where extra rifles were stored. Two men had been sent to outlying farms to warn other settlers of the invasion. Broome cared nothing for any of it.

A child approached him and stood with head tilted, staring at him. He looked down at her.

'What do you want?'

'Are you crying?' she asked.

'Yes,' he admitted.

'Why?'

The question was so ludicrous that Broome began to giggle. The child laughed with him, but when his eyes filled with tears and racking sobs shook his spare frame, she backed away and ran to the Parson. His face streaked with mud, the red-headed preacher moved to Broome's side.

'It does not look good, Meneer,' he said. 'You are frightening the children. Now stand like a man and do some work, there's a good fellow.'

'We are all going to die,' whispered Broome through his tears. 'I don't want to die.'

'Death comes to all men – and then they face the Almighty. Do not be afraid, Meneer Broome. It is unlikely that a maker of breakfasts has done much to offend Him.' The Parson put his arm around Broome's shoulder. 'We are not dead yet, Josiah. Come now, help the men with the ditch.' Broome allowed himself to be led to the ramparts; he stared out over the valley.

'When will they come, do you think?'

'When they are ready,' said the Parson grimly.

Work ceased as the sound of a walking horse was heard in the woods behind them, then they heard the lowing of cattle. Three milk cows were herded into the clearing, their calves beside them. Jon Shannow rode his stallion up to the ditch and stepped down from the saddle.

'I thought these might be of use,' he said. 'If you slaughter the calves for meat, you'll be able to milk the cows to feed the children.'

'Where did you find them?' the Parson asked.

'I heard the shooting this morning, and watched your flight. I rode to a farm and cut these from the herd there. The owner was dead – with his whole family.'

'We are grateful, Shannow,' said the Parson. 'Now if you could come up with around a thousand shells and a couple of hundred rifles, I would kiss your feet.'

Shannow grinned and reached into his saddlebag. 'These are all the shells I have – they're for Hellborn rifles or pistols. But I'll fetch some weapons for you; I hid them yesterday about four miles from here.'

'Walk with me aways,' said the Parson, leading him through the camp. They stopped by a stream and sat. 'How many of them are there?' he asked.

'As near as I could see, more than a thousand. They are led by a woman.'

'The black whore,' the Parson hissed.

'She's not black; she has golden hair and she looks like an angel,' Shannow told him. 'And they are not from Beyond the Wall.'

'How do you know that?'

'I just know it. Speaking of the Wall, the last earthquake ripped a hole in it. I would think we would have more chance of survival if we can get there and go through it. A few men would then be able to hold the gap, allowing the rest of the community to find a safe camping place.'

'We have around three hundred people here, Shannow. Everything they had has been taken from them. We have no food, no spare clothing, no canvas for tents, no shovels, axes or hammers. Where can we go that is safe?'

'Then what is your plan?'

'Wait here, hit them hard and pray for success.'

'I agree with the praying,' said Shannow. 'Look, Parson, I don't know much about warfare on this scale, but I do know that we're not going to beat these reptiles by sitting and waiting for them. You say we need supplies – axes, hammers and the like. Then let's get them. And at the same time, let's pick up a few guns.'

'Where?'

'Back in the town. There are still wagons, and there are oxen and horses aplenty wandering the meadows. Not all of the buildings were destroyed, Parson. I studied the town through a long glass. Groves' shop still stands; he had powder there, and lead for ammunition. Then there's the smithy – and the whole of Tent Town is untouched.'

'But what of the reptiles?'

'They're camped just south of the town. I think they're afraid of another quake.'

'How many men will you need?'

'Let's say a dozen. We'll swing round to the west and come in by night.'

'And you expect to load up wagons and drive them away under the noses of the enemy?'

'I don't know, Parson. But it's surely better than sitting here and starving to death.'

The Parson was silent for a while, then he chuckled and shook his head. 'Do you ever think of defeat, Shannow?'

'Not while I breathe,' said the Jerusalem Man. 'You get these people to the hole in the Wall. I'll fetch the tools you need, and some supplies. Can I choose my own men?'

'If they'll go with you.'

Shannow followed the Parson back to the camp and waited as the preacher gathered the men together. When he outlined Shannow's plan and called for volunteers, twenty men stepped forward. Shannow summoned them all and led them from the gathering to a small clearing where he addressed them.

'I need only twelve,' he said. 'How many have wives here?' Fifteen raised their hands. 'How many with children?' he asked the fifteen. Nine hands went up. 'Then you men get back; the rest gather round and I'll tell you what we need to do.' For over an hour Shannow listed the kinds of supplies they would require and ways to obtain them. Some men offered good advice, others remained silent, taking it all in. Finally Shannow gave them a warning.

'No futile heroics. The most important thing is to get the supplies back. If you are attacked and you see friends in trouble, do not under any circumstances ride back to help. Now you will not see me, but I will be close. You will hear a commotion in the enemy camp – that is when you will move.'

'What you going to do, Shannow?' asked Bull.

'I'm going to read to them from the Book,' said the Jerusalem Man.

24

For two days Chreena had studied the Pledging Pool, analysing the crystal-clear water that flowed away beneath the cliffs to underground streams and rivers. She sat now in the shade of the Chaos Peak, a tall, spear-straight tower of jagged rocks and natural platforms from which the more reckless of the Dianae men would dive.

Shir-ran had climbed almost to a point just below the crest of the Peak. He would have gone further had the crown of the rock not jutted from the column, creating an overhang no man could negotiate. His dive had been flawless and Chreena remembered him rising from the water with his dark hair gleaming, the light of triumph in his golden eyes.

She pushed back the memory. There had to be something in the Pool that had affected Shir-ran's genetic structure. To dive from such a height meant that he would have plunged deep into the water . . . perhaps the problem was there. Chreena closed her eyes and let her spirit flow over the rocks of the Pool and down, down into the darker depths. She knew what she was seeking – some toxic legacy from the Between Times. Drums of chemical waste, nerve gases, plague germs. The Betweeners had rarely given any thought to the future, dumping their hideous war-refined poisons into the depths of the ocean. One theory back at Home Base had been that the Betweeners must have known their time was short. Why else would they poison their rivers and streams, strip away the forests that gave them air and pollute their own bodies with toxins and carcinogens? But the theory was offered more as a debating point for children than a serious topic for study.

Now Chreena blanked such thoughts from her mind and drew from her memories everything she had been taught concerning water: the essence of life. In the Between Days it had covered 70.8 per cent of the earth's surface, but now the figure was 71.3. Water made up two-thirds of total body weight. Man could survive months without food, but only days without water. *Think! Think!* Two parts hydrogen to one part oxygen. She honed her concentration, adjusting her focus, shrinking, ever shrinking deeper into the Search-trance, analysing the trace elements at the bottom of the Pool. One by one she dismissed them – reactive silica, magnesium, sodium, potassium, iron, copper, zinc. There were minute traces of lead, but these could not have been harmful unless a person drank around sixty gallons a day for who knew what number of years.

She returned to her body and leaned back exhausted. The sun had moved past the Chaos Peak and her naked skin was burning. Moving several yards to her left, she looked around for Oshere. He was lying asleep in the shade; there was little of humanity left in him, and his voice was almost gone.

Not the water. What then? She glanced up at the sky and the awesome Sword of God pointing to the heavens. She shivered. Not that!

Her eyes flicked to the Peak. Was it something there? Chreena stood and stretched, then dressed swiftly and made her way to the base. There were many handholds in the heavily barnacled rock and she began to climb slowly. Her mind fled back to the last time she had clung to a rock face, almost three years before, when the *Titanic* had been breached and she had carried her son Luke from the doomed ghost ship and down the sheer face of the mountain above the ruins of Balacris.

Then she had been Amaziga Archer, widow of Samuel and a teacher to the children of the Guardians. Guardians? All the knowledge of the Betweeners had been held by them for future generations, yet the work had been ruined, corrupted by one man: Sarento. He had longed to see Rebirth, the world back as it was. His patience had worn thin and he had begun, through the Motherstone, to manipulate events. He had given Bloodstones to a growing nation that became the Hellborn; he had encouraged their warlike tendencies, giving them the secrets of automatic weapons. 'In war,' he said, 'man is at his most inventive. All great historical advances have come through the battlefield.'

With the power of the Motherstone he had reassembled the wreck of the *Titanic* as it lay broken upon the mountainside over Atlantis. He had made it Home Base for the Guardians. But his doom had been sealed when the Hellborn took Donna Taybard as a blood sacrifice, for that alone had led the Jerusalem Man to Balacris and the *Titanic*.

Amaziga remembered that awful night when Sarento used the Motherstone to duplicate the first voyage. Though the ship remained on the mountain, those on board – under its glittering lights and beautiful saloons – could gaze out on a star-filled sky over a black and shining ocean.

But Shannow had fought Sarento in the subterranean cavern of the Motherstone, killing him and sealing off the power of the Stone. The *Titanic* had once more struck the iceberg and a sorcerous sea filled the ship, destroying the Guardians and obliterating the knowledge of eons.

And Amaziga had climbed down from the wreck and walked away without a backward glance.

The Jerusalem Man had come to her.

'I am sorry,' he said. 'I do not know if my actions were right – but they were just. I will lead you to a safe place.'

They had parted at a small town hundreds of miles to the north, and Amaziga had journeyed with her son to the lands of the Wall.

She climbed higher and glanced down at the shimmering Pool below. Her fingers were tired and she hauled herself on to a ledge to rest. There was nothing harmful here that she could feel. 'You are getting old,' she told herself. She had lived more than a century, her youth guaranteed by the Sipstrassi carried by the Guardians. But that was gone now and silver flecks highlighted her tightly curled hair. How old are you in real terms, Amaziga? she asked herself. Thirty-five? Forty?

Taking a deep breath, she rose and climbed on. It took her an hour to reach the ledge beneath the Peak and as she scrambled over it, her hand gripped a sharp stone which split the skin of her palm. She cursed and sat with her back to the rock-face, heart hammering. She could detect nothing baleful in the rock of the Peak. The climb had been a waste of time, and had served only to bring her bitter memories and a painful wound. Settling herself down, preparing her body for the return journey, she thought of jumping to the Pool far below, but dismissed the idea; she had never been comfortable in the water. The sun bathed her and she felt warm and curiously refreshed. Her pulse slowed. When she lifted her injured hand, ready to apply pressure to stop the bleeding, the cut had disappeared. She rubbed her fingers at the skin but there was no mark. Reaching out, she picked up the stone with the serrated edge. Blood had stained it. Carefully she rose to her knees on the narrow ledge and turned to the rock-face. Above her the overhang jutted from the Peak, and above that the Sword of God and the tiny crosses that surrounded it. She closed her eyes, her spirit flowing into the barnacled stone. Deeper she moved, coming at last to shaped marble and beyond that to a network of golden wire and crystals. She followed the network up to a silver bowl, six feet in diameter. At the centre of this lay a huge Sipstrassi Stone with golden threads inches wide.

Her eyes snapped open. 'Oh God!' she whispered. 'Oh God!'

The Chaos Peak was not a natural formation. It had become encrusted as it lay beneath the ocean. It was a tower, and the Sipstrassi Stone was still pulsing its power after 12,000 years. Amaziga gazed down at the sleeping Oshere – and understood.

The healing powers of Sipstrassi!

There had been no intention of harming the Dianae. The almost mechanical magic of the Stone had bathed Shir-ran and the others – it had repaired them, eliminating the promoter genes and the carefully wrought genetic engineering. It had returned them to a state of perfection. 'Dear God!'

Amaziga rose and pushed her back to the face, then stared down at Oshere. Normally a wielder would need to touch a Stone to direct its powers . . . but with something of this size? Her concentration grew and far below Oshere stirred in his sleep. Pain lanced him and he roared, his great head snapping at unseen enemies. His body twisted and he sank back, his new fur shrinking, his limbs straightening. Amaziga pictured him as she remembered him, holding the vision before her eyes. Finally she relaxed and gazed down at the naked young man lying asleep in the sunshine.

Without a moment's hesitation she stepped forward and dived, her lithe ebony frame falling like a spear to cleave the water below. She surfaced and swam to the edge, heaving herself up on to the rocks beside Oshere. Removing her wet clothes, she let the sun dry her skin.

Oshere stirred and opened his golden eyes. 'Is this a dream?' he asked.

'No. This is the reality dreams are shaped of.'

'You look so . . . young and beautiful.'

'So do you,' she told him, smiling. He sat up and gazed in wonder at his bronzed body.

'Truly this is no dream? I am returned?'

'Yes.'

'Tell me. Tell me everything.'

'Not yet,' she whispered, stroking his face. 'Not now, Oshere. Not when I have just dived for you.'

*

Clutching her Bloodstone to her breast, Sharazad stepped through the gateway. Her mind swam, her vision blurred with colours more vivid than any she had seen in life. She held herself steady until the whirling movement before her eyes ceased; she had moved from a star-filled night to a bright dawn and for a moment or two she felt disorientated.

The King was sitting by a window, staring out at his

armies engaged in their training manoeuvres on the far fields.

'Welcome,' he said softly, without turning.

She dropped to her knees with head bent, golden hair falling over her face.

'I cannot tell you how wondrous it is to be once more in your presence, Lord.'

The King swung round and smiled broadly. 'Your flattery is well timed,' he said, 'for I am not best pleased with you.' She looked up into his handsome face, seeing the sunlight glisten on his freshly curled golden beard and the warm, humorous – almost gentle – look in his eyes. Fear rose. She was not fooled by his easy manner, nor the apparent lightness of his mood.

'In what way have I earned your displeasure, Great One?' she whispered, averting her eyes and staring at the ornate rug on which she knelt.

'Your attack on the barbarian village – it was badly timed, and appallingly led. I took you for a woman with a mind, Sharazad. Yet you only attacked from one direction, allowing the enemy room to flee. Where you should have delivered a crushing blow, you merely drove them into the woods to the south, there to plan and prepare a defence.'

'But they cannot defend against us, Great One. They are merely barbarians; they have no organisation, few weapons and little skill.'

'That may be so,' he agreed. 'But if you are so bereft of ideas, strategies and skills, why should I allow you to command?'

'I am not bereft of ideas, Lord, but it was my first engagement. All generals must learn. I will learn; I will do anything to please you.'

He chuckled and stood. He was tall and well-built, his movements easy and graceful as he raised her to her feet. 'I know that you will. You always have. That is why I allow you your . . . small pleasures. Before I make love to you, Sharazad, I want you to see something. It may help you to understand.'

He lifted a Sipstrassi Stone from a gold-embroidered pouch at his belt and held it in the air. The far wall vanished and she found herself gazing down on the Dagger encampment; their low, flat leather tents were bunched together on a rocky slope by a stream. There were guards posted all around the camp, and two sentries on the rocky escarpment above.

'I see nothing amiss,' she said.

'I know. Watch . . . and listen.' The wind sighed across the hillside and the whisper of bats' wings could be heard. Then she caught the sound of lowing cattle; there was nothing else. 'You still cannot sense it, can you?' said the King, laying his hand on her shoulder and unbuckling the straps of her golden breastplate.

'No. They are natural sounds of the night, are they not?'

'They are not,' he said, lifting her breastplate clear and removing the belted dagger at her waist. 'One of them is out of place.'

'The cattle?'

'Yes. They rarely move at night, Sharazad, therefore they are being driven. And they are moving towards the Daggers. A gift, do you think? A peace offering?'

She could see the herd now – a dark, shifting mass moving slowly across the plain towards the camp. Several of the sentries stopped their pacing to watch them approach. Suddenly a shot sounded from behind the herd and a series of hair-raising screams followed. The cattle broke into a run, thundering towards the camp. Sharazad watched with growing horror as the sentries opened fire on the lead beasts; she saw the bulls fall, but the herd ploughed on. Daggers slithered from their tents and ran, diving into the stream or sprinting up the scree-covered slope. Then the stampeding cattle swept through the camp and were gone. As the dust settled, Sharazad gazed down on the ruins where some thirty bodies lay crushed and torn.

The King's hands moved to her silk tunic, untying the laces and sliding the garment down over her shoulders, but she could not tear her eyes from the carnage.

'Look and learn, Sharazad,' he whispered, his fingers sliding over the skin of her hips. The scene shifted to a gulley some three hundred paces from the camp where a man was sitting on a tall, black horse. The rider leaned back in the saddle and removed his hat. Under the moonlight she could see his features clearly, and remembered the man who had bowed to her in the Traveller's Rest.

'One man, Sharazad, one special man. His name is Shannow. He is respected and feared among these barbarians; they call him the Jerusalem Man, for he seeks a mythical city. *One man*.'

'The camp is nothing,' she said. 'And thirty Daggers can be replaced.'

'Still you do not see. Why did he stampede those cattle? Petty revenge? That man is above that.'

'What other reason could there be?'

'You have patrols out?'

'Of course.'

'Where are they now?'

She scanned the plain. The three patrols, each with twenty warriors, were hurrying back towards the ruined camp. Once more the scene shimmered and she found herself looking at the town.

'Of course you searched the town and destroyed anything that might be of use to the enemy?'

'No. I . . . did not . . .'

'You did not think, Sharazad – that is your great crime.' She saw the men at work, loading wagons with food, tools, spare rifles from the gunsmith's store and other weapons still lying beside the dead Daggers. The King moved away from her, but she did not notice, for she saw the man Shannow riding slowly along the main street, watched him dismount before the gunsmith's store. Hatred surged through her blood like a fever.

'Can I have the Hunters?' she asked. 'I want that man.'

'You can have anything you want,' said the King, 'for I love you.'

His whip snaked out, lashing across her buttocks. She screamed once, but did not move.

And the long day of pain began.

*

The King gazed down on Sharazad's sleeping form as she lay face down on the white silken sheets with her long legs drawn up to her body. She looked like a babe, all innocence and purity, thought the King. He had whipped her until she had collapsed, the blood flowing to stain the rug beneath her feet. Then he had healed her.

'Foolish, foolish woman,' he said. A tremor shook the city, but the power of the Sipstrassi Motherstone beneath the temple cut in, repairing cracks in the masonry and shielding the inhabitants from the quakes that rippled across the surrounding countryside.

The King wandered to the window. Below the palace, beyond the tall marble walls the people of Ad were moving about their business. Six hundred thousand souls born in the greatest nation the earth had ever seen – or ever would see, he thought. Through the power of the Stone from Heaven the King had conquered all the civilised world and opened gates to wonders beyond imagination.

Fresh conquests meant little to him now. All that mattered was that his name would ring like a clashing shield down through the ages of history. He smiled. Why should it not? With Sipstrassi he was immortal and therefore would be ever present when his continuing story was sung by the bards.

A second tremor struck. They were beginning to worry him, they had increased so much of late. Clutching his Stone, he closed his eyes.

And disappeared . . .

He opened them to find himself standing in the same room overlooking an identical view. There were the marble walls, beyond them the city, and the docks silent and waiting. It was perhaps his greatest artistic achievement: he had created an exact replica of Ad in a world unpeopled by

Man. Here there were no earthquakes, only an abundance of deer, elk and all the other wondrous creatures of nature.

Soon he would transfer the inhabitants here and build a new Atlantis where no enemies could ever conquer them, for there would be no other nations.

He returned to his room and considered waking Sharazad for an hour of love-making, then dismissed the thought, still angry at her stupidity. He did not mind the deaths of the Daggers; the reptiles were merely tools and, as Sharazad so rightly pointed out, could be replaced with ease. But he hated undisciplined thought, he loathed those who could not see or understand the simplest strategies. Many of his generals dismayed him. They could not comprehend that the object of war was to win, not merely to engage in huge and costly battles with a plethora of heroics on either side. Defeat the enemy from within. First convince him of the hopelessness of his cause and then strike him down while he sits demoralised. But in victory, be magnanimous, for a defeated and humiliated enemy will live only for the day when he can be revenged. Blame the war on the defeated leaders and court the people. But did the generals understand?

Now a new dawn was beginning for Atlantis. The King had seen a world of flying machines and great wonders. So far the links had been tentative, but soon he would open the gateway wider and send out scouts to learn of the new enemy.

His thoughts returned to Sharazad. The world she had discovered was not worthy of their attention – save for the weapons known as guns. But now they had seen them, they could duplicate them – improve on them. There was nothing there of interest. Yet he would allow Sharazad to play out her game to the end; there was the faintest glimmer of hope that she would learn something of value. And if she did not, there was always the whip and her deliciously satisfying screams.

The man Shannow, at least, was of transient interest. The Hunters would kill him, of course, but not before he had provided great sport. How many to send? Five would ensure success. One would give Shannow a chance. Then let it be three, thought the King. But which three?

Magellas must be one; haughty and proud, he needed a tough task. Lindian? Cold, that one, and lethal – not a man to allow into your presence with a weapon of any kind. Yes, Lindian. And to complete the mixture, Rhodaeul. He and Magellas hated one another, constantly vying for supremacy. It should be a fascinating mission for them. They had mastered the new guns with rare brilliance.

Now it was time to see if they could use them to good purpose against an enemy of great skill.

The King lifted his Stone and concentrated on Shannow's face. The air rippled before him and he saw the Jerusalem Man heaving a sack across the back of his saddle.

'You are in great danger, Jon Shannow,' said the King. 'Best to be on your guard!'

Shannow swung as the eerie voice filled his mind. His gun swept up, but there was no target in sight.

The sound of mocking laughter drifted away into echoes.

25

The withdrawal took place just after dawn. The Parson and twenty of the men moved out to flank the straggling column as it headed across the valley towards the great gash the quake had ripped into the ancient Wall. The Parson carried a short-barrelled rifle, his pistols jutting from the belt of his black cassock. The rescued wagons carried some of the children, but most of the three hundred survivors of the raid – reinforced by farmers and settlers from outlying regions – walked in silence, casting nervous glances around them. Everyone expected the reptiles to attack, and the Parson had been hard pressed to convince the refugees of the need to move from the seeming sanctuary of the woods.

Edric Scayse had returned in the night with two wagons loaded with food and spare guns. He had volunteered with thirty others to man the defensive trench in the woods.

'This is partly my fault,' he had told the Parson before the column moved out. 'Those demons are carrying guns I supplied, may God forgive me.'

'He has a habit of forgiving people,' the Parson assured him.

As he walked, the Parson prayed earnestly. 'Lord, as you saw your chosen people from the clutches of the Egyptians, so be with us now as we walk across the valley of the shadow. And be with us when we enter the realm of the Great Whore, who, with your blessing, I will cut down and destroy, with all the beasts of Hell over whom she reigns.'

The wagons were raising dust and the Parson ran back to the column, organising children to scatter water around the wheels. In the distance the Wall loomed, but if they were found here there would be no defence. He loped back to the flanking men.

'You see anything?' he asked Bull.

'Not a movement, Parson. But I feel like I'm sitting on the anvil with the hammer over me – know what I mean? If it ain't the reptiles, we've still got to walk into the land of the Lion-men.'

'God will be with us,' said the Parson, forcing sincerity into his voice.

'Hope so,' muttered the man. 'Surely do need some edge. Look there! More survivors.'

The Parson followed his gaze and saw a wagon moving down to join them. He recognised Beth McAdam at the reins, a black-bearded man beside her. Waving them into the column, he strode across.

'I am pleased to see you are well, Beth,' he said.

'This ain't well, Parson. I just built my god-damned house, and now I'm being run out by a bunch of lizards. What's worse, I got a sick man in the back and this bumping around is doing him no good at all.'

'Within a couple of hours, God willing, we should be behind the Wall. Then we can defend ourselves.'

'Yeah, against the reptiles. What about the other beasts?'

The Parson shrugged. 'As God wishes. Will you introduce me to your friend?'

'This is Nu, Parson. He healed the convoy; he's another man of God – getting to be so I feel hip-deep in them.'

Nu climbed down from the wagon and stretched. The Parson offered his hand, which Nu shook, and the two men strolled together.

'Are you new to this country, Meneer?' the Parson asked.

'Yes and no,' replied Nu. 'I was here . . . a long time ago. Much has changed.'

'Do you know of the lands Beyond the Wall?'

'Not much, I am afraid. There is a city there – a very old city. It used to be called Ad. There are temples and palaces.'

'It is inhabited now by beasts of the Devil,' said the Parson. 'Their evil keeps the Sword of God trapped in the sky. It is my dream to destroy their evil and release the Sword.'

Nu said nothing. He had seen the city in his spirit-search, but there were no signs of beasts or demons. The two men walked together with the flanking gunmen and soon the Parson, tiring of the silence, moved away. Nu strode on, lost in thought. How, he wondered, could a man who professed to believe in the supreme power of God be so convinced that such an awesome power would need his help? Trapped in the sky? What kind of petty creature did this man believe God to be?

The convoy moved slowly across the landscape.

A horseman came galloping across the valley. The Parson and his flankers ran to intercept him; the man was one of Scayse's riders.

'Better move fast, Parson,' he said, leaning over the saddle of his lathered mount. 'There's two groups of the creatures. One is moving on Meneer Scayse in the woods, the second and largest is coming to intercept you. They're not far behind.'

The Parson swung to gauge the distance to the Wall – it was over a mile. 'Ride in and get the wagons moving at speed. Tell everyone to run.' The horseman dug his heels into the flanks of his weary horse and cantered down to the leading wagons. Whips cracked and the oxen strained into the traces.

The Parson gathered his men. 'We can't hold them,' he said, 'but we'll keep together at the rear of the convoy. When we see them, we can at least slow their advance. Let's go.'

The morning sun blazed down on them as they ran into the dust-cloud left by the fleeing convoy.

*

As the mocking laughter faded, Shannow stepped into the saddle. He cast his eyes around the silent street. There in the dust by the Traveller's Rest lay Mason, his body riddled with bullet holes. Some yards to the left was Boris Haimut, who would now never find the answers to his questions. The crippled hostler lay in the street by the livery stable with an old shotgun in his hands. Elsewhere were the bodies of men, women and children Shannow had never known in life. Yet all must have nurtured their own dreams and ambitions. He turned the stallion's head and rode out into the valley.

He had been lucky at the gunsmith's store. As he had hoped, Groves had made more of the Hellborn shells, obviously planning on larger orders from Scayse. Shannow now had more than a hundred bullets. He had also gathered a short rifle, three sacks of black powder and sundry other items from the debris of the general store.

As he rode, he thought back to the voice that had whispered in his mind: *Be on your guard?* When in the last two decades had he not been on his guard, or in peril? Neither the voice nor the implied threat worried him unduly. A man lived, a man died. What could frighten a man who understood these truths?

For some time Shannow rode in sight of the wagons, but there was no pursuit and he cut his trail at right-angles and rode for the hills to the east. If the Parson took his advice and moved his people, then the valley would become the place of greatest danger.

Shannow rode warily, altering direction often, allowing no hidden observer to plot his path. The ground rose and he guided the stallion up into the boulder-strewn hills, dismounting and tethering him. Then he lifted the sack and opened it, spreading the contents on the ground before him. There were seven clay pots with narrow necks stopped with corks, six packets of small nails and a coil of fuse wire. He filled each pot with black powder mixed with nails, tamping them down firmly. With a long nail he pierced each of the corks and fed lengths of fuse wire into them. Satisfied with his handiwork, he returned the pots to the sack and sat down to wait. With his long glass he studied the valley below; in the far distance he saw the wagons reach the woods and, later, watched as the convoy began its slow progress towards the Wall.

For an hour he sat and then the first of the Daggers came

into view, running towards the woods. Shannow focused the glass and watched the enemy closing in on the makeshift fortifications. Another movement caught his eye – several hundred of the reptiles were running towards the south. A horseman cut across them and thundered away. Shannow stood and heaved the sack over the back of his saddle. Taking the reins, he mounted and steered the stallion through the trees towards the eastern slopes. Shielded by the hills he rode at speed, ignoring the danger of pot-holes or rocks. The stallion was sure-footed and strong, and he loved to run. Twice Shannow was forced to duck under overhanging branches that would have swept him from the saddle, and once the stallion surged over a fallen tree. As the hills levelled out, Shannow swung his mount to the west, into a shallow gulley that led out on to the plain. Shots whistled by him and he could see the reptiles closing fast as he leapt from the saddle, dragging the sack with him and pulling one of the pots clear. He struck a match and applied it to the fuse, which crackled and spat. Shannow heaved it over the gulley edge and then lit another. The explosion was deafening and red-hot nails screamed overhead. Three more pots sailed into the advancing ranks of the Daggers before Shannow grabbed the pommel of his saddle and vaulted to the stallion's back.

Kicking the beast into a run he headed him west, glancing back once to see the Daggers regrouping. There were many bodies lying on the long grass, but many more were still standing.

Shells came close, but the speed of the stallion soon carried the Jerusalem Man out of range.

*

Edric Scayse reloaded his rifle. The reptiles had charged the slope just once, but the withering volley fire from the defenders had scythed through their ranks. Now they were more cautious, creeping forward and waiting until the defenders skylined themselves. Eleven men were down and Scayse knew the position was hopeless.

He was angry with himself. All of his dreams were ashes now – and all because of the gold supplied by the woman, Sharazad. She had first come to him three months before, claiming to be from a community far to the east. Could he get her weapons? Of course he could if the price was right. And the gold was of spectacular quality. Now he was pinned down in a wood – his silver mine deserted, his town destroyed, the people who would have made him their leader decimated and scattered. He reared up and pumped three shots down the hill before dropping back behind the earthworks.

A man to his left screamed and fell, a ghastly wound in his temple. 'We'd best be thinking about leaving,' said another man beside him.

'Seems like a good time,' Scayse agreed. Word was passed along the line and the eighteen survivors moved back from the ditch into the woods. Shots screamed into them from the trees and Scayse dived for cover, his wide hat ripped from his head. He rolled into the bushes and sprinted off to the right as shells ricocheted from the trees around him. One struck the butt of his rifle, spinning it from his numbed hand, but he drew his pistol and ran on. A reptile reared up before him, with a serrated dagger in its hand, but Scayse triggered the pistol point-blank and the creature fell. Hurdling the body, he ran on. Behind him came the screams of the dying. He looked back once to see the dark, scaled forms of the reptiles were giving chase. He loosed two shots in their direction, but hit nothing. Ducking behind a tree, Scayse fed shells into the cylinder of his pistol and waited.

'Get down, Scayse,' came a voice, 'and cover your ears.' A clay pot soared overhead and exploded in the path of the hunters. A second followed it. Scayse dived for the ground as the explosion ripped into the woods, then he was up and running.

Shannow rode into his path, offering his hand. Scayse swung up behind him and the stallion cantered away through the woods.

They rode for two miles before Shannow halted to allow the stallion to rest; its breathing was laboured, its flanks covered with lather. Scayse climbed down and patted the beast. 'Some horse, Shannow. If ever you feel like selling, I'll buy.'

'With what?' asked Shannow, stepping down. 'All you own is what you're wearing.'

'I'll get it back. Somehow I'll find a way to beat those creatures – and that damned woman.'

'You should be grateful to her,' said Shannow. 'She's surely not a general. With a hundred well-armed, well-mounted men we could destroy them in a day.'

'Maybe,' Scayse agreed. 'But I'd say she has the upper hand around now. Wouldn't you?'

Shannow did not answer and the two men walked on for some time. Finally, Shannow turned the horse on to a narrow side trail leading up to a cave. The opening was less than four feet wide, but inside the cave itself was huge and almost circular. Shannow unsaddled the stallion and rubbed him down. 'We'll stay here for an hour or two, then I guess we should find a way to get over the Wall.'

'Easier said, Shannow. By now those reptiles will be swarming over it like bees on honey. By the way, thanks for the timely rescue. I'll pay you back one day.'

'That's an interesting thought,' answered Shannow, taking his blankets and spreading them for a bed. 'Wake me in an hour.'

'We could be trapped in here. Shouldn't we move on?'

'It's unlikely they'll hunt for long. Having removed your force, they'll congregate at the Wall.'

'And if you're wrong?'

'Then we'll both be dead. Wake me in an hour.'

*

The great Wall had been torn asunder by the quake, a huge gash appearing more than twenty feet across. On either side massive stone blocks hung precariously, looking as if a breath of wind would tumble them down on the rumbling wagons.

The Parson watched the column inch its perilous way along the stone-strewn pathway. Behind them the explosions had stopped – as had the headlong advance of the enemy.

'Shannow?' asked Bull and the Parson nodded. 'He don't give up, do he?'

With the last wagon through the gap, the Parson sent a group of men to scale the Wall and lever down the hanging blocks. They crashed to the ground, sending up clouds of dust.

'We should be able to hold them here for a while,' said Bull. 'Mind you, I think them beasts could climb over anywheres they chose.'

'We'll head south,' said the Parson. 'But I'd like you and a dozen others to hold this breach for a day . . . if you're willing?'

Bull chuckled and ran his fingers through his long, sandy hair. 'Given the choice between this and having boils lanced, I'd surely plump for the knife, Parson. But I reckon it needs doing. Anyways, I think it would be neighbourly to wait for Meneer Scayse and the others.'

'You're a good man, Bull.'

'I know it, Parson. And don't you forget to tell the Almighty!'

Bull sauntered among the men, choosing those he felt he could trust in a tight spot. They unloaded extra ammunition, filled their water canteens from the barrels on the wagons and took up positions on the Wall or behind fallen blocks to await the enemy.

From the north came the sound of gunfire and two more muted explosions.

'He surely does get around,' observed Bull to a young rider named Faird.

'Who?'

'The Jerusalem Man. Hope to God he makes it.'

'I hope to God *we* make it,' said Faird with feeling.

'Goddammit, there's that second sun again.' The brilliance was overpowering and Bull shielded his eyes. He felt the rumble beneath his feet.

'Get back from the Wall!' he bellowed. Men started to run, then the tremor struck and they were hurled from their feet. Jagged lines scored the surface of the Wall, blocks shifting and falling. A chasm opened across the valley and a great roaring filled the air, as flames spewed from the pit.

'Son of a bitch!' whispered Bull as the smell of sulphur blew across him. He pushed himself to his knees. Another massive section of the Wall had collapsed and from out of the dust-storm walked a tall reptile, his right hand held before him. Faird levelled his rifle. 'Hold it,' said Bull, and he rose and walked out to meet the beast, halting some three paces short.

The creature snorted dust from its slitted nostrils, then fixed Bull with its golden eyes.

'Speak your mind,' said Bull, his hand resting on the pistol butt at his side.

'Yess. Sspeak. Thiss war no good, U-man. Much death. No point.'

'You began it.'

'Yess. Great sstupidity. We only soldierss. You understand? No choicess. Now Goldenhair ssays talk. We talk.'

'Who is this Goldenhair?'

'Sharassad. Leader. She ssays to give uss the man Nu and we will leave you in peace.'

'Why should we believe her?'

'I don't believe her,' said the reptile. 'Treacherouss woman. But she ssays sspeak so I sspeak.'

'You're telling me not to trust your own leader?' asked Bull, amazed. 'Then why the Hell come here in the first place?'

'We are *Ruazsh*-Pa. Warriors. We fight good. We lie bad. She ssay come, talk, tell you words. I tell you words. What answer you?'

'What answer would you give?'

The reptile waved his hand. 'Not for me to ssay.' He snorted once more, then began to cough.

'You want some water?' asked Bull. He called Faird over.

'Yess.' Faird brought a canteen and handed it gingerly to the creature, who lifted it high and poured the cool liquid over his face. Immediately the dry scaled skin took on a healthy glow. The reptile handed back the canteen, ignoring Faird.

'Very much bad, thiss war,' he told Bull. 'And these,' he added, patting the pistol at his hip, 'no good. Battle sshould be fought close, daggerss and swordss. No win souls from sso far. I, Szshark, kill twenty-six enemies with dagger, face close, touch their eyess with my tongue. Now . . . bang . . . enemy fall. Very much very bad.'

'You seem like a decent sort,' said Bull, aware that the others had gathered close. 'I . . . we . . . never seen nothing like you before. Shame we got to go on killing one another.'

'Nothing wrong with killing,' hissed the creature, 'but it musst be according to cusstom. What answer you give treacherouss woman?'

'Tell her we need time to think about it.'

'Why?'

'To discuss it amongst ourselves.'

'You have no leader? What of the red-headed one in black? Or the Deathrider?'

'It's hard to explain. Our leaders need time to discuss it. Then maybe they'll say yes, maybe no.'

'It sshould be no,' said Szshark. 'It would lack honour. Better to die than betray a friend. Yet I will take your words to Goldenhair. Water wass good. For that gift I will kill you the right way, with dagger.'

'Thanks,' said Bull, grinning. 'That's nice to know.'

Szshark bowed stiffly and loped back to the Wall. With one leap he cleared a ten-foot block and was gone.

'What the Hell do you make of that?' Faird asked.

'Damned if I know,' answered Bull. 'Seemed a reasonable . . . thing, didn't he?'

'You could almost like him,' agreed Faird. 'We'd better get back to the Parson – tell him about the offer.'

'I don't like the feel of it,' said Bull. 'No way.'

'Me neither. But my wife and children are with that convoy, and if it comes to a choice between a stranger and them, I know where my vote goes.'

'He saved you and your wife on the trail, Faird. You surely don't go too long on gratitude in your family.'

'That was then, this is now,' snapped Faird, swinging away.

26

The bodies of the three sacrificial victims were carried from the altars. The High Priest lifted the three gleaming Bloodstones and placed them in a golden bowl.

'By the Spirit of Belial, by the blood of the innocent, by the law of the King,' he chanted. 'Let these tokens carry you to victory.'

The three men remained kneeling as the High Priest brought the bowl to them. From his jewel-encrusted throne the King watched the ceremony with little interest. He could see the giant Magellas and feel the warrior's discomfort as he knelt. The King smiled. Beside Magellas, the slender Lindian showed no expression; his grey eyes were hooded, his face a taut mask. On the extreme right Rhodaeul waited with eyes closed, mind locked in prayer. All three looked like brothers with their snow-white hair and pale faces. The High Priest gave them their Stones, then blessed them with the Horns of Belial. They rose smoothly and bowed to the King.

He acknowledged their obeisance, gestured them to follow him and strode to his rooms. Once there, he stood by the window and waited as the three warriors entered. Magellas was by far the largest, his black and silver tunic stretched by the enormous muscles of his shoulders and arms. Lindian looked almost boylike beside him. Rhodaeul moved some paces to the right.

'Come,' invited the King. 'Meet your enemy.' He lifted his Sipstrassi, the wall shimmered and disappeared and they saw a man standing beside a tall, black horse. Another man was sitting close by. 'That is the victim you seek,' said the King. 'His name is Shannow.'

'He is old, sire,' said Magellas. 'Why are the Hunters needed?'

'Find him and see,' the King told him. 'But I do not want him killed from ambush, or destroyed from distance. You will face him.'

'It is a test then, Father?' asked Rhodaeul.

'It is a test,' the King agreed. 'The man is a warrior and I suspect he is – as you are – Rolynd. His disadvantage is that he was not fed with Sipstrassi strength while he was in the womb, nor tutored as you have been by the finest assassins in the Empire. Yet still he is a warrior.'

'Why three of us, Lord?' asked Lindian. 'Would not one suffice?'

'Most probably. But your enemy is a master of the new weapons – perhaps you will acquire something from him. To that end my reward will be great. The Hunter who kills him will become Satrap of the Northern Province of Akkady; his companions will receive six talents of silver.'

The three warriors said nothing, but the King could see their minds working. No unity of purpose now. No combined plan. Each of them was plotting to defeat not only Shannow but each other.

'Are there no questions, my children?'

'None, Father,' volunteered Magellas. 'It will be as you say.'

'I will watch your progress with interest.'

The three having bowed and left the room, the King sealed the chamber with his Stone and settled back on a silk-covered divan. The wall shimmered once more and he gazed down on the land of the Wall. At last Sharazad had begun to think; she had laid the seed of division within the enemy and was moving her troops to encircle them. He looked further, into the heavily wooded hills to the west of the refugees. Then he chuckled.

'Oh, Sharazad, if only I could tire of your beauty. Yet again you conspire to snatch defeat from the jaws of victory.' He touched the Stone and viewed the lands to the south. His body arched upright as he saw the distant city. As he stood, his pale eyes widening, his mouth was dry and for the first time in decades a lance of fear smote him.

'What demonic trickery is this?' he whispered aloud. Leaving the image shimmering, he summoned his astrologers. There were four men, all appearing to be in their middle twenties.

'Look, and tell me what you see,' ordered the King.

'It is the City of Ad,' said the leader, Araksis. 'Bring it closer, Majesty. Yes, it is Ad. But see the way the statues are worn and the roadways buckle. Move further south, Lord. Find the tower.' But there was no tower, only a barnacle-encrusted peak. For some time the Atlanteans stared at the Sword of God. 'It is baffling, my Lord,' said Araksis. 'Unless someone copied the city, or . . .'

'Speak!' ordered the King.

'We could be looking at the city as it will one day be.'

'Where is the sea? Where are the ships?'

The astrologers looked at one another. 'Show us nightfall, sire, on this world.' The King touched his Stone and the astrologers grouped together to study the star-filled sky.

'We will return to the tower, Lord,' said Araksis. 'We will study more closely and report back to you.'

'By midday, Araksis. Meanwhile, send Serpiat to me.'

The King sat lost in thought, staring at the vision before him. He did not notice the arrival of the general, Serpiat. The man was squat and powerfully built, wearing golden armour and a jet-black cloak.

'Not good, sire,' he observed, his voice rough and grating, 'to allow an armed man easy access to your chambers.'

'What? Yes, you are right, my friend. I did not secure the chamber. But my mind was occupied with that,' said the King, pointing to the distant city. Serpiat removed his black-plumed helm and approached the vision. He rubbed at his beard.

'Is it real?'

'All too real. Araksis is returning here at midday, but when he left his face was white, his eyes frightened. It frightens me also. With the Towerstone we have opened gates to other worlds – and conquered them. But this . . . this is no other world, Serpiat. What have we done?'

'I do not understand, sire. What is it you fear?'

'I fear that!' shouted the King. 'My city. I built it. But where is the ocean – and where am I?'

'You? You are here. You are the King.'

'Yes, yes. Forgive me, Serpiat. Gather ten legions. I want that city surrounded and taken – all its records. *Everything.* Capture its people. Question them.'

'But this was to be Sharazad's realm, was it not? Do I serve under her?'

'Sharazad is finished. The game is over. Do as I ask and prepare your men. I will open a wide gateway three days from now.'

*

The Parson listened to the reports of his scouts. The southland was wide and open; there was evidence of past cultivation, and an incredible number of lion tracks on the plain before the city. Several prides had been seen moving in the distance. To the east, he was told, there were other tracks, bigger, showing talon marks of prodigious size.

'Did you see any beasts?' he asked the rider.

'No, sir. Nothing unnatural, like. But I seen some big bears – biggest I ever saw. High up in the timber country. I didn't get too close.'

They had camped by a lake where the Parson ordered trees to be felled and dragged to the lakeside, forming three perimeter walls. Within this rough stockade he allowed tents to be erected and cook-fires lit. The people moved through their chores like sleepwalkers. Many of the women had lost husbands in the attack on the town. Other men, who had chosen to go to church on that fateful morning, knew their wives and children had been butchered. All had lost. For some it was only a building, or a tent or a wagon. For others it was loved ones. Now the survivors were in shock.

The Parson gathered them together and prayed for the souls of the departed. Then he allocated tasks for the survivors – gathering wood for the fires, helping to erect tents, preparing food, scouting the woods for root crops, tubers, wild onions.

In the distance he could see the glistening towers of the Whore's city, and wondered how long it would be before her satanic legions fell upon them.

Bull's arrival with Faird was a surprise – yet even more surprising was his news of the meeting with Szshark.

'You spoke with one of the Devil's minions?' he said, aghast. 'I hope your soul was not burned.'

'He seemed . . .' Bull shrugged. '. . . honest, at least, Parson. He warned us to beware of the woman.'

'Don't be a fool, Bull. He is a creature of darkness and he knows nothing of the truth. His ways are the ways of deceit. If the woman has made us an offer, we must regard it as honest – if only because the demon says otherwise.'

'Hold on there, Parson. You didn't speak to him. I did. I kinda trust what he says.'

'Then the Devil has touched you, Bull, and you are not to be trusted.'

'That's kinda harsh, Parson. Does that mean you'd consider giving up the Healer to them creatures?'

'What do we know of him – or his connection with them? He could be a killer. He could have brought this doom upon us all. I will pray on it and then the men will vote. You ride back and keep an eye on the enemy.'

'Don't I get a vote, Parson?'

'I will make it for you, Bull. I take it you are against any . . . trade?'

'You couldn't be more damn right!'

'I hear what you say. Go now.'

The Parson summoned Nu to him and the two walked together on the shores of the lake.

'Why are these creatures hunting you, Meneer?' he asked.

'I spoke against the King in the temple. I warned the people of coming disasters.'

'So then they consider you a traitor? It is not surprising, Meneer Nu. Are we not told in the Bible to respect the power of Kings, as they are ordained by God himself?'

'I am not versed in the lore of your Bible, Parson. I follow the Law of the One. God spoke to me and He told me to prophesy.'

'If He was truly with you, Meneer, He would have kept you safe from harm. As it is, you fled before the law of your King. No true prophet fears the way of kings. Elijah stood against Ahab, Moses against the Pharoahs, Jesus against the Romans.'

'I do not know of Jesus, but I read Shannow's Bible concerning Moses, and did he not run away to the desert before returning to save his people?'

'I will not bandy words with you, sir. Tonight the people will decide your fate.'

'My fate is in God's hands, Parson. Not yours.'

'Indeed? But which God? You know nothing of Jesus, the Son of God. You do not know the Bible. How can you be a man of God? Your deceit is colossal – but it does not fool me for the Lord has given me the gift of discernment. You will not leave this camp-site. I will give orders to see that if you attempt it you will be confined in chains. Do you understand?'

'I understand only too well,' Nu replied.

As the sun set the Parson called the men together and began to address them. But Beth McAdam strode into the circle.

'What do you want here, Beth?' the Parson asked.

'I want to hear the arguments, Parson. So do all the women here. Or did you think to exclude us from this meeting of yours?'

'It is written that women should be silent at religious meetings, and it is not fitting that you should question holy law.'

'I don't question holy law – whatever the Hell it might be. But two-thirds of the people here are women and we've got a point to make. Nobody lives my life or makes decisions for me. And I've sent the souls of men who've tried to Hell. Now you're deciding on the fate of a friend of mine and, by God, I'll have a say in it. *We'll* have a say in it.'

Beyond the circle the women crowded in and Martha stepped forward, her hair silver in the gathering dusk.

'You weren't there on the trail, Parson,' she said, 'when Meneer Nu healed all the people. He had him a Daniel Stone – and we all know what one of them is worth. It could have made him rich, given him a life of ease. But he used it up for people he didn't know. I don't think it a Christian deed to hand him to a bunch of killers.'

'Enough!' stormed the Parson, surging to his feet. 'I call upon the men here to vote on this matter. It is obvious that the Devil, Satan, has once more reached into the hearts of Woman – as he did on that dreadful day when Man was cast from the joys of Eden. Vote, I say!'

'No, Parson,' said Josiah Broome, pushing himself to his feet and clearing his throat. 'I don't think we should vote. I think it demeans us. I am not a man of violence, and I fear for all of us, but the facts are simple. Meneer Nu, you say, is not a true man of God. Yet the Bible says, "By their works shall ye judge them." Well, by his works I judge him. He healed our people; he carries no weapons; he speaks no evil. The woman, Sharazad, whom you urge us to believe, bought guns from Meneer Scayse and then loosed the demons upon our community. By her works I judge her. To vote on such a trade would be a shame I will not carry.'

'Spoken like the coward you are!' shouted the Parson. 'Do not vote then, Broome. Walk away. Turn your back on responsibility. Look around you! See the children and the women who will die. And for what? So that one man – whom we do not know – can escape the penalties of his treason.'

'How dare you call the man a coward?' stormed Beth. 'If you are right, he just accepted death rather than shame. I've got two kids and I'd give my life to see them happy and healthy. But I'll be damned before I give someone else's.'

'Very well,' said the Parson, fighting to control his anger. 'Then let the vote take in all the people. And let the Lord God move in your hearts when you do so. Let all who wish the man Nu to be returned to his people walk over here and stand behind me.'

Slowly some of the men began to shift and Faird rose.

'You go with him, Ezra Faird, and you don't come back to me,' shouted a woman. Faird shifted uneasily, then sat down. In all, twenty-seven men and three women moved to stand behind the Parson.

'Looks like that settles it,' said Beth. 'Now let's see to the cook-fires.' She turned to leave, then stopped. Slowly she approached Josiah Broome.

'We don't always see eye to eye, Meneer, but for what it's worth I am sorry for the things I said to you. And I'm right proud to have heard you speak tonight.'

He bowed and gave a nervous smile. 'I am not a man of decisive action, Beth. But I too am proud of what the people did here tonight. It's probably meaningless in the long run, but it shows what greatness Mankind is capable of.'

'Will you join my family and me for a meal?'

'I would be glad to.'

27

Shannow and Scayse walked to the crest of the last hill and found themselves looking down on a lake of dark beauty. The moon hung in the sky between two distant peaks, and the surface of the water shone like silver. By the shoreline the camp-site was lit by fires, the wagons spread like a necklace of pearls to reinforce the perimeter walls. From where they stood, all seemed peaceful.

'This is a beautiful country,' said Scayse. 'God-forsaken, but beautiful.'

Shannow said nothing. He was scanning the horizon, seeking any sign of the reptiles. He and Scayse had passed through the gap in the Wall and come across many tracks, but of the enemy there was no sign. Shannow was disturbed. As long as he knew where his enemy was, he could plan to defeat or avoid him. But the Daggers had vanished, the tracks seeming to indicate they had headed for the woods to the west of the camp-site.

'Not much of a talker, are you, Shannow?'

'When I have something to say, Scayse. There seems to be a meeting going on down there,' said Shannow, pointing to the centre of the camp-site.

'Well, let's get down there. I don't want decisions taken without me.'

Shannow walked ahead, leading the stallion. A sentry spotted them, recognising Scayse, and the two men were ushered through a break in the perimeter wall. As the Parson strode to meet them, Shannow saw that his face was flushed and his eyes angry.

'Trouble, Parson?' he asked.

'A prophet is not without honour – save in his own land,' snapped the Parson. 'Where are the other men?'

'All dead,' replied Scayse. 'What's going on?' Swiftly the

Parson told them of the meeting and what he described as its satanic outcome.

'It might have been different had you been here,' he told Shannow, but the Jerusalem Man did not reply; he led his horse to the picket line by the lake, stripped the saddle and brushed the stallion down for several minutes. Then he fed him grain, allowed him to drink at the lakeside and tethered him to the line.

Shannow wandered through the camp-site seeking Beth McAdam. He found her by her wagon, sitting at a fire with Josiah Broome and Nu, her children lying asleep beside her wrapped in blankets. 'May I join you?' asked the Jerusalem Man.

Beth made a space for him beside her, but Broome stood. 'Thank you, Beth, for your company. I will leave you now.'

'There's no need to rush, Josiah. Where is there to go?'

'I think I'll get some sleep.' He nodded to Shannow and walked away.

'The man does not like me,' said Shannow as Beth passed him a cup of Baker's.

'No, he doesn't. You heard what happened?'

'Yes. How are you faring, Nu?'

The shipbuilder shrugged. 'I am well, Shannow. But your Parson is unhappy; he feels I am a devil's disciple. I am sorry for him. He is under great strain, yet has performed wonders holding the people together. He is a good leader, but like all leaders he has a belief that only he is right.'

A burst of gunfire came from the western woods, more than a mile away. Shannow stood and gazed across the open ground, but he could see nothing and the sound faded.

Returning to his seat, he finished his drink. 'I think I know how I might get home,' said Nu. 'The Temple at Ad had an inner sanctuary, where once a year the Elders would heal supplicants. They had Sipstrassi. If the end came suddenly, perhaps the Stones are still hidden there.'

'A good thought,' said Shannow. 'I am riding there myself. Come with me.'

'What do you plan there?' asked Beth.

'It is said – by the Parson and others – to be a city of beasts ruled by a dark queen. I shall go to her, tell her of the reptiles and the attack.'

'But she is evil,' protested Beth. 'You'll be killed.'

'Who is to say she is evil?' answered Shannow. 'The Parson has never seen her. No one has come Beyond the Wall in years. I trust my own eyes, Beth McAdam.'

'But the beast back in the town, the lion-creature. You saw it. It was terrifying.'

'I also met such a creature when I was in need, Beth. He healed my wounds and tended me. He told me of the Dark Lady; he said she was a teacher who worked among the people of the Lion, the Bear and the Wolf. I will not trust to rumour. I will make no judgements.'

'But if you are wrong . . .'

'So be it.'

'I will come with you, Shannow,' Nu said. 'I need a Stone. I need to return home. My world is about to die and I must be there.'

Shannow nodded. 'Let us walk a while. There are matters we must speak of.' The two men strolled to the lake and sat by the waters. 'When we spoke on the hillside,' said Shannow, 'you told me of the King and his evil. But you did not say his name. Tell me, is it Pendarric?'

'Yes. The King of Kings. Is it important?'

'I owe the man my life. He saved me twice. He came to me in a dream three years ago and showed me his sword – saying that if ever I saw it in life and had need of it, I should reach for it and it would come to me. When I fought Sarento in the cavern of the Motherstone, I saw the image of the sword carved on an altar. I stretched out my hand and the blade appeared. Later, when the cavern flooded and I was dying, Pendarric's face appeared beside me, leading me to safety.'

'I do not understand all this, Shannow. What are you trying to tell me?'

'I owe him. I cannot go against him.'

Nu picked up a flat stone and skimmed it across the

water. 'There was a time when Pendarric was a good King – even a great one. But the Sons of Belial came to him and showed him the power of Sipstrassi when fed by blood. He changed, Shannow. Evil swamped him. I have seen children hauled up by their ankles over the altars of Molech-Belial, their throats cut. I have seen young women slaughtered in their hundreds.'

'But I have not. Though I know you speak the truth, because Pendarric told me he was the King who had destroyed the world. He will fall whatever I do, or do not do.'

Nu skimmed a second stone. 'I build ships, Shannow. I shape the keels, I work the wood. Everything in its place and its rightful order. You cannot start with the deck and build around it. It is the same with Pendarric. You and I are servants of the Creator and He also believes in order. He created the universe, the suns and moons and stars. Then the world. Then the creatures of the sea. Lastly He placed man upon the earth. All in order.'

'What has this to do with Pendarric?'

'Everything. He has changed the order of the universe. Atlantis is dead, Shannow; it died twelve thousand years ago. Yet it is here, its sun shining alongside our own. The spirit Pendarric who saved you is yet to be. The King beyond is not yet him. You understand? The evil ruler who is trying to conquer worlds beyond imagination has not yet met you. Only *after* the doom of Atlantis will he come into your life. Therefore you owe him nothing. There is another thought too, Shannow. You have already gone against him and perhaps he now knows of you. Perhaps that is why he came to you three years ago. He already knew you, though you had no knowledge of him.'

'My mind feels like a kitten chasing its tail,' said Shannow, smiling, 'but I think I understand. Even so, I will not go against him directly.'

'You may be forced to,' Nu told him. 'If two ships are lashed together in a storm and one is holed, what happens to the other?'

'I do not know. They both sink?'

'Indeed they do. Then think on this, my friend. Pendarric has joined our two worlds together. There is a gateway to the past. What happens when the oceans rise?'

Shannow shivered and gazed at the stars. 'In Balacris,' he said, 'I had a vision. I saw the tidal wave sweeping towards the city – higher than mountains, and black as the pit. I watched it roar. It was a terrible sight. You think it would pour through the gateway?'

'What would stop it?'

Both men were silent for a while, then Shannow reached into his pocket and removed the golden coin he had found in Shir-ran's cave. He stared down at the engraving.

'What is it?' asked Nu.

'The Sword of God,' Shannow whispered.

*

Bull reined in his horse and listened to the sudden flurry of gunshots. He had followed the Daggers at a discreet distance, watching them climb into the timberline, guessing their objective was to circle the camp-site and attack under cover of darkness. He had been just about to ride back and warn the Parson when the shots shattered the silence. He glanced back at the distant camp with its twinkling fires. If he returned now, he would have little to report. He drew his gun and checked the loads, then with pistol in hand he steered his horse into the trees. He rode slowly, following a deer trail, stopping often to listen. The wind was picking up and the branches above him whispered and crackled, but every now and then the wind would drop and then Bull thought he heard the sounds of roaring beasts. Sweat beaded his brow.

He pulled his hat from his head and wiped his face with the sleeve of his shirt. 'You gotta be crazy, boy,' he told himself, touching his heels to the mare's side. She was a good cattle pony, mountain-bred for stamina and speed over short distances, but her ears were pressed flat against her skull and she moved skittishly, as if a scent on the night breeze frightened her. The wind died and Bull heard a terrible growling from ahead. He pulled on the reins and considered riding back; instead he dismounted, looped the pony's reins around a branch and crept forward.

Pushing aside a thick bush, he gazed on a scene of carnage. The bodies of reptiles littered the clearing beyond, and giant bears were ripping at their flesh. At the centre of the clearing he saw a flash of golden hair as the body of the woman Sharazad was dragged away into the night. Swiftly he did a count. There were some forty huge creatures here, and he could hear growling from all around him. He backed away, his pistol cocked.

Suddenly a colossal beast reared up alongside. Bull rolled and put a shot into the gaping jaws that towered over him, but a massive taloned arm swept out, hammering him to the ground. He landed heavily, but managed another shot as the beast moved in, its mouth spewing blood.

Szshark leapt from the undergrowth with a serrated dagger in his hand. He landed on the bear's back and the knife plunged into the beast's right eye. It fell with a great crash. Bull scrambled to his feet and ran back for the pony, the reptile moving alongside. Reaching his mount, Bull scrambled into the saddle, dragging the reins clear. From all around him came the sounds of huge bodies crashing through the undergrowth. Szshark hissed and waited, his bloody dagger raised. Instinctively Bull stretched out a hand.

'We'd best get out of here,' he shouted. Szshark reached up, took the hand and vaulted up behind Bull. The little pony took off down the deer trail as if its tail was on fire. They emerged on to open ground and galloped clear of the trees.

'Much good fighting,' said Szshark. 'Many soulss.'

Bull dragged on the reins and glanced back. The bears had halted by the tree-line and were gazing after them. He allowed the pony a short breather and then headed in a walk towards the camp-site.

'I ain't sure as how you'll be too welcome, Szshark,' he said. 'The Parson's likely to boil you in oil.' The reptile said nothing, its wedge-shaped head resting on Bull's shoulder. 'You hear me?'

There was no movement and Bull cursed and rode on. The sentries allowed him through, then saw his passenger. Word swept the camp-site faster than a fire through dry grass. Bull climbed down, twisting to catch Szshark's falling body. He laid him on the grass, then saw the awful talon cuts on his shoulders and back. Blood seeped to the ground as Szshark's golden eyes opened.

'Many soulss,' he hissed. He blinked and looked up at the faces gazing down. His eyes misted, his scaled hand reached up and took Bull's arm. 'Cut out my heart,' he said. 'You . . .' The golden eyes closed.

'Why did you bring this demon here?' asked the Parson.

Bull stood. 'They're all dead, Parson, God be praised. This one was Szshark; he rescued me back in the woods. There's creatures there, damn big – ten, twelve feet tall. Look like bears. They wiped out the reptiles. The woman's dead too.'

'Then we can return to Pilgrim's Valley,' said Beth McAdam. 'Now that's what I call a miracle.'

'No,' said the Parson. 'Don't you understand? We were led here, like the children of Israel. But our work is only beginning. There is the Great Whore to be destroyed, and the Sword of God to be loosed over the land. Then, in truth, God will bless us, the wolf will lie down with the lamb and the lion eat grass like the cattle. Don't you see?'

'I don't want no more fighting,' declared Beth. 'I'm going home tomorrow.' Murmurs of agreement came from the listeners. 'Listen, Parson, you've done right proud by all of us. If it weren't for you, we'd all be dead. I'm grateful – and I mean that. You're always welcome in my home. But that's where I'm going – home. I don't know anything about this whore of yours, and I don't care a damn about some sword.'

'Then I will go on alone,' said the Parson. 'I will follow God's path.'

He walked away from the group and saddled a horse.

Shannow moved across to him. 'Be sure of God's path, Parson, before you attempt to ride it,' he said.

'I have the Gift, Shannow. No harm will befall me. Won't you ride with me? You are a man of God.'

'I have other plans, Parson. Take care.'

'My destiny lies with the Sword, Shannow. I know it. It fills my mind, it swells my heart.'

'God be with you, Parson.'

'As He wills,' replied the other, stepping into the saddle.

28

Araksis pushed the computations from him and stared at the midday sun. He was a frightened man. He had been four hundred and twenty-seven years old, sick and dying, when Pendarric first had him summoned to the winter palace at Balacris. But the Sipstrassi had changed his life. The King had healed him, given him back his lost youth. Yet since that time there had been many astrologers, and seventeen had been put to death for causing the King displeasure. It was not that Pendarric did not wish to hear bad omens, rather that he expected the astrologers to be exact in their predictions. However, as all initiates knew, the study of the Fates was an art, not a science. Now Araksis faced the same predicament as many of his erstwhile colleagues. He sighed and rose, gathering his parchments.

A doorway appeared in the wall and he stepped through, holding his head high, pulling his slender shoulders back.

'Well?' said the King.

Araksis spread the parchments on the table before Pendarric. 'The stars have moved, sire – or rather, the world has shifted. There is great difficulty in deciding how this occurred. Some of my colleagues believe that the world – which as we know, spins around the sun – gradually changed its position. I myself tend towards the theory of a cataclysm that tipped the earth on its axis. We exhausted two Stones in an effort to discover the truth. All we could determine for certain is that the land you showed us was once below the ocean.'

'You are aware of the prophecies of the man Nu-Khasisatra?' asked the King.

'I am, sire. And I thought greatly before bringing this theory to you.'

'He says the earth will topple because of my evil. Are you telling me you concur with his blasphemy?'

'Majesty, I am not a leader, nor a philosopher; I am a student of the Star-magic. All I can say on the question you raised is that all the evidence points to Atlantis resting for thousands of years on the sea bed. How this will occur I cannot determine. Or when. But if Nu-Khasisatra is right, it will happen soon. He said the year's end would see the doom of Atlantis – that is six days from now.'

'Has there ever been a king with more power than I, Araksis?'

'No, sire. Not in all recorded history.'

'And yet this cataclysm is beyond my control?'

'It would appear so, sire. We have seen the future City of Ad, and our own Star-tower encrusted with seashells and the muck of oceans.'

'Serpiat will be leading his legions through into that world in three days. Then we will see. Is it possible that we can learn from the future and alter the present?'

'There are many questions hidden in the one, sire. The future will tell us what *happened*. But can we change it? In the future the cataclysm has already taken place. If we avert it, then we change the future, and therefore what we have seen cannot exist. Yet we have seen it.'

'What would you advise?'

'Close all the gateways, and hold all the City Mother-stones in readiness for any shift in the earth. Focus all the power of Sipstrassi on holding the world in balance.'

'All the world? That would take all the power we have. And what are we without Sipstrassi? Merely men . . . men who will decay and die. There must be another way. I will wait for Serpiat's report.'

'And Sharazad, sire?'

'She is dead . . . killed by stupidity. Let us hope it is not an omen. What do my stars show?'

Araksis cleared his throat. 'There is nothing I can tell you that is not already obvious, sire. This is a time of great stress, and greater peril. A journey is indicated, from which there is no return.'

'Are you speaking of my death?' stormed the King, drawing a gold-adorned dagger and holding it to the astrologer's throat.

'I always swore to be truthful, majesty. I have remained so,' whispered Araksis, staring into the gleaming eyes of the monarch. 'I do not know.'

Pendarric hurled the astrologer from him.

'I will not die,' he hissed. 'I will survive – and so will my nation. There is no other law in the world than mine. There is no other God but Pendarric!'

*

Clem Steiner hauled himself up from the bed in the wagon and pulled on his shirt. His chest wound dragged on the stitches and his leg felt numb, but he was healing well. He dressed slowly and climbed over into the driver's seat. Beth was fixing the traces to the oxen but she stopped as she saw him.

'Damn if you ain't as stupid as you look,' she stormed. 'Get back and lie down. You break those stitches and I won't put them back.'

Samuel giggled, and Steiner smiled down at the blond boy. 'Don't she get fired up easy?' Samuel nodded, his eyes flicking to his mother.

'Suit yourself,' said Beth. 'If you're so anxious to be up and moving, climb down and help Mary with the breakfast. We're leaving in an hour.'

Shannow arrived as the injured man was negotiating the painful climb down. Clem was out of breath by the time he made it to the ground and clung to the brake, his face chalk-white. Shannow took his arm and helped him to the cook-fire. 'Always there to rescue me, Shannow. I'm starting to look on you as a mother.'

'I'm surprised you're alive, Steiner. You must be tougher than I gave you credit for.'

Clem managed a weak grin, then lay back as Shannow

sat beside him. 'I hope you have purged yourself of the wish to kill me?'

'I have that,' Steiner answered. 'It would be downright bad manners. What was all the commotion during the night?'

'The reptiles were wiped out. Your friend Bull can give you the details.'

A sentry gave out a shout of warning and Shannow left Steiner and ran to the perimeter. More than a hundred of the bears were moving slowly across the open ground. One man levelled a rifle, but Shannow shouted, 'Don't shoot!' and reluctantly he laid down the weapon. The beasts were of prodigious size, with massive shoulders and hairless snouts. Their arms were out of proportion to their bodies, and hung low to the ground before them. Mostly they walked on their hind legs, but occasionally they dropped to all fours. Shannow climbed over the perimeter log and walked out to meet the animals.

'You a crazy man?' shouted Scayse, but Shannow waved him to silence. He walked slowly forward and then stood, his hands hooked in his belt.

Close up, the creatures reminded him of Shir-ran. Though their bodies were bestial and twisted, their eyes were round and humanoid, their faces showing glimpses of past humanity.

'I am Shannow,' he said. The beasts stopped and squatted down, staring at him. One, larger than the rest, dropped to all fours and moved in. Shannow found his hands itching to grasp the pistol butts . . . yet he did not. The beast came closer still, then reared up before him, its taloned arms flashing past his face and coming to rest on his shoulders. The creature's face was almost touching his own.

'Sha-nnow?' it said.

'Yes. That is my name. You have killed our enemies and we are grateful.'

A talon touched Shannow's cheek; the great head shook. 'Not enemies, Sha-nnow. Rider brought one to your camp.'

'He is dead,' Shannow said.

'What do you want in the land of the Dianae?'

'We were driven here – by the reptiles. Now the wagons will return to the valley Beyond the Wall. We mean no harm to you – or your people.'

'People, Sha-nnow? Not people. Things. Beasts.' He growled, lifted his talons from Shannow's shoulders and squatted on the grass. Shannow sat beside him.

'My name is Kerril – and I can smell their fear,' said the creature, angling his head towards the camp.

'Yes, they are afraid. But then so am I. Fear is a gift, Kerril. It keeps a man alive.'

'Once I knew fear,' said Kerril. 'I knew the fear of becoming a beast; it terrified me. Now I am strong and I fear nothing . . . save mirrors, or the still water of pools and lakes. But I can drink with my eyes closed. I still dream as a man, Sha-nnow.'

'Why did you come here, Kerril?'

'To kill you all.'

'And will you?'

'I have not decided yet. You have weapons of great power. Many of my people would be struck down – perhaps all. Would that not be wonderful? Would that not be an answer to prayer?'

'If you want to die, Kerril, just say the word. I will oblige you.'

The beast rolled to its back, scratching its shoulders on the grass. Then it reared up, its talons once more touching Shannow's cheek, but this time it felt the cold metal of his pistol resting under its chin.

A sound close to laughter came from Kerril's fanged mouth. 'I like you, Sha-nnow. Take your wagons and leave our lands. We do not like to be seen. We do not like grubbing in the ground for insects. We wish to be alone.'

Kerril stood, turned and ambled away towards the distant woods, his people following him.

*

Magellas lay on his stomach, watching the scene, enhancing

his vision and hearing through the power of the Bloodstone. Beside him Lindian's cold gaze also rested on the Jerusalem Man.

'He handled that well,' said Magellas. 'And did you note the speed with which his pistol came into action?'

'Yes,' answered Lindian. 'But how did he know the beast would not kill him? Can he read minds? Is he a seer?'

Magellas elbowed himself back from the skyline and stood. 'I don't know – but I would doubt it. The Lord, our Father, would have warned us of such talent.'

'Would he?' Lindian queried. 'He admitted it was a test.'

Magellas shrugged. 'We will see during the next three days. Why have you remained with me, Lindian? Why did you not ride off, like Rhodaeul?'

The slender warrior smiled. 'Perhaps I like your company, brother.' He walked off towards his horse, leaving Magellas staring after him.

Curiously, he realised, his words had been true: he did like Magellas. The giant had helped him many times when they were growing in the War-pens, when Lindian had been small and weak. And Magellas was easy company – unlike the arrogant Rhodaeul, always so sure of victory.

He vaulted into the saddle and grinned at Magellas.

It will be no pleasure to kill you, thought Lindian.

But that was the real secret of the test. Smaller and weaker than the other hunters, Lindian had developed skills of the mind. He had watched and studied, learning the secrets of men. Pendarric loathed Rhodaeul and disliked Magellas. Yet each of them, in their own way, had the talent to succeed the Atlantean King. And that was the doom they carried. For, with Sipstrassi, a king needed no heirs, and the last talent a man should develop in Pendarric's presence was that of charismatic leadership.

No, better to be like me, thought Lindian – efficient, careful, and undeniably loyal. I will make a good satrap of Akkady, he thought.

The two Hunters rode together for most of the morning. In the distance they saw lions, and they passed a small deserted settlement of tiny huts that aroused Magellas' interest. He dismounted and ducked to his knees to enter a doorway. Moments later he emerged. 'They must have seen us coming and scampered off to the trees. Fascinating.'

They rode on, guiding their mounts up a steep slope and halting on the crest. The city lay before them.

Lindian disguised the shock he felt, but the breath hissed from Magellas' throat, turning into a foul obscenity. He studied the Wall, the line of the docks, the distant spires of the temple.

'Where is the sea?' he whispered.

Lindian swung in the saddle, his eyes scanning the mountains and valleys. 'It is all different. Everything!'

'Then this is not Atlantis, and that . . . monstrosity . . . is merely a replica of Ad. But why would anyone build it? Look at the docks. Why?'

'I have no idea, brother,' said Lindian. 'I suggest we complete our mission and return home. We must have passed a score of places where we could waylay Shannow.'

Magellas could not tear his eyes from the city. 'Why?' he asked again.

'I am not a seer,' snapped Lindian. 'Perhaps the King created it to disturb us. Perhaps this is all some dark game. I do not care, Magellas. I merely want to kill Shannow and return home – that is if Rhodaeul does not beat us to the quarry.'

At the sound of his enemy's name Magellas jerked his gaze from the white-marbled city. 'Yes, yes, you are right, my brother. But Rhodaeul's arrogance is, I think, misplaced this time. You recall the teachings of Locratis? First study your enemy, come to know him, learn of his strengths and in them you will find his weaknesses. Rhodaeul has come to expect victory.'

'Only because he is skilful,' Lindian pointed out.

'Even so, he is becoming careless. It is the fault of these new weapons. A man can at least see an arrow in flight, or hear the hissing of the air it cuts. Not so with these,' he said, drawing the pistol. 'I do not like them.'

'Rhodaeul does.'

'Indeed he does. Though when has he faced an enemy as skilled in their use as the man Shannow?'

'You are taking a great risk in allowing Rhodaeul to make the first move. How will you feel if he rides in and kills the Jerusalem Man?'

Magellas chuckled. 'I will bid him a fond farewell on his journey to Akkady. However, it is wise when hunting a lion to consider the kill – not where one will place the trophy. There is a stream yonder. I think it is time to locate our brother and watch his progress.'

29

Nu-Khasisatra felt awkward on the horse he had borrowed from Scayse. He had never enjoyed riding and on every slope he closed his eyes and prayed as he swayed in the saddle, his stomach churning.

'I would sooner ride a storm at sea than this . . . this creature.'

Shannow chuckled. 'I have seen sacks of carrots ride with more style,' he said. 'Do not grip with your calves, just the thighs, letting the lower leg hang loose. And when going downhill, keep her head up.'

'My spine is being crushed,' grumbled Nu.

'Relax, settle down in the saddle. By Heaven, I've never seen a worse rider. You're unsettling the mare.'

'The feeling is mutual,' said Nu. They rode on through a wide valley, leaving the wagons far behind. The sun was obscured by clouds and the threat of rain hung in the air.

Towards noon Shannow spotted a rider approaching them; he reined in and took out his long glass. At first he thought the man was elderly, for his hair was bone-white, but as he focused the glass he saw that he was mistaken. The rider was young and wearing a black and silver tunic with dark leggings and high riding boots. He passed the glass to Nu and the shipbuilder cursed.

'It is one of Pendarric's killers. They are the Hunters. He is searching for me, Shannow – best you ride away.'

'It is only one man, Nu.'

'Maybe so – but such men you would not want to meet. They are reared in War-pens; they fight and kill each other from their earliest days; they are bred for strength, speed and stamina, and there are no fighting men to equal them. Believe me, Shannow, ride away – while there is still time! Please – I do not want to see you come to any harm.'

'We share that wish, my friend,' Shannow agreed, watching as the rider moved ever closer.

Rhodaeul smiled as he saw the men waiting for him. Truly his rewards would be great, for the second rider was the traitor Nu-Khasisatra – a prophet of the One God, and a man opposed to violence. He could not decide whether to kill him here, or take him back to face Pendarric's justice.

He halted some twenty paces from the pair. 'Jon Shannow, the King of Kings has spoken the words of your death. I am Rhodaeul the Hunter. Do you have anything to say before you die?'

'No,' said Shannow, palming his gun and blasting Rhodaeul from the saddle. The Atlantean hit the ground hard, a hammering pain in his chest; he tried to draw his pistol, but Shannow rode forward and fired a second shot that smashed his skull.

'Sweet Chronos!' exclaimed Nu. 'I cannot believe it.'

'Neither could he,' said Shannow. 'Let us move on.'

'But . . . what of the body?'

'That's why God made vultures,' answered Shannow, touching heels to his stallion.

Two miles away, Magellas opened his eyes and gave a deep, throaty chuckle. 'Oh joy,' he said. Lindian returned his Stone to its pouch and shook his head but Magellas laughed again, the sound rich with humour. 'What I would have paid to see that scene! The satrapy of Akkady? That and ten more like it. Did you see the look on Rhodaeul's face as Shannow fired? Was it not wonderful? Shannow, I am in your debt. I will light candles to your soul for a thousand years. Oh, Belial, how I wish I could see it again.'

'Your grief for your brother is deeply touching,' said Lindian, 'but I still do not understand what happened.'

'That is because your eyes were on Rhodaeul. For myself I cannot – could not – stomach the man. Therefore I watched Shannow. He drew his gun as he spoke; there was no sharp movement, and the weapon was almost clear before Rhodaeul realised he was in peril.'

'But surely Rhodaeul must have known Shannow would attempt to fight?'

'Of course – but that is where timing is all-important. He asked Shannow a question and was waiting for a response. How many times have we both done exactly that? It has never mattered, because we dealt with sword and knife. But these guns . . . they are sudden. Rhodaeul expected conversation, fear, nervousness . . . even pleading or flight. Shannow merely killed him.'

Lindian nodded. 'You guessed, didn't you? You expected this?'

'I did – but the outcome was beyond my greatest hopes. It is the guns, Lindian. We can master their uses with ease, but not the great changes they create in man-to-man battles. It's what I tried to say earlier. With the sword, the lance or the mace, battle becomes ritualised. Opponents must circle one another, seeking openings, risking their lives. It all takes time. But the gun? A fraction of a heartbeat separates man from corpse. Shannow understands this, he has lived all his life with such weapons. There is no need for ritual or concepts of honour. An enemy is there to be shot down and forgotten. He will light no candles for Rhodaeul.'

'Then how do we tackle him? We cannot kill him from ambush; we must face him.'

'He will show us his weakness, Lindian. Tonight we will enter his dreams and they will give us the key.'

*

Shannow and Nu made their camp in the lee of a hill. The Jerusalem Man said little and moved away to sit alone, staring at the city they would visit in the morning. His mood was dark and sombre. A long time ago he had told Donna Taybard, 'Each death lessens me, Lady.' But was it still true? The execution of Webber had been a first: an unarmed man made to stand, humiliated, in front of his peers and then gunned down. The other man in the crowd had done nothing but speak – for that he too was dead.

'*What separates you from the brigand now, Shannow?*'

There was no answer. He was older, slower, more reliant on skill than speed. And worse, he had cocooned himself within his reputation, allowing the legend to awe lesser men into bending to his will.

'For what?' he whispered. 'Is the world a better place? Is Jerusalem any closer?'

He thought back to the white-haired young man who had accosted them on the trail. Was that a duel, he asked himself? 'No, it was a murder.' The young warrior had no chance. You could have waited and met him on equal terms. Why? Honour? Fair play?

Why not? You used to believe in such virtues. He rubbed at his tired eyes as Nu strode over to him.

'Do you wish to remain alone?'

'I will be alone whether you join me or not. But sit anyway.'

'Talk of it, Shannow. Let the words bring out the bile inside.'

'There is no bile. I was thinking about the Hunter.'

'Yes. He was Rhodaeul, and he had killed many. I was surprised at the ease with which you sent him to the grave.'

'Yes, it was easy. They are all easy.'

'Yet it troubles you?'

'Sometimes, in the dark of the night. I killed a child once, ended his life by mistake. He troubles me, he haunts my dreams. I have killed so many men, and it is all becoming so easy.'

'God did not make Man to be alone, Shannow. Think on it.'

'You think I have not? I tried once to settle down, but I knew before I lost her that it was not for me. I am not a man made for happiness. I carry such guilt over that child, Nu.'

'Not guilt, my friend. Grief. There is a difference. Yours is a skill I would not wish to acquire – yet it is necessary. In my own time there were wild tribes bordering our lands; they would raid and kill. Pendarric destroyed them, and we all slept easier in our beds. As long as Man remains the hunter-killer, there will be a need for warriors like you. I can wear my white robes and pray in peace. The evil can dress in black. But there must always be the grey riders to patrol the border between good and evil.'

'We are playing with words, Nu. Grey is only a lighter shade of black.'

'Or a darker shade of white? You are not evil, Shannow; you are plagued by self-doubt. That is what saves you. That is where the Parson is in peril. He has no doubts – and therefore is capable of enormous evil. It was the downfall of Pendarric. No, you are safe, Grey Rider.'

'Safe?' repeated Shannow. 'Who is safe?'

'He who walks with God. How long since you sought His word in your Bible?'

'Too long.'

Nu stretched out his hand, holding Shannow's leather-covered Bible. 'No man of God should be lonely.'

Shannow took the book. 'Maybe I should have devoted myself to a life of prayer.'

'You have followed the path set for you. God uses both warrior and priest and it is not for us to judge His purposes. Read a little, then sleep. I will pray for you, Shannow.'

'Pray for the dead, my friend.'

*

As the horse reared and died, Shannow leapt from the saddle. He hit the ground hard, rolled and came to his knees with guns in hand. The roaring of the pistols and the screams of his attackers faded. A sound from behind! Shannow swivelled and fired. The boy was hurled from his feet. A small dog began yapping; it ran to the boy, licking his dead face.

'What a vile man you are,' came a voice and Shannow blinked and turned. Two young men stood close by – their hair white, their eyes cold.

'It was an accident,' said Shannow. 'I was being attacked . . . I didn't realise.'

'A child-killer, Lindian. What should we do with him?'

'He deserves to die,' said the smaller of the two. 'There is no question of that.'

'I never meant to kill the child,' Shannow repeated.

The tall man in the black and silver tunic stepped forward, his hand hovering over the gun butt. 'The King of Kings has spoken the words of your death, Jon Shannow. Do you have anything to say before you die?'

'No,' said Shannow, palming his pistol smoothly. A bullet smashed into Shannow's chest, the pain incredible as his own gun dropped from his twitching fingers and he sank to his knees.

'You should not try the same trick twice, old man,' whispered his killer.

Shannow died . . .

And awoke beside the fire on the hillside. Nu was sleeping soundly beside him, the night breeze was cool. Shannow built up the fire and returned to his blankets.

He was standing at the centre of an arena. Seated all around him were men he had killed: Sarento, Webber, Thomas, Lomax, and so many others whose names he could not remember. The child was leaning back on a golden throne, blood dripping steadily to stain the breast of the white tunic he wore.

'These are your judges, Jon Shannow,' said a voice and the tall white-haired warrior stepped forward. 'These are the souls of the slain.'

'They are evil men,' stated Shannow. 'Why should they have the right to judge me?'

'What gave you the right to judge them?'

'By their deeds,' answered the Jerusalem Man.

'And what was his crime?' stormed his accuser, pointing to the blood-drenched child.

'It was a mistake. An error!'

'And what price have you paid for that error, Jon Shannow?'

'Every day I have paid a price with the fire in my soul!'

'And what price for these?' shouted the warrior as down the central aisle came a score of children – some black, some white, toddlers and infants, young boys and girls.

'I do not know them. This is trickery!' said Shannow.

'They were the children of the Guardians, drowned when you destroyed the Titanic. *What price for these, Shannow?'*

'I am not an evil man!' shouted the Jerusalem Man.

'By your deeds we judge you.' Shannow saw the warrior reach for his pistol.

His own gun flashed up, but at the moment he fired the man disappeared and the bullet smashed into the chest of the boy on the throne. 'Oh dear God, not again!' screamed the Jerusalem Man.

His body jerked and he came awake instantly. Beyond the fire sat a lioness and her cubs. As he sat up, the lioness growled and moved back, the cubs scampering after her. Shannow banked up the fire and Nu awoke and stretched.

'Did you sleep well?' he asked.

'Let's pack up and move on,' Shannow answered.

*

As always when the Parson needed to pray in solitude he headed for the high country, bordering the clouds. His route took him through the woods of the Bear-people, but he cared nothing for danger; a man on his way to speak with his Maker, he knew that nothing would keep him from that appointment.

His soul was heavy, for the people had rejected him. He should have expected that, he knew, for it was always the way with prophets. Did they not reject Elijah, Elisha, Samuel? Did they not spurn the Son of God himself?

The people were weak, thinking only of their bellies or their small needs. Just like the monastery, with their constant prayers and works of little good.

'The world is evil,' the Abbot had told him. 'We must turn our faces from it, and seek the greater glory of God through worship.'

'But God made the world, Abbot, and Jesus himself asked us to go among the people as yeast to dough.'

'No, He did not,' the Abbot answered. 'He asked His disciples to do that. But this is Armageddon, these are the

End days. The people are not for saving; they have made their choices.'

He had left the monastery and taken a meagre living in a mining town, preaching in a bell-shaped tent. But the Devil had come to him there and found him wanting. Lucifer had led the girl to his sermon, and Lucifer had put the carnal thoughts in her mind. Oh, he had fought the desires of the flesh. But how weak is man!

His people – not understanding his temptations, nor the inner battles that went with them – had driven him from the town. It was not his fault! It was God's judgement when the girl hanged herself.

The Parson shook his head and looked around him, realising he had come deep into the woods. He saw the dismembered body of a reptile, then another. Drawing the horse to a halt he looked around. Bodies lay everywhere. He dismounted and saw that by a bush, her corpse wedged beneath the jutting roots of an old oak, lay Sharazad. There were terrible rips and tears on her body, but her face was remarkably untouched.

'Shannow was right,' said the Parson. 'You do look like an angel.' By her hand lay a red-veined Stone and he lifted it; it was warm and soothing to the touch. He dropped it into the pocket of his black cassock and mounted his horse, but his hand seemed to miss the warmth of the Stone, and he drew it out once more. He rode on, ever rising, until he came out on to a clearing at the crest of the range. It was cold here, but the air was fresh and clean, the sky unbearably blue. Dismounting once more, he knelt in prayer.

'Dear Father,' he began, 'lead me to the paths of righteousness. Take my body and soul. Show me the road I must walk to do your work, fulfil your word.' The Stone grew hot in his hand and his mind blurred.

A golden face appeared before him, bearded and stern, pale-eyed and regal. The Parson's heart began to hammer.

'Who calls on me?' came a voice in the Parson's mind.

'I, Lord, the humblest of your servants,' the Parson whispered, falling forward and pressing his face to the ground.

Miraculously the image remained before him, as if his eyes were still open.

'Open your mind to me,' said the voice.

'I do not know how.'

'Hold the Stone to your breast.' The Parson did so. Warmth enveloped him, and for a while there was peace and serenity; then the glow faded and he felt alone once more.

'You have sinned greatly, my son,' said Pendarric. 'How will you cleanse yourself?'

'I will do anything, Lord.'

'Mount your horse and ride a little way to the east. There you will find the survivors of the . . . reptiles. You will lift the Stone and say to them: "Pendarric". They will follow you and do your bidding.'

'But they are creatures of the Devil, Lord.'

'Yes, but I will give them the opportunity to redeem their souls. Go to the city, enter the Temple, then call for me again and I will guide you.'

'But what of the Great Whore? She must be destroyed.'

'Do not seek to contradict me!' thundered Pendarric. 'In my own time will I bring her down. Go to the Temple, Nicodemus. Seek out the Scrolls of Gold hidden beneath the altar.'

'But if the Whore tries to prevent me?'

'Then kill her and any who stand with her.'

'Yes, Lord. As you bid. And the Sword?'

'We will speak again when you have accomplished your mission.' The face faded . . . the Parson rose.

All his anguish left him.

At last he had found his God.

30

Back at her cabin Beth was happily surprised to find no damage from the earthquakes. In the fields below there were still pits and chasms, and several trees had fallen; but on the flat ledge of the hillside where Bull had chosen to place the McAdam home, there was no evidence of movement at all.

The sandy-haired rider grinned at Beth. 'If you say "I told you so", Bull, I'll crack your skull,' Beth said to him.

'Me? The thought never crossed my mind.' He tethered his horse and helped Beth carry the wounded Steiner into the house.

'I can walk, dammit,' Steiner grumbled.

'I ain't having those stitches opening again,' Beth told him. 'Now keep quiet.'

Bull and the children manhandled the furniture from the wagon, while Beth fuelled the iron stove and set a pot of Baker's to simmer. As dusk stained the sky, Bull rose.

'Best be getting back to Meneer Scayse,' he said. 'I reckon there'll be enough to do there. You want me to bring you anything tomorrow?'

'If there's anything left in the town, I wouldn't mind some salt.'

'I'll fetch it – and some dried beef. You're looking mighty low on stores.'

'I'm short on Barta coin, Bull. I'll have to owe you.'

'You do that,' he said. She watched him ride off and shook her head, allowing a smile to show. Now he wouldn't make a bad husband, she thought. He's caring, strong, and he likes the kids. But the face of Jon Shannow cut across the smiling image of Bull. 'Damn you for a fool, Shannow!' whispered Beth.

Samuel and Mary were sitting by the stove, Samuel's

head resting against the wall, his eyes closed. Beth walked to him, lifting him from his feet. His eyes opened and his head dropped to her shoulder. 'It's bed for you, snapper-gut,' she said, carrying him into the back room and laying him down. She didn't bother to strip his clothes, but removing his shoes she covered him with a blanket.

Mary came in behind her. 'I'm not tired, Ma. Can I sit up for a while?'

Beth looked into the child's puffy eyes. 'You can snuggle in next to your brother, and if you're still awake in an hour you can sit with me.' Mary grinned sheepishly and climbed under the blanket; she was asleep within minutes.

Beth returned to the main room and lit the fire, then walked out on to the porch where Bull had erected a bench seat made from a split log, planed and polished. She sat back and stared over the moonlit valley. The Wall was down everywhere, although some sections still reared like broken teeth. She shivered.

'Nice night,' observed Steiner, limping out to sit beside her. His face was pale, dark rings staining the skin beneath his eyes.

'You're a damn fool,' said Beth.

'And you're as pretty as a picture under moonlight,' he told her.

'Except for the nose,' she replied. 'And it's no good making up to me, Clem Steiner. Even if I let you, it would kill you for certain.'

'There's truth in that,' he admitted. Beth continued to stare at the horizon. 'What are you thinking?' he asked.

'I was thinking about Shannow – not that it's any of your business.'

'You in love with him?'

'You're a prying sort of fella, Steiner.'

'You are then. You could do worse, I guess – except I don't see you travelling the world looking for some city that don't exist.'

'You're right. Maybe I should marry you.'

'That's not a bad thought, Frey McAdam,' he responded, smiling. 'I can be right good company.'

'You've been hiding that light under a bushel,' she said sharply.

He chuckled. 'Come to think of it, that *is* a pretty big nose.' She laughed and her tension eased. Clem stretched his wounded leg out in front of him and rubbed at it. 'Does Shannow know how you feel?' he asked, his voice low and serious.

Beth cut off a sharp retort. 'I told him – in a way. But he won't change. He's like you.'

'I've changed,' he said. 'I don't want to be a pistoleer; I couldn't give a damn about reputations. I had a father who beat the Hell out of me. He said I'd never make anything of my life and I guess I've been trying to prove him wrong. Now I don't care about that no more.'

'What will you do?'

'I'll find a nice woman. I'll raise kids and corn.'

'There's some hope for you yet, Clem Steiner.' He was about to answer when he spotted two riders angling up towards the house.

'Strange-looking pair,' said Beth. 'Look how the moon-light makes their hair seem white.'

*

Shannow was ill at ease as they rode. The dreams had unnerved him, but worse than that he had the constant feeling he was being watched. Time and again he would turn in the saddle and study the skyline, or alter the direction in which they travelled, dismounting before the crest of every hill.

But now the city was ahead of them, and still the feeling would not pass.

'What is troubling you?' Nu asked. 'We should have been at the city hours ago.'

'I don't know,' admitted Shannow. 'I feel uncomfortable.'

'No more than I feel, perched on this horse,' responded Nu.

A rabbit darted across their path and Shannow's guns swept up. He cursed softly, then flicked the stallion's flanks with his heels.

The city was protected by a great Wall, but the recent earthquakes had scored it with cracks. There were no gates, but as they entered the city Shannow could see deep holes in the stones where hinges had once been placed.

'The gates,' Nu told him, 'were of wood and bronze, emblazoned with the head of a lion. And this entrance would take you through the Street of Silversmiths, and on to the Sculptors' Quarter. My home was close by.'

People in the streets stopped and stared at the riders. There was no animosity here, only curious gazes. There were more women than men, Shannow noticed, and they were tall and well-formed – their clothes mainly hide, beautifully embroidered.

He halted his horse. 'I seek the Dark Lady,' he said, removing his hat and bowing. The nearest woman smiled and pointed to the east.

'She is in the High Tower with Oshere,' she answered.

'God's peace upon you,' Shannow told her.

'The Law of the One be with you,' she replied.

The horses' hooves clattered on the cobbled street. 'In my time, no beasts were allowed into this quarter,' said Nu. 'The residents found the smell of manure less than appealing.'

A bent and crippled shape loomed before them, and Shannow's mind was hurled back to Shir-ran. His stallion reared, but he calmed it with soft words. The Man-beast ambled past, not able to lift his huge, misshapen head.

'Poor soul,' said Nu, as they walked their horses on.

The street widened into a statue-lined road that stretched, arrow-straight, towards a tall palace of white marble. 'Pendarric's summer home,' explained Nu. 'It also houses the temple.' The road ended at a colossal stairway more than a hundred paces wide, slowly rising to an enormous archway.

'The Steps of the King,' said Nu. Like the road the steps

were lined with statues, each one carved from marble and each bearing a sword and a sceptre. Shannow urged on the stallion and rode the steps; Nu dismounted and led the mare after him. As the Jerusalem Man reached the archway a slender black woman moved from the shadows to greet him. Shannow recalled the moment he had first seen her, carrying her son from the wreck of the resurrected *Titanic*. 'Amaziga? You are the Dark Lady?' he said as he climbed down from the saddle.

'The same, Shannow. What are you doing here?' He noted the tension in her voice, the lack of warmth in her eyes.

'Am I such an unwelcome visitor?'

'There are no evils here for you to slay, I promise you that.'

'I am not here to kill. Do you think me such a villain?'

'Then tell me why you are here.'

Shannow saw a movement behind her, deep in the shadows of the archway. A young man appeared; once he must have been strikingly handsome, but now his face was distended and his shoulders bowed. Guiltily Shannow averted his eyes from the man's deformities. 'I asked you a question, Shannow,' said Amaziga Archer.

'I came to warn you of impending perils – and also to see the Sword of God. But it would be pleasant if we could talk inside somewhere.' Nu reached the archway, saw Amaziga and bowed low. 'This is my companion, Nu-Khasisatra. He is from Atlantis, Amaziga, and I think you should hear what he has to say.'

'Follow me,' she said, turning on her heel and striding back through the archway. The deformed man followed her silently, Nu and Shannow bringing up the rear. They found themselves in a wide, square courtyard; Amaziga crossed it, passed a circular fountain and continued on through a huge hallway. Shannow tethered his stallion and Nu's mare in the courtyard and entered the building. It was ghostly quiet within, and their footsteps created eerie echoes.

They mounted a long circular staircase and emerged into

a room where Amaziga had already seated herself behind a mahogany desk on which were scattered papers, scrolls and books. She looked younger than Shannow remembered, but her eyes seemed full of sorrow.

'Say what you want to say, Jerusalem Man. Then leave us in whatever peace remains.'

Shannow took a deep breath, stilling the rise of anger he felt. Slowly he told her of the attack on the township of Pilgrim's Valley, and their flight beyond the fractured Wall. He spoke of the woman, Sharazad, and the Parson, and the fears that she was some evil goddess. And he told her of Pendarric. She listened without comment, but her interest grew when Nu began his tale; she questioned him sharply, but his soft-spoken answers seemed to satisfy her. At last, when both men had finished, she asked the deformed man to fetch some drink. Neither Shannow nor Nu had stared at him, and after he had gone Amaziga fixed her eyes on the Jerusalem Man.

'Do you know what is happening to him?' she asked.

'He is turning into a lion,' Shannow answered, holding her gaze.

'How did you know?'

'I met a man, named Shir-ran, who suffered the same horror. He rescued me, gave me aid when I needed it, healed my wounds.'

'What happened to him?'

'He died.'

'I said what happened to him?' Amaziga snapped.

'I killed him,' said Shannow.

Her eyes grew cold, and her smile chilled Nu. 'Now *that* has a familiar ring, Shannow. After all, how many stories are there concerning the Jerusalem Man when he doesn't kill something – or someone? Have you destroyed any communities lately?'

'I did not destroy your Home Base; Sarento did that when he sailed the *Titanic*. I merely blocked the power of the Motherstone. But I will not argue with you, Lady, nor debate my deeds. I will leave now and seek the Sword.'

'You must not, Shannow! You must not go near it.' The words hissed from her. 'You do not understand.'

'I understand that the gateway between past and present must be closed. Perhaps the Sword of God will close it. If not, when the disaster befalls Atlantis we could be dragged down with it.'

'The Sword of God is not the answer you seek. Believe me.'

'I will not know until I have seen it,' Shannow told her.

Amaziga's hand came up from below the desk and in it was held a Hellborn pistol. She cocked it and pointed the barrel at Shannow. 'You will promise me to stay away from the Sword – or you will die here,' she said.

'Chreena!' came a voice from the doorway. 'Stop it! Put the pistol away.'

'You don't understand, Oshere. Stay out of this!'

'I understand enough,' said the Man-beast, moving clumsily forward and placing the silver tray on the desk. His deformed hand closed over the pistol, gently removing it from her grasp. 'Nothing you have told me about this man suggests he is evil. Why would you wish to harm him?'

'Death follows wherever he rides. Destruction! I can feel it, Oshere.'

She stood and ran from the room and Oshere laid the pistol on the desk. Shannow leaned forward and uncocked it. Oshere eased himself into the chair Amaziga had used, his dark eyes fixed on the Jerusalem Man.

'She is under great strain, Shannow,' he said. 'She thought she had found a way to cure me, but it was only a temporary respite. Now she must suffer again. She loved my brother, Shir-ran, and he became a beast. Now . . .' He shrugged. 'Now it is my turn. Your arrival made her distraught. But she will gather her strength and consider what you have said. Now, have some wine, and rest. I will see your horses are taken to a field nearby where there is good grass. Through that door you will find beds and blankets.'

'There is no time to rest,' said Nu. 'The end is near, I can feel it.'

Shannow pushed himself wearily to his feet. 'I had hoped for aid. I thought the Dark Lady would be a person of power.'

'She is, Shannow,' Oshere assured him. 'She has great knowledge. Give her time.'

'You heard Nu. There *is* no time. We will ride on to the Sword – but first Nu needs to search the Temple sanctuary.'

'Why?' Oshere asked.

'There could be something there that will help me to return home,' Nu told him.

The sound of gunshots came from close by, followed by screams of terror.

'You see!' shouted Amaziga Archer from the doorway, pointing at Shannow. 'Where he rides, death always follows.'

31

The Parson rode boldly into the clearing where twenty-three survivors of the Daggers' force had gathered. Several were wounded, their scaled limbs bound. Others were keeping watch, rifles poised, for any attack from the Bears. Holding the Bloodstone high, the Parson guided his mount in amongst his enemies and voiced the single word that his God had commanded him.

'Pendarric,' he said, as rifles were aimed at his chest; the guns were lowered instantly. 'Follow me,' ordered the Parson, riding from the clearing. The reptiles took up their weapons, formed two lines and marched out behind his horse. The Parson was exultant.

'How mysterious are the ways of the Lord,' he told the morning air. 'And how great are His wonders.' On the plain before the city lions gathered in great numbers, padding forward to stand in the Parson's path. He lifted his Stone. 'Give way!' he bellowed. A black-maned beast reared up in pain, then ran to the left. The others followed it, leaving a path through which the Parson heeled his mount.

He led the reptiles to the northern gateway and then turned in the saddle. 'All who resist the Will of God must die,' he declared. Confident that the awesome power of the Creator was with him, he entered the gateway. Beyond it he saw many people. None stood in his way; they gazed with frank, open curiosity as the marching reptiles and the Parson rode on through white-walled streets.

A young woman with a child stood close by, holding the toddler's hand. 'The Temple,' enquired the Parson. 'How shall I reach it?' The woman pointed to a high domed building and he approached it. The Temple pillars were massive, and close-set. He dismounted and walked up the long stairway with the reptiles behind him.

An old man moved out to stand before him. 'Who seeks the wisdom of the Law of One?' he asked.

'Step aside for the Warrior of God,' the Parson told him.

'You cannot enter,' replied the old man pleasantly. 'The priests are at prayer. When the sun touches the western wall, then may your entreaties be heard.'

'Out of my way, old man,' the Parson ordered, drawing his pistol.

'Do you not understand?' asked the High Priest. 'It is not allowed.'

A shot echoed in the Temple corridors and the High Priest fell back without a sound, blood pumping from a hole in his brow. The Parson ran into the Temple, the reptiles swarming after him. Taking their new master's lead, they began firing on the priests inside who ran for shelter. Ignoring the carnage, the Parson scanned the building, seeking the Inner Sanctum. There was a narrow doorway at the end of the long hall and he ran to it, kicking it open. Within was an altar and another old man was hastily gathering scrolls of gold foil. He looked up and struggled to rise, but the pistol bucked in the Parson's hand and he fell. The Parson knelt by the scrolls and lifted his Stone.

'Hear me, Lord. I have done your bidding.'

Pendarric's face shimmered before him. 'The scrolls,' he said. 'Read them.'

The Parson lifted a section of gold foil and unrolled it. 'I cannot make out the symbols,' he said.

'I can. Discard that one. Take another.'

One by one the Parson opened the foils, his eyes scanning the curious stick-like symbols. At last, when he had finished, he looked into the eyes of God and saw they were troubled.

'What must I do, Lord?' he whispered.

'Bring the Sword of God to the earth,' Pendarric told him. 'Today. There is a peak to the south. Climb it – but first lay your Stone upon the body of the priest beside you. Place it on his blood. There it will gather strength. When you have climbed the peak, lift the Stone and call upon the Sword. Bring it to you. You understand?'

'Yes,' answered the Parson. 'Oh, yes. My dreams fulfilled. Thank you, Lord. What then must I do?'

'We will speak again when you have obeyed me.' The face disappeared.

The Parson laid his Stone on the bleeding chest of the priest, watching as the blood seemed to flow into it, swelling its veins. Then he took it once more and rose.

From outside came the sound of more gunshots. He ran through the hallway, down the steps, and leapt to his horse. Ignoring the reptiles, he galloped back to the main gateway, and on to fulfil God's wishes.

*

Shannow ran from the room when the first shots sounded, pushing past Amaziga and taking the steps two at a time. The courtyard was deserted, save for the two horses tethered there. More shots came from the Temple building and Shannow drew his pistols and advanced across the courtyard. A reptile ran into view with a rifle in his hands. As Shannow's pistol came up, the reptile spotted him and swung his weapon to bear. Shannow's gun fired, the creature spun back into the wall and fell to his face on the stones.

The Jerusalem Man waited for several seconds, watching the entrances, but no other reptiles came in sight. He ducked past the fountain and ran across the open space to the rear of the Temple, where a wooden door blocked his access. Lifting his foot, he crashed it against the lock and the door burst inwards. A shot splintered the wood of the frame as he dived through and rolled to his left. Bullets hissed and whined around him, ricocheting from the mosaic floor. As he came to his knees behind a pillar, he heard the sound of running feet from his right. Twisting, he levelled his pistols . . . three reptiles died. He watched the Parson run from a doorway to the left; two Daggers moved aside to let him pass and Shannow killed them both. A shell tore through the collar of his coat and he returned the fire, but missed. Then he was up and running for a second pillar as bullets hissed by him. A Dagger ran into his path with knife raised. Shannow shot twice into the beast's body. All around, the reptiles were running for the great doorway.

Silence fell within the Temple as Shannow reloaded his pistols and stood. Amaziga appeared in the doorway, Nu and Oshere with her, and ran to the room Shannow had seen the Parson emerge from. The Jerusalem Man returned his guns to their scabbards and followed them. Within the small chamber, Nu was kneeling with Amaziga beside a dying priest. He was old, white-bearded, and his chest was stained with blood.

'I am the leaf,' whispered the priest as Nu lifted his head and cradled him.

'God is the tree,' Nu responded softly.

'The circle is complete,' said the man. 'Now I will know the Law of the One, the Circle of God.'

'Now you will know,' said Nu. 'The streams flow into the rivers, the rivers into the sea, the sea into the clouds, the clouds into the streams. The rich earth into the tree, the tree to the leaf, the leaf to the earth. All life forms the Circle of God.'

The dying priest smiled. 'You are a Believer. I am glad. Your circle goes on.'

'What did they want? What did they take?' asked Amaziga.

'Nothing,' answered the priest. 'He read the sacred scrolls, and summoned a demon. The demon told him to bring the Sword of God to the earth.'

'No!' Amaziga whispered.

'It is of no matter, Chreena,' said the priest, his voice fading. His head fell back in Nu's arms; the shipbuilder gently lowered the body to the floor and rose.

'They were fine words,' Shannow told him.

'They are part of the writings of the One. There is perfection only in the circle, Shannow: to understand that is to understand God.' Nu smiled and began to walk around the chamber, searching the carved walls, studying each projection. Shannow joined him.

'What do you seek?'

'I'm not sure. The Stones would have been kept in this room but I have no idea where – only the High Priest knew, and he passed the knowledge to his successor.'

The room was small and square, though the altar was circular. The limestone walls were splendidly sculpted, graceful figures with painted eyes and long, tapering hands that reached for the sky. Shannow walked to the altar and stood gazing down on the flat, polished surface. Engraved there, and filled with gold leaf, was a wondrous tree with golden leaves. He ran his fingers lightly over the surface, tracing the branches. The design was beautiful and restful to the eye. Around the rim of the altar birds were carved – some in flight, some nesting, others feeding their young. Again the principle was the circle from the egg to the sky. His fingers traced over the carvings, resting at last on the nest and the single egg. It moved under his fingers and taking a firm grip, he lifted the egg clear. It was small and perfectly white; but once in his hand it became warm, the colour growing from white to cream, to yellow and finally to gold.

'I have what you seek,' he said and Nu came to him and took the golden egg from his palm.

'Yes,' Nu agreed, his voice low. 'You have indeed.'

'The Stone from Heaven,' said Oshere. 'Wondrous. What will you do now?'

'It is not mine to take,' replied Nu. 'But if it were, I would return to my land and try to save my wife and children from the coming cataclysm.'

'Then take it,' Oshere told him.

'No!' cried Amaziga. 'I need it. You need it. I cannot watch you change again.'

Oshere turned away from her. 'I . . . wish you to have the Stone, Nu-Khasisatra. I am a prince of the Dianae. The High Priest is dead and I have the right to bestow the Stone. Take it. Use it well.'

'Let me have it just for a moment,' pleaded Amaziga. 'Let me make Oshere well again.'

'No!' Oshere shouted. 'The Sipstrassi will not work

against itself, you have seen that. It made me what I am. The power is too great to waste on a man like me. Can you not understand that, Chreena? I am a lion who walks like a man. Even magic cannot change what I am . . . what I will become. It does not matter, Chreena. You and I, we will see the ocean and that is all I want.'

'What about what I want?' she asked him. 'I love you, Oshere.'

'And I love you, Dark Lady . . . more than life. I always will. But nothing is for ever, not even love.' He turned to Nu. 'How will you find your way home?'

'There is a circle of stones beyond what was once the Royal Gardens. I shall go there.'

'I will walk with you,' said Oshere and the three men left the chamber. Amaziga stayed beside the dead priest, staring at the golden scrolls.

The circle of stones had been largely untouched by the centuries, though one had cracked and fallen. Nu walked to the centre of the circle and offered his hand to Shannow.

'I learned much, my friend,' he said. 'Yet I did not discover the Sword of God as I was commanded.'

'I'll find it, Nu . . . and do what needs to be done. You find your family.'

'Farewell, Shannow. God's love be with you.'

Shannow and Oshere walked out of the circle and Nu lifted the Stone and cried out in a language Shannow could not understand. There was no flash of light, no drama. One moment he was there . . . the next he had gone.

Shannow felt a sense of loss as he turned to Oshere. 'You are a man of courage,' he said.

'No, Shannow, I wish that I were. But Sipstrassi has made me what I am. Chreena used the magic of the Stones to reshape me, but almost immediately I began to revert. She is a stubborn woman and she would use all the Stones in the world to hold me. Such a gift from God should not be wasted in that way.'

The two men walked slowly back to the Temple. Crowds had now gathered and the bodies of the slain priests were being carried from the building. 'Why did they not fight?' asked Shannow. 'There were so few of the enemy.'

'We are not warriors, Shannow. We do not believe in murder.'

Inside the Temple Amaziga joined them, her face set and hard.

'We must talk, Shannow. Excuse us, Oshere.' She led the Jerusalem Man back into the Inner Sanctum; the priest's body was gone, but blood still stained the floor. Amaziga swung on him. 'You must follow the killer, and stop him. It is vital.'

'Why? What harm can he do?'

'The Sword must be left as it is.'

'I still do not see why. If it serves God's purposes . . .'

'God, Shannow? God has nothing to do with the Sword. Sword? What am I saying? It is not a sword, Shannow; it is a missile – a nuclear missile. A flying bomb.'

'Then the Parson will blow himself to Hell. Why concern yourself?'

'He will blow us *all* to Hell. You have no conception of the power of that missile, Shannow. It will destroy everything that you could see from the tower. For two hundred miles the earth will be scorched and laid bare. Can you comprehend that?'

'Explain it to me.' Amaziga took a deep breath, trying to marshal her words. As a Guardian and a teacher, her memory had been enhanced by Sipstrassi and she could summon all the facts concerning the missile, yet none of them would serve to help her explain it to Shannow. It was an MX (Missile eXperimental). Length: 34.3 metres. Diameter: 225 centimetres at first stage. Speed: 18,000 miles per hour at burn-out. Range: 14,000 kilometres. Yield: 10 X 350 kilotons. Ten warheads, each with the capacity to destroy a city. How could she explain that to an Armageddon savage?

'In the Between Times, Shannow, there was great fear and hatred. Men built awesome weapons and one was used on a city during a terrible war. It destroyed the city utterly;

hundreds of thousands of people were killed by that single blast. But soon the bombs were made even more powerful, and great rockets were constructed that could carry the bombs from one continent to another.'

'How did the nations survive?'

'They didn't, Shannow,' she said simply.

'And these bombs caused the earth to topple?'

'Not exactly. But that is not important. The . . . Parson? . . . must not be allowed to interfere with the missile.'

'Why does it stand in the sky? Why is it surrounded by crosses, if not from God?' he asked.

'Come back to my rooms and I will tell you as best I can. I do not have all the answers. But promise me, Shannow, that when I have explained it to you, you will ride to stop him.'

'I will decide that *when* you have explained it all.'

He followed her to her chambers and sat down opposite her desk. 'You know,' she said, 'that this land was once below the oceans? Where we are now was once an area of sea known as the Devil's Triangle. It acquired that name because of the unexplained disappearances of ships and planes. You understand about planes?'

'No.'

'Men used to . . . It was discovered that it was possible for machines to take to the skies. They were called planes; they had wide wings, and engines that propelled them at great speeds through the air. What you will see clustered in the sky around the . . . Sword, are not crucifixes or crosses, but planes. They are trapped in some sort of stasis field. . . . Dear God, Shannow, this is impossible!' She poured a goblet of wine from the pitcher on her desk and drank deeply, then she leaned forward. 'The Atlanteans used the power of a great Sipstrassi Stone and aimed it at the sky. Why, I do not know, but they did it. When Atlantis sank beneath the oceans, the power of the Stone continued. It trapped more than a hundred planes and ships. It would have been more, but the field is very narrow; the power has been decreasing over the years, and the ships fell to earth. You can still find their ruined hulks out on the desert beyond the Chaos Peak. How it trapped the missile, I can only guess. When the earth toppled for the second time, there were massive earthquakes. By then the weapons centres were run by computers and they probably registered the enormous earthquakes as nuclear strikes, and responded. That's why the levels of radiation are still so high over most of the world. The earth toppled, missiles were released and any opportunity of salvaging some remnants of civilisation was gone. This missile was probably fired from somewhere in a country called America. It crossed the stasis field and has remained there for three hundred years.'

'But surely the Between Timers would have seen – as we do – the planes hanging in the air? If they had such great weapons, why did they not destroy the Stone?'

'I don't think they *could* see the planes. I think the Sipstrassi was originally programmed to hold the objects in another dimension, invisible to us. Only when the power began to drain did they become visible.'

Shannow shook his head. 'I do not understand any of this, Amaziga; it is beyond me. Planes? Stasis fields? Computers? But I have been having strange dreams lately. I am sitting in a crystal bubble inside a giant cross high in the sky. There is a voice whispering in my ear; it is someone called Tower and he is telling me to assume a bearing due west. My voice – and yet not my voice – tells him we do not know which way is west. Everything is wrong . . . strange. Even the ocean does not look as it should.'

'The crystal bubble, Shannow, is the cockpit of a plane. And the voice you heard was not from someone called Tower, but the Control Tower in a place called Fort Lauderdale. And the voice that was yours – and yet not yours – was that of Lieutenant Charles Taylor, flying one of five Navy Avenger torpedo-bombers on a training run. You can still see them in formation close to the missile. Trust me, Shannow. Stop the Parson.'

He rose. 'I don't know that I can. But I will try,' he told her.

32

Beth McAdam awoke with her head pounding, her body sore. She sat up – and saw the two men who had dragged her from her cabin. Grabbing a rock, she pushed herself to her feet. 'You slimy sons of bitches!' she hissed. The taller of the men rose smoothly to his feet and moved towards her. Her hand flew up, with the rock poised to smash his temple, but he blocked the blow with ease and backhanded her to the ground.

'Do not seek to annoy me,' he said. His hair was chalk-white, his face young and unlined. He knelt beside her. 'You will come to no harm, you have the promise of Magellas. We merely need you to help us to complete a mission.'

'My children?'

'They are unharmed. And the man Lindian struck was only unconscious – there was no lasting damage.'

'What is this mission?' she asked, tensing herself for a second attack.

'Do not be foolish,' he advised her. 'If you choose to be troublesome, I will break both your arms.' Beth let the rock fall from her fingers. 'You ask about our mission,' he continued, smiling. 'We are sent to despatch Jon Shannow. He holds you in some esteem and he will give himself up to us in return for your safety.'

'In a pig's eye!' she retorted. 'He'll kill you both.'

'I do not think so. I have come to know Jon Shannow; to respect him – even to like him. He will surrender himself.'

'If you like him, how can you think of killing him?'

'What has emotion to do with duty? The King, my Father, says Shannow must die. Then he *will* die.'

'Why don't you just face him – like men?'

Magellas chuckled. 'We are executioners – not duellists. Had I been instructed to face him on equal terms, then I would have done so – as would my brother Lindian. But it is not necessary and therefore would constitute a foolish risk. Now we will proceed with – or without – your willing help. But I do not wish to break your arms. Will you help us? Your children need you, Beth McAdam.'

'What do you want me to say?'

'That you will stay with us – and not try any more foolishness with rocks.'

'I don't have a lot of choices, do I?'

'Say the words anyway. It will make me feel more relaxed.'

'I'll do as you say. That good enough for you?'

'It will suffice. We have prepared some food and it would be our pleasure if you joined us for a meal.'

'Where are we?' Beth asked.

'We are sitting in one of your holy places, I believe,' answered Magellas, pointing to the star-filled sky. Several hundred feet above them, glistening silver in the moonlight, hung the Sword of God.

*

Amaziga Archer sat alone after Shannow had gone. On her desk now were the Sacred Scrolls guarded by the Dianae. Her husband Samuel had spent four years teaching her the meaning of the symbols, which resembled the cuneiform writings of ancient Mesopotamia. For the main part the gold foils were covered with astrological notes, and charts of star systems. But the last three – including one missed by the Parson – contained the thoughts of the astrologer Araksis.

Amaziga read the words of the first two and shivered.

There was much here that was beyond her, but it tallied with ancient legends concerning the doom of Atlantis. They had found a great power source, but had misused it, and the oceans had risen up, the continent been buried beneath the waves. Now Amaziga understood. In opening the Gates of Time, they had altered the delicate balance of gravity. Instead of spinning contentedly around the sun, the earth was exposed to the gravitational pull of a second sun, and perhaps more. The earthquakes and volcanic eruptions outlined in Araksis' scrolls were merely indications of a tortured world, pulled in opposing directions and teetering on its axis. The earthquakes now were exactly the same; with two colossal suns in the sky, the gravitation drag was causing the planet to tremble.

Shannow was right: the imminent fall of Atlantis represented a deadly danger to the new world. One of the great mysteries the Guardians had never been able to solve was the eye-witness accounts of the Second Fall, when ten thousand years of civilisation were ripped from the surface of the planet. Those eye-witnesses had spoken of two suns in the sky. Amaziga had been educated in the theory that what had been seen was, in fact, a nuclear explosion. Now she was not so sure. The gold scrolls spoke of a gateway to a world of flying machines and great weapons. The circle of history? When Atlantis fell, did it drag the twenty-first century with it? And what of the twenty-fourth . . . What of now? Dear God, was the earth to fall again?

The dusk breeze was cold against her skin. Rising, she drew the heavy curtains and lit the lanterns on the wall. What is it about our race, she wondered, that leads us always along the road of destruction?

Returning to her desk, she picked up the last scroll and traced the words under the dim, golden light of the lanterns. Her eyes widened.

'Sweet Jesus!' she whispered and taking her pistol, she ran from the room and down the stairs to the courtyard. Nu's mare was still tethered there and she climbed into the saddle and raced through the city. Beyond the main gate the lions were feasting on the bodies of the reptiles; they ignored her and she lashed the mare into a gallop.

*

Shannow did not follow the Parson at speed. The stallion was weary and in need of rest; also, the light was failing and he knew he would be too late if any mishap should befall the horse. The Jerusalem Man swayed in the saddle. He also was tired; his mind reeled with all that Amaziga had told him. Once upon a time the world had been a simple place where there were good men and evil men and the hope of Jerusalem. Now all had changed.

The Sword of God was just a weapon created by men to destroy other men. The crown of crosses was planes from out of the past. So where was God? Shannow lifted his water canteen and drank deeply. Far ahead he could see the outline of the Chaos Peak. As the clouds parted he saw the Sword, glittering like silver in the night sky.

'Where are you, Lord?' said Shannow. 'Where do you walk?'

There was no answer. Shannow thought of Nu, and hoped the shipbuilder had returned home safely. The stallion plodded on and dawn was breaking as Shannow angled his mount up the rocky slope leading to the Chaos Peak and the Pledging Pool. Glancing back, he could see in the distance a rider coming towards the Peak. Taking his long glass, he focused it and recognised Amaziga. The mare was all but finished, lather-covered and scarcely moving. Returning the glass to his saddlebag, Shannow crested the last rise. His eyes were burning with fatigue as he headed the stallion down to the Pool, then dismounted and gazed about him. The Peak reared like a jagged finger, and he could see the Parson almost at the last ledge. It was a long shot for a pistol.

'Welcome, Shannow,' came a voice and the Jerusalem Man spun, his pistols levelling at the speaker. Then he saw Beth McAdam. A slender, white-haired man had his arm about her throat, a pistol pointed to her head. The speaker – the man from his dreams – stood several paces to the left. 'I have to say, Shannow, that I am grateful to you,' Magellas told him. 'You killed that arrogant swine, Rhodaeul, and that did me a great service. However, the King of Kings has spoken the words of your death.'

'What has she to do with this?' asked Shannow.

'She will be released the moment you lay down your weapons.'

'And that is the moment I die?'

'Exactly. But it will be swift.' Magellas drew his pistol. 'I promise you.'

Shannow's guns were still trained on the young man, hammers cocked, fingers on the triggers. 'Don't listen to him, Shannow. Blow him away!' cried Beth McAdam.

'You will let her go?' Shannow asked.

'I am a man of my word,' said Magellas and Shannow nodded.

'Then it is done,' he agreed.

At that moment Beth McAdam lifted her booted foot and slammed it down on Lindian's instep. Ramming her head back into his face, she tore loose from his grip. As Lindian cursed and raised his pistol, Clem Steiner reared up from behind a rock. Lindian saw him and swung, but he was too late. Steiner's pistol boomed and the slender warrior was hurled to the ground with a bullet in his heart.

As Beth made her move, Magellas fired and the shell swept Shannow's hat from his head. The Jerusalem Man triggered his pistols. Magellas staggered, but did not go down. Again Shannow fired and Magellas sank to his knees, still struggling to lift his gun. The pistol dropped from his fingers and he raised his head. 'I like you, Shannow,' he said, with a weak smile. Then his eyes closed and he toppled forward.

Shannow ran to Steiner. The wound in his chest had opened, and his face was ghostly as he sat back on a rock.

'Paid you back, Shannow,' he whispered.

Beth approached him. 'You're crazy, Clem . . . but thanks. How the Hell did you get here?'

'I wasn't out for long. Bull came by to see me and I left the kids with him and followed the tracks. Looks like we should be safe now.'

'Not yet,' said Shannow.

The Parson had reached the ledge and was now out of range. They watched him lift his hand.

The Sword of God trembled in the sky.

*

Shannow ran to the base of the Peak and stripped off his black coat, dropping it to the ground. Then he reached up, took hold of a jutting rock and hauled himself up. The Peak loomed above him. His fingers reached for other holds and the slow climb began.

Beth and Steiner sat down to watch his progress. High above, on the ledge, the Parson began to chant broken verses from the Old Testament.

'A sword, a sword, drawn for the slaughter, polished to consume, and to flash like lightning . . . For thus saith the Lord God: When I shall make thee a desolate city . . . when I shall bring up the deep upon thee, and great waters shall cover thee . . . I shall make thee a terror, and thou shalt be no more; though thou be sought for, yet shall thou never be found again, saith the Lord God.' His voice echoed on the wind.

Amaziga stumbled over the crest of the hill, the mare dead on the slope. She ran down to the poolside and saw Shannow inching his way up the rock-face.

'No,' she shouted. 'Let him be, Shannow. Let him be!' But the Jerusalem Man did not respond. As Amaziga drew her pistol and aimed it at him, Beth ran across the stones and hurled herself at the other woman. The pistol fired, splintering the rock by Shannow's left hand; he flinched instinctively and almost fell. Beth tore the gun from Amaziga's hand and threw the woman from her.

'We have to stop him!' said Amaziga. 'We have to!'

A rumbling roar came from the sky . . . the base of the Sword was becoming flame and smoke. Shannow climbed on. Minutes fled by. On the rock-face Shannow was tiring, his arms trembling with the effort of dragging himself upwards. But he was close now. Sweat bathed his face as he forced his weary limbs to respond.

He could hear the Parson's voice above him: 'I will breathe out my wrath upon you, and breathe out my fiery anger against you . . . Wail and say Alas for that day . . . a time of doom for the nations.'

As the missile trembled, several planes on the edge of the stasis field broke clear, the sound of their engines roaring over the desert beyond the Peak. Shannow reached the ledge and hauled himself over it. For several seconds, exhausted, he could do nothing.

The Parson saw him. 'Welcome, brother. Welcome! Today you will hear a sermon unlike any other, for the Sword of God is coming home.'

'No,' Shannow told him. 'It is no sword, Parson.' But the man did not hear him.

'This is a blessed day. This is my destiny.' With a terrifying roar, the missile burst clear of the field and began to rise. 'NO!' screamed the Parson. 'No! Come back!' He held up his hand. The missile slowed its rise and began to turn in the air. The tower rumbled. A great flash of lightning seared the sky to the south, the air parting like a curtain, and a second sun shone in the sky. Shannow pushed himself to his knees. From the ledge he could see the immense gateway opened by Pendarric and the massed ranks of his legions beyond it. The light was unbearable. In the sky, the missile had almost completed its turn. Shannow drew his pistol. The earthquake hit just as he was about to fire on the Parson. A huge crack snaked across the desert . . . the Pool disappeared . . . the tower buckled, great slabs of stone peeling from the walls. Shannow dropped his pistol and grasped a jutting rock. The Parson, concentrating on the missile, lost his footing and tumbled from the ledge, his body shattering on impact with the rocks below where once the Pool had been.

Clem Steiner, Beth and Amaziga ran from the edge of the new chasm, taking shelter higher on the slopes. Shannow pushed himself upright. The missile was coming back towards him.

He stared sullenly at the weapon of his own destruction, wishing he could hurl the monster through the gaping gateway. In response to his thoughts, the missile wavered and twisted in the air. Shannow did not understand the miracle, for he did not know of the Sipstrassi Stone pulsing its power beyond the rock, but his heart leapt with the realisation that the Sword of God was responding to *his* wishes. He concentrated with all the strength he could muster. Like a spear, the silver missile sped through the Gate of Time. Pendarric's legions watched it pass . . . on it flew, one section breaking away. For some moments Shannow experienced a sense of bitter disappointment, for nothing had happened. Then came the light of a thousand suns and a sound like the end of worlds.

The gateway disappeared.

33

Nu-Khasisatra opened his eyes to find he was standing within the circle of stones beyond the Royal Gardens, two hundred paces from the Temple of Ad. Stars shone brightly in the sky and the city slept. He ran from the circle, down the tree-lined Avenue of Kings and on through the Gates of Pearl and Silver. An old beggar awoke as he passed, stretching out his hand.

'Help me, Highness,' he said drowsily, but Nu ran by him. The man sent a whispered curse after him and settled down to sleep beneath his thin blankets.

Nu was breathing heavily by the time he reached the Street of Merchants. He slowed to a walk, then ran again, coming at last to the bolted gate by his own gardens. Glancing left and right, he grasped the iron grille and began to climb. Once over the top, he dropped to the earth and loped towards the house. A huge hound bore down on him, but when Nu knelt and held out his hand the hound stopped short, sniffing at him.

'Come on, Nimrod. It hasn't been that long,' said Nu. The black hound's tail began to wag and Nu rubbed at the beast's long ears. 'Let's find your mistress.'

The house doors were also bolted, but Nu pounded on the wood. A light flickered in an upper window and a servant stepped out to the balcony.

'Who is it?' came a voice.

'Open the door. The master of the house is home,' called Nu.

'Sweet Chronos!' exclaimed the servant, Purat. Moments later the bolts were drawn back and Nu stepped into the house. Purat, an elderly retainer, blinked as he saw the strange garb worn by his master, but Nu allowed no time for questions. 'Rouse the servants,' he said, 'and pack all your belongings – and food for a journey.'

'Where are we going, Lord?' Purat asked.

'To safety, God willing.' Nu ran up the winding staircase and opened the door to his bedroom where Pashad was asleep. He sat on the wide silk-covered bed and stroked her dark hair and her eyes opened.

'Is this another dream?' she whispered.

'It is no dream, beloved. I am here.' She sat up and threw her arms around her husband's neck.

'I knew you would come. I prayed so hard.'

'We have no time, Pashad. The world we know is about to end, even as the Lord Chronos told me. We must get away to the docks. Which of my ships is in harbour?'

'*Arcanau* alone stands ready. She will carry a shipment of livestock to the eastern colony.'

'Then *Arcanau* it is. Fetch the children, pack warm clothes. We will go to the dock and seek out Conalis the Master; he must be prepared to sail at dusk tomorrow.'

'But the manifest has not been cleared, beloved. They will not allow us to sail; they will close the harbour mouth.'

'I do not think so – not on this coming Day of Days. Now dress swiftly and do as I bid you.'

Pashad pushed aside the silk sheet and rose from the bed. 'Much has happened since you left us,' she told him, slipping from her nightgown and pulling a warm woollen dress from the chest by the window. 'Half the merchants and artisans from the east quarter have vanished; it is said that the King has taken them to another world. There is great excitement in the city. You know my second cousin, Karia? She is married to the court astrologer, Araksis. She says that a huge Sipstrassi Stone has been taken to the Star Tower; it is set to catch a great weapon our enemies are sending against us.'

'What? The Star Tower?'

'Yes. Karia says Araksis is very concerned. The King told him that enemies in another world will be seeking to destroy the Empire.'

'And they have set up a Stone to prevent it? Listen to me, Pashad. Take the children and find Conalis; tell him to prepare for a dusk sailing. I will join you at the dock. Where is *Arcanau* berthed?'

'The twelfth jetty. Why are you not coming with us?'

He strode to her, taking her in a powerful embrace. 'I cannot. There is something I must do. But trust me, Pashad. I love you.'

He kissed her swiftly and then ran from the room. Two of the retainers were waiting in the courtyard; beside them were hastily packed chests, while Purat was leading a horse and wagon along the pathway from the gate. The dawn was bright in the sky now.

'Purat! Harness the chariot. I need it now.'

'Yes, Lord. But the white pair have been loaned to Bon-antae. There is only the bay mare and a gelding and they are not a team.'

'Do it.'

'At once, Lord.'

Within minutes Nu-Khasisatra was lashing the team back along the Avenue of Kings towards the distant Star Tower. The gelding was stronger than the mare, and it was hard to control the wooden chariot, but Nu drove recklessly, relying on his strength to keep the beasts under control. The chariot bounced on a jutting stone, lifting Nu from his feet, but he steadied himself and raced on through the doomed city.

The Lord had commanded him to find the Sword of God . . . he had failed. But Shannow had promised to find it and do what needed to be done. At last Nu understood what that meant. Shannow would send the Sword through the gateway and this was how the world would end. The Sword of God was the bright light of Nu's vision, and Araksis was using Sipstrassi power to stop it.

The sky was bright now, the morning upon him as Nu swung the chariot into the courtyard below the Star Tower. Two sentries ran to him, seizing the bridles of the sweating horses.

Nu leapt to the ground. 'Is Araksis here?' he asked.

The men eyed his strange clothing and exchanged glances.

'I have to see him on a matter of great urgency,' stated Nu.

'I think you should come with us, sir,' said one of the sentries, moving towards him. 'The captain of the guard will want to question you.'

'No time,' said Nu, his huge fist clubbing into the man's jaw. The sentry dropped like a stone. The other man was struggling to draw his sword when Nu leapt at him; Nu's fist rose and fell and the second sentry fell alongside his companion.

The door to the Tower stairs was bolted from the inside. When Nu slammed his shoulder against it, the wood buckled but did not give. He stepped back and hammered his foot against the lock; the door exploded inwards.

Taking the steps two at a time, Nu climbed to the Tower. A second door was not locked and he stepped inside. A dark, handsome man wearing a golden circlet on his brow was leaning over a desk, working on a large chart. He glanced up as Nu entered.

'Who are you?' he demanded.

'Nu-Khasisatra.'

The man's eyes widened. 'You have been named as a traitor and a heretic. What do you want here?'

'I have come to stop you, Araksis . . . in the name of the Most Holy.'

'You don't know what you are saying. The world is at risk.'

'The world is dead. You know that I speak the truth; you have seen the future, Astrologer. The King's evil has destroyed the balance of harmony in the world. The Lord Chronos has decreed his evil should end.'

'But there are thousands – hundreds of thousands – of innocents. We have a thousand years of civilisation to protect. You must be wrong.'

'Wrong? I have seen the fall of worlds. I have walked in

the ruins of Ad. I have seen the statue of Pendarric toppled by a shark in the depths below the oceans. I am not wrong.'

'I can stop it. I *can*, Nu. This Sword of God is only a mighty machine. I can hold it with the Sipstrassi . . . send it where it can cause no killing.'

'I cannot allow you to make the attempt,' said Nu softly, glancing at the clear blue sky.

'You cannot stop it, traitor. The power is spread across the gateway like a shield. It also covers the city. Any metallic object in the sky around Ad will be trapped – nothing can get through. You can kill me, Nu-Khasisatra, but that will not change the magic. And you cannot approach the Stone and live, for there are mighty spells protecting it.'

Nu swung to look at the giant Sipstrassi Stone. Golden wires were welded to its surface and these led to six crystal spheres supported on a framework of silver. 'Get out while you can,' said Araksis. 'Since we are linked by marriage, I will give you an hour before I notify the King of your return.'

Nu ignored him. Striding to the desk, he swept the parchment from it and pushed his hands under the oak top. The heavy desk lifted.

'No!' screamed Araksis, hurling himself at the larger man. Nu released the desk and turned just as the astrologer's body struck him. As both men fell, Nu sent a back-hand blow into Araksis' face; stunned, yet still he clung to Nu. The shipbuilder surged upright, hurling Araksis against the far wall; then he turned again to the desk, hoisted it high above his head and, with a grunt, threw it into the silver framework. Lightning lanced around the room, shattering a long window and setting fire to the velvet curtains that hung there. The silver framework melted. One of the crystals had been smashed by the desk, three others had fallen to the floor; Nu seized a stool and hammered them to shards.

'You don't know what you've done,' whispered Araksis, blood seeping from a cut on his temple.

A shout went up from the courtyard. Nu cursed and ran

to the window. Three more guards had appeared and were kneeling by the bodies of the sentries.

Nu raced down the stairs. Two of the guards were entering the doorway as he came into sight and he dived at them, his weight sending them sprawling to the ground. Running into the sunlight, he ducked a sweeping sword-cut and back-handed the wielder from his feet. Then leaping into the chariot, he took up the whip and cracked it over the heads of the two horses. They surged into the traces and hurtled out through the gateway.

In the high Star Tower Araksis struggled to his feet. Four of the crystals were ruined and he had no time now to repair the damage. Two still hung in place – enough to send a beam of power over the City of Ad. If the Sword was directed towards Ad, the Stone could still catch it in the sky and nullify its awesome power. If it missed the city, then it could explode harmlessly in the wide ocean beyond. Araksis moved to the great Stone and began to whisper words of power.

As the racing chariot sped towards the city, Nu hoped he had done enough to wreck Araksis' plans. If he had not, then Shannow's world would face the agony of Pendarric's evil.

The horses were tired and it was two hours before Nu guided the chariot into the docks. The *Arcanau* was berthed at the twelfth jetty as Pashad had told him. He left the chariot and ran up the gangplank. Conalis saw him and moved from the tiller to usher him below deck.

'This is madness, Highness,' said the burly master. 'The tides are against us, we have no manifest and the livestock are still being loaded.'

'This is a day of madness. Is my wife here?'

'Yes, and your sons and your servants; they are all below decks. But there is an inspection planned. What will I tell the Port Master?'

'Tell him what you please. Do you have a family, Conalis?'

'A wife and two daughters.'

'Get them on board now.'

'Why?'

'I wish to give them a great present . . . you also. That should suffice. Now I am going to sleep for a couple of hours. Wake me at dusk. Now tell any of the crew who have wives or sweethearts to bring them aboard also. I have presents for all.'

'Whatever you say, Highness. But it would be best for me to say the Lady Pashad has presents; you are still named as a traitor.'

'Wake me at dusk – and put off the inspection until tomorrow.'

'Yes, Highness.'

Nu spread himself out on the narrow bunk, too tired even to seek Pashad. His eyes closed and sleep overcame him within seconds . . .

He awoke with a start to find Pashad sitting beside him. His eyes were heavy with sleep, and it seemed only moments before that he had lowered himself to the bunk.

'It is dusk, my lord,' said Pashad and he rose.

'Are the children well?'

'Yes. All are safe, but the ship is crowded now with the wives and children of the crew.'

'Get them all below. I will speak to Conalis. Send him to the tiller.'

'What is happening, Nu? This is all beyond me.'

'You will not have long to wait, beloved. Believe me.'

Conalis met him at the tiller. 'I do not understand this, Highness. You said you wanted to sail at dusk, but now we are full of women and children who must be put ashore.'

'No one is going ashore,' Nu told him, scanning the sky.

Conalis muttered a curse – at the far end of the dock a squad of soldiers was marching towards them. 'Word must be out that you are here,' said the Master. 'Now we are all doomed.'

Nu shook his head. 'Look there!' he shouted, his arm lancing up, finger pointing to the sky where a long silver arrow was arcing across the heavens. 'Cut the ropes,' bellowed Nu. 'Do it now if you value your life!'

Conalis lifted an axe from a hook near the stern and hammered it through the docking rope. Running forward, he did the same at the prow. The *Arcanau* drifted away from the jetty and Nu pushed the tiller hard left. Feeling the ship move, many of the women and children surged up to the deck. On the dock the soldiers ran to the quayside, but the gap was too great to jump. Across the mouth of the bay a long trireme waited, its bronze ramming horn glinting in the light of the dying sun.

'It'll sink us,' shouted Conalis.

'No, it will not,' Nu told him. In the distance a colossal burst of white light was followed by an explosion that rocked the earth. A terrible tremor ran through the city and the *Arcanau* trembled.

'Shall I loose the sail?' Conalis shouted.

'No, a sail would destroy us. Get everyone below.'

The sky darkened. Then the sun swept majestically back into the sky and a hurricane wind roared across the city. Nu took his Sipstrassi Stone from the pocket of his jacket and whispered a prayer. The tidal wave, more than a thousand feet high, thundered across the city and Nu could see giant trees whirling in the torrent. If any were to strike the *Arcanau*, the vessel would be smashed to tinder. Their prow slowly swung until it pointed straight at the gigantic wall of water. Clutching the Sipstrassi, Nu felt the shock of the wave. The ship was lifted as if by a giant hand and carried high into the roaring swell, yet not one drop of water splashed the decks. Up and up soared the vessel until it crested the wave and bobbed on the surface. Far below them, the trireme was lifted like a cork and hammered against the cliffs on the outer curve of the bay; the ship exploded on impact and disappeared beneath the torrent. To the east, the plume of the wave raced on.

In the sudden silence Conalis moved alongside Nu, his face ashen.

'It's all gone,' he whispered. 'The world is destroyed.'

'No,' said Nu. 'Not the world. Only Atlantis. Raise the sail. When the waters subside, we must find a new home.'

The lowing of the livestock brought a wry smile from Nu. 'At least we'll have cattle and sheep,' he said.

Pashad came on to the deck, leading her sons, Shem, Ham and Japheth. Nu strode to meet her.

'What will we do now?' she asked. 'Where shall we go?'

'Wherever it is, we will be together,' he promised.

34

Shannow sank back on his haunches. Suddenly he felt good – better than he had in years. It was a most curious sensation. Despite his lack of rest, he felt such strength in his limbs. A crack opened on the ledge and he felt the Tower move. Swiftly he levered himself over the side and began to climb down. The Tower shivered, the top section breaking away and crashing down. Shannow hugged himself to the wall as the rocks and stones plunged past him, then slowly he completed his descent.

Beth ran to him. 'My God, Shannow. Look at you! What the Hell happened up there?'

'What's wrong?' he asked.

'You look young,' she said. 'Your hair is dark, your skin . . . It's incredible.'

A low groan came from the left and Shannow and Beth walked to where the Parson lay, his body broken, blood seeping from his right ear, his left leg bent under him. Shannow knelt by the man.

'The Sword . . . ?' whispered the Parson.

Shannow cradled the man's head. 'It went where God intended.'

'I'm dying, Shannow. And He won't appear to me. I failed Him . . .'

'Rest easy, Parson. You earned the right to make mistakes.'

'I failed Him.'

'We all fail Him,' said Shannow softly. 'But He doesn't seem to mind much. You did your best and you worked hard. You saved the town. You did a lot of good. He saw that, Parson. He knows.'

'I wanted . . . Him . . . to love me. Wanted . . . to earn . . .' his voice faded.

'I know. Rest easy. You're going home, Parson. You'll see the glory.'

'No. I've . . . been evil, Shannow. I've done such bad things.' Tears welled in the Parson's eyes. 'I'll be in Hell.'

'I don't think so,' Shannow assured him. 'If you hadn't come to this Peak, then maybe the world would have toppled again. None of us is perfect, Parson. At least you tried to walk the road.'

'Pray for . . . me . . . Shannow . . .'

'I'll do that.'

'It wasn't God . . . was it?'

'No. Rest easy.' The Parson's eyes closed and the last breath rattled from his throat. Shannow stood.

'Did you mean that?' Beth asked. 'You think he won't roast in Hell?'

The Jerusalem Man shrugged. 'I hope not. He was a tortured soul and I like to think God looks kindly on such men.'

Amaziga Archer approached. 'Why did you shoot at me?' asked Shannow.

'To try to change the past, Shannow. I read the gold scrolls.' Suddenly she laughed. 'The circle of history, Jerusalem Man. Pendarric took over the mind of the Parson – or Godspeaker, as he was named in the scrolls of Araksis. Through him Pendarric learned that a great weapon would be hurled at Atlantis, that through this weapon the world would topple. Do you know what Pendarric did? He had Sipstrassi transferred to this tower, and ordered Araksis to set the power to trap the Sword when it came over Ad. Do you understand what I am saying? Twelve thousand years ago, Pendarric set this stasis field in operation in order to catch a missile. And it caught it – twelve thousand years later. Can you see?'

'No,' said Shannow.

'It's so disgustingly perfect. If Pendarric had not learned of the missile and had made no effort to catch it – then it would not have been here at all. You can't change the past, Shannow. You can't.'

'But why did you try to kill me?'

'Because you just destroyed two worlds. If you had not sent that bomb into the past, our old world could not have been destroyed. You see, Pendarric was also responsible for the Second Fall. I thought I could change history . . . but no.' She looked at Shannow and he saw the anguish and hatred in her eyes. 'You're not the Jerusalem Man any more, Shannow. Oh, no. Now you are the Armageddon Man: the destroyer of worlds.'

Shannow did not reply and Amaziga turned from him and strode to the ruins of the Tower. The encrusted rocks had been dashed away, the white marble showing through. There was a broken doorway and Amaziga pushed her way inside. A dust-covered skeleton lay close to the Sipstrassi, which had fallen from its bowl; there were rings on the skeletal fingers and a gold band still circled the brow. Then Shannow, Beth and Steiner entered the chamber. Shannow led Steiner to the Sipstrassi and touched the pistoleer's hand to it; the veins of gold were thin now but still the power surged through him, healing his wounds.

Outside they could hear the roaring of engines as the once trapped planes continued to circle, seeking places to land.

Amaziga knelt and lifted a scroll of golden foil. 'The Sword,' she read, 'did not pass near Ad. But then a noise came, and a pillar of smoke. A strange phenomenon has just occurred. The sun, which was setting, has just risen again. And I can see dark storm-clouds racing towards us. Dark, blacker than any storm of memory. No, not a storm. The traitor was right. It is the sea!' Amaziga dropped the foil and stood. 'The missile was the final touch to a world straining on its axis.' She turned to the skeleton. 'I would guess this was Araksis. Even the Sipstrassi could not save him from the tidal wave he saw. God, Shannow, how I hate you!'

'Stop your whingeing!' snarled Beth McAdam. 'It wasn't Shannow who destroyed the worlds – it was Pendarric. He opened the gates; he set up whatever it was you called it, to trap the Sword of God. And it destroyed him. What right have you to condemn a man who only fought to save his friends?'

'Leave her alone,' said Shannow softly.

'No,' answered Beth, her cold blue eyes locked to Amaziga. 'She knows the truth. When a gun kills a man, it is not the weapon that goes on trial, but the man whose finger is on the trigger. She knows that!'

'He is a bringer of death,' Amaziga hissed. 'He destroyed my community. My husband died because of him, my son is dead. Now two worlds have toppled because of him.'

'Tell me, Shannow,' asked Beth, 'why you came to the Sword?'

'It does not matter,' answered the Jerusalem Man. 'Let it rest, Beth.'

'No,' she said again. 'While Magellas and Lindian held me captive, they used their Power Stones to observe you and they let me see. It was *you*,' she said, swinging once more to Amaziga, 'who urged Shannow – pleaded with him – to come here and stop the Parson. It was you who sent him scaling that Peak and risking his life. So whose finger was on the trigger, you bitch?'

'It was not my fault,' shouted Amaziga. 'I didn't know!'

'And he did? Jon Shannow knew that if the Sword passed through the gate it would destroy two worlds? You make me sick. Carry your own guilt, like the rest of us. Don't seek to palm it off on the man who just saved all our lives.'

Amaziga backed away from Beth's anger and walked out into the sunlight.

Shannow followed her. 'I am sorry for your loss,' he said. 'Samuel Archer was a fine man. I don't know what else to say to you.'

Amaziga sighed. 'The woman is right in what she says and you are just part of the circle of history. Forgive me, Shannow. Nu-Khasisatra said he was sent to find the Sword of God. He found it.'

'No, he didn't,' said Shannow sadly. 'There was no Sword – only a foul instrument of mass death.'

She placed her hand on his arm. 'He found the Sword, Shannow, because he found you. You were the Sword of God.'

'I hope Nu survived,' said Shannow, changing the subject. 'I liked the man.'

Amaziga laughed. 'Oh, he survived, Jon Shannow. Be assured of that.'

'Is there something else in the scrolls then?'

'No.' She shook her head. 'Nu is the Arabic form, and Khasisatra the Assyrian name, for Noah. You remember what he said about the Circle of God? Nu-Khasisatra came to the future and read of Noah's survival in your Bible, Shannow. So he went home, rescued his family and, I should imagine, with the aid of the Sipstrassi, created a ship that was storm-proof. How's that for a Circle of God?' Her laughter was almost hysterical . . . then the weeping began.

'Come away,' said Beth McAdam, taking Shannow by the arm and leading him back towards the horses.

Some planes had already begun to land on the hard-baked sand of the desert. 'What are they?' asked Beth.

'Nothing that I would see,' he told her, as Flight 19 touched down four centuries after take-off.

Together Shannow and Beth rode from the desolated Pool.

'What will you do now, Shannow?' she asked. 'Now that you are young again, I mean? Will you still seek Jerusalem?'

'I have spent half a lifetime pursuing that dream, Beth. It was a mistake. You don't find God across a distant hill. There are no answers in stone.' Turning back in the saddle, he gazed at the broken Peak and the forlorn figure of Amaziga Archer. Reaching out he took Beth's hand, lifting it to his lips. 'If you'll have me, I'd like to come home.'

EPILOGUE

Under the leadership of Edric Scayse and the Committee, led by Josiah Broome, Pilgrim's Valley prospered. The church was rebuilt and, for the want of a preacher, a young bearded farmer named Jon Cade took the service. If any noted the resemblance between Cade and a legendary killer called Shannow, none mentioned it.

Far to the south a beautiful black woman walked with a golden, black-maned lion at her side and climbed the last hill before the ocean. There she stood staring out to sea, feeling the cool of the ocean breeze, watching the sun's broken reflection on the rippling waves.

Beside her the lion turned his head and focused on a herd of deer grazing on a distant hillside. He did not know why the woman had stopped here, but he was hungry and padded off in search of food.

Amaziga Archer watched him go, tears welling to her cheeks.

'Farewell, Oshere,' she said.

But the lion did not hear her . . .